Edited by
Trip Galey, Robert Berg, and C.L. McCartney

BONA

First published in Great Britain in 2024 by Bona Books Ltd

Copyright © Bona Books Ltd

Trip Galey, Robert Berg, and C.L. McCartney have asserted their rights under the Copyright, Designs and Patents Act 1988, to be identified as the editors of this work.

Copyright for individual texts rests with the contributors.

ISBN: KICKSTARTER EDITION: 978-1-0687311-0-5;
ISBN: EBOOK: 978-1-0687311-2-9;
ISBN: PAPERBACK: 978-1-0687311-1-2

Edited by Trip Galey, Robert Berg, and C.L. McCartney
Typeset by C.L. McCartney
Illustration and Cover Design by Stephen Andrade

Printed and bound in Great Britain by
CPI Group (UK) Ltd, Croydon CR0 4YY

BONA
www.bona-books.com

For all the twinks we obliterated along the way

Contents

Introduction

May 2023. Three humble editors are sitting around a kitchen table, doomscrolling through Twitter. Someone laughs, WhatsApp pings, and the latest iteration of an old meme pops up on all our screens. It probably involves Timothy Chalamet.

I WANT THAT TWINK OBLITERATED!

One of us says, 'That'd be a great name for an anthology', and out of nowhere, without realising, our conversation has turned *deadly*. Because we hoot with laughter and we joke about what kind of anthology it would be. Pulp, obviously. SFF, *obviously*. Unsparingly Queer, DUH.

'We should totally make this happen.'

More laughter, then a pause. A long, inevitable, life-twisting pause.

'We really could, you know. We're writers. Editors. We've *literally* got the skills.'

And just like that… there go our evenings, weekends, sleep schedules, and hairlines. Over the next year we founded Bona Books, we commissioned the best cover artist ever (thanks, Stephen!), we assembled a stable of stunningly talented authors—we hauled together a whole-arsed book.

But before we get into all that, what's this meme about? Well. Back in the faded history of 2019, someone posted a WattPad (don't ask) screencap to Twitter, containing five fateful words: 'i want that twink Obliterated'.

The phrase ate; it was a serve heard 'round the world. Soon, whenever an overly online queer decided a pretty, svelte twenty-something needed to be destroyed (whether socially, sexually, or as much-deserved comeuppance), those five words appeared. Then, after spreading through meme culture, they escaped containment into the wider world. In July 2020, a certain Anthony Oliveira (yes that one, whose mind-bending story, *'Ganymede'*, closes this anthology!) dropped the iconic phrase into his critically acclaimed Marvel comic, *Lords of Empyre: Emperor Hulkling* #1, where a mysterious alien really, *really* wanted rid of the young gay superhero Wiccan.

When we set out to create this anthology, we knew we needed a strong core cohort of queer writers. Anthony was top of our list of invitees, but we were delighted and honoured as the roster filled up with the likes of Adam Sass, Aliette de Bodard, Brent Lambert, Caleb Roehrig, Christopher Caldwell, and James Bennett.

We also knew that we wanted open submissions, because—if we could make this anthology work—it would be an incredible opportunity to spotlight fresh and underheard queer voices. We reserved six slots initially, but the runaway success of our Kickstarter let us up that to *ten*! We're particularly humbled by the number of trans and nonbinary authors who have trusted us with their words, and delighted that for a few authors this represents their first professional-level sale.

Speaking of, we were unprepared for how satisfying it would be to pay queer people proper rates for their art—honestly, bliss.

So yes, welcome to the pages of *IWTTO!* Bailey Maybray, Charlie Winter, Derrick Webber, John Berkeley, Julie Danvers, Kieran Craft, Malcolm Schmitz, Rien Gray, William C. Tracy, and Ng Yi-Sheng.

And what has this talented cast of heartbreakers, frighteners, and thrillseekers created for you? Well, first and foremost: *Pulp*.

The pulp style emerged in the short fiction magazines of the early 20th Century, so-named for the cheap 'pulp' paper they were printed on. The term rapidly became synonymous with stories that were lurid, thrilling, sensationalist, formulaic, of popular appeal, sometimes questionable in quality, and—above all—*fun*.

Full disclosure, they *also* tended to be sexist, racist, homophobic, and prone to the whole host of societal ills that plagued the time. In pulp, men were *men*. Women screamed in revealing dresses, queers were sissies and perverts, and non-white characters tended to be either savage brutes or exotically mystical.

Utter nonsense, in other words.

This was the period that brought us Buck Rogers, John Carter of Mars, Conan the Barbarian, Sam Spade, Zorro, Flash Gordon, the Cthulhu mythos, and Tarzan (who you can find adroitly deconstructed by James Bennett in just a few pages' time…). The legacy of these stories was long, and their tropes (for good or ill) were absorbed into much that came after. You'll find their echoes in golden age comics, in mid-century film noir, and in the Space Opera excesses of the 80s.

Amidst all that, pulp was *camp as tits*. Over-muscled, sweat-soaked heroes who always felt half an inch from kissing. Femme fatales who made you snap your fingers and cry 'Mother!' Gender-bending, queer-coded villains, once intended by their authors to be sinister and unsettling, who now just look like a slay. The writers took their exaggerated straight-male-ness *so* seriously, they never noticed they'd leapt into self-parody.

So it made perfect sense to us that *I Want That Twink OBLITERATED!* would be pulp—it *had* to be pulp. It needed to embrace the camp and reclaim the style from the bigotry. Masculinity (and its infinite boundaries) belongs to everyone, particularly if you're queer. So what happens to pulp science fiction, fantasy, and horror if that's your starting point?

We looked specifically for stories that would reclaim the idea of pulp for a queer audience, centre masculinities in a new light, and take us on a damn fun ride. Pulp parody, pulp pastiche, and pulp deconstruction.

The stories in this volume run the gamut(s!) between funny, horny, heartbreaking, thrilling, horrific, explicit, and more. Not every tale will make you wince, but several bring the heat, and a few bar no holds. For those who like them, we've included content notes in the back (p.349).

We are unspeakably excited to share these tales with you. Prepare to be thrilled/scandalised/aroused/gripped-by-existential-dread [choose your own adventure!].

Trip, Robert, and Chris
London, July 2024

In the Garden of the Serpent King

James Bennett

The Congo Basin, 1913

The great stone phallus thrust from the fetid earth of the swamp, ten-foot high and veined in liana, its fat, rounded glans mist-polished and worn.

'Good lord!' ejaculated Lord Roland Moss, adding in a needless bluster. 'What the devil is it?'

His son and heir, Lysander Moss, was the only one among the party to laugh, struggling to conceal his eighteen-year-old nature behind a muddy hand. The others—those who remained—went through a series of varying reactions. Mr Bell, the swarthy rifleman, shouldered the weapon in question, grunted, and spat. The portly Dr Montgomery Ives, a ball of sweat-drenched khaki under his salacot, gasped and fumbled for his camera case. The two tribesmen leading the mules fell to their knees, venerating the monolith in a muted babble and letting all present know that it was sacred to the Mbuti. The so-called "ape-man", standing lean and pale in his loincloth (his only concession to fashion), narrowed his eyes and was silent.

'Heavens, it's a giant tallywhacker, Father.' Lysander offered this with customary relish, hands on hips and smirking up at the shadowing column. 'One can only marvel at the ancient hand that raised such an erection.'

Lord Roland spared him a disapproving glance. He'd yet to forgive the lad for his indiscretions at Oxford last summer, as more than a few guineas had changed hands with the Dean to save him from being expelled. What would his mother think? She'd already had a fit of the vapours over his expulsion, though she tended to turn a blind eye to Lysander's precocious behaviour at home. To stave off thought of the ailing Eunice, oceans away in rural Bedfordshire, he strode over to the ape-man, whom the tribes called Kabou, and enquired after what the guides were saying.

'They're saying, sir,' Kabou replied, 'that it marks the boundary of the temple of Mboo, the primordial python god.'

'Thunderation! Then the Stanley map was right.'

'Indeed. They're also saying they'll go no further.'

At this, Lysander hastened forth, lithe as the draping vines on the *muyovu* trees. He raised his whip over his shoulder. His son seemed determined to take out his temper on every poor tribesman they met along the way. Or *had* until Roland threatened to pull down his breeches and give him a jolly good spanking in front of all and sundry, which he would've gladly done had he not feared that Lysander would never forgive him for it and Mr Bell rather enjoy the spectacle. As it happened, Kabou stood in the youth's path and that was enough to make him think better of it. For a moment, the midges swarmed and the bonobos sang, the heat rippling through the morass. Then the whip sank to Lysander's side and there came the expected pout.

'I hope you're not suggesting that *I* lead the mules,' he said, blond and trembling in his sodden brown shirt.

'Let them go,' Roland said, ignoring his son and speaking to the canopy, the lattice of leaves growing dimmer by the minute. 'We have you, Kabou, and you shall show us the way. According to the map, we should reach the temple by nightfall.'

Come dusk, Lord Roland sat in his tent, sipped a little whiskey, and scribbled in his diary:

Three days out from Kinshasha, following the arc of the Congo River. Oh, Eunice, woe has dogged our every step, as if the very jungle reviles our presence. First, our steamship ran aground at Matoko, near where the Congo and Ubangi fork, forcing us to continue into the forest on foot. Edward, the cartographer, fell afoul of quicksand on the first day, sinking without trace. We've seen lions and leopards near the camp at night. To add to our troubles, we had to leave Captain McFadden behind in a Mbuti village—and with the greatest reluctance of the chief—because his drunkenness was becoming too much for us and we feared malaria had him in its clutches. I only pray that the natives can withstand him! Then crocodiles took one of the guides during the night. The next day, our bungling Dr Ives lost the compass and so we've followed the rudimentary sketches judging by the sun, the map gleaned from the prior Stanley expedition (and the munificence of the Royal Geographical Society, of course). We mean to force our way to the temple, out here where the villages and the lake names run out. I'm afraid to tell you that the worst of our ills is undeniably our son, who appears more unruly by the day and makes me regret with every step that I decided to bring him along, sparing you the burden in your sickness.

Nevertheless, Kabou, the famous "ape-man", assures me that we draw near our prize! Why, this very afternoon we encountered a stone marking the gates of the ancient kingdom, a granite pillar of untold centuries, featuring the graven face of Mboo himself. Should we find the seat of the erstwhile 'python god', that forgotten icon of masculine desire, then we have every reason to hope that the legend of the night orchid will also prove true. Once plucked under a full moon, I shall speed home to you at once with its curative properties!

Linger yet, sweet Eunice. I labour for your life. Though the jungle may shriek and the mosquitoes sting, each arduous step brings me closer to your side, with a flower in my faithful grip.

Your dearest husband.

The letter, he knew, would never be sent. It was a nightly habit for his own comfort, easing him where the whiskey could not. Chuffing his pipe, Lord Roland resolved to take in the air and stumbled out into the gloaming, tobacco smoke wreathing with the mist. It pleased him to find Dr Ives stoking the fire and he wandered on to the edge of the little camp, peering down through the purple trees towards the gleam of the river. At this hour, the forest was most alive, a chorus of birds and beasts shaking off the heat. Its many perils would keep the party close to camp, and yet at first he could see nothing but the doctor and the mules, one coughing and slapping at the midges, the others with heads in nosebags. It was only when he made out a muffled titter that he shuffled down a slope and spied Lysander crouched behind a fallen limba tree. What in blazes was he about? Squinting beyond, he caught sight of Kabou by the river, and Lord Roland's cheeks coloured under his beard. The ape-man stood, loincloth discarded on a branch, washing himself in the shoals. In his usual steady manner, the famed 'lord' who'd relinquished his title to languish here in the African wilds, was sluicing water over his chest, his neck, and his considerable groin, providing Roland's son with a private spectacle. The swift jigging of Lysander's elbow in the gloom forbade any hiss of fatherly chastisement, the unspoken laws of gentlemen far exceeding those of patriarchal outrage.

Appalled, and hoarding a lungful of smoke, he moved to retreat as quietly as possible. It was then that he spied Mr Bell, the rifleman, standing some distance away on the other side of the glade, his grin faded in the murk and his gaze fixed firmly on Lysander.

From that furtive trio of watchers, Roland slipped away unseen, an unbidden image of the ancient pillar swimming in his mind and with it a niggling unease.

Late morning saw the party battling up an overgrown hill for a better view of the surrounding landscape. Below, the 'Lungs of Africa' spread wide and throbbing, a sea of green that plunged from the range and into the navel of a broad and shadowy valley. The raffia and palms were particularly thick here—so thick, in fact, that Dr Ives questioned Kabou about his navigation twice on their struggle to the summit and Roland was moved to remind him, a little churlishly, that he had been the one to lose the compass.

A streak of sinew in the scrub, the ape-man paid neither of them any mind, strolling ahead as if they were on their way to a Hyde Park picnic and not stuck here in the middle of the blasted jungle. True to form, Lysander whined the whole way up, about exhaustion, the flies, the unfairness of Oxford deans and the lack of Bolly. When he slipped on mulch and went tumbling backwards, he was caught—not without grace—by a grim-faced Mr Bell, who was leading the mules and chugging up the rise like an old coal train, a cigar clutched between his teeth. How the lad wriggled and squealed! Peafowls flapped from the brush and somewhere okapi scurried, and it took a bark from Roland to calm the confusion, his son wrenching himself free from the unwanted embrace and clinging to dignity as he did his best to prance up the slope.

In this fashion, the four of them emerged on the summit of the nameless hill and were treated to a breathless panorama of the forest and a rigid Kabou, their guide standing with spread legs and pointing ahead into the distance.

'By George, can it be?'

Roland slipped off his hat and snapped his fingers for the telescope. Dr Ives obliged him and in gasping wonder, the intrepid lord surveyed the haze miles yonder. There was the unmistakable swell of ruins below, peeping through the settling mist. The structures, he saw, were cylindrical and worn, reminiscent of the monolith they'd spied the day before. Two low, round, and crumbled turrets flanked the taller central one—a thick, vine-choked stub of granite that rose to an expected dome, its tip split crosswise in a narrow opening like an eye, presumably to let in the sunlight. Who knew what ancients had worshipped there?

Well, a tribe, according to the tomes that Roland had studied, who had made sacrifices of bread and blood in return for virility and their hearts' desires. From afar, the explorers greeted the phallic impression without mirth, their sheer fatigue forbidding it. No doubt remained, however, of the sight which they beheld. The temple of the serpent king, Mboo, the 'python god' of the Mbuti—or of their ancestors, long since faded and forgotten in these lands.

'Another day, no more,' Kabou informed them in his educated tones. 'Should you wish to proceed, sir. The tribes never come here. They say the gardens of the king are cursed.'

Lysander guffawed.

'What the devil do you mean?' blustered Dr Ives. 'We haven't come all this way for nothing, sir.'

'They say the earth itself holds the power of the god. They say that every step closer to the temple will addle and drive men mad.'

'Savages!' Lysander spat, but the disdain was wiped from his face by a cocked eye from the ape-man.

'I've read the legends, Mister Kabou,' Roland told their guide. 'One can only pray that the tale of the orchid holds as true. Fear not, we shan't tarry long. Tomorrow the moon waxes to full and signals the start of our return. Come along, Mr Bell. We'll stop for lunch at the foot of this blasted hill.'

The rifleman, rank and sour, muttered something about 'pork pies' and continued to badger the mules across the bluff. Dr Ives pocketed his telescope. Lysander, nose high, afforded the ape-man a smug look and skipped after his father.

'We stand on the brink of a grand discovery,' the youth trilled to no one in particular. 'We'll be the toast of England. Dining with Asquith himself. A flower to cure all ills and make heroes of us all!'

Kabou followed in silence.

Come late afternoon—hot, weary, and the jungle singing—the four men entered a broad clearing in the valley and stumbled across further ruins. Chimps scattered from the litter of spherical stone objects. Snakes slithered into cracks. The stench of mud and lobelias hung heavy in the air along with the pervasive reek of sweat. Each of the spheres—Roland counted nine in all—was the size of an automobile, the debris strewn without regard across the low vegetation. Somewhere, an elephant hooted to announce the party's emergence from the forest, the lot of them blinking in the sun.

It was Dr Ives who hobbled to the first of the stones, ignoring a hiss from Roland and stroking its weathered surface. Under the moss, it was hard to notice the carvings at first, but the doctor picked them out with increasing fervour, one chubby hand rubbing at the rock.

'Great Scott, Rollo!' the anthropologist expounded. 'Runes. Pictograms. Can you believe it? Look. This represents a man bending to pick up rocks for construction. And the man behind him is—oh. Oh, my goodness.'

'Well, what is it, man?'

Where Roland expressed frustration, Lysander became immediately curious, craning his neck to peer at the sphere. A schoolboy to the last, he snickered, relishing the reddening face of Ives and the way that the little man shuffled and coughed.

'I must confess my knowledge falls short, sirs. I imagine I've misinterpreted the—'

'These are the shattered balls of Mboo,' Kabou interjected, as calm as ever. He slipped forth to examine the stone. 'The tribe of old was a sex cult, concentrated on male desire. If my memory of the dialect serves, this was a sacred court dedicated to the instruction of youths in the carnal arts, their efforts and their seed given to the glory of the god. Once deemed a man, each would then return to their tribes, presumably to share whatever they'd learnt, to please their wives, sire children, and so forth. The balls hold many secrets. The essence of life itself.'

Roland himself was blushing now, more crimson than his sunburn. Dr Ives squirmed. Mr Bell gave a grunt, chuffing smoke. Lysander clapped his hands and trumpeted.

'Goodness, Father. We stand in a shrine to buggery and forni—'

'That's quite enough.' Roland cuffed his son around the ear, perturbed by the self-righteous look of him. To the wider gathering, he said, 'All of this is of great interest, but it's by-the-by. Do remember that we came here for the flower. Every minute we linger draws poor Eunice closer to the grave.'

Thus sobered, Mr Bell set about making camp, turning to the mules with a veiled sneer. Dr Ives nodded, half-interested, then turned again to peer at the stone, his spectacles perched on the end of his nose.

'There's magic here,' Kabou said, grabbing the doctor's wrist. 'Old magic. It wouldn't do to touch them.'

As if stung, the doctor withdrew, turning his mind to the building of a fire.

Lysander stared at the ape-man. When Kabou met his gaze, he winked.

The once-titled lord shook his head and went in search of water.

That night in his tent, Lord Roland wrote:

Oh, Eunice. There's such an ache in me. Perhaps it's the insufferable heat. Perhaps it's the subliminal prurience that haunts this tangled thicket of myth, making me thirst and yearn so. Twice today, I've found myself thus discomforted, an unbidden throbbing betwixt my legs. Why, it's as if the legend itself grips me, cupping my family jewels with tenderness and then slowly becoming a vice. Well, it's doubtful you shall read this and so I vent my lust, on paper instead of at your breast. How I miss you! Why, I'm reminded of that time at Broadstairs in the park when you reached under the hat in my lap and took me firmly in hand, the both of us wary of passersby yet determined to see out our need...

They found Dr Ives in the morning, a little after dawn. It was Lysander who screamed and Kabou who came running, urging Lord Roland from his tent. Roused from dreams in which a thousand powdered ladies had chased him through a park and torn at his clothes until, bloodied and naked, they set upon him at the edge of a lake, a whirligig of ravenous hands and questing mouths... He wasn't best pleased to find himself shaken from sleep. Less so when he stumbled out and, like the others, saw Monty on the stone.

'By fuckery,' growled Mr Bell, summing up the sight.

Lysander laughed. A shrill sound, more shocked than amused.

Atop the granite sphere, Dr Ives laboured. His sabaton had fallen off as well as his spectacles, both discarded in the grass. At some point in the night, the little man had scaled the rubble, wrenched down his trousers and, rump exposed to the rising sun, begun humping away at the stone, having found some fissure or crack that pleased him. But there was horror in the sight. Such horror! How long the doctor had struggled here, pale-faced, his tongue lolling, his eyes rolled up to show the whites, could only be guessed at by the blood. Runnels of the stuff were trickling down the sides of the sphere, dripping over the moss and the pictograms, reddening the sward. Either unaware or unashamed of their presence, Ives continued his ill-advised congress, his thighs slapping at the stone, abandoned.

'Christ in heaven!' Roland roared, aghast. 'Get the poor man down!'

Mr Bell fumbled with his rifle, apparently unable to think of what to do without it. Lysander winced and tittered and danced, useless as a boiled carrot. It was Kabou, blessed Kabou, who leapt up onto the sphere and, on nimble feet, dislodged the groaning, pumping doctor from his plight. With a watery sigh, Montgomery Ives rolled from the stone and slumped into the grass, lying sprawled on his back and leaving no one in doubt as to his ruin. Only a red, tattered, and mangled mess remained between his legs.

Roland looked away, thunderstruck. He met the gaze of the ape-man, who'd descended from the sphere as if it were a burning coal, the heat of it bright in his eyes.

'Magic,' Kabou told them. 'A curse.'

There was no time to bury the doctor. Roland had done what he could, making the man comfortable, promising to send his love to his wife who waited in distant Buckinghamshire. The man had lost too much blood. The flies were having a heyday. Kabou, mouth downturned and peering at the sun, urged them to proceed. It wouldn't do to linger, he said. Their intrusion on the ruins and the plucking of the orchid must needs be swift, if they hoped to make it out at all. Tonight, the moon would be full.

Lysander, naturally, complained. He wanted to go home. Father had said nothing about a curse. Another man lay dead. *Monty!* He wanted Dear Mummy. Moved by his whining, the gruff Mr Bell stepped forward to calm the lad, and, with a queasiness in the pit of his stomach, Roland watched his son wriggle then surrender to his embrace, sobbing into the rifleman's chest like some hammy Shakespearean actor in a Lyceum romance. It was all Roland needed to call the dwindled party to saddle up. Another life lay in peril, miles away. To lose her would see him undone.

Take Ives as your sacrifice then, you bastard god, the lord thought without charity, *and surrender to us your bounty.*

Nevertheless, for all of Kabou's steadfast guidance (they said he spoke to the animals), the going that day was hard. And in quite literal terms. It was as if the air of the valley were water, packed between the hills and swimming with midges, seeping into every crack and crevice. Between thighs and hairy buttocks. Baboons watched their progress from the sheltering branches, yawning in the strengthening sun. Turacos called, barking. Even the wind, for which all were thankful, sighed through the liquid trees in a ceaseless chant, rendering the forest dreamlike, their steps slow.

And a certain fervour was dogging Roland. His nerves tingled with every drop of sweat to run down his back, seemingly pooling at his groin. His swollen member throbbed throughout the morning and into the afternoon. No matter how he pictured his grandmother—a shell of a woman in white lace coughing up bile on her deathbed—or the buckets of worms he'd seen slithering in a cookpot in one of the Mbuti villages, he couldn't dissuade himself from his passion. Come lunchtime, it dawned on him that he wasn't alone in his experience, for Lysander lagged some yards behind, his usual prideful strut reduced to an awkward lope. Mr Bell, that captain of mules, kept pausing to tug at the front of his trousers, shifting in obvious discomfort, and at one point he pulled out his shirt to drape over his thighs in an attempt at modesty. After they'd dined on stale ham and apples, Kabou returned to them from scouting ahead and the game was up. A loincloth was no good for discretion and the engorgement of the ape-man was evident to all, his rigid rudder seen plain through his skins—and one that put Roland's to shame, a spicket as thick as a vine and doubtless as smooth to the touch if only—

Good heavens. Get a hold of yourself, man!

None in the party mentioned it, of course. The unspoken laws of gentlemen would never brook such a discussion, yet all noticed and sensed the growing disquiet, the mystery between the trees. Red-cheeked, with furtive glances and coughs, the four of them pressed on towards the temple, each occupied by his own thoughts. And Kabou kept prudently ahead, sniffing out any hidden threat, lions and traps and suchlike. If any had scorned the ape-man's tale of magic, they had cause to regret it now. There was something in the air, something in the blood, preying upon them as it had on the poor Dr Ives. While thought of the tragedy seemed unable to soften Roland, the gruesome outcome of the power in these lands kept him upright and walking, his machete swinging.

He meant to steal nectar from the gods. He told himself the trek would be worth it.

Dusk descended on the forest, a settling shroud. *The last dusk before victory*. Roland told himself that too. Aching, dizzy, and not a little sore, the party at last reached the forecourt of the temple, their boots ringing on stone cracked, crumbling, and weed-choked. Mr Bell went off to check the camp perimeter. He was gone for some time. Kabou had yet to appear on an overhead branch or come swinging, as was his wont, on some dangling vine or other. As darkness crept over the encampment, Roland found himself glad of it, veiling as it did the surrounding statues and columns, each one graven with runes and resembling the block-shouldered figures of men. *Oh, to what dark places you've taken me, Eunice.* Unease danced in his nerves and not all of it was due to archaic impropriety, his modern mores at odds with the ruins around him. He'd thought Lysander enough of a handful. The statues lining the atrium disabused him of the notion. It was hard to ignore the protuberance of each — moss-covered, weatherworn and thick, a row of exaggerated priapi leading to the narrow mouth of the temple. There, steps led steeply upward, the great domed tower soaring above, its narrow eye awaiting the moon.

The attack, when it came, was silent and swift. The ageing lord had been instructing his son in the building of a fire—a frustrating effort at best—when a shadow detached itself from the foot of the nearest plinth and leapt for Lysander, fangs bared. The lad screamed as a sudden velvet weight flung him to his belly in a strew of kindling—unlit, thank God. The boy at least had the sense to cover his head, the beast snapping for the softer parts of him. Blood sprayed across the flagstones in a black fan. Another second and he would've been torn apart by the very jungle he reviled, but in this he was fortunate. Another shadow sprang from the murk and, steadying his boots against stone, Mr Bell took aim, butt against his shoulder. His rifle rang out, shaking dust from the statues, setting night birds to flight. The leopard yelped and rolled clear, a scrabble of claws and tail. Encouraged, Mr Bell stepped forth—his belt loose, shirt disarrayed—and fired again, the echoes discordant, and then the beast lay still.

'Got the bastard,' the rifleman grinned, trembling in the gloom regardless. 'That'll make a fine skin to take home to Dartford.'

Roland regarded the crazed look in his eye. His concern, naturally, was for his son.

Lysander lay groaning, the back of his khaki shirt damp and shredded.

Nevertheless, they'd come too far to turn back now.

'Get him up, damn you. We have this night, and this night only.'

Kabou, when he returned, refused to enter the temple.

'It does not do to steal from the gods, sir.' The ape-man stood, filthy and engorged, his hooded eyes piercing the narrow mouth of the edifice. For the first time on their journey, Roland detected fear in him. 'Let the leopard serve as your last warning, my Lord, as if the pillar, the balls, and your doctor weren't enough. Will you deafen yourself to reason, man?'

Considering the squeals and sniffles of Lysander, bandaged as best they could manage and presently propped on Mr Bell's shoulder, Roland wished that he *were* deaf. The moon hung fat above the gardens of the serpent king. The time had come. In his heart, his need spoke loudest of all.

'You know my cause, sir. I'll not let my wife perish. It ill behooves you to suggest it.'

'Faugh! I merely speak to nature, that all must follow its natural course. And for men like you it was ever thus, to tread uninvited in strange lands and imagine yourself a king. All that comes of it is suffering and pain—and chiefly for the native.' Kabou shook his head. 'I shall wait without. On your head be it.'

'Such was our agreement.' Roland was rather curt in his consent, and too anguished between the legs, from the smell of blood to his own cephalic deprivation, to argue. 'I shall return victorious and you shall lead us from this hell.'

'Farewell, Lord Moss.'

'Enough now.' He swayed a little, dizzied. 'We proceed.'

Then, calling to Mr Bell to attend him and unable to hide a sneer at his whimpering son, Roland turned and ventured into the temple mouth.

Along with Roland's own growing discomfort, the party shared the restless ache of desire—even Lysander in his distress, the front of his pantaloons taut and bulging—and the temple seemed set to make a mockery of them. The stairway that greeted them was more akin to a ladder, a lichen-and-vine ravel that soared at a nigh on eighty-degree angle into the heights of the shrine. The slick stone and the stagnant air caused both Mr Bell and himself to avail themselves of the handles on either side—priapic, round-headed members of stone curving outward from the wall. The atmosphere throbbed with expectation, with the ruttish blood in their veins, with echoes like laughter at all that made them men.

'Gar!' Mr Bell exclaimed halfway up, perspiring under the weight of his sobbing burden. 'One can scarce breathe in here. The wind… the wind… it's unnatural. A man could lose a hold of… his senses.'

'Hush, Mr Bell. We're drawing close to the summit.'

Nevertheless, the rifleman spoke true. The moonlight fell in slender beams through narrow apertures above, rendering all an illusion of breadth and dimension, the walls fluid and looming, the staircase at one time short and at another interminable. Yet it was the ceaseless shifting of the air that caused him the greatest complaint, tugging at Lord Roland's khakis, cooling the sweat on his skin, caressing the polished dome of his head. The higher he climbed, the more the absurdities took hold. Graven faces leered from the walls, tongues out as though to lick the impressions of his footfalls in the dust. Spiders scuttled, gigantic in the adumbration, suspended like ripe, hirsute plums from webs of milk and gossamer. And the wind became as a serpent, coiling around his limbs, slipping up his trouser legs, pressing and pushing against his manhood with such an alien rhythm and force that he found himself emerging on the dais in a panting, shivering heap. In his mind, Eunice swam, *en deshabille* on a silken eiderdown in some fine mansion or other, her legs spread to embrace him. The torment deepened with every breath, strange, sinful thoughts of depravities needling through his more commonplace appetites. Helpless to repel them, gasping on the stone, he found himself afflicted by musings of how the carved protrusions of the ladder might feel to the touch, the taste—and the depth of the sensation were such a corpulent todger to penetrate him, skewer him to the rock, lost in the mindless pounding of his own blood, of ancient, sorcerous drums…

Christ in heaven. Desist!

Battling the sensory assault, Roland drew himself up on his knees, alarmed to discover that Lysander and his grizzled crutch, Mr Bell, had fallen some distance behind. He could barely see them in the gloom, a wavering, indistinct shape on the steps below. But the moon—*oh, the moon!*—was high and shining in dull argent through the eye of the dome, a broad and singular beam falling on the altar before him. There, to his breathless delight, he observed the uncoiling of a sprig of green, slipping through a crack in the stone. Even as he watched, petals of a rich velvet blue unfurled from the questing stamen, each one hand-sized and ablaze in the radiance, calling to him through his physical plight. In that moment, Eunice, Lysander, and the rifleman were forgotten. Kabou's warning was as if the man had never spoken. *The legend was true!* Upon the altar sprouted the marvel of the night orchid, which Roland had crossed oceans to find, braving the jungle and the hoodoo of the serpent king for its promise of hope and salvation. Not to mention the medical find of the century. Press interviews. Prizes. And money.

Shuddering, every nerve aflame and fit to climax, Lord Roland Moss reached out for the flower.

Before his fingers closed on his bounty, the shadows around the altar shifted and bulged. Dazed as he was, he might've thought it another mirage, a phantasm spun by moonlight and fatigue, and continued in his desperate plucking of the orchid. Alas, it wasn't to be. When the shifting bulk above him eclipsed the moonlight falling through the roof of the strangled temple, he knew. The pale, fat, veinous coils that detached themselves from the crumbled plinth held an unmistakable impression of life. At first, he imagined the beast a snake of some kind—a striped python thirty feet long—but the pinkish length of the thing gave him pause. As the creature stiffened and drew itself to its full height, its hood of folded skin slipped back, revealing a plump and glossy head, all a swollen, wicked purple. Its mouth (or perchance an eye) was no more than a vertical slit in its blind, freakish countenance, regarding him with outrage.

Gads! The size of the thing!

The beast pulsed, rearing, some doubtless noxious fluid glittering around its narrow orifice. Roland had faced diabolical creatures enough in his explorations of the Dark Continent to anticipate an imminent attack and threw his arms up, surrendering the flower. However, it was this hasty retreat that proved the end of his endeavour. His boot-heel slipped on the edge of the dais and, with nothing to grasp at but air, he found himself wheeling away from the rigid serpent—the living symbol of primordial Mboo—and plunging backwards down the steep stone steps.

There was naught to catch him as he fell, a cry for dear Eunice flying from his throat. Over and over, he tumbled into the awaiting gloom. In a blur, he passed poor Lysander and Mr Bell, and thus bore witness to one final terror. His poor boy lay sprawled on his back, cold and silent on the stone, his injuries having at last overcome him. Poised above, the rifleman laboured, trousers yanked down around his knees, buttocks pumping for all they were worth at the youth's defenceless face. Blood dripped down the steps, for Mr Bell had selected the dubious portal of an eye socket for his ghastly pleasure, and maddened, laughing, had given no regard to the pallid corpse that had once been his employer's son.

The sight alone confirmed damnation. Not a one of them were to leave the temple alive, claimed and devoured by the serpent king. Then all was air, blankness, and regret, and Roland fell head over heels into the dark. None remained to hear his intrepid bones crack and shatter on stone.

It was dawn when Kabou emerged from the forest to survey the vine-choked temple, tall, bulbous, and abandoned for aeons by the tribes hereabouts, with none but the foolish venturing thither. Mist-shrouded, dense, the Congo kept her secrets and among them dwelt the wise. Since his retreat, the ape-man had availed himself of a potion from a nearby village, part venom and part river mud, that allowed him to stand on the bluff in grim quietude, observing the scene of the expedition's undoing without the hindrance of jungle magic. Without lascivious thoughts.

Magic, Kabou had told them. *A curse.*

Yes, he had tried to warn them. It was only polite, a remnant from his days as a gentleman with lands and a title, years ago in long-forgotten England. It had been no use. Men such as those never listened.

And others would come, he knew, just as they always came, seeking treasures, empires, slaves. If they asked, Kabou told himself, he would oblige as ever and lead them to the temple. It was the way of things. His pact with the forest. What little he could do.

Shaking his head, he turned away. Turacos shrieked in the thicket, taking to the air, but none could ever grate on him as much as the carping and snivelling of Lord Roland's son.

Grabbing a vine, Kabou swung off into the jungle, glad of the comparative peace.

Dusk and Dawn in the Grand Bazaar

John Berkeley

The Grand Bazaar isn't so much the sort of place that people go looking for trouble as it is the sort of place that trouble goes looking for dinner. I had a whole heap of trouble behind me, and I figured it could use a meal.

Call me a soft touch.

The sandstorm already had dinner sorted, but the assassins and spies and mercenaries were probably getting peckish. They'd spent a few days chasing me through the Noctis Labyrinth and the upper Mariner Valley, after all.

When an offworld government offers three times the asking price to deliver a simple cryocrystal, you just know it's too good to be true. The official I dealt with in the Commonwealth High Commission at Pavonis was fat and charming in the way only a diplomat could be. Just a single cryocrystal with a message in it. How hard could it be? It was only when I realised that both the Americans and the Soviets were after it, along with a bunch of others, that I decided I was going to need to get creative as I couriered it to the ruined Pyramid of Podor down in Argyre.

I had the Nectaris Mountains ahead of me and practically half the galaxy beating a path down the Mariner Valley behind. And a sandstorm just about to blow in off Noachis, just to make things interesting.

Well, in for a penny, in for a pound, as they used to say on—

—*Bang*!

I ducked and swerved as something whip-cracked off the roof of my drift-rover. The short-range scope was clear; I zoomed the range out—whoever-it-was must have taken a potshot from over a kilometre away.

I was out of options and needed somewhere safe, fast. Just my luck that the nearest station was Nectaris.

But that shot was from something big—and the sandstorm was getting closer, too.

Just one night. I just had to stay alive *one* night. I could worry about how I was going to make it to Podor in one piece in the morning.

So I swore and thumbed the comm.

'This is Jarazan Crael, Tharsis Courier Service, to Nectaris Station, requesting entry to the Grand Bazaar.' I tapped my ident on my drift-rover's console screen. My hair was the wrong colour and I had more stubble than I like (in that I had any at all), but I was still scrawny, and the cheekbones and chin were about right.

It was an older ident, but it checked out.

'*Greetings, [Mister] [Crael]*,' said the Bazaar's autocomp in its androgynous monotone, as an equally androgynous holographic avatar-head appeared on my dashboard. '*In the name of the Six Bardos, welcome [back] to Nectaris Market, the Grand Bazaar of Mars—*'

'—Yes, I know, I—'

It was going to keep talking, wasn't it?

'*–Nectaris Market is a free colony of the Mariner Valley Protectorates, independently governed by the Six Bardos of the Bazaar (may their names be blessed)—*'

—*Bang*!

—A second round ricocheted off the canopy and sent a crack haring down the left of the windscreen—

'—*All visitors are advised to familiarise themselves with local contract law before entry.*'

I glanced at the fresh crack in my windscreen and chuckled. Usually, I'd have brushed that last comment off, but with the week I was having, I'd actually spent the last few hours reading some of the more obscure laws.

'Already done,' I assured the autocomp. 'Tell the Six Bardos I say hi.' No one really knew who or what the Six Bardos were, other than '*not to be screwed with*'—and that usually dealt with the other questions too.

Today, I was counting on it.

'*The Six Bardos can be reached in the usual fashion via their Factor's office. Stand by; you are being scanned prior to entry.*'

I'd already spotted the scout drone on my scope; as I watched, it cast a flickering blue light over my drift-rover.

Anywhere else, it would have been checking me out for contraband and suchlike. But contraband wasn't a thing at the Grand Bazaar, so all they were doing was seeing what I was carrying so the Six Bardos' security would know what they were shooting at if things came to it.

Hopefully whoever-it-was shooting at me would see the scout drone and hang back.

'Please tell the Factor I need to speak to them urgently,' I said as levelly as I could.

'*Courier status confirmed; diplomatic packet recognised. Access to the secure bays is [granted]. I have notified the Factor's office. Do you require directions to the—*'

'—Got it, and no, thanks, I'll walk when I get there,' I cut in as soon as the scanner finished, waving a hand as it prattled.

'*Very well. The Factor will speak to you now, [Mister] [Crael]. Have a good day.*'

'We'll see about that,' I muttered as the channel blinked and the autocomp's head was replaced by a flashing standby dot.

The dot was replaced by a hologram of a bald, almond-shaped head with great, mournful turquoise eyes and a stylish rebreather, accented in black and gold to offset the wearer's fawn skin.

'*Crael? I say, Crael! Welcome back! In a hurry, I see... (gasp)*'

Houhnhof voices were hard to tell apart because of their rebreathers, but I definitely recognised that one. No one knew for sure what the Six Bardos actually *were*, but everyone knew their Factor.

'Evening, Grace. Good to hear you,' I said. It was, as always, at least partly true.

'*Likewise. Now (gasp), what can I do for you?*'

I checked that that damned cryocrystal was still in my safe pouch—and then I checked my long-range scope just to be sure. Still nothing. Maybe whoever was after me was hanging back after all.

'Grace, I need to invoke the old sanctuary laws. I don't have much time.'

The drone had long since flitted away—I was now driving down a sandstone ravine wide enough for three drift-rovers to pass lengthways and curving steadily towards the foot of the mountains ahead.

Grace cocked zyr head to one side. '*Well, you certainly have (gasp) my attention. Whether you have the Bardos', we shall see. As Factor, I can, of course, provide—*'

I gave zyn a tight smile. '—No, not *your* sanctuary, Grace; the Bardos'.'

Zyr vast turquoise eyes widened and then narrowed, asterisk-like, along all three axes of symmetry at once—it's always disconcerting being scrutinised by a houhnhof, even a holographic one. Grace and I went way back, good and bad. Only ever business, and I was never great at reading alien expressions, but zy certainly seemed... uncomfortable.

Zy coughed into zyr rebreather. '*You… wish to invoke sanctuary with the* Six Bardos? *Crael, no one has made such a bargain since the time your Commonwealth made the first (gasp) human landfall.*'

I gave zyn a smile. 'So it's been done before, then?'

'*Well… (gasp) I suppose there* is *precedent,*' zy conceded, rocking zyr head back and forth thoughtfully. '*You will need to tread very carefully, though.*'

That was the point. I cocked my head, mirroring zyr gesture. 'Why?'

'*Well, each Bardo has their own… preoccupation. And they are, of course, (gasp), extremely powerful and private individuals with whom it is best not to trifle. Which of the six do you wish to petition?*'

'All of them.'

Those eyes went wide again. Grace blinked at me and seemed to focus on something else—presumably tapping a few commands on zyr desk. Whatever response zy got seemed to satisfy zyn.

'*(gasp) Well, you have their attention, at least…*'

The idea of being watched by the Six Bardos made me feel… oddly carefree, actually. They could probably already tell my pulse had quickened by scrutinising me over the comm. Not licking my lips right then would at least tell them I was able to retain a degree of self-control.

So, I licked my lips.

'*…However, only the Bardo Kyenay is prepared to grant you sanctuary at this time. Do you accept?*'

I tried not to stare too obviously. I hadn't expected *any* of them to actually agree. I tried to remember which one Kyenay was. The Six Bardos had many names, because of course they did, and no one really knew who or what they all were, because of course they didn't, but the one thing most agreed on was that they had something to do with the six stages of life, or was it death, or was it reincarnation, or was it consciousness? It was easy to lose track—which was just how the Six Bardos liked it.

Didn't Kyenay have something to do with life? That sounded better than the death one, anyway.

'I accept. Please give Kyenay… my thanks.'

Those eyes narrowed on the horizontal axis, which told me that Grace was smiling under zyr rebreather. Zy wasn't actually called Grace—houhnhofs have a whole thing about names—but, even so, if I had Grace's name, I'd abbreviate it too.

'Then… ah, yes. On behalf of and in the name of Kyenay, Bardo of Life of the Grand Bazaar of Nectaris (may her name be (gasp) blessed), I, the Graceless Insufferable Pedant, Factor of the Six Bardos, grant you, Jarazan Crael, sanctuary of the Grand Bazaar of Nectaris. In exchange, you shall grant the Bardo Kyenay this same right, should she ever have (gasp) need of it from you, and you shall perform a single equitable task for her that will neither prejudice your life nor your position.'

I remembered what I could of those pages of legalese I'd read on the way in. 'And I promise not to be a burden during my stay.'

'That (gasp) would be appreciated.'

And the less said about the folks after me, the better.

'I hope to be leaving in the morning anyway, once the storm has passed. Work to do.' Again—not untrue.

'Yes, it has come to my attention that you have resumed your career as (gasp) a courier. I assume you are here on business rather than pleasure?'

I quirked a smile. 'Is it too much to ask for both?'

Zy shrugged. 'If you cannot find it at Nectaris Market, such a thing does not exist.'

'Exactly.'

'Though, I'm sure you had different colouration the last time we spoke.'

My hand went to my hair—sea green rather than the usual mouse-blond. 'This? I… fancied a change,' I lied.

Zy scowled at something. 'Curious. (gasp) Our scan shows your drift-rover appears to have taken fire from a military-grade anti-materiel rifle.'

Well, shit.

I said as much, too.

Grace blinked at me. '*I have never understood the human tendency to use bodily functions as expletives. Have you ever met anyone who does not, as you so eloquently put it, (gasp) shit?*'

That threw me enough for me to say, 'I have, actually, but that's beside the point' before I could stop myself.

Grace was watching me with what I thought was a tinge of sadness. '*I trust you know what you are doing, Crael.*'

I certainly did, but not in the way zy meant. 'Thank you for giving me the… opportunity.' I nearly said *warning*, but houhnhofs could be funny about things like that. Better to give zyn the impression of having done zyr duty. 'But you know how it is.'

Grace bowed zyr head. '*Indeed. Under usual circumstances, I would suggest we go for a drink, but this time I will politely request you remain in the Lower Market for the duration of your (gasp) stay.*'

I felt my jaw set. So much for waiting the night out in comfort.

'Yeah. I hear you,' I said, managing not to make it sound rude.

'*In that case, I believe our business is concluded. (gasp) May you sail on fragrant seas, Jarazan Crael of Cydonia.*'

I was so surprised to receive the honoured houhnhof farewell that I briefly forgot that I'd told zyn where I was from.

The channel died.

I indulged in that baffling human tendency to use bodily functions as expletives again. Then I sighed and focused on driving.

Well, it didn't look like anyone was behind me. But then, I'd never seen who it was who shot at me with a sodding anti-materiel rifle…

The track headed into a cleft in the reddish basalt at the tip of the Nectaris Mountains. Some cave or other—a lava tunnel, probably—led into the rock, and past large floodlit caves with all sorts of vehicles, both human and otherwise. The indicator boards flashed for me to continue into the secure bays.

No one had followed me in, which could have been as suspicious as it could have been normal.

On the one hand, there was a sandstorm coming in and people would be hunkering down... On the other hand, given the choice between the storm and the Grand Bazaar, most people might prefer their chances in the sandstorm. I figured both would have assassins and mercenaries, but the sandstorm wouldn't have bars or the potential for attractive company.

Call me old-fashioned.

The secure bays were pretty deserted—a few robots tending drift-rovers here, a youngish green-skinned Venusian guy cleaning a racer there (speaking of attractive company...). No other drivers, at least.

Looking at him a second time, under other circumstances I might have offered to buy the (shirtless) Venusian a drink. As it was, I made a swift exit, hoping he'd be here next time—and that there would *be* a next time.

The walkway to the main bazaar was open to the elements, but it would be less crowded than a shuttle train, particularly with the storm coming in.

A dusk-bloated sun was lumbering to the canyon-floor horizon behind me through the first traces of the storm. According to my sidenote, Saravan Crater had already gone dark in more ways than one, a hundred miles or so southeast. At least the villagers would be safe in their lava tunnels and rice burrows.

The breeze was becoming stale as I climbed the red basalt steps; the few closed stumps of rhubarb trees showed that even the local plant life was hunkering down. I suppose I was doing the same—in my own way.

In the rock face ahead, the vast, pearlescent outer doors were open to the sunset; the throat of the market was a tunnel fully fifty yards across and a hundred or more deep. The more permanent outside stalls were already shuttered; the less-permanent ones were being dismantled by the concession-holders as I watched.

Thinking of the place's name, someone-or-other (probably either some meddling human or a houhnhof with a sense of humour) had trained fruit trees from Earth to climb the walls around the tunnel entrance. Whoever-it-was had long ago left them to their own devices, and the trees had become something... *else*, withered and contorted but refusing to die as their roots burst the containers of Earthsoil and quested for water and nutriment in the alien stuff of Mars instead. I could swear those fruit glow, sometimes.

I felt my back straighten as I stepped into that vast basalt tunnel. Something about getting inside just before a storm always made me free to walk that bit taller.

Let's see the mercs follow me in here.

The last rays of sunset were filtering in through the outer doors as they closed, spilling into the nearest of the main cavern halls ahead of me.

And where they hit, they shattered against spun glass and polymer signs and artworks—mosaics and fabricants of a hundred different traditions and none. Static, animated, neon, holographic, phosphorescent, bioluminescent, and some which were decidedly none of the above, all jostling for attention in a flurry of human and alien languages.

Above everything loomed a camphor tree from Earth, grown colossal in Mars' lighter gravity—and which seemed to almost hold up the cavern roof, let alone the signs, stalls, and art festooning it. The hubbub of stalls and semi-permanent shops were arrayed in dizzying rings around a central plaza at its bole.

Each hall had something different at the centre—most had plazas or food courts, but some had gambling floors or a showroom of expensive racers at their heart; and, if not that, everything from a beer hall (or what passed for one on Mars), to a Venusian spa, a park, or the legendary Nectaris Stock Exchange, which was supposed to be the ace in the Six Bardos' collective hole, giving them power over fully half of Mars.

The stallholders were as eclectic as the wares they sold: robots, from the rusted to the glittering from every species, competed with Venusians who could be mistaken for humans but for their green, violet, or paint-white skin; slender, rebreather-wearing houhnhofs with spidery fingers, long robes, and huge, expressive eyes; great, rotund, metal-hued egesterians, with their pairs of drooping tentacle-trunks like prehensile, inquisitive moustaches—and more besides. There were a few scatterings of humans here and there too, usually manning the shabbier stalls. There was even an ilhinovetch flittering ponderously over a stall of remarkable fruits and vegetables.

'Parts for your drift-rover! The latest specs at prices you can afford!'

'*Fine new clothes, (gasp), straight from the Looms of Isdis!*'

'The purest lutherium the Bardos will allow, the best in all of Tharsis!'

You learn soon enough to slightly un-focus your gaze, almost as if pretending to be drunk. Making eye contact with the stallholders was always the first mistake.

'Fresh fruit from the gardens of the Three Worlds and beyond! Get your swamp-apples here! Nectarines, half price!' (That was usually the second.)

I wandered for a bit and decided to head for Gulliver's Rest—a wedge of one of the outer circuits of the plaza under a branch of the camphor tree.

The last of the sunlight had died and the night lamps had flickered into bioluminescence by the time I made my way to the bar—a great beaten metal thing salvaged from heaven-knows-what mix of scrap. I could have sworn that the patch I leant on had the remains of an old Commonwealth Space Agency decal on it. Like everything else in the Grand Bazaar, it belonged in a museum—but no museum could afford it.

Night might only just be falling outside, but Gulliver's Rest was the sort of place where it was always a quarter to midnight. There was a press of people around the bar and around some of the gaming tables. Plenty of intimate booths at the back and around the upper levels.

What with being followed all the way from Pavonis, shot at outside, and being under the dubious protection of one of the sodding Bardos, I needed a drink about as much as I really shouldn't have had one.

I wasn't sure whether or not to be grateful I didn't recognise anyone; Gulliver's was busy enough that I could get something weak and some food and sit unobtrusively in a corner for however long I liked. If it were a normal visit, I might have sat at the bar and had a chat with Gulliver, the sonorous egesterian who ran the place. This wasn't normal, of course.

I was most of the way to a likely-looking corner when someone seized my shoulder.

'Hey, Eddie!'

I found myself face-to-face with a dark, slender human woman with a set jaw and rage in her eyes.

'Do I know—'

—*Smack!*

I blinked the stars out of my eyes and raised a hand to my cheek as a few '*ooh*'s went up from the nearby patrons.

'What the hell?' I asked, at about the same time as the woman gaped and said, 'Ohmygodyou'renotEddieI'msosorry.'

'What?'

Her eyes were almost as wide as her American accent. 'I'm *so* sorry, I thought you were my—it doesn't matter, my *god*, I'm so sorry, are you okay?'

Nothing seemed to be permanent. 'Um… yeah, I'm fine. Who's Eddie?'

She shook her head. 'Doesn't matter. He's got long hair like yours. Are you okay, can I get you anything?'

I blinked in surprise—I'd been starting to wonder if my hair was a bit too much of a giveaway. Clearly I wasn't the only skinny twentysomething human guy on Mars with dark green hair worn below the shoulders (don't ask – it's better than my natural colour).

'I… I'll be fine, thank you.'

'You sure?' She was squeezing my arm as if willing me to brush it off. Which, I decided, I was always going to.

'I'm sure. I hope you… find? Don't find? …that other guy.'

'Oh, I'll find him,' she assured me, letting me go. 'See you 'round.'

Turns out it's hard to settle down when you know there are god-knows-what special forces after you. At least my cheek stopped aching, though it felt oddly tight after the smack the woman had given me.

The only way you could tell the night was wearing on was that the crowds around the gambling tables got louder.

Eventually, I decided nothing else was going to happen—or at least, nothing new. No one else tried to hit me, at least. Maybe having one of the Bardos look out for me was actually paying off.

I paid the deposit for a cubby-room off one of the upper walkways. It was little more than a doorway to an enclosed bed, and once I was in it, I found it even harder to settle down.

Even so, I lost track of time and slept for a bit. I checked my sidenote when I woke up—four and a half hours. I supposed that was four and a half more than I'd have gotten otherwise.

I threw my clothes back on, checked I still had both the cryocrystal and the decoys, and ducked into the bathroom. I always hated the phrase 'freshen up' but this was one of those situations where that's both what I needed and what I did. I considered myself in the mirror—I *definitely* needed to shave when I got a chance.

It was either so late it was early or so early it was late, but it was the Grand Bazaar, so someone would be selling food. I made my way back towards the floor of Gulliver's—heading along one of those upper galleries with a good view of the bazaar cavern that everyone forgets about.

At which point the wall punched me.

I didn't just walk into it or anything: a rock-coloured fist appeared from it and hit me squarely on the nose.

So, I did what any reasonable person would do and went down clutching my face.

'What the fu—' I lashed out with a foot as I went and hit something that felt like a shin, but at that point I'd stopped paying attention.

My concussion revolver was kicked skittering across the floor. I couldn't tell how many there were, but it felt like more than one person. At least two. Both men, and both... oddly hard to focus on, as if they were wearing chameleon gear.

Okay, so they *were* wearing chameleon gear. Shit.

It was me versus at least two—maybe more? I   couldn't tell, and that was the sodding point. I rolled and kicked out again, this time scuffing something rather than connecting properly.

Hands fell from the sky and tried to grapple me—so I grabbed them back, and *twisted*. There was a cry of pain and suddenly I had space to move.

That's the thing with fingers. If you know how to grab them—

—Another half-visible fist struck sparks from the world. I fell back.

This was getting old, fast.

Then a black shape dropped from above.

I had the sense of something moving over me, and then something connected with a distortion in the air. A human—or Venusian?—figure staggered out of it and toppled over the railing with a strangled noise of surprise.

They were moving quickly and unerringly—whoever these guys were, it looked like they had been relying on their camouflage—and whoever this was, that didn't seem to matter. A second load of chameleon gear flickered out, and a second attacker went down, this time with the muted thud of what sounded suspiciously like my concussion revolver.

'Take him out!' one of the attackers hissed—I didn't know whether they meant me, or the person laying into them.

I hunkered down in the mouth of a passageway—I couldn't see my attackers in any case, and this new person seemed able to handle them.

Eventually, the sounds of the struggle died away. Something slumped to the floor with an apologetic note of finality.

Still breathing hard, I sneaked a glance at the force of nature that had come to my aid.

Well, with their chin-length black hair, achingly sharp cheekbones, and full lips being what they were, it was impossible to tell *what* exactly they were, beyond *human* and *dangerous*.

'You can come out, you know.' They were breathless, but their voice was deeper than I'd expected. It had a smooth edge that implied a different and altogether more alarming type of danger than the simply lethal.

I stood up slowly. 'Oh, I came out ages ago,' I heard myself say. 'Didn't do me any good.'

He was a head or so shorter than me, and the longer I looked, the… more there was to appreciate. Beneath a short, loose jacket, he was wearing close-fitting black clothes showing a gymnast's build.

He was also wearing just enough of a smile to be dangerous and just enough eyeliner to be a fire hazard.

'Pleased to meet you,' I decided. It was the first time I'd greeted someone entirely truthfully since I arrived—and it was the time I was most confident I'd come to regret before the night was out.

His eyes were wide with amusement and something which made me tempted to flee as he took me in. 'So, what do we have here?'

I spread my hands. 'I'm just a courier…'

He gave me a wicked grin and a golden laugh. 'Oh sure, and I'm the Khedive of Xanthe.'

'Guess you know who I am already,' I supposed, leaning deflated against the cavern wall.

I got a smirk for my trouble. 'Maybe I do.' He twirled his—no, *my*—concussion revolver thoughtfully. 'Felix Zakaryan. Pleased to meet you, too.'

'We'll see about that,' I grated. 'Who are you working for? The Soviets?' He shook his head—but then, he *would*. 'America? Arcadia? The Bardos?'

Felix made a so-so gesture as he rolled an unconscious assailant over with a foot. Full face mask, of course. 'Not quite, Courier Boy.' Then he wrinkled his nose. 'It's complicated.'

I frowned. 'But—'

He rolled those exquisite eyes. 'I'm trying to keep you *alive*, idiot. Honestly, did you think those Spetsnaz just happened to get lost in the ravines yesterday?'

I blinked—I'd been quite proud of shaking whoever-it-was. 'Wait, that was *you*? Hang on—*Spetsnaz?!*'

He rolled his eyes again. 'No, it was the Great Mariner Serpent—what do you think? Not sure about these amateurs though...' He trailed off and gave me a look as if he'd just spotted a fly on me.

'But how could you *see* them? They had active camo—'

'—Of *course* they—oh, for—hold still.' Felix lifted a hand to my cheek. For one moment, I thought he was going to smack me, too. Instead, he dug a fingernail under something unexpected and hard, and *ripped*—

'—*Ow*!' It felt like he'd waxed my face. Not for the first time that night, my hand went protectively to my cheek.

Then I realised what he was holding: a clear film of something, visible only because he was holding it. And as I looked, there was the faintest imprint of a circuit.

'What's that?' I asked, knowing the answer and dreading it.

'A trace. It's how they were going to track you.'

I swore.

Felix was considering it. 'I mean, given where it was… I'm guessing you didn't apply it yourself?'

'No,' I groaned, thinking back to Gulliver's Rest. 'That damn woman.'

He blinked. 'Pardon?'

'Oh, she… thought I was someone else and gave me a smack round the face for… well, for no good reason. But still. Damn.'

Felix pursed his lips. 'Well, I shan't pry,' he said, sounding revolted.

I raised a hand to forestall the inevitable—and inevitably wrong—assumption. 'Nothing like that. Just—'

'—If you say "business", I'm going to slap this back right where I found it—'

'—a mistake,' I tried, with emphasis. 'She said.'

His gaze took on a volcanic glint for a moment, then softened. 'Better.' The trace he was holding seemed to draw his narrowed gaze for a moment. Almost nonchalantly, he let it twirl to the floor.

Then he fired my concussion revolver at it in the sort of gesture I hoped I might be able to manage if I really worked hard at it in front of a mirror.

The trace vanished in a thud and a puff of curling smoke, leaving a scorch mark, an acrid smell, and me feeling thoroughly shown up (but appreciative of the view).

Felix glanced at the revolver as if he had only just realised he was holding it, flicked the safety back on, and handed it back without a word. Then as if paying for that moment of looking awesome, he blinked and half-raised a hand to his eye, and looked around.

'You okay? Get eyeliner in your eye?' I couldn't help the dig.

He glared at me. 'What, you think *this* is just for show? Right.' And before I could stop him, Felix grasped my chin in one slender hand and raised a stylus in the other. 'Close your eyes.' It was not a request.

Something cold, wet, and slightly grainy was scored hard around my eyes.

The fingers holding my chin tilted my head this way and that. 'That'll have to do.' He paused to consider something. '…Aaaand, we only live once.'

Suddenly, lips pressed against mine—mine unsuspecting, his warm and taut in a grin. The kiss was so brief I wasn't sure it was actually happening before it was over. Then that golden laugh came again as my chin was relinquished.

'Open your eyes, Courier Boy.'

I did, blinking in more than just the light. The world looked the same as it had before. Felix was smirking up at me as if he had just shared a secret. Damn him, but he'd done a good job keeping that stuff out of my eyes. I tried not to dwell on how he'd done a good job of sneaking a kiss, too, but it was *hard*.

'What…?'

'The kohl. Squint, then blink hard.'

I did so—and then I gasped like a houhnhof. As I squinted, the tiniest amount of eyeliner bled coldly into my eyes, and the world became… different. Colours flattened to undifferentiated grey, and then there appeared colour of a different kind. *So much* colour, in lines that went beyond mere objects and thrust through the air itself. Almost like…

Felix spread his hands as if revealing a magic trick. 'Behold, the magnetic world.' He was dull and flat as everything else—but his eyes shimmered and I could see the faint impressions of other tech about him too. I made a mental note of a few things—some of which I might even ask him about.

Then I frowned as I processed what he'd said. 'Hang on, isn't light just part of the *electro*magnetic spectrum? So, what's… this?'

'You're seeing the *fields*, not the waves.'

I blinked again—and then blinked a few more times as the two worlds became hopelessly blurred and muddled before the visible world began to reassert itself. I'd raised my hand instinctively towards my—

'—Don't you *dare* wipe your eyes; it'll hurt, and you'll look like a panda.'

'You're enjoying this, aren't you?' I asked, letting my vision clear.

Felix arched an eyebrow. 'Every *second* of it. Come on, this way. Let's get out of here.'

From the next level, the damage seemed insignificant.

With Felix's magnetic kohl, the bazaar was electric on a whole new level. The signs, the materials, even the vast camphor tree—everything had its own fields which flexed and flowed. A vast florescence of magnetism to one side made me blink. The ilhinovetch stallkeeper was eye-catching in normal light; in magnetism, he radiated field lines like a diagram of the sun itself.

Like half of Mars, it felt like, Nectaris Market was built in what used to be a set of lava tunnels. As with the rest of the planet, the Ancient Martians did something to the place (there was an entire campus of Xanthe University here somewhere trying to work out exactly what) and then they did what they did and went extinct centuries before the houhnhofs and the egesterians and the robots and the Venusians and the humans and the ilhinovetch and what-have-you all showed up.

The walls might have been basalt, but they *swam* with currents and fields. That must have been how Felix saw my attackers.

A hand—slender, firm, and warm—seized mine and led me back down to the main floor.

After a few paces I squinted and blinked the world back into normality.

We walked in silence, Felix leading, and me not particularly minding being led, until we reached the outer door to the walkway to the secure bays.

A hologram of what looked like a bronze sculpture of a female angel was standing in the doorway.

Breath hissed in Felix's teeth. He pulled up. The corridor around us was deserted.

'Who…?' I asked. This was no autocomp.

The ghostly bronze statue smiled at me. 'Greetings, Jaz Crael. We are Kyenay, Bardo of Life of the Grand Bazaar.'

Oh, shit.

'I'm… pleased to meet you…? …And, thank you for your hospitality,' I added, bowing my head hurriedly. Beside me, Felix bowed his head too.

'It was our… pleasure,' Kyenay seemed to decide, cocking her head with a wry smile at Felix.

'Have you come to… see me off?' I asked, deciding not to press the issue.

'We have come to make sure you *leave*,' she said, more firmly. 'And to remind you of the hospitality rite which we shared with our Factor.'

That earned a raised eyebrow from Felix.

I licked my lips. 'I apologise for—'

A bronze hand waved in dismissal. '—The damage to the market was superficial and not yours to fix. Keeping you safe has been… *interesting*—that you were assaulted at all was an… oversight. But the rite entailed a promise, Jaz Crael. We are entitled to a boon: a favour of your service which we now feel is richly earned.'

My heart sank. 'You are, yes. Have you come to collect?'

'Not yet, Jaz Crael, but we will. Once you are no longer *of interest* to certain… other parties, a retainer will be lodged with the Tharsis Courier Service.'

I swallowed. A retainer for one of the Six Bardos of the Bazaar. That could only end badly.

'Thank you,' I lied.

'As for you, Felix Zakaryan, continue as you have done, and your debt shall be repaid.'

'I will,' he told the floor.

It was my turn to raise an eyebrow.

Kyenay simply smiled and faded out of existence.

'Well, that was reassuring,' Felix sighed, in about the same tone of voice as I'd thanked the hologram. 'What?'

'...you? *You* were how she was keeping me alive?'

He rolled his eyes. 'Sort of? As I said, it's complicated. And technically I still am, so lead on, Courier Boy.'

That brought me up short.

We walked out in silence. The air was crisp and blue-grey; the remains of the sandstorm were out of sight, with the barest wisps of cirrus above. The rhubarb trees had ventured out of their stumps again, their great, black-blue leaves waving languidly in a fresh morning breeze.

Felix flickered his eyelashes at me for a moment as the first rays of sunshine brushed the Nectaris Mountains behind him. 'Tell me, is it always this dramatic, being a courier?'

'Well, we made it through one night. And since you're coming along for the ride,' I sighed, 'I expect you'll find out the hard way.'

And his laughter echoed off the basalt cliff.

Shoggothtown

Julie Danvers

G uys in my line a work don't do vacations too often.

But my pal Jimmy Kretz knows a guy does summer work for some Big Cheese in the Vineyard. Jimmy's guy says the Cheese and his family only use their house one week outta the year. Says he'll lend me the key if I want it.

The beach, though? People prefer my kind stick to the shadows. What with the tentacles and all. I'm told they're unsettling.

'You gotta stop worryin' about what people think,' Jimmy says. ''Sides, it'll be good for ya to get outta town for a while. You haven't had a case in months.'

A coupla my eyes might've flashed a little greener at that, because Jimmy shuts his gob and don't say anything more. But what he's thinkin' is written all over his face. Lately I'd been tryin' to drown myself in work and Mabel's bathtub gin, and one of those things was in short supply.

But the look in my eyes must've reminded Jimmy that, in addition to bein' a highly capable albeit underemployed private dick, I'm also an Immortal Scion of the Oldest Gods, while he's just a guy. So he don't say no more about my temporary indignities of finance or profession.

'Stead he goes real quiet. 'Lou. I'm worried aboutcha.'

Considerin' I was about three-quarters of the way through a bottle a Mabel's—that stuff'll take the enamel right off your fangs—I
figure he's right. My left tentacle's wrapped around the bottle so
tight it coulda shattered the glass like an opera singer's whine. I
know I need to unwind, but any rookie flatfoot can tell you: the
moment you let your guard down, that's when the hellmouth opens.

Even so. I need a break.

And Jimmy owes me a favour, on account of how I cleared his
wife when the rich broad she cleaned for accused her a stealin'
money. Like mosta my clients, Jimmy can't afford to pay much. He
figures he'll swing me a free vacation and we'll be square.

So I tell Jimmy, sure, maybe a few days outside the city will do
me some good. If nothing else, it'll make my pal feel like we're
even stevens.

I guess no good deed goes unpunished.

The beach ain't bad if you give it half a chance. The Vineyard
house has private access to a strip of coastline, and the fresh air's
a welcome change after the smog in the city. It actually feels good
to leave my hat and trench coat on the rocks after wearin' em for
so long. I scuttle down toward where sea meets sand, the grit of it
creating pleasant friction between the thousands of suckers lining
my limbs. I brought a book with me—some crime paperback that
promised to be trashy yet titillatin'—but lyin' there with the sun
beating down on my unfurled wings makes most of my eyelids too
heavy to keep open.

I'm almost driftin' off to sleep when a shadow blocks out the sun.

'Hey, Lou,' he says, his voice cool and steady, like he hadn't ever
ripped my heart out and left it bleeding on the plains of a distant
battlefield.

Carl is half-and-half, born of the goddess Idrah and some jamoke
in the wrong place at the right time, depending on how you look at

it. He's a shape-shifter, like his mother. He could take a thousand different forms, but the version of Carl that meets me on the beach is the one I'm most familiar with. He's all lean angles, with a mop of burnished copper-coloured curls that overspill his forehead and brush against deep-set brown eyes. I used to tell Carl any guy his age would *have* to be a shape-shifter to get cheekbones as smooth and high as his.

He never did get the shifting down perfect, though. A stray tentacle nestles amongst his curls, and he self-consciously tucks it behind an ear with his slender, elegant hand.

Carl isn't immortal like me; he has one life to live on Earth, and as a shape-shifter he has the chance to find his place in it. But my place is on the outside, lookin' in. He'd always wanted me to come in from the cold, and I wanted him to see the power in immutable darkness. We were great together until we weren't.

And now, out of all the beaches in all the galaxies, he washes up on mine. There's no way that's by coincidence. He needs a favour.

'You look good,' he says. 'I never took you for a beach bum, but it's workin' for ya.'

I lift my wings in a shrug. 'Guess I've changed.'

'You still a private detective?'

This throws me, because if there's one thing he didn't want to hear about when we were together, it was my job. 'Look, Sunshine, if you've tracked me down just to let me know once again how much you disapprove of my career choices…'

'No, Lou. You got it all wrong. Thing is… I got a case for ya.'

Turns out Carl's at the Vineyard 'cause he's been goin' round with this hoity-toity fella Harry. Real nice guy, he says. Good family, good job, summer home. Respectable. He coulda passed through a lotta important doors on Harry's arm, 'steada gettin' thrown out like three-day-old fish the way it always happens with me.

But, alas, Perfect Harry wasn't long for this world. Poor sap washed up dead on the other side of the island yesterday, and Carl suspects foul play.

'Let the authorities handle it,' I tell him. 'I'm on vacation.' And truth be told, I don't wanna spend my vacation investigatin' my ex's love life. I wish I was a better guy, but there it is.

Carl hesitates, then says, 'I can't go to the cops. They're not equipped to deal with this.'

'And I am?'

He looks me in the eyes. 'I think the Oldest were involved. The marks on Harry's body… they look like shoggoth bites, Lou. Cops wouldn't know what to do with that.'

Shoggoths. They're all teeth and digestive tract, which makes 'em good, efficient killers. Their venom's one of the only things that can infect abominations, demons, or horrors—which is why our Family have always kept a pack of our own.

'But why would anyone sic shoggoths on your boyfriend?' I'm not just wonderin' about motivation, either. Usin' a shoggoth to kill a human is like usin' a flamethrower to kill a hamster. It'll get the job done, but so would a lot of other things.

'That's what I want you to find out. Harry was good people, Lou. He never did nothin' to nobody, and he didn't deserve to die like that. He was the first human I ever told about bein' half-Oldest.'

'You told him?' The Carl I'd known would've kept any secret to fit in, even if it meant hiding his truest self.

'He deserved to know what he was gettin' into. I was afraid he'd think I was a monster, but he said he loved me, even knowin' what I really was.'

His eyes glimmer with tears. He's always wanted to fit in, and soon as he gets his chance, it's ripped away from him. Despite what happened between us, I can't help feelin' it ain't fair.

Then again, life ain't fair. 'Why come to me?' I say. 'Why not get one of the Family to help you out?'

'Brute force alone won't solve the case. I need answers. And I know that once you get started on a case, you'll never let go.'

'Thought that was a problem for you, back when we were together.' His eyes are twin pools of hurt and longing, and it all comes rushing back: the sleepless nights, the arguments, the making it up to each other afterward. I always had more to make up for than he did.

Carl swallows, and I wonder if he's remembering, too. 'That was a long time ago,' he says. 'Please. You gotta help me, Lou. Tell me who killed Harry.'

'And then what?'

'Then I'll get my revenge. Maybe I'll get my mother to throw them into the sun. One way or another, somebody's gotta pay.'

'I'm on vacation,' I say again, but we both know I'm gonna take the case. Because I know—and he knows I know—there ain't nothin' more painful than to love and lose.

I learned that from him.

Carl shows me the part of the beach where Harry's body was found. The shore's littered with broken seashells and the empty carapaces of dead horseshoe crabs. There's a little pile of ash; Carl thinks he mighta been tryin' to ward himself. 'I showed Harry a few simple tricks,' he says. 'I taught him some spells and gave him an amulet and one of my old grimoires. Just in case he ever needed an extra layer of protection. Y'know, like at family reunions.'

But whatever he'd taught Harry, it hadn't been enough. I can tell by the signs on the beach that the shoggoths got 'im; gobs of black, tarry slime dot the sand amid clumps of shells and seaweed strands. The slime has a sulfur smell that would've been like the sweetest nectar to shoggoths: a single drop of it could attract one from half a galaxy away.

But seein' the crime scene gives me a break: whoever had done Harry in wasn't necessarily one of the Family. The killer coulda been any schmuck who happened to get his hands on a vial of summoning slime, maybe from some black-market shop or shady flea market. All the galoot would've had to do was wait till Harry was alone, and pour out the slime, and the shoggoths woulda come runnin'.

'Don't step in it,' I warn Carl. I ain't just tryin' to protect his shoes. Once the shoggoths attack the person they've been summoned to kill, they're supposed to return home, but they ain't exactly smart or obedient. I didn't want either of us to be here in the event they came back to slurp up what's left of their favourite slime. 'Why don't you go spend some time with Harry's family, and I'll check in with Azathoth.' It's his job to leave viscera out on the astral plane for the shoggoth herd. If someone's been interfering with them, *he'll* know.

'Thanks,' he says as he turns to leave, and also, 'Sorry.' He knows how I feel about Az.

I extend my index claw, tearing a hole in the fabric of space and time, and step through to find myself in the middle of a party in the stars. I can barely move amidst the dancing beings, most of them swaying multiple limbs and bobbing dual heads. Az has the background noise from the birth of the universe turned up so loud I can barely hear myself think. For a second, I wonder if coming here was a bad idea, but it's too late; he's already seen me in the crowd.

'Hey, man! Drinks are over there!' he shouts, pointing to the polar ice caps of Mars.

'No, thanks. I'm here on a case,' I say.

'A case? Naw, brah, we just got single cans.'

'I need to talk to you! Where are your shoggoths?'

'Goths? Okay. Niche, but we can summon some goths if that's your jam.' He opens a second spacetime tear, but I immediately close it before things get weird.

'Your *shoggoths*,' I scream. 'Are they all accounted for?'

Az shakes his head. 'My brah, this is a *party*. We don't have accountants here.' The beady little eyes above his cavernous stoma peer into mine. 'Dude, you need to relax. Have you ever considered taking… a vacation?'

The billion tentillum beneath my nostrils bristle. Carl always said I loved solving crime more than I loved him. Maybe that was true. Maybe I was a fool. One thing was certain: I wasn't going to get any information out of Azathoth. They don't call him the blind idiot god for nothing.

I open a spacetime rift to get back to the beach, but just as I'm stepping through, a barbed hook wraps itself around my waist and pulls me out of the party and into a dark alley between realities.

The thing about fighting between realities is, it's not just hard to punch or kick. It's hard to *exist*. I can feel myself fading, even as I try to wrap tentacles I don't have around the neck of an unseen attacker who both is and isn't there.

I'm suffocating, even though technically my air sacs are nebulous and undefined in that liminal space. Is this the end? Am I—an eternal who simultaneously contains and transcends life and death—about to meet my demise as I began: in a place defined by nothingness?

The despair reminds me of the old days when the ennui threatened to consume me. I'd cared little for the daily affairs of mortal beings because their lives were pointless. All life would inevitably succumb to destruction in the name of Cthulhu.

I got bored. All-powerful or not, it's dreary to have a single purpose that only becomes relevant at the end of time. For a few millennia, I wallowed. Then I decided, screw it. I was getting a hobby. If ignoring mortal affairs left me depressed, I was going to do the opposite.

I found a cold, grey city reminiscent of home, and opened the detective agency.

And right up until that moment in the alley, it worked. Sure, the corruption of humanity usually meant a bleak outcome for most of my cases. But at least things were *interesting* again. I made friends.

I solved puzzles, even if I was usually too late to do anything about it. I met a few dames, and then I met Carl. Carl, who'd complained that he'd never understood my obsession with my work but who was still waitin' for me to come back. He'd just lost one person he'd depended on. I feel my vision fading around the edges, and I think, he can't be left wonderin' what happened to me.

And what happens is gonna be an untimely death in a dank and despairing place, if I don't get the upper hand on whatever's tryin' to pin me down real quick. It's got fangs, and I have to keep twistin' out of the mandibles faster than they can bite down.

But thinkin' about Carl makes me feel a little more substantial within the void. Which gives me an idea. I turn my mind away from the cosmic vortex, and I try to think less like an Oldest God and more like a detective.

This bum is lookin' to thrash me but good, I think.

It helps. I feel even more solid, so I keep goin'.

C'mon, Lou. The big galoot ain' t even packin' a heater. You can take 'im.

Finally I get one tentacle pushing back on what feels like a jaw, and I get another one wrapped around a chest, and I squeeze real hard. I think, *I'm supposed to be on vacation, I oughta be drinkin' quality rotgut in a fancy clip joint 'steada tusslin' with this goon*, and with that, we both pop out onto the beach, and I'm holding my attacker's dead body.

Turns out it's not a who but a *what*. It's a shoggoth, and it's a good thing it didn't get a bite in, because that venom woulda messed me up real good.

More importantly, it confirms all the suspicions that had crept into my mind about that schmuck, Harry, the moment I saw the beach where he'd died.

I take another look at that small pile of ash, the stuff Carl'd thought Harry had been using to ward himself. The pools of slime are still there on the beach, including one with a skid mark from a tentacle. Well, shit. I must've accidentally stepped in it earlier. And since that slime is like wearin' a sign that says 'C'mere, kitty kitty,' that shoggoth must've been huntin' me from the moment I left the beach.

But I wouldn't'a been the original target. And neither would Harry.

I'm startin' to see the case come together. It never did add up that somebody from the Family would've set the shoggoths on Harry. There's lots of more efficient ways to murder a human. And why would any of the Oldest care if he lives or dies? Nobody'd do it just to hurt Carl, either; that' be riskin' his mother's ire, which is a one-way trip to Tortureville.

There's only one person involved who'd have any reason to summon shoggoths. Someone lookin' to kill a monster.

Poor, sweet Carl had loved Harry enough to tell him who he really was. Even taught him some basic spells, so he'd know how to handle himself. And Harry had gone and used that knowledge against him. Maybe he was scared, or maybe he just didn't like that Carl was different. Doesn't really matter why, though. Carl thought he'd found what he'd always wanted: a guy who could accept and love him as his real self. Instead, Harry had seen a monster.

So he'd gone and summoned the shoggoths himself, only they'd done for him instead of Carl, because they ain't intelligent creatures. Like I said, they're all teeth and digestive tract.

Telling Carl will break his heart. But if I lie, try to pin it on someone else in the Family, he won't rest until he gets revenge. Then either some other poor sucker gets killed, or, worse, Carl gets killed in the process. Course, I could say nothing at all, tell him I'm dropping the case. But if I do that, he'll hate me forever...

Option C is the safest for Carl.

I tell him I'm dropping the case on another beach, a pretty one, where the wind blows through the tall grass and the sun warms our shoulders. I thought that would make it easier, but it doesn't.

His laugh is bitter as cigarette butts. 'So it's like that, Lou? Now that there's something *I* need, a crime *I* want solved, you're all tentacles-off and there are *more important things to worry about?* Screw you, pal.'

He turns to leave. Without thinking, I whip a tentacle out to spin him around and pull him close against my trench coat. He presses himself against my lapels, tears filling his eyes. 'I know you know something,' he says. 'You've found something out and you think I can't handle it. Don't lie to me.'

I look into his glassy eyes, and I break. I never could resist him. I come clean and give him the truth, even though the last thing I want to do is hurt him more than I already have.

I'd hoped to never see that look of hurt and betrayal on his face again, but there it is: his warm brown eyes darken to obsidian, and I can tell by the tightness of his jaw that he's fighting to hold back tears of anger, or grief, or maybe both. 'That's a low blow, even for you. Makin' up a story like that about Harry, just so's you can try and win me back.'

'It's no lie, sweetheart. He called them; they came, and he got more than he bargained for. Harry wanted you dead. How else do you explain it?'

'Then… then… oh, I *hate* you!' He pounds his fists against my chest, then sinks into the folds of my coat and cries, and I hold him, because the world ain't a kind place to people like us.

It's hard when you're wrong about the person you love, and it's even worse that he'd been right about me. If things had worked out between us, maybe he'd never have had to deal with that ass, Harry.

In the end, he leaves. I let him go, because I know that's what he wants. It's funny. The whole time we were together, he complained that I could never let go of anything, but now here I am watching him walk away, without doing a thing to stop him.

But then I see it, in one of Carl's footprints in the sand—a trace of summoning slime. Just a drop, if that. But for a shoggoth, it would be enough.

I race frantically over the bluff, onto the street. He hasn't gotten far, and I'm screaming his name.

He looks over his shoulder and hesitates.

'Carl, honey.' I'm begging him. 'Please. Come back. I can help.'

His face is all twisted, trying not to cry. 'Dammit, Lou. If I don't leave you now, I might never be able to leave again.'

'Then don't. Don't leave. Come back and we'll work things out. I'll do anything.' There's no time to explain. I just say whatever gets him close to me, so I can protect him. But as I'm saying it, I realise I mean every word. This isn't me trying to save Carl's life, this is me trying to find a life worth living again. A life that includes *him*.

And against all odds, it works. He turns back. He's walkin,' then runnin' towards me. He falls into my waiting tentacles, and I hold him close. For one sweet moment, everything's all right.

Then I hear the gnash of feral teeth, the sizzle of acid venom, and Carl goes limp in my arms. It all happens so fast that he doesn't even have time to scream. The shoggoth is already scuttling away, back to the netherworlds with its mission accomplished.

Leaving me holding nothing but a shell.

I shake Carl's body, even though I know it's useless. 'C'mon, kid. Wake up. It's just one bite. One little bite. You'll be all right.'

But shoggoth venom works fast. Too fast for a sweet half-human just tryin' to find somewhere in the world he belongs. Isn't that what we all want? To belong? I wish Carl coulda found what he was lookin' for, but this ain't that kind of story. Most days, no matter how warm the beach, how sweet the sun, there's no escapin' that we're still in Shoggothtown.

Jenseti, You in Danger, Girl

Brent Lambert

This was the tenth inquisitor who Jenseti had worked to heal with the Touch. Only dedication to his craft kept him from walking away and leaving the writhing man strapped down to the altar, hurling his insults through pain and injury: filthy queer, caged scumbag, sex fiend. But then the ungrateful warrior would die from the lapis-maggots happily latched to the gash in his side. The brightly coloured grubs typically ate their way through the decaying bellies of the gold-eye arctodus, a beast employed by the Princes of Ka, bitter enemies of this warrior's Church of Hazzrian. Lapis-maggots devoured living, smaller hosts much more slowly (some believed they knew how to be cruel) so this hateful wretch's agony would last for months to come. But pettiness was not a source the Touch gathered power from so Jenseti quieted the Inquisitor with Hazzrian religious doctrine.

'Words transform the spirit. Would you make yours so ugly, Inquisitor?' Part of Jenseti's training with the Unmatched Queers of Gisara, Peerless in Name, Elders of the Touch involved rigorous study of religions. Almost all of them involved hierarchy and at the tops of those were shameless charlatans who warped the minds of their faithful to hate queer people. Studying their wickedness was no antidote for hate, but knowing their scriptures, songs, and histories better than the bigots did give him a roadmap to humiliate them.

Belief in the power of transformation was central to those who followed Hazzrian, especially its inquisitors. The butterfly god, in all its various incarnations, was depicted in the cathedral's towering stain-glassed windows. From a caterpillar covered in thorns to a ridged brown chrysalis hanging from a gnarled tree limb to a butterfly with wings spread wide, the windows were beacons of faith. Jenseti knew they were crafted with glass imported from Nzolagrad, a vassal-nation of the Ashtari Empire. Jenseti remembered his mother (always with a cold shiver) and her commanding baritone, speaking highly of the Nzolapi work ethic and how they valued art like the lion valued its teeth. These butterflies of silver, gold, and red cast against majestic landscapes proved her right.

The inquisitor's insults vanished and only a low moan remained. The sound scandalised the worshippers crowding the Grand Chrysalis Cathedral. Jenseti smirked and let the simple crowd drum up their assumptions. They probably thought he had removed his chastity cage and inserted a gift into the inquisitor's mouth. He wished his teachers had done a better job of keeping that part of their lives secret. These people assumed those who knew the Touch sent fits of lust into whoever they gazed upon. Silly. Superstitious. Comical.

The inquisitor rattled and coughed, gripping his chest and, for a startling moment, lapis-maggots spewed fountain-like from his side. The inquisitor fell alarmingly still. Jenseti thought his rude patient might have died until a smile stretched wide across his spittle-covered face. The inquisitor started to tap his fingers along his chest.

'You're right—words transform the spirit. Names do too.' The inquisitor's eyes looked at Jenseti with murderous intensity. 'You would know all about new names and new lives, wouldn't you? The Heir Who Refused.'

Jenseti hated fear and thought his time with the Unmatched Queers of Gisara had rid him of it, but it was always a lie. It rumbled up from his gut and poured out his skin as sweat. And as happened to a million people in a million places, that fear became anger.

'My name is Jenseti. You speak madness.' The words were declared with the speed of a man desperate to flee. Jenseti would have gone to his iron-auroch and bolted right then, but he saw the inquisitor's eyes—pink and growing brighter. The air around Jenseti became smoky and scratched at his throat. A hint of pine and burnt cinnamon. The lapis-maggots, once so thoroughly attached, had turned grey and fell to the ground like dropped coins. He knew what this was.

The inquisitor was possessed.

Jenseti steadied himself, trying to not let his mind race to possibilities that would paralyse him. He leaned down, bringing his nose close to the inquisitor's. He didn't want the parishioners spying; he hoped they had the good sense to see something was wrong and depart. 'Since names are important, what's yours? You have taken a body that does not belong to you.'

'There are so many names, and they *all* want to kill you. But *I'm* Mondari, babe. Of the Gomi-Han-Bale. You know of us. Everyone does.'

The need to empty the Grand Chrysalis Cathedral became paramount. Jenseti kept his closeness to the possessed inquisitor and yelled at his highest pitch, 'Oh I'll be your little slut! I'm so close to cumming! Know the Touch!'

The proclamation made the worshippers wail and holler in indignation and rush out of the cathedral as intended. For while the followers of Hazzrian believed in the transformative power of sex, their beliefs centred on the creation of a life, not public sex before their god. It would be a long time before the butterfly worshippers stopped cursing his name.

Mondari fell into cachinnation. 'I wasn't going to pluck their little wings, babe. Wanton slaughter is an extra charge in my line of work.'

'Gomi-Han-Bale have a *reputation*.' Jenseti poured all the insult he could muster into the word. They were a group of killers, centuries old, and only worked at the behest of the rich and powerful. The money they made from their murderous work funnelled right back into their lives of unbridled debauchery. The parties the Gomi-Han-Bale threw were as celebrated as their assassinations were feared.

The inquisitor's body jittered, clearly trying to resist Mondari's control. The mercenary's voice slithered out anyway. 'Then you know you're already dead, babe. And your handsy friends too.'

Jenseti sucked his teeth, annoyed at the unbridled confidence. The inquisitor's back arched and his eyes became more pink and more swollen by the second. They grew to the size of small apples before exploding. Jenseti covered his face and called upon the power of the Touch to repel the eruption of pink ooze, which splattered over the inquisitor's corpse and along the cathedral floor.

Once his shock passed, an incipient fear gripped Jenseti, more primal than the last. He knew what this pink substance was and the confirmation it provided. Angry again at the fear worming through him, Jenseti quickly dipped the tip of a finger into the ruined cavern of the inquisitor's left eye socket. Using the Touch, the poison did him no harm, but he could immediately decipher its origin. The egg cream of a Southern Lynxpus. The animal had all the feline features of a lynx, with bright pink quills covering its feet and tail. It gave birth by producing large egg saccs with thick, poisonous embryonic fluid. Jenseti could still recite the names of all the familial rivals killed by the toxin.

The Southern Lynxpus was a beloved pet of Emperor Osangia, sixty-sixth child of the Tourmaline Warlock, Conqueror of the Ravenblood Seas, and High Speaker of the Caiman Elite. Master of the Ashtari Empire.

Jenseti's father.

The skin of his shoulder ached and cracked, the transformation familiar and annoying to Jenseti. The flesh sloshed around like wet mud before an old, gnarled face with a small horn above its nose popped up. It yawned with a mouth full of wide-set teeth and smiled with a smugness that made Jenseti wonder daily why he hadn't excised the parasite. 'Ooooo! Jenseti, you in danger, girl.'

Macentor's symbiotic attachment to Jenseti stretched decades. Before him, it had been joined with the rhino god, Adann. But after Adann's death, Macentor had saved Jenseti from Bonedrinkers under a Grey Rainbow in the lands of Dhamill Karr. The obligations of a Grey Rainbow dictated that Macentor was allowed to ask one boon without refusal, and its request had been bondage. Though it worded it as companionship…

'Be quiet.' Macentor delighted in aggravating him, and Jenseti was in no mood. 'It could still all be a lie.'

'HA! You don't believe that. Poison's right out of your father's usual repertoire. You told me he even executed people who used that poison without his blessing. Am I supposed to believe that the emperor of the Ashtari Empire has suddenly become magnanimous? HA! I'd sooner believe—never mind. Don't want to hurt your little feelings.' The parasitic face started to hum an old funeral song. Jenseti's sister had been fond of singing it when she performed live surgeries on war prisoners for her own amusement. Macentor knew how to strike a nerve. 'This is your own fault, you know? Should have been ready for your family to come at you.'

Family—an ominous thought rushed through Jenseti. Macentor was right; he was in danger, but he wasn't the only one. 'Handsy friends' had been Mondari's phrasing and that could only mean one thing. His mentors, the family he chose and love, the Unmatched Queers—they were in real danger.

The way back to Gisara would be a long, treacherous one. It had taken him many years to wander his way to the lands of Hazzrian and he would need to return in a fraction of the time. The towns-people had been so eager to get rid of him that they showered Jenseti with provisions. A blessing born of contempt.

Jenseti took no offence, focused only on not losing the people who had given him purpose after his family cast him out. Almost a century ago, his exile brought him to Gisara, his spirit pulverised by cruelty. His refusal to continue the Ashtari Empire's endless thirst for violence left him a broken child. They took that child and showed him how to be a man. Mondari had been right about one thing; names had power and when Jenseti left the empire, he didn't have one. The Unmatched Queers of Gisara, Peerless in Name, Elders of the Touch had tutored and sheltered that broken youth and, through their kindness and validation, made him whole again.

Unravelling the pain visited on him by his family had required infinite patience from the Unmatched Queers. Even now, his family's actions still came to him vividly: his father denied him his rights as heir and banished him from the only home he knew; his siblings tried to kill him with the emperor's approval; and his mother erased his name by holy rite. It removed him from every imperial record and even snatched the name from Jenseti's own mind.

A small mercy saved him; his grandmother gave him the iron-auroch to flee the Ashtari Empire. The beast had stayed with him, the only remnant of his old life Jenseti held on to. Its innards had been replaced with the magic metal only the Ashtari knew how to forge, granting it a long life. Jenseti hoped it would survive many centuries more for the iron-auroch was always better company than the god-parasite.

'You really shouldn't go back,' Macentor said, emerging from Jenseti's shoulder once the Hazzrian worshippers were far enough away. 'The Gomi-Han-Bale do not play. I heard once they ransacked the whole city of Rihog Annog-a just to make room for a thou-sand-man orgy. They're persistent about whatever they want and they make it look effortless. Not the kind of people you want to

go chasing after. I just think we'd be better off getting our asses…
well, *your* ass, and just find somewhere nice and cosy. Loosen up
that cage of yours a little, have some fun, and let your family get
bored with chasing.'

Jenseti refused to see Gisara plundered, and wouldn't entertain a
second of the parasite's cowardice. Violence would not command
his life anymore. The Gomi-Han-Bale were notorious for three
things: dispensing unbridled death, partaking in enough drugs to
kill a metropolis, and looking undeniably handsome while doing
it. But they were monsters, and no amount of muscle and easy
smiles could varnish that fact.

He ignored Macentor's continued pleas and made final preparations for the journey west. Jenseti regretted not making more
genuine allies in his decades-long eastward march. His life since
leaving Gisara was a continuous cycle of a limited number of actions:
heal someone so his magic grew stronger, service a man sexually so
his magic grew stronger, or deny himself orgasm so his magic grew
much stronger. Most of his collected magic resided in the chastity
cage—an instrument focused on restraint and subservience. It was
a perfect receptacle. No one could see it and he had been taught
to never reveal it. Jenseti supposed a part of him always knew his
family would come for him one day, and he had been gathering
the power to prepare.

'You have me, you know,' Macentor said with a huff. 'Though
I'd rather not fight.'

'Normally, this is where we align. But my family has forced my
hand.' Abhorring violence had led Jenseti to refuse the throne of
the Ashtari Empire. His mother had foreseen the 'defect' and tried
to cleanse him through the tutelage of one brutal combat master
after another. At the time, his love for his mother had trumped
his disgust and so he was an excellent student. But she always saw
through him.

'Then you better fight, because I know you can, girl. Your people ain't all there and I refuse to have them throw me in a stew or something!'

They came first to the Achian Desert—a wide expanse of sand white as bone with massive, jagged blocks of obsidian littering the landscape like fleas on a dirty dog. The harsh air smelled like simmering charcoal. With every gust of wind, the iron-auroch made its displeasure known. Jenseti was more concerned with the obsidian wreckage. He knew them to be the shattered pieces of an Ujan World-Ship. His father told him that nothing could ever truly quiet a World-Ship. The air around them was full of whispers, repeating voices older than ancient.

Hazzrian is grateful for your service to the Inquisitors. You have the god's favour. A blessing will fall upon you.

Jenseti kept the revelation to himself. He didn't want to get Macentor's hopes up. World-Ships were known to say seductive things and he heard many stories of people meeting their ends for believing them. For now, he'd keep its assurance of a blessing close.

'I hate being back here. Too many voices from Adann's day,' Macentor said, sucking his teeth. 'Just talking nonsense. Girl, couldn't we have taken an airship or something?'

'I don't like my feet not touching the ground.' Jenseti patted the iron-auroch. 'Neither does he.'

Despite the urgency of his need to return to Gisara, he wasn't entirely sure he had the power needed to face the threat. So when he found a group of nomads, he saw an opportunity to lessen that doubt and performed the Touch on them. Each had long been deprived of pleasure, making Jenseti's chastity cage quiver imperceptibly as it gathered magic. One of the nomads he found irresistibly beautiful and Jenseti allowed himself to be pleasured in return, but not to the point of release. That was key. A deep attraction combined with a withheld orgasm was an oasis of power, and he would need all of it. The Touch could be used in arts of healing and pleasure, but also combat. Anything the hands could perform, the Touch could empower. But Jenseti had never used it for violence before, and he tried to avoid considering what it might mean to.

The desert changed. Its sands became blood-coloured, and black, withered acacia trees replaced the World-Ship's obsidian wreckage and constant whispers. This portion of the Achian Desert was a good deal more dangerous.

The black acacia trees were home to nests for assa-assa, bee-like creatures the size of sparrows, their red chitin dotted with white. Jenseti's sister had kept a small nest of them in one of the many royal animal bazaars. She talked incessantly about them being like her—rare, deadly and a small size that shouldn't be underestimated.

Macentor hated the insects because they were known to devour any parasite of any origin, even ones that had come from gods. It pleased Jenseti to imagine Macentor squirming away from an assa-assa's spiky proboscis. He wouldn't let it happen, of course, as he admittedly might miss the judgmental cretin; the parasite annoyed him every day, but the two had developed a teasing kinship over the decades. And Macentor had *power*—a devastating scream capable of plaguing all living things that heard it with cancers that mutated and consumed them. They didn't often use it because of how drained it left Jenseti, but when they had it saved his life.

Jenseti didn't push the iron-auroch hard, knowing too much hoof-trampling would easily awaken the bull scorpions slumbering beneath them. And besides, the beast deserved a break. Pushing it too hard would mean having to find lilac-oil to salve its fatigue. Such maintenance would cost him more time than taking a slower pace now.

They passed through the rest of the Achian Desert without encountering an assa-assa. A miracle that made him start to believe a little more in what the World-Ship had told him. The Ship had promised a blessing, without specifying what it would be. Avoiding those lethal pests felt a sufficient payment.

Over the next week, they navigated a forest of mushrooms large as trees. The ground beneath them was blanketed by singing orange spores, which packs of horned rodents would dig up from the ground to devour. Wrapped around the bases of the mushrooms were caravan-long centipedes, each in turn covered with birds pecking fungus from their carapaces. This would be the most peaceful stretch of their journey and Jenseti tried to enjoy it.

The forest faded into hills covered with a small, poisonous cacti. His iron-auroch's hooves crushed the plants, sending creamy white juices flying upwards. Macentor lapped the splashes from his lips, marking his first appearance since the desert, but still the parasite didn't speak to Jenseti. Perhaps he had pushed the teasing too far. After a long day, they approached a wide river with a bridge of iron; a dozen iron-aurochs could have crossed it shoulder to shoulder with room to spare. Off to one side stood a bronze statue of a weeping woman holding a basket of glittering butterflies.

'Much rather not know her story,' Macentor said. 'Got a feeling she was the one out here snatching people's eyes.'

'She was a saint of Hazzrian. Their ministries once reached far.' Jenseti mouthed the traditional words of blessing for Hazzrian as they trotted across the bridge, sparing the statue one last glance. 'May the chrysalis protect us from all harm. And may your wings guide us home."

And with the promise of the World-Ship fresh on his mind, he thought: *If your gratitude for me saving your Inquisitors still applies then help me protect those I love.*

The cacti on the other side were smaller and slowly gave way to ashen bushes shaped like hands reaching up to the sky. An hour more of riding and the bushes grew tall, taking on hues of milky white and dark red. A day more and those bushes faded too, giving space to grey trees, thin and narrow but too thick to be bamboo, their bark dotted with pulsating, gelatinous green squares. Riding through the forest would be impossible, so Jenseti dismounted and let his faithful beast follow carefully behind.

Before night fell, they found an ankle-high pool surrounded by a perfect circle of pitifully tiny rocks. The water shimmered with all the colours of the rainbow. Macentor recognized it and screeched. 'You cheap cunt! We could have just taken an airship!'

Jenseti bent down to touch a finger against the cool surface, making ripples of rainbow. 'I already told you why.'

'You should have said…' Macentor feigned hurt. 'Not like we aren't permanently attached or anything. I swear sometimes it's like you'd rather I just pluck myself off and go crawl off a cliff. You drag me across this part of the world and it all changes too damn quick and you're too cheap to fly and you'd rather use some portal around these trees that give me the ick and Adann use to—'

'Men like me always keep secrets.' Jenseti said quietly. He was an exiled son. A wandering healer, welcomed when there were wounds and rejected when there was lust. He wore a cage no one knew about, brimming with power. What choice did he have but secrets, to keep parts of himself locked away.

He stared into the pool—excited by thoughts of Gisara and fearful of what he might find there.

The trees rustled behind him. 'Getting yourself all wet at the thought of some old men? That's a bit pathetic—even for you, babe.'

Jenseti kissed his teeth and looked over his shoulder, finger still hovering over the pool. 'Muscles and insults. That's all you Gomi-Han-Bale come packaged with.'

Mondari was a specimen—no denying that. Log-carrying shoulders, neck-crushing thighs, and a chest you could rest your head on. It was the accessories that ruined it for Jenseti. His spiky, platinum blonde hair and silver eyes were obviously worked by magic, and that growling koala tattoo covering his neck had such a desperate 'don't you want me?' vibe. Jenseti wouldn't waste the Touch on someone like Mondari, exquisitely built or not.

'You forgot magnetism.' Mondari ran his tongue across his top teeth. 'Everyone wants to be us. Men will say all kinds of things hoping just to get a whiff. Learned a few things about you that way. Like how you got that ugly parasite stuck on your shoulder.'

'You little assbag!' Macentor shouted. 'I've chewed bugs harder than you, why don't you come and try it, you—'

Oh no. Jenseti knew what this was.

Mondari drew a pink dagger and tapped it against one of the thin, grey trees. He crossed his legs and leaned against it, grinning. 'I made some friends with *your* friends, babe. They've been wanting to catch up for *so* long.'

Jenseti looked up and saw his 'friends' clinging like murderous monkeys to the trees. Bonedrinkers. When he had escaped Dhamill Karr's wasteland with Macentor, he'd known they survived. But Dhamill Karr was so far away... he never suspected they might track him down. Part of him always assumed the Bonedrinkers were more animal than human, forgoing the hunt if their prey became too laborious. Like a gazelle in the grasslands, he thought distance meant safety.

He had been wrong.

The Bonedrinkers were garbed in tattered black robes and their ragged breathing misted the air with red, a digestive byproduct of the marrow they consumed. Men once, an ancient, hateful quest had left them like this: skin ashen and cracked like an unfinished cremation, lines of rusty tears encrusted permanently on their cheeks, and mouths devoid of teeth that never quite closed. Somehow Mondari had found a way to converse with these cursed creatures—to offer Jenseti up as a vengeful meal.

'There were *so many* names wanting to kill you. They have them, you know.' Mondari winked and gave one of the Bonedrinkers a thumbs up. 'Couldn't get them to shut up after I gave them Gisara as a snack.'

No… no… it couldn't—that would mean…

Jenseti noticed the many small, jagged bones poking out of their faces—white and glistening. That only happened when they were engorged—their endless hunger filled to a physical, if not mental, brim. They had feasted recently. The bastards! His journey to Gisara failed before it even began. The Unmatched Queers were gone, his new family butchered by the old. All his fault.

"Jenseti…" Macentor said his name weakly, confirming the horror. He was only kind when there was reason to weep.

He risked everything the day he became the Heir Who Refused, forsaking a life of total power and disgustingly decadent comfort because he didn't want responsibility for the violence that came packaged with it. Every combat tutor his mother forced him through only calcified his position on the useless cruelty of war and all its subsidiaries. The day Jenseti rebuked his family, he thought he was saving countless lives. Instead, he had brought an onslaught of savagery to the people who taught him a way past pain and brutality to a life of servitude and sensuality. The Unmatched Queers of Gisara, Peerless in Name, Elders of the Touch were gone, and they had doomed themselves the second they opened their doors to the Heir Who Refused.

'Don't believe him! The Touch—'

Jenseti's self-loathing wail drowned out Macentor's words and he charged. The Bonedrinkers jumped out of the trees with arms spread wide and landed without a single collision. These were not the shambling beasts Jenseti had encountered decades ago, barely able to avoid crashing into each other in their rush to devour his skeleton. These were organised and swiftly surrounded him. The only avenue of escape was a quick backpedal into the pool portal, but he hadn't made his destination clear to it yet. For all he knew, he could go in and come out inside a volcano or deep in an ocean.

No, he wasn't running away. These monsters had feasted on the people he cared about the most. If he left now, the shame would haunt him the rest of his days. He swallowed all his grief, choosing anger to carry him forward.

Jenseti charged once more, tears flying from his eyes as he deflected the first of the Bonedrinkers' hands. In a dark irony, these fiends *ate* through touch. A fingertip was all it took to start the process. In his first encounter with them, he had watched them feed on a few small flightless birds. The poor wretches crumbled into sacks of boneless flesh, clinging to agonising life for a few scant moments before expiring.

The Bonedrinkers wouldn't do that to him. The Touch allowed him to withstand it, flinging their hands away. He controlled the recoil, sending some Bonedrinkers crashing into the trees and knocking others backward into their nearest fellow. Two quick fingers from Jenseti crushed a windpipe, a precise chop to the neck broke a spine, his palm to the sternum crushed a heart. This push, shove, tap, and kill was a dance from one of the warrior arts his mother forced on him. In the end, she had won. The Ashtari Empire was in him no matter how he tried to escape it.

Wouldn't it be better to stop now? Gisara was gone. And every Bonedrinker he killed was a stamp of approval for what his family always wanted him to be. Wasn't this just a different kind of death?

A scream bellowed from his shoulder, Macentor unleashing a howl of god-adjacent rage. Jenseti's moment of despair had nearly allowed the remaining Bonedrinkers to fall on him like an assa-assa swarm. But they fell back, clasping at their throats as their bone growths grew and twisted like eager vines. Pustules and tumours exploded across their flesh and, Jenseti knew, inside their bodies as well. The Bonedrinkers tried to scream but their tongues had become unmanageable masses of flesh that grew until their jaws broke. For a moment Jenseti savoured the violence Macentor had brought down on the monsters that destroyed Gisara.

Was this revenge? Or had he just granted his family another victory? Revelling in what would on any other day repulse you?

'Whew, that was nasty!' Mondari grabbed two plugs from his ears and threw them to the ground. 'I research my targets, you know. Even the little parasite you got stuck in you. One and done on that scream for a while.'

Jenseti fell to one knee from the fatigue of Macentor's power and could feel the parasite retreating. He had to rest. 'You used them...'

'Of course! Ugly, stupid, and obsessed with eating everything. Those are the kind of people you get rid of quick.' Mondari hadn't moved closer but twirled his pink dagger. 'I do my research, babe. I hate an unnecessarily hard job. So I needed you mad enough to not think too hard as you used up all your goods. Empty the Touch right out of you. Gisara getting fucked by monsters you should have killed felt like the perfect lesson for a wimp who keeps avoiding violence.'

Jenseti wanted to rip Mondari's throat out. Exhaustion kept him floored.

With a pitiful pout of his lips that switched to a murderous smile, Mondari rushed him, the dagger stabbing through Jenseti's chest with enough force to lift him off the ground. The Gomi-Han-Bale grabbed Jenseti by the back of his neck and forced him to lock eyes. 'You gave up an entire empire! To do what? Fix people who think you're a freak and to fuck people with no reward?'

It would have taken so much effort to respond. Every part of his body felt far away, but dying meant Gisara's murders went unanswered. He refused to accept that. Jenseti groaned and struggled, pouring all the anger he had left into one hand so he could reach into his pants. There was a loud snap, and he smiled as a torrent of power flooded through him. He withdrew his hand, holding his now-unlocked chastity cage. Mondari's eyes widened right as Jenseti headbutted him. Falling to the ground with the dagger still in his chest, Jenseti yanked it out painlessly and with not a drop of blood on it.

'Can't research something I've never done before.' The next word was a satisfaction better than sex. 'Babe.'

I could not protect your family healer. But I can protect you. Jenseti smiled, knowing this was the moment gratitude would be repaid.

A cacophony filled the forest as dozens of glittering stone butterflies flew out of the trees and swarmed around them. Gifts from Hazzrian delivered by their saint. In the end, the inquisitors he saved proved the source of his own salvation.

Mondari looked around, frantic and confused. Jenseti had used the Touch when their heads collided, performing an act that could only come from the power of releasing the cage. Jenseti poured parts of himself into the killer. The burden of his brutal family's expectations. Gone. The fear they might one day find him. Gone. The grief of failing Gisara. Gone. The hesitation at using his skills to inflict violence. All of it gone.

The Touch was used to ease pain, but that did not mean it was incapable of giving it.

Mondari clutched at his head, mumbling to himself. He fell to his knees and his lip quivered, on the verge of tears. A century's worth of emotion had been forced into his mind in a single moment. Not even the most hardened would have been able to cope.

'I will tell the Gomi-Han-Bale where to find you.'

Mondari held out a trembling hand. 'NO! Please—'

The butterflies screeched and daggers of light zipped through the air. Jenseti felt the heat of each and closed his eyes, not wanting to see what would happen to Mondari. There was no enjoyment to be found. It had been a mistake to feel it with the Bonedrinkers. All this was because Jenseti had run from his family when he should have confronted them. He left the Ashtari Empire when he should have worked to bring it down. He realised now that it wasn't enough to abhor violence. Running away from a festering wound didn't make it heal.

Jenseti opened his eyes and heard Macentor weakly laughing. 'What?'

'Look how many times the bastard got stabbed in his groin. HA! What he deserves for talking down to me. Stupid little mortal with his bad hair and—'

'Macentor. Please.' Jenseti struggled to not laugh. 'None of this should have happened. Even the Gomi-Han-Bale got drawn into this because of my cowardice. I can't keep running away.'

'Ehhh, you don't have to. You're safe again, girl.'

Still holding the pink dagger, Jenseti walked to Mondari's bloodied body and kneeled. He closed the killer's eyes with a new resolve. He had once refused to take a throne. Now he refused to allow that throne to exist at all.

'No, Macentor. I'm still in danger.' He looked over his shoulder as the stone butterflies flew homeward, then retrieved his chastity cage and moved to lock it back into its proper place. 'But now… so is everyone else.'

Dotch Masher and the Planet `mm`

William C. Tracy

In the latter half of the twenty-fourth century, the universe is but a plaything for the minds of the most powerful beings...

DOTCH MASHER—Space Explorer, planet conqueror, face of Krill Crème™ hair product (Sticks in place no matter the gravity!), and three-time winner of the Alpha Centauri tightest-space-pants contest— ponders his perfectly coiffed, glistening blond hair in the shiny silver wallplate of his XL-2000 SuperGO Space Speeder™.

His faithful assistant, the ever-optimistic TWERKY, stands slightly behind him and to the left...

'Your jumpsuit is clashing with the interior again, Twerky,' Dotch said. 'Why do you always go for the pink?'

'I d-didn't even notice the colour, sir,' Twerky answered, brushing a nervous hand down his front. 'It's always so dangerous out in space, I opted for the flame-retardant, gravity-retardant, ice-retardant, and Destruct-O-Ray™-resistant option. It *only* comes in pink.'

'And the pink pumps?'

'Oh, they w-were included.'

'That's why you're still the assistant, Twerky,' Dotch reprimanded. He puffed up his lithe frame, turning his head side to side—he was certain his hair hadn't moved a micrometre. 'You're younger and less experienced, even if those sweet chubby cheeks of yours light up every room you enter. Expand-O-Weave™ is the way to go! See how the threads stretch and compress as needed? Never a wrinkle, and it shows off my every advantage in the situation!' Dotch flexed a bulging arm, and the Expand-O-Weave™ instantly compensated.

Twerky blinked his large, dark eyes, obviously trying not to swoon. 'But d-does it resist Destruct-O-Rays™? I'd hate for anything to harm your excellent suit, sir, and especially that physique. Why, your arms are as b-big around as my thighs!'

Dotch waggled a finger. 'Don't get coy with me, mister. You've made it clear you never sample the wares.'

Twerky blushed. 'Y-yes sir, I prefer to look.'

Dotch opened his mouth to reply, but the Commun-O-Matic Insta-Feel-O-Gram™ *binged* for attention.

'A message. This must be our next mission, Twerky!' Dotch examined the rows of buttons on the communication device—settings for different galaxies, atmospheres, nebulae, quark rotation, and lunch menus. He flipped a switch at random. The set continued to *bing* for attention.

'Blasted thing never works right,' Dotch said. He flipped the galaxy to Andromeda, the lunch to bologna, and the quark rotation to 'Charmed, I'm sure'. The projection set continued to display an angry blob of plasma, devoid of meaning.

Dotch punched it, his Expand-O-Weave™ keeping his toned forearms and triceps on display as he did. It blobbed blobbily but did nothing else.

'A-are you certain it's Bologna Week, sir?' Twerky asked. He sidled up to the console, flipping far too many switches. The blob of plasma reflected garishly off his jumpsuit.

'The switches go sideways too?' Dotch exclaimed. 'They must have updated this one while I wasn't looking.'

'T-terribly rude of them, sir,' Twerky replied, still flipping switches. 'Those engineers keep fixing things.'

Dotch would have replied, but a wide, purple, and blotchy face swam into view, like an eager biologist who'd found a new single-celled organism.

'Doctor Thrombosis!' Dotch snapped to attention, hand clenched into a fist in front of his stomach. 'I answered as soon as I heard you *bing*. What's our next mission?'

One of the good doctor's eyes expanded to fill the Commun-O-Matic Insta-Feel-O-Gram™ projection field before it moved to display his mouth, surrounded by wiry hairs like he'd eaten an angry hedgehog.

'…got no choice left, Masher!' The doctor seemed mid-rant, judging by the spittle around his mouth. Dotch wiped a speck of moisture from his cheek. 'That malicious Melvin is at it again! He's got some ridiculous vendetta against one of the solar golf courses we've built, and he's taking it out on our production. Those vagrants he's allied with keep helping him. We can't stop him, Masher. He's outmanoeuvred us!'

'Melvin! That mischievous miscreant!' Dotch cried—the best way to break the doctor's rant. 'What's he done this time?'

'He's blocked us, Masher.' Doctor Thrombosis pulled back from the Feel-o-Gram so his whole head was in view, wispy hair surrounding an unhealthy purple skin tone, like cotton candy glued on a bowling ball. The collar of his doctor's coat fluttered at the edge of the display, supporting the projection of his head. Twerky peered at the back of the display, frowning at the rear of Doctor Thrombosis' head. 'Every last mine, manufacturing rig, and milling process has been bought up or destroyed! We're down to our last three-day supply of Texttostergo Maximus.'

'That sounds important, Doctor!' Dotch said. 'Why would this malevolent creature do such a thing?'

'Why, Texttostergo Maximus is only the most virile element, Masher! And it's up to you to get more for the Associated Satellite and Stationary Mining Unified New Colonisation Hierarchy (ASSMUNCH™)!' Doctor Thrombosis leaned forward, his nose threatening to push Dotch into the reflective wall of his Space Speeder. 'Now listen up, Masher. The only known remaining source of Texttostergo Maximus is on the secretive planet "MM", which has never before been charted. All attempts have ended in failure!'

'Never fear, Doctor.' Dotch struck a pose, making sure his Expand-O-Weave™ showed his midsection off to its best effect. 'Dotch Masher, Space Explorer is on the case!'

'Best be quick, Masher,' the doctor grumbled, his eyes blood-shot. 'That murderous Melvin is already speeding toward planet "MM"! Not only that, but that malefactor has blocked all our hardiest space warriors from getting there before him. We've got nothing left but you, Masher! Can you do it? Can you catch the evil Melvin in time and save the last supply of Texttostergo?' A vein pulsed dangerously above his left eye. The good doctor looked like he was about to have a stroke.

'You can count on me, Doctor,' Dotch said. 'And if it were up to me, this would be the last you'd hear of that malicious malcontent, the meddling Melvin!'

'It *is* up to you, Masher,' Doctor Thrombosis cried and pounded his holographic fist onto something in front of him, at which point the communication ended in a burst of blobby static.

'Well, bully for that,' Dotch said.

'I'm s-sure you'll do m-marvellously, sir,' Twerky added.

'Step back, Twerky. I've got to plot the fastest course possible to overtake Melvin before he gets to planet "MM"!' Dotch stroked his chin, standing before the Project-O-Plot™ board, making sure his right side (the better side) was in full view.

'Now, if we fly straight through the Nebula of Madness here, we can cut off five hours of flight time.'

'Th-the one that drives everyone mad, sir?' Twerky asked.

'Ye-es. Well, maybe that isn't the best choice. How about sling-shotting around the radioactive Przybylski's Star?'

'Thrusters will get c-cooked by the radiation.'

'Cut through the nursery of black holes?'

'We'll be trapped until the end of the universe, sir.'

'The Gas Cloud of Mad Gods? Gyre of Perturbed Warrior Aliens? Starlanes of the Mecha-accountants?'

Twerky only shook his head. 'Just the p-paperwork to get into the starlanes will take the whole three days, sir.'

Dotch folded his arms, his Expand-O-Weave™ flowing over his chest like a smooth band of starlight. 'Well, I'd like to see *you* plot a course.'

Twerky toddled up to the Project-O-Plot™ board in his pink pumps, a stick of Ethereal Chalk in his hand. 'We can always drop into the s-subspace race lanes here—' He made a mark. '—catch the slipstream behind the migration of s-starwhales *here*—' Another mark. '—and then thread the needle on the phasing asteroid field r-right here, sir.' He made the last mark.

'Exactly what I was thinking,' Dotch proclaimed. 'Now, let's get moving!'

They had barely caught up to the starwhale pod when the Commun-O-Matic Insta-Feel-O-Gram™ *binged* again.

'I can't get any piloting done with these incessant communications!' Dotch took a big bite of his pastrami sandwich (it hadn't been Bologna Week after all) and removed his elegantly pointed Magnet-O-Clamp™ strolling loafers from the dashboard. 'Take over, Twerky.'

'Y-yes sir,' Twerky said, already furiously switching buttons, pushing wheels, and turning switches.

'Now, Twerky, you're already working up a sweat and we're barely halfway across the galaxy.' Dotch stood in front of the communicator, considering the bank of switches. Which one had it been last time?

The projector screen bloomed into life, without any action whatsoever.

'Huh. Must have still been on,' Dotch mused.

'I have programmed your Commun-O-Matic Insta-Feel-O-Gram™ without your knowledge thanks to my gigantic intellect,' said the mysterious figure in a sonorous, nasally voice from the projection area. They were dressed to the nines, wearing a segmented green tutu, red tie, and a green bowler hat that cast their face in shadow. Only two huge, lovely white eyes peered out from the depths of the shadows. 'You will never catch up to me, Dotch. Your commanders never told you what they will do with the Texttostergo Maximus of planet "MM". Now it will all be mine!'

Dotch shook his head to keep from staring into those eyes. He'd never seen Melvin in person before. Then he realised he hadn't seen a mouth move. Where had that voice come from?

'Melvin!' Dotch clenched his hand into a fist, noting how the Expand-O-Weave™ displayed the fine muscles of his forearm. 'How dare you break into the sanctum of my personal Space Speeder! But you will never get there before me! I've enacted a daring path—'

'I b-believe I enacted it, sir,' Twerky said from the controls.

'—My trusty assistant has enacted a daring path and I'm flying at top speed right now—'

'Except I'm flying the speeder now, sir.'

'—My trusty assistant is flying me at top speed right now toward planet "MM" so I can stop you from getting the last of the supply of Texttostergo Maximus!'

'Oh dear,' Melvin said from the projector. 'That won't do at all. Prepare to be exploded!'

The figure produced a Threat-Answerer X5™ from his green tutu and pointed it out of the projector. Dotch laughed.

'You can't fire from inside a Commun-O-Matic Insta-Feel-O-Gram™! That's preposterous!'

There was a *bang*, and something bounced off Dotch's Expand-O-Weave™-protected chest.

'You can if you have a gigantic intellect.'

'Ow, that stung!'

'And this will sting more.'

Dotch was thrown sideways as the whole speeder swerved.

'Watch your piloting, Twerky!' he growled.

'S-sorry, sir. Just dodged a missile aimed directly at us.'

'Is that so? Well, I'll just fire one back!' Dotch bounded to the controls and mashed the large red button marked 'MISSILE'. The ship bucked and a rounded shape shot away.

Dotch looked back to the projection where Melvin's shadowy face and bright white eyes still lurked. The projection shook, Melvin's elegant poise faltering for just a moment.

'How about that?'

Melvin shook his head. 'Quite unfortunate. I shall have to do something to rectify this.' One hand reached out and the projection helpfully zoomed back to show a single finger pressing an even larger, even redder button marked 'LARGER MISSILE'.

Dotch gulped as the shadow of something nearly as large as his ship loomed over them.

'I've g-got it, sir!' Twerky cried and flipped an entire bank of switches. The XL-2000 SuperGO Space Speeder™ jumped like a porpoise, bucked like a bronco, and stretched like a cat.

When he came to, Dotch found himself suspended from the ceiling by his Magnet-O-Clamp™ strolling loafers. Twerky's pink pumps seemed to have stabbed into the control panel, anchoring him in place around the hissing sparks. Dotch's well-Krill-Crème™-d hair had been mussed. He looked into the upside-down blackness of Melvin's face.

'Of course, you realise this means war!' he said.

The chase continued for hours, neither ship gaining a lead. They had barely left the starwhale lanes before the Space Speeder—now marred by dozens of laser punctures, missile scars, and pinholes from Twerky's pumps—raced side by side with Melvin's bulky warship, each striving to reach planet 'MM' first.

'You will never defeat me, Dotch.' Melvin preened from the projector.

'We'll see about that!' Dotch mumbled from underneath the bank of controls, wires gripped in his teeth.

'It's impossible to get away from my gigantic intelle—'

The projector blobbed back into a floating orb, severing the connection. Dotch dusted off his hands.

'Enough of that meddling mealymouth,' he said and stomped to the pilot's seat. 'Give me back the controls, Twerky! It's time to dive into the phasing asteroids, right?'

'T-that's right, sir.' Twerky pushed a button and a joystick rose from the console in front of Dotch, who gripped it hard. 'You'll see I've mapped out the path through the obstacles, t-taking into account the probability of each asteroid as it moves in and out of our dimension, sir.'

Dotch glanced at the map. 'It's too slow. We've got to get ahead of Melvin.' He bore down on the joystick and the speeder jumped into the asteroid field.

'O-of course, sir. Just w-watch out for that… eee! And the other one t-there… aaaah!'

'These asteroids are no match for the Space Speeder!' Dotch exclaimed, mashing the 'FIRE LASERS' button. The rock ahead burst into three pieces just as it phased back into reality. One piece immediately phased again, another shot away to the side, and the

third transformed into a very-briefly asphyxiating Florian carnivorous slug before the speeder turned it into a sticky mist.

'T-there's no telling what these asteroids will do if you hit them
while they're phasing, sir!' Twerky had one hand covering his round
face while the other danced across the control board, recalibrating
the shielding screens to face fully forward.

'We'll just have to risk it. After all, "Danger" is my middle
name, Twerky!'

'I believe your middle name is in fact "Francis",' came a languid
voice behind them.

'Blast it, Melvin!' Dotch Francis Danger Masher sprang from
his chair while Twerky grabbed for the joystick and wrestled the
speeder around a large asteroid. 'I disabled the projector. How
are you here?'

'It is simply a natural product of my—'

'Gigantic intellect, yes, you've said. I'd shoot a missile at you,
but we're going too fast.'

'You will never survive, you realise.' Melvin's large white eyes
stared out from under his green bowler hat. Dotch tried to see
anything else of his face, but it was impossible. 'I calculate you have
less than a 3% chance of making it through this asteroid field. You
will never catch me.'

'You can't tell me the odds if I do *this*!' Dotch ran his hand
over the controls for the Commun-O-Matic Insta-Feel-O-Gram™,
switching settings. Melvin's background changed from blue to pink
to green to dancing toasters. Deli meat of all kinds flew past. Melvin
only laughed, an oddly pleasant sound.

'Oh ho ho, Dotch. You can't turn me off so easily. You will have
to keep me turned on.'

'How about *this* then!' Dotch ran back to the controls, acknowl-
edging there was perhaps a design flaw in a speeder that required
one to move three metres between the controls and the communications systems.

'Where's his ship?' he demanded, and Twerky pointed to an oblong, tapered shape in front of them.

'R-right there, sir, but he's keeping the phasing asteroids between us.'

'Perfect!' Dotch mashed down on the 'FIRE LASERS' button again and again, targeting each asteroid between them as it phased in and out of their dimension.

'W-watch out, sir!' Twerky cried as chunks of asteroid zipped off in all directions, turned into cephalopods and gastropods of all shapes, and exploded in the fireworks of dying dimensions.

'Oh, dear. Your chances are getting lower all the time, Dotch,' Melvin called, swimming through slices of blue pepperoni. Twerky was jerking the joystick around like he was milking a cow on roller skates. Chunks of asteroid bounced off the hull while Dotch gritted his teeth and kept punching the button.

He was rewarded with an 'Oh my' from the projector as the ship in front of them received a large asteroid chunk directly up its tailpipe, spinning it around in a large circle, ploughing through asteroids. The projector snapped back to an amorphous blob.

'Now, Twerky!' Dotch removed his finger from the 'FIRE LASERS' button and grasped his own joystick. 'Together, to planet "MM"!'

On the viewscreen loomed a planet covered with swirling milky clouds, its surface almost completely obscured. Melvin's large warship was hopefully far behind them, and the projector had been quiet.

'Almost there, my trusty assistant!' Dotch exclaimed. 'We need only land, claim the surface for ASSMUNCH™, and get as much of the Texttostergo Maximus as we can. Now, shall I take us down, or shall you?'

'Oh, I j-just prefer to watch,' Twerky deferred.

Suddenly, a familiar, yet dented warship zipped in from the side, blocking their path to the surface. A calm voice emanated from the secondary voice communications.

'I'm afraid I shall have to obliterate you utterly, Dotch,' Melvin lamented. 'No one shall have the Texttostergo Maximus but me! ASSMUNCH™ will only abuse it, just to swell their already-en-gorged holdings. Turn back now.'

Ten different cannons rotated out from hidden ports on the warship, pointing directly toward the Space Speeder.

'Never!' Dotch pushed forward on the joystick.

'Ah, sir, w-we're getting dangerously close!' Twerky squeaked.

'He can't shoot us if we're closer than his laser range!'

All cannon mounts were charging up, glowing with radio-active energy.

'I b-believe that's missiles, not lasers, sir,' Twerky corrected.

'Faster, then!' Dotch rammed the joystick all the way forward, speeding toward the warship. 'He'll have to move out of the way!'

'I'll never surrender planet "MM",' Melvin pronounced from the speaker system. 'Firing now!'

But the Space Speeder was going faster than the warships' cannons could charge and punched straight through the other ship like a metallic hot dog turning a bread loaf into a bagel. With explosions.

'Ha ha!' Dotch exclaimed.

'Urg!' Twerky shouted.

'Goodness,' Melvin intoned.

Then Dotch jerked forward in his seat as the speeder caught on something, starting the ship twirling. Planet 'MM' wove in and out of their view. Dotch felt his pastrami starting to fight its way out of his stomach.

'It's the speedfins!' Twerky called from somewhere to Dotch's left. Or down. 'They're t-tangled, sir!'

'I hate it when that happens,' Dotch said. 'They're just too big to go through another ship. Catches every time.'

'You will never take me down, Dotch,' Melvin's voice said. 'Even if you're inside me, I can still control where we're going.'

The speeder jerked to the side as Melvin's warship accelerated.

'Not on my watch!' Dotch found the joystick, now somewhere above his head, and pulled in the opposite direction. Their spinning only increased, as both ships—locked together—went nowhere.

'You can't see me, but I am pushing my "MORE ENGINES" button,' Melvin said. The speeder jerked again.

'Two can play at that game!' Dotch found his yellow 'HOTTER ENGINES' button and jammed it down.

'Sir, I c-calculate if Melvin runs his engines any hotter, we'll—'

'I am running my engines even hotter. You cannot win.'

'—fly directly into planet "MM".'

Both ships dropped from the sky like slabs of intertwined salami.

Dotch regained awareness surrounded by the wreckage of his XL-2000 SuperGO Space Speeder™. He glanced down, glad to see his Expand-O-Weave™ was wrinkle-free, carefully arranged on his prone form to show his abs in the best light—which changed as a shadow passed across the now-cracked viewscreen.

'We're s-surrounded by strange shapes, sir!' Twerky exclaimed. His pink jumpsuit was covered with soot, but at least his pumps still had their heels. 'Fortunately, the air is breathable here. I th-think there's more holes than ship.'

'Then we'd best see what's out there!' Dotch unlatched the auto-engaging restraining belt that had looped itself around him when they crashed, dropping to the splintered floor of the wrecked speeder.

The exit ramp wheezed open halfway, stuck, then dropped the rest of the way to clang on the ground. Dotch's jaw followed it.

The ground of planet 'MM' glowed softly, in blues, pinks, and purples. The giant shapes they'd seen from the cockpit were plants, shooting up all around them, growing incredibly fast.

'It m-must be the effect of the Texttostergo M-Maximus, sir, the most virile element!' Twerky poked a lengthy stalk next to him and it curved around his finger, growing toward him. Twerky hastily stepped back. 'Oh, p-pardon me. I'll just watch from back here. I prefer to do that.'

Fleshy growths, with long stalks and bulbous sacks beneath, sprang up around them, blossoming into tightly curled flower heads.

'This is amazing!' Dotch said. He caressed a bunch of mushrooms poking up from the surface, each growing as big as a baby's arm in moments. 'Now I've seen the power of the Texttostergo Maximus firsthand.'

'Unfortunately, this view shall have to be your last.'

Dotch spun to see another figure crawl from the wreckage, then brush his green tutu off carefully. He straightened his tie, but his bowler hat had stayed firmly in place. Wide eyes met Dotch's from the shadows under the hat. Dotch ran a hand across his Krill Crème™ coif.

'Sticks in place no matter the gravity!' Dotch grinned at Melvin.

'Your time has run out, Dotch. The Texttostergo Maximus shall all be mine.'

'Never, Melvin! Despite your mysterious magnetism, I will resist you! Twerky, start collecting as much of the virile element as you can.' Dotch turned to Twerky, his arms already full of suggestive plants, but when he turned back, Melvin's hand held a Destruct-O-Ray™ gun.

'This planet does not seem to be big enough for the two of us.' Melvin's nasal voice had turned lugubrious.

Dotch straightened, showing off his Expand-O-Weave™-suited chest. 'You wouldn't dare!'

Time slowed as Melvin's finger tightened on the trigger.

Dotch finally realised he should have gotten that Destruct-O-Ray™ resistant upgrade.

'Noooooooooo!'

A flash of pink flew in front of Dotch and the deadly rays bounced off to fry the nearby plants.

Twerky fell to the ground, a grisly burn marring the front of his jumpsuit, his pumps scratching furrows in the ground.

'How rude. Now I shall have to wait several minutes for my Destruct-O-Ray™ to recharge.' Melvin's large eyes turned down to his gun as Dotch knelt beside his trusty sidekick.

'Twerky, can you hear me? You're hurt! I thought your jumpsuit repelled Destruct-O-Ray™!'

'And f-flames, gravity, and ice, sir,' Twerky whispered.

Dotch carefully inspected the wound, wincing. This wasn't good. He caught sight of the tag, flapping from the ragged edge of the jumpsuit.

'Twerky, this says the jumpsuit is only Destruct-O-Ray™ *resistant*. This fine print says, "May not repel Destruct-O-Ray™ at close range."'

'I'm v-very sorry, sir,' Twerky breathed.

Nearly every action was fair game in the job of the Space Explorer, but Dotch drew the line at anything that hurt his faithful assistant Twerky.

'You win, Melvin,' Dotch hissed. 'You can have all the Texttostergo Maximus on planet "MM". Just help me heal him.'

For once, Melvin's eyes looked worried. 'You do care for him, don't you?'

'Of course I do! What kind of a question is that?' Dotch frowned, still unable to see any part of Melvin's face except those lovely, large eyes.

'You know, of course, Texttostergo Maximus has marvellous medicinal properties. There is plenty here to start your assistant's healing process.'

'And you'll let me do that? You just tried to shoot me.'

'You have given up your claim. I no longer need to fight you over planet "MM".'

Dotch considered that. 'You really just want the Texttostergo Maximus?' Maybe Melvin *was* afraid of ASSMUNCH™ abusing it.

'I would like to p-point out that I'm in quite incredible pain, sir,' Twerky wheezed.

'My apologies, Twerky.' Dotch slowly reached for the nearest growth, a sizable mushroom. He looked up to Melvin, catching a glimpse under the green tutu.

'My, you really do have a gigantic...'

'Intellect, yes,' Melvin finished. 'The plants here are safe to eat. I have scanned them already for compatibility.'

'Afraid you can't watch this one, Twerky.' Dotch placed the end of the mushroom in front of him. 'The whole thing. Best to start at the tip and work your way down to the base.'

Dotch and Melvin watched Twerky eat the mushroom, listening to the slurping sounds.

'He really can swallow it down, can't he?' Dotch commented.

'Quite talented,' Melvin said. 'But I feel I must explain.'

'How so, my manipulative nemesis?'

'Were you told why ASSMUNCH™ needs so much Texttostergo Maximus?'

'Something about a golf course and vagrants. With that many capitals, it had to be important,' Dotch hedged. 'Besides, it's the most virile element.'

'Used to fuel ASSMUNCH™'s expansionist tendencies and keep the old and decrepit leaders like your Doctor Thrombosis in power. With it, they can live far past their years, swallowing down vast amounts of resources, blocking growing systems from needed sustenance.'

'Nothing wrong with keeping yourself fit and ready,' Dotch said, but his heart wasn't in it. Doctor Thrombosis had been directing his missions since he was barely out of Explorer Cadet school. 'I suppose you have a better use for it?'

'I shall be taking it to my planet of refugees—not vagrants—displaced by ASSMUNCH™'s expansion into my solar system. We can barely sustain our species without the Texttostergo Maximus to help grow crops and increase our birth rate. I tried to tell you, but you wouldn't listen.'

Twerky made a heroic swallow, the last of the mushroom disappearing down his throat. 'He's correct, sir. The Marchians were m-moved from their home system to make room for a solar golf course.'

Things suddenly made more sense.

'Melvin the Marchian was marooned with his many mates by the meddling machinations of the mining managers?'

'It w-would appear so, sir.' Twerky sat up, the grievous wound in his flesh knitting back together. His pink jumpsuit, unfortunately, was unaffected. Dotch feared what outfit Twerky would purchase next.

'Well, that's just despicable.' Dotch stood and offered a hand to Melvin. 'I propose a new plan: I help you take the Texttostergo Maximus to your people. Nothing less would appease my sense of decency as a Space Explorer!'

'And Doctor Thrombosis?'

Dotch made a rude noise. 'The man hasn't seen the outside of a space station in years. As far as I'm concerned, he's revoked his Space Explorer licence!'

Twerky brushed off his jumpsuit, arranging it as best he could. 'Ah, sir—*sirs*—there is s-still one problem. Both spacecraft are wrecked.'

'I'm sure everything can be fixed with a judicious application of gigantic intellect,' Dotch said, smiling at Melvin.

'My XL-2000 SuperGO Space Speeder™ is even better than before!' Dotch exclaimed.

'Because it uses a lot of *my* Warmaker 2001™ warship.' Melvin dusted off his hands and straightened his red tie, having connected the last luncheon-compensating drive circuits.

The new ship was erected proudly on the surface of planet 'MM,' held in place by a scaffolding of giant plant stems. Longer than either the original speeder or warship, it now boasted two sets of engines at the back end, nestled in double-rounded enclosures at the base of the shaft.

'Cargo is loaded, s-sirs!' Twerky saluted from the command module. 'I've stuffed as much Texttostergo Maximus as p-possible in the expanded cargo space.'

'We'll leave a little for Doctor Thrombosis and his cronies, eh, Melvin?' Dotch asked as they climbed aboard.

'Quite.' Melvin raised a single finger. 'But I see a problem with this construction.'

Dotch glanced around. 'The projector system was pretty badly damaged, but I think we can get it up and running before the new lunch menu comes out.'

'Not that. There appears to only be one captain's seat.' Melvin pointed to the swivelling chair in front of the control bank. Twerky had taken his usual place as co-pilot.

'Oh, that.' Dotch winked. 'That was intentional. I figured it was a shame not to share the captain's responsibilities, as well as that gigantic… intellect of yours.' He gestured to the seat. 'After you.'

Melvin considered Dotch for a long moment, his large eyes taking in the smooth expanse of Expand-O-Weave™ across Dotch's chest, arms, legs, and abdomen. The Expand-O-Weave™ was doing more work than usual to keep that latter area smooth. He took a seat in the swivel chair and patted his green tutu.

'Ready to blast off, Dotch Masher.'

…*and so, faithful TWERKY pulls a curtain across the scene, hiding Melvin and Dotch from sight.*

   'T-that's all, twinks!' he says, then turns back to the scene. 'I'll j-just watch from here.'

Hazard Pay

Malcolm Schmitz

'A pleasure garden,' I said, 'isn't the traditional place to talk about a *job*.'

The breeze ruffled my hair; the scent of jasmine hung on the wind. The marble walls around us trailed rose bushes and clinging religolds; my client and I sat in a pavilion covered in silks, on pillow-covered benches.

I couldn't complain; it was a fine place to meet, in theory. Much better than the darkest corner of the dodgiest tavern. But if a client invites you to their *home*… they're either very honest or very stupid.

In practice, it's usually the same thing.

'You're not a traditional man, are you?' Lord Lendemere's eyes narrowed. He gestured to one of his flock of servant girls—the one holding a platter of fruit and doing her best to look invisible. When she came over, he grabbed a bunch of grapes, and popped one into his mouth.

I've been told I have a good poker face, but what I have is a *babyface*. Doe eyes bigger than one's waist give a certain *innocent* look, whether or not that's what one wants. It took me everything I had not to roll them.

'I'm not,' I said. 'Just surprised. People who want my services go to the Tattered Banner and ask for Nic.'

'That's not your name, Mister Vezian... or *was* it "Miss"?'

'Mister,' I said. 'And no. Nic's not my name.'

I wasn't going to spell it out for him. My hints should have been enough. If Lord Lendemere didn't realise an unlicenced adventurer would have reasons to work *privately,* that meant one of two things: either he was trying to throw me under a cart, or he was a flaming idiot.

Maybe, I thought, I should assume he's an idiot. That way I could assume he'd heard about the job where I'd disguised myself as a courtesan or of my short-lived drag act and not my *very public* transition. And then I wouldn't be tempted to argue with the idiot.

Arguing with a potential client is a great way to not have a client.

'I suppose it doesn't matter,' he said. 'And it doesn't matter that you're *here,* either. I'm not asking you to do anything... underhanded.'

'Of course, of course,' I said. 'But if you don't want underhanded... why me? You could go to the Guild—'

'Two reasons.' Lord Lendemere held up a hand. 'First, the Guild's raised its prices again.'

'That'd do it.' I tsked sympathetically. 'I have to warn you, I don't come cheap.'

'But you'll *work* for your money, won't you?'

I nodded, not trusting myself to speak. The servant girl glanced at me, and for a moment, we shared the deep and profound connection of Those Who Had To Deal With This Terrible Man. Then she looked away, and I took a deep breath.

'What's the other reason?' I said.

'I've heard,' Lord Lendemere said, 'you have... *abilities* that other adventurers don't.'

Did a cold wind blow through the pleasure garden, or was it just me? I tried not to bristle. My sword hung heavy on my back.

'Where did you hear that?' I asked, calmly.

'You're a legend. Honestly, I expected you to be more... muscular,' Lord Lendemere said. 'But that's one of your powers, isn't it? The strength of the gods—'

I sighed.

'Whatever you've heard, it was probably exaggerated,' I said. 'I'm just an... acquisition specialist. I use the odd magic item here and there, but...'

'Regardless,' Lord Lendemere said. 'You are a specialist.'

'Yes. And you still haven't told me what I'm acquiring.'

Lord Lendemere handed the grape branch, now empty, back to the serving girl. She vanished into the hedge maze. It felt like we were alone—but I knew there were a hundred eyes on us.

'If it's something from one of the other Houses...' I raised an eyebrow and steepled my fingers. '...you'll need to wait until their spies forget I was here.'

'I *said* it wasn't going to be anything underhanded,' Lord Lendemere said. 'You'll need to travel into the Dreadlands, but...'

'So you want me to steal from a Dark Lord.'

'Yes? I thought that's what adventurers *did*.'

'It is,' I said. 'Wanted to make sure we were on the same page.'

'Have you ever heard,' Lord Lendemere said, 'of the Eye of Cotora?'

It took everything I had to keep a straight face. 'It's a magic item, right? A *very famous* magic item?'

'Yes. A gem with the power to reveal the truth,' Lord Lendemere said, giving me the explanation I was trying to avoid. 'It's currently in the possession of the dread lich Belzarian.'

'Undead wizard? Bit dramatic? Turns people into salamanders? Skeleton army?'

'That's the one.'

I took a deep breath. 'If you're sending me after a lich—especially *that* lich—I'm going to need hazard pay. And I'll need it upfront.'

Lord Lendemere frowned, but I kept talking.

'This is an incredibly dangerous job,' I said. 'Stealing a powerful artefact from a dangerous creature? If I'm going to return from this, I'll need better equipment—'

'Fine. Fine.' Lord Lendemere sat up, pushing aside his mountain of pillows. 'Say, six hundred gold?'

'Mm. If I don't come back from this, my poor dear mother will need something to live on. Say, a thousand?'

'Eight hundred. That's my final offer.' Lord Lendemere scowled.

Eight hundred gold was enough to feed a family for a year and a day. It was also much, much cheaper than Guild rates. He knew, and I knew, that this was the best deal he'd get.

He fumbled at his belt and pulled out a purse. It clinked *ever* so satisfyingly. I pocketed it, carefully—wouldn't do to flash my magic items.

'My valet will deliver the rest,' he said. 'Until then…'

'Pleasure doing business with you.' I stuck my hand out; we shook on it.

The deal was done. Now I just had to do the deed.

It was a long journey from the City of Crystal into the Dark Lands, but I didn't mind. I wouldn't be riding the world's most elderly gelding if I wanted to move *quickly*. I had time to daydream, to simmer over ideas and schemes, and to think of a plan.

My main strategy was simple: climb the wall, slip into Belzarian's tower, and take things from there. But there was always the danger of a complication. Contingency plans were much more difficult than regular plans, and so they were what took up most of my attention as I rode onward.

The wheat-gold plains around the City of Crystal gave way to dark-green pine forest. The sky overhead grew cloudy as the trees grew taller and sparser. It began to drizzle, and the air smelled like sulphur. The trees grew blackened, twisted, and gnarled; my horse picked his way over the roots, nickering softly.

'Easy, boy,' I muttered. 'Easy.'

Something in the air smelled strange, strong enough to drown out the sulphur. It was the unmistakable, bright scent of holy magic—like cold air mixed with pepper. I crested the last hill before Belzarian's stronghold... and cursed under my breath.

A crowd of holy knights in shining armour stood at the gate. Some of them brandished blazing swords; some hoisted a battering ram; some led bright white horses to a makeshift pen. One knight in ostentatious bleached-white armour was giving a speech—I couldn't make out the words, but it was something between a sermon and a battle speech—bleating at the top of his lungs:

'—AND THE EARTH SHALL BE CLEANSED OF EVIL!'

The paladins cheered raucously.

And there's the complication... I couldn't walk right in the front door with these idiots trying to besiege it.

I could have fought my way through, of course. Lord Whats-His-Face hadn't been wrong—my family sword *did* have powers, and they made me a much better swordsman than I had any right to be. It'd be so easy to raise the sword, murmur the incantation, and fight my way through these chumps. But I didn't want to fight if I could help it—much better to let Belzarian's traps and spells do the dirty work for me.

'Easy, easy,' I said. My horse—the second-most patient creature on the planet—stopped in its tracks. I found a patch of scraggly crabgrass at the foot of a blighted tree and hitched him up.

A crow croaked in the tree's highest branches. Another landed beside it. They tilted their heads, in the way of birds, and then the first opened its beak and spoke to me.

'BODY AND SOUL,' it said.

'Yeah, yeah, hello to you too.' I sighed and looked up at it.

'THE DARK LORD WILL TAKE YOU, BODY AND SOUL,' it screeched. A wind blew through the tree, moaning hollow and long.

'Tell your dark master that if he wants to talk to me, he should send me a messenger who knows what they're saying.'

The crow croaked.

'BODY—'

'And soul. I get it.'

BAM! The stronghold's drawbridge clattered open and a horde of skeletons spilled out. They moved like puppets with half-cut strings, jerking back and forth wildly as they swung their scimitars. The paladins, in their gleaming armour, tried to hold a line.

Bless their hearts. My unintentional allies would make this a damn sight easier. With everyone distracted, it'd be much simpler to slip inside.

I snuck through the dark forest, around the back. The stronghold's high obsidian walls bristled with spikes and grotesques, just *begging* to be climbed. Every gargoyle a foothold; every spike a piton. I clambered over griffins' beaks, bat wings, laughing imps, and skeletal hands, and pulled myself over the wall. Its top was wider than it looked from beneath, a perfect place to sit and catch a breath beside a crenellation.

The easy part was done. Now, I had to get to Belzarian's tower.

He'd been a wizard, hundreds of years ago. Of course he had a tower, twice as covered in grotesques as his fortress' walls, and three times as high. If I hadn't known better, I'd say he was compensating for something.

I knew how liches did things, and in particular how *this* lich did things. When he had a problem, his first tactic was to throw bodies at it, and when he ran out of bodies, he'd switch to spells. I had to get to him before the paladins breached the gate. It was just a matter of time——he only had so many skeletons. If they reached him before I did, they'd kill their bogeyman. And heroes—whether holy warriors of light or grizzled barbarians—*always* looted their kills.

If they killed Belzarian before I got there, I'd never forgive myself.

It started to rain. Cold water trickled down my spine, making my hair prickle; it pushed my hair into my eyes and drenched my bare hands. Yet another complication—did they ever cease? I wrapped my cloak around myself, pulled up my hood, and strode forward across the top of the wall.

Time to climb the lich's tower.

In my hubris, even with the rain, I thought it'd be easy. The tower's gargoyles were even more twisted than those on the outer walls, snarling and contorted, with teeth like cats and eyes like snakes. More handholds and footholds than a thief could have asked for. I pulled myself up as easily as a lizard climbing a wall, reaching out, grabbing a gargoyle's jaw—

CHOMP! The gargoyle bit down.

Its teeth weren't as sharp as you'd think, but its grip was tighter than pliers on a cheap lock. I struggled against it, trying to yank my hand from its mouth, but it was no good.

In the distance, an alarm clanged. Bones clattered against each other; they drew closer and closer. I'd distracted Belzarian's skeleton army. Unfortunately, skeletons aren't the brightest. They'll go for the nearest threat—or what *looks* like a threat—no matter how big the thing behind them is.

'Shoo!' I said. 'Don't you have paladins to fight?'

The skeletons turned to look at each other and then back at me. They could really only pay attention to one thing at a time.

My other hand slipped off the wet stone. In the distance, an alarm bell clanged and clattered, loud as thunder.

Damnation and hellfire. Here I was, dangling by one hand from the mouth of a gargoyle, while skeletons milled around the base of the tower. A few of the brighter ones tried to chuck things at me—bones, pebbles, a flame-eyed skull, y'know, the usual—but skeletons aren't good shots. Couldn't hit the broad side of a bronze dragon, much less me.

I could draw my sword and dive. Cleave my way through, like some kind of bloody *hero*. But no, things weren't quite that dire. I could still *think* my way out of this.

I scrabbled for a handhold. A bird-like gargoyle squatted just above my head; I grabbed its beak—making sure it was *closed*—and pulled myself up just before I could fall. The other gargoyle's teeth stayed clamped around my hand. I kicked desperately at its throat—and it let go. My hand throbbed, but I pulled myself up.

My flailing cloak snagged on the gargoyle's teeth. I undid the clasp and let it fall. Finally I found a foothold. A second foothold. Took a deep breath.

The cloak dropped on top of a skeleton, covering it like a ghost from a children's pantomime. It lurched forward, trying to shake off the fabric—and the other skeletons drew their scimitars. They fell upon each other like army ants, ready to tear each other bone from bone.

That was fine by me. Belzarian would put them back together soon enough. Assuming I didn't get to him first.

I pulled myself through the nearest window—into the maze of staircases that was Belzarian's Tower.

There was a *reason* I'd wanted to climb the walls, rather than going through the door. Two giant, rusty saw blades spun in front of me, the gears that powered them creaking.

'Saw blades *again?*' I groaned. 'Could you be *any* less original?'

They blocked the staircase up—and they weren't the only danger I'd have to face. Every floor of this stupid tower was a gauntlet of half-baked traps, until you got to Belzarian's quarters at the summit. There was a gap in the enormous spinning blades just big enough to slip between if you timed it right. I dashed through and ran up the stairs.

By this point, I could avoid these traps in my sleep. I dodged the giant rock that rolled down the next flight of stairs. The scythes that swung through the next room were a little trickier—one of them nicked my shoulder. The *worst* were the tripwires, which were nigh-invisible, and set off cutlight beams. Not wanting to be sliced to ribbons, I moved with all the caution and grace of a fly in a forest of spiderwebs.

By the top of the stairs, I was out of breath, sweaty, and pissed off. *Focus,* I told myself. *Remember why you're here. You need to get to Belzarian.*

The door to Belzarian's study was as grandiose as the outside of the tower—festooned with monstrous faces twisted in snarls, twining briar-and-thorn motifs, and carvings showing the great deeds he accomplished in life. It was twice as tall as I was, with heavy brass handles and keyholes I could have fit my fist into.

It also stood ajar.

Well, that solved one problem; I wouldn't have to get out my lockpicks. It did pose another: did Belzarian even know he was being attacked? He was in there, I was sure of it—but was he on high alert, or was he oblivious? If he knew what was going on, he might get *twitchy.* He'd cast magic missile first and ask questions later.

There was only one way to find out. I took a deep breath and stepped into his room.

After climbing his dark tower on a dark, rainy night, the candlelight was dazzling. It bounced off the golden ceiling, shone off his polished cauldron, glinted off his gilded wardrobe. Belzarian had filled the room with candlesticks, and some were new since I was last here—silver and gold alike, ornate and overwrought. I blinked, trying to make my eyes adjust.

Belzarian was lounging in his study by the roaring fire, in an armchair that was as overstuffed as it was velvet.

The most infuriating thing about Belzarian—more infuriating than his love of traps, or his bad habit of going on and on about magical minutiae, or even his avalanche-loud snoring—was how he always managed to look *elegant.* Even though his head was a skull with flaming eyes, even though his body was gaunt and blue-fleshed, and even though he was holding a tome an inch away from his skull, his demeanour would rival any elf prince. Maybe it was the delicate way he held his wrists, the careful positioning of each long-nailed finger. Maybe it was the easy grace in his crossed legs, the subtle tilt of his shoulders.

Or maybe it was just his peacock-fine wardrobe. At home, he wore a sky-blue silk dressing gown, imported from the far-off West. An entire scene—a bridge over a river, with pale pink petals falling from a tree like rain—covered his chest and back, embroidered in whisper-fine thread. He'd tied it at the waist with a pink silk belt—I knew for a fact that it wasn't the one that he'd gotten with the dressing gown. But somehow, *somehow*, he made it work.

Like I said, *infuriating*.

He looked up from his book. Set it down on his lap, one skeletal finger slipping between the pages. Tilted his head and gazed at me. His skull was always locked in a rictus grin, but I could hear the smile in his voice.

'Vezian,' he said. 'To what do I owe this pleasure?'

I laughed.

'You *really* need to fix your trap gauntlet, darling. I got through it in twenty minutes.'

'Twenty whole minutes? You're losing your touch,' Belzarian said.

'In my defence, I had some things on my mind… Did you know there's *paladins* outside?'

'Oh, heavens no.'

Belzarian closed the book, properly this time. My gaze lingered on those long, strong fingers of his. It had been too long since we—

Focus, I told myself.

'What's the point of all your alarms if you don't listen to them?'

'I listen more often than not.' Belzarian stood and walked to his telescope—the one by the window, as opposed to the one on his desk. He peered outside, squinting again, those blue flames in his sockets turning to slits.

'You could stand to listen a bit more.' I sighed. 'Did I mention the paladins—'

'You did, dearest. But what are *you* doing here?'

'Do you want the short answer or the long one?' My hand crept towards my belt pouch again.

'They're both going to be long, aren't they?' Belzarian sighed. 'You do so love your epics.'

'Epics, schmepics.' I waved his words off, even though I knew he wasn't *wrong*. 'I've got a delivery for you, and I'm running a game on someone else.'

'A game.' Belzarian turned his head—all the way around, so that his skull was on backwards. 'Are you doing the hazard pay scam *again*?'

'Oh, *darling*, you know me too well.' I grinned.

'Anyone I should be worried about?'

'Nah, just a twopenny noble. But listen, we've got a problem—'

CRASH! Down below, the tower's door smashed open. The paladins were marching ants from up here—marching ants that pushed aside the white specks of skeletons.

Belzarian squinted down.

'That's a *plethora* of paladins,' he said.

'I was *trying* to tell you,' I said.

'Vezian,' he said.

'Yes?'

'What did you do?'

'*I* did nothing. They were there when I got here.' I folded my arms. 'I've been *trying* to warn you—'

Belzarian looked at me. I looked at him.

I took a deep breath and reached for the scabbard on my back.

'Let me guess. You want me to take care of it?'

'Please,' Belzarian said. 'I've exhausted my spells for the day—'

'*How?*'

'...I wanted to read, and my spectacles have disappeared.' He rubbed the back of his neck. 'Eyesight is precious.'

'We can talk about *that* later,' I said, 'but if you want me to protect you—'

'Yes, yes, you can spend the night,' Belzarian said. *'Go!'*

I drew my sword and held it up in front of my eyes. It was a gaudy thing—a cross guard shaped like a figure eight made of twisting thorns, a blade studded with rubies, and an unblinking eye at the pommel. It even had a name: the Sword of Hopes. I hated it, but it had been in my family for generations. There was no way I was going to replace it—especially because its powers *were* handy.

I looked through the cross guard.

'By the power of Hope's Wings—' I said.

The transformation took longer than you'd think. A white glow surrounded me, enveloping me from head to toe. My body burned; white lines of pain ran down my muscles as they grew. My shoulders broadened; my wiry arms became thick as tree trunks, and my soft stomach flattened into a washboard you could use to grate diamonds. My legs lengthened, till I was nearly twice as tall, and my shirt shredded to rags.

That was *half* my outfit gone. I'd have to steal one of Belzarian's robes at this rate.

Before I'd transitioned, I'd used the Sword's powers all too often—it got me closer to the body I'd needed to have. But after, it made me feel like a parody of myself. It felt *wrong*—too large, too powerful, unable to fit down a chimney or up a dumb waiter. I didn't like to use them if I didn't have to, not anymore.

But needs must, and my lover needed me. I held the sword high, and thunder rolled in the distance.

'The power is mine!' I shouted.

Thank gods, it was over. I took a deep breath, and ran to the door—hitting my head on the doorframe.

'*Why does* it have to make me so *tall?*' I grumbled.

I pointed my sword down the stairs. Below, I heard the sound of clattering sabatons—the *clank* of a scythe blade hitting a breast-plate—the screams of paladins dodging a giant rolling rock.

'Ah!' Belzarian said. 'The mechanisms *did* work! They're resetting—'

'They're not working well enough,' I said. 'Get back!'

The paladins' leader crested the stairs. I brandished the Sword of Hopes and prayed to anyone that would listen that I looked like I knew how to use it.

I didn't have much time. The spell lasted twenty minutes, at most, and I had to concentrate to keep it going. And while mild dysphoria certainly keeps your attention, so does a pitched battle.

'Get back,' I told him.

'Foul Dark Knight,' the paladin said, 'get thee behind me!'

He drew his sword. I groaned.

'We can do this the easy way,' I said. 'Go home, and we'll forget this ever happened.'

The paladin launched himself at me.

In this state, I was twice his size, and twice as strong. Even though I *barely* knew how to use a sword—even though I was trying to use the flat of my blade, because I didn't want to *kill* the idiot—I was able to force him down the stairs.

A few of his buddies came up behind him—one in a helmet shaped like a boar's head, one with a shock of red feathers bursting from the back of his helmet. I swung my sword like a club. It hit the idiot's snout with a satisfying clank; he fell down the stairs, landing on the bannister.

'Anyone else want to try?' I yelled.

The lead paladin swung his shield at my face. I tried to sidestep, but my body was bigger than I was used to—twice as big. He clipped me in the ribs, knocking the breath right out of me. I faltered; I lost my concentration. My false strength left me. My body shrank, till I was back to my scrawny self.

He shoved past me into Belzarian's sanctum.

I caught myself before I could fall down the stairs—or worse, drop my sword. The feathery paladin ran for me… and stumbled, falling to the ground with a sound like a thousand plates smashing on a thousand stairs. He'd hit a tripwire, and the beam of cutlight sliced the feathers right off his helmet. No great loss for him—they'd been tacky *before* he'd stuck the tinsel in.

Behind me, the lead paladin charged. Straight for Belzarian. I turned on my heel, swinging my sword, but I was too weak. The tip barely scraped his back.

Everything moved too slowly, like I was underwater. The paladin lunged for Belzarian… the tip of his sword nicked Bel's skull… Belzarian chanted something. A burst of light filled the room. Light and *heat*.

I managed to shield my face and duck—I'd heard him cast this spell before. The paladin wasn't so lucky. Bel's fireballs hit like a stampede; the sheer force of it knocked the paladin out the window. He hit Belzarian's telescope—and every gargoyle—on the way down. The other paladins looked at each other. They looked back at me, and Belzarian behind me.

'Boo,' Belzarian deadpanned.

One paladin screamed. The other grabbed his wrist, and turned tail. As they ran back down the stairs, we heard the clatter of a hundred traps. One way or another, they wouldn't be bothering us again.

'Waste of a good spell slot,' Belzarian muttered. He rolled his sleeves back down and glanced over at me. Then he ran to me, and his bony arms pressed around me. He pulled me to my feet and into a tight embrace.

I pressed into him, my face in the crook of his neck. He was so warm—warmer than usual—and he smelled like old books and strange spices. I could have stayed in his arms forever, but he pulled back, gazing fondly down at me.

'Are you hurt?' he said.

I shook my head.

'I'm gonna have some bruises,' I said. 'But nothing worse.'

'Thank Dark S'tradyol.' His voice was as warm as his arms. 'I was worried something terrible had happened.'

'Nah, nah. I'm fine.' I grinned ruefully. It *did* still sting when I breathed in deep, but that was all. 'Thought you were out of spells, though.'

'That one's not a spell. It's a spell-like ability,' he said. 'I can cast it without seeing my target.'

'Right,' I said. 'Because you lost your spectacles.'

'Yes.' He sighed.

'Your spectacles, and the incredibly powerful, magical gem you used for the lenses,' I said.

'You don't have to rub it in.' Belzarian massaged his brow. I knew full well he couldn't get headaches—he was just being dramatic, as usual. 'The Eye of Cotora's going to be *impossible* to replace.'

'Mm-*hm*.' I let him stew in his exquisite despair for a long, long moment, but couldn't hide the smirk that crept up the corners of my mouth.

'What's so funny?' Belzarian said. The flames in his eye sockets dimmed.

'Well,' I said. I opened my belt pouch, slowly, letting the buckles slip apart and the flap fall open. I reached inside and drew forth the thing I'd come here for: a golden frame, with two faceted diamonds set inside. The diamonds were clearer and purer than any I'd ever seen. If you held them up to the candlelight, they almost glowed. A delicate chain hung off the back—a chain shaped to keep the spectacles on a head that had no ears.

Belzarian gasped and rubbed his socket.

'*No*,' he said. 'Where did you get—you had them this entire time?!'

He reached out; I placed the spectacles, gently, on his bony palm.

'I did. Because *someone* left them at my place. And *someone* didn't think to check with me.' My smirk stretched wider.

'I've been busy.' Belzarian donned the glasses with an elegant flourish. They sat on his face perfectly—they'd been made for him, after all. The flames flickered behind the diamonds, casting blue light across his face and off the walls. He glittered like an undead prism.

'You could have sent me a bird,' I said. I closed my pouch and gave him a long, hard look. Had he had any flesh on his cheeks, I would have sworn he was blushing.

'You haven't visited me in ages—' Belzarian said.

'A *bird*-bird, not an omen crow,' I said. 'They never say anything useful.'

On cue, a familiar screeching drifted in from the woods outside: 'THE DARK LORD WILL TAKE YOU, BODY AND SOUL! BODY AND SOUL!'

'They tell you how much I want you,' Belzarian purred.

'You still could have *asked* me.'

'Is that why…?' The sorcerer put his arm around my shoulder.

'Why I came in the first place? Yeah.' I leaned into his touch. 'I've been carrying these for weeks. Thought you'd ask for them back any minute. And when you didn't…'

'You didn't have to keep them on you!' Belzarian sounded so offended. Cute.

'Unlike *some* people, I didn't want to lose them,' I said. 'It's where they were safest.'

'Wait. You said you were doing a hazard pay scam,' Belzarian said. 'Did you agree to steal my spectacles—'

'While they were in my pocket. Yes.'

'You *ridiculous little man.*' Belzarian rumpled my hair; I pretended to bristle. 'I could kiss you right now.'

'Then do it,' I said.

His face pressed against my cheek. I kissed him where I could reach—his cheekbones, his jaw, the hollow where his skull met his throat. He cupped my face in his hand and pressed his forehead to mine. Outside, the paladins' horses cantered away, followed by the creaking charge of a skeleton horde.

'You wanted to stay the night?' he asked.

'It's been a *long* day.' I leaned into his touch, closing my eyes. 'Of course I want to stay.'

'Good,' he said. 'I'll send a skeleton for your horse, and…' A grin crept into his voice, matching his grinning skull. 'I'll trade you my glasses for what *you* left here last time.'

'Oh gods,' I muttered. The tips of my ears—and only the tips— flushed, warm as the roaring fire. 'My trousers…?'

'*And* your packer.'

The warmth crept down my face.

'I've been looking all over!' I exclaimed. 'I thought I was gonna have to replace— Why didn't you—'

'You didn't ask. All's fair in love and war.'

'Next time, send me a bird! You can just go to a coop—'

'If I have to go into town,' Belzarian said, 'I want hazard pay.'

I pressed closer still.

'Oh no,' I said. 'I am but a poor, humble thief. How will I ever give you what you require?'

He laughed and pushed me to the bedroom door. I pulled him back towards me. My face burned; my heart fluttered with anticipation.

'Let's just say,' he said, 'I've got some *ideas*.'

In Sheep's Clothing

Caleb Roehrig

When God created man, it was an honest mistake; but when man created the Trojans, it was with malice aforethought. We were told they were the future. We were told they were a triumph of science, technology, and the human spirit. We were told they were the key to our survival as a species.

Later, when they finally told us to be afraid, it was too late.

The light was just beginning to shift toward evening on the day I found myself unexpectedly summoned to Dean Cawdor's office. Classes were over, and the hallways were deserted, which meant I had nothing to distract me from my ominous thoughts. I wasn't exactly a prize pupil, so whatever he wanted me for, it couldn't be good.

'Mr Leino.' The dean glanced up when I entered the room, gesturing to a chair across from his desk. 'Please have a seat.'

He wasn't smiling, but then he didn't appear angry, either, and I discreetly wiped my hands on my thighs. Outside his window, the stars were coming out; but it was Cawdor's other guests who had my attention—a man in a uniform jacket, and a blonde woman clutching a glass of wine like a life preserver. I knew who she was, of course, and my stomach cramped with nerves.

'You already know our head of security, Mr Keough.' Cawdor indicated the man. 'But I don't think you've ever met Director Brundle. It's rare she has time to sit down with students, so—'

'Oh, for Pete's sake, Aurelius.' The woman's knuckles were as white as the string of pearls at her throat. 'Enough of this—let's just get to business.'

The words were alarming, and the dean cleared his throat. 'Right. Well, Mr Leino—Zeph—this is obviously not an ordinary check-in. You're here—'

'You failed your midterm exams,' Director Brundle stated bluntly. 'On top of multiple behavioural infractions, and one very… *inappropriate* incident in the shower block over the summer term.'

My cheeks blazed. I'd been caught with my then-boyfriend, Ozzy Dillinger—which was a major no-no, according to the Avernus Academy code of conduct. As a rule, I never hooked up outside of my dorm room, but I'd been especially horny that day and not thinking clearly.

Ozzy was one of the Good Kids at Avernus. Top of his class and a member of the Echelon Society—an elite student organisation for academic overachievers—and the only guy who'd ever made me want to be Somebody's Boyfriend. He was serious and smart… and only interested in a relationship as long as we kept it secret. Apparently, dating a troublemaking burnout wasn't great for his image.

In the end, it was his best friend, Kai Wharton, who'd caught and reported us to administration. Our love story didn't survive the publicity.

'I've already made arrangements to retake two of my exams,' I bluffed, trying not to sweat. 'And it's not like I'm the only one who's ever messed around in those showers. Maybe the rich kids—'

'That's enough.' The director was emphatic. 'The point is that you aren't performing at the level we require of students here. You don't fit in.'

I stared from one face to the next, starting to get dizzy—*guilty on all counts*. A lifelong 'problem student', Avernus was the third academy I'd attended in as many years. I'd been kicked out of the first one, 'invited to leave' by the second, and only accepted here—a boarding school on one of the few habitable exoplanets in this sector of the galaxy—because my dad was an old friend of the dean's. It was my last chance at graduating with a degree. If I failed, my options were the military or one of the mining colonies on Parcae 2—and I didn't know which was worse.

My tongue dry as dust, I croaked, 'Am I… am I being expelled?'

The silence lasted until I couldn't bear it, and then the director's shoulders slumped. 'No, Mr Leino. I wish things were that simple, but no. You're not being expelled.'

'Zeph.' Dean Cawdor bore a fretful expression. 'The reason you're here is because we want to offer you a second chance. Something has come up, something we need to deal with urgently and discreetly, and…" He swallowed audibly. '…you might be able to help us.'

A silence fell, the adults trading loaded glances, and then Mr Keough took over. 'Here's the deal, kid: we've got good reason to believe that there's a Trojan on campus.'

'A… a *what*?' My eyes popped open so wide they hurt. 'You're not serious. In this star system, that's a Class-One felony—'

'They're forbidden on terra firma, yeah, but that leaves a loophole.' Mr Keough turned to the window, to the vast, purpling depths of the sky. 'They're legal as cargo, so long as they stay up there. But apparently one was smuggled to the surface.'

'And enrolled.' The director's voice was hollow. 'Here.'

A chill settled over the room. What they were suggesting was the sort of worst-case scenario that conspiracy theorists loved to warn against—but even the most hardened sceptics took the threat of Trojan infiltration seriously. Avernus even had an entire behavioural sciences unit on learning to identify them.

It involved watching dozens of prerecorded interviews and guessing which subjects were human and which were not. After that came a field trip to an orbiting research station with legally sanctioned Trojans on staff, where interviews could be conducted, face-to-face.

'Are you sure?' I swivelled toward the door, half-expecting a Trojan to kick it down. 'I mean, don't you scan for them? Don't you do *background checks*?'

Dean Cawdor did his best to sound calm. 'The latest models are just too sophisticated for the antiquated tech we have here.'

'These days, you need a sample of bone marrow or brain tissue for conclusive determination.' Keough let out a dark chuckle. 'And that's not exactly something we can just demand from this student body.'

'Not yet, anyway.' Director Brundle began to pace. 'If we're not fast enough to stop… what we've been told is about to happen, tissue samples may become a non-negotiable part of the application process.' Another snort. 'Provided the Avernus Academy even exists after tonight.'

I sat up. 'What happens tonight?'

'Governor Mannerheim is coming for an official visit.' The dean sighed. 'Her current goodwill tour includes a luncheon to honour the students of Avernus's Echelon Society. This evening at the Gateway Club.'

'Where,' Mr Keough picked up the thread, 'according to the intel we received, a Trojan posing as one of our students is planning to assassinate her.'

My hands were sticky on the chair's armrests. 'What does this have to do with me?'

'As Mr Keough points out, we can't subject the Echelon students to invasive testing. And even if we could, we don't have the time.' Dean Cawdor spread his hands. 'Neither can we cancel the event. Not without explaining why.'

I shook my head. 'So explain it!'

'We can't,' the director groaned, sounding like she'd aged two hundred years in ten seconds. 'We'd be ruined. Parents would pull their children en masse, benefactors would withdraw their endowments… and how do you tell a senator or a judge that the child they're taking home might be a decoy? That you suspect one of *them* of being responsible?'

'I don't know… have you tried?' I snapped, waiting for someone to make sense. 'Shouldn't you at least tell the governor that her life is in danger?'

'That was the first call I made!' For the first time, the dean raised his voice. 'But Mannerheim's people said she refuses to be intimidated by extremists. They're convinced it's just another crank. The governor's… a divisive figure.'

I didn't follow politics, but even I knew that Hespera Mannerheim was either loved or hated, with nothing in between. She had aims for executive office in the Triangulum Galactic Coalition and was staunchly against the Trojans, calling for them to be destroyed and their creators—the GeneSys Corporation—to be tried for crimes against humanity.

Robots were nothing new; but in the old days, if someone wanted to harvest cadmium on a moon too hostile to support human life, they had to count on clumsy minions made of wires and steel. They were heavy, expensive, and difficult to service, and they couldn't react to sudden environmental changes.

And then GeneSys introduced the Trojan: a class of android that was lighter, smaller, and nimbler than anything seen before. They had fine motor skills and could replicate human movement; but what made them truly revolutionary was that each model came with a biosynthetic brain, capable of storing vast amounts of complex information.

Capable of storing an entire human consciousness.

That was the selling point. The Trojan itself was just a shell, a hardwearing frame that could withstand temperature extremes and caustic atmospheres; but its brain could be… well, anyone's. Any person willing to have their consciousness mapped and downloaded onto a GeneSys server could have their every thought, feeling, and memory reuploaded into the body of a robot. Copy and paste.

The process was long but painless; and every nine months, the GeneSys technicians promised, all uploads would be permanently retired and deleted. Every nine months, their fleet of androids would be reset, wiped clean, and prepared to take on the identities of new volunteers. But every upload meant a matching human consciousness brought to life on the fringes of civilisation—indentured servants stranded on planets unfit for habitation. Many of them felt deceived, abused, and traumatised.

Many more felt vengeful.

The Y1s gave way to the X Class, the first to feature biosynthetic exteriors; and those gave way to the X2s, and then the Centurions and the Zeroes. With each iteration, the Trojans became more lifelike—inside and out—no longer being marketed exclusively as workers but also as companions: friends for the friendless, lovers for the loveless, children for the childless.

GeneSys maintained that they were harmless, even after a group of malcontented Centurions attempted to blow up one of their facilities; even when androids were linked to terrorism and organised crime. The problem was, Trojan brains were giant receivers: all you needed was a model's serial number and you could hack its operating frequency—make it do anything you wanted, from dancing a jig to assassinating a visiting dignitary.

They were the ultimate sleeper agents, virtually indistinguishable from humans; and now there was one hidden among the students at Avernus.

'One last time,' I began, afraid I already knew the answer to my next question, '*what am I doing here?*'

'You're here,' Dean Cawdor replied, 'because when we tested the student body on how to recognise Trojans based on behavioural patterns, you blew the rest of your classmates out of the water.' He turned his data screen to face me. 'You had an 87% accuracy rate for recorded interviews, and in person, you scored 92%.'

Mr Keough leaned forward. 'What's your secret?'

'I don't know, I just…' I shrugged, not sure how to explain. 'I paid attention? I mean, they look like us, but they're still machines, right? And all machines glitch. Some of them repeated gestures, or laughed when no one made a joke, or lagged when answering personal questions…' I struggled to articulate it. 'It's like playing poker. Everyone's got a tell, you just have to watch them until you spot it.'

'That's what *we* told *you*.' Keough rolled his eyes. 'But you're the only one who developed an actual instinct for it. Which is great, because we need someone who can sit down across from a friendly face and tell whether they're human. Without scraping their frontal cortex, I mean.'

I tensed. 'You want *me* to smoke out your assassin?'

'Please.' The director covered her eyes with her hand. 'We have no intention of putting you in harm's way, we just want you to, to—'

'To mingle with your classmates,' the dean supplied. 'Enjoy a free meal, chat, see if anyone has a "tell".' He knitted his hands together on the desk. 'All three of us will be there. If you spot a Trojan, you just signal us and leave.'

He almost made it sound like a favour. 'And what's in it for me?'

'You won't be expelled.' Director Brundle stared me down.

'We can also provide a financial reward,' the dean added quickly. 'Let's call it a scholarship. How does that sound?'

It sounded too simple, but I needed money as badly as I needed to graduate; so I nodded.

'Splendid.' Director Brundle downed the rest of her wine. 'Be at the Gateway Club this evening at six sharp, and keep this conversation a secret. Do you have any questions?'

'Just one, I guess,' I said, getting to my feet. 'If this party is for the Echelon kids, then what's my excuse for being there? They'll know I'm not a member.'

'By this evening, you will be.' She hesitated. 'And Mr Leino? Thank you.'

The Gateway Club was smack in the heart of town, built on private acreage and boasting a pool, a golf course, and a man-made lake. It was the sort of place that people bragged about going to; the sort of place that wouldn't have someone like me as a member. Until that evening, anyway.

By the time I arrived, I'd managed to do a little research on Hespera Mannerheim. She called herself a 'radical humanist', who believed Trojans posed an increasing existential threat. Her views were revolutionary, and her political agenda against android technology stood to topple the Coalition's industrial giants like dominos. Once treated as a kook by the media, she'd gained immense support from the working class in recent years—and made some very powerful enemies among the wealthy.

Still, even if Mannerheim's people were overly hasty in dismissing the threat, I nevertheless expected to walk away empty-handed tonight. I didn't exactly run in the same circles as the Echelon kids, but we had classes together, shared the same living space, the same shower block. For better or worse, I already knew them all personally: Kai Wharton, Lyra Hassan, Jupe Darcy, Samson Caulfield, Selene Washington. And Ozzy.

If one of them was a Trojan, and my instinct for 'tells' was worth a damn, I'd have picked up on it by now… right?

The Gateway's doorman wore a green uniform and had the snooty attitude of someone who licked boots for a living. The way he curled his lip at my scuffed shoes and threadbare jacket would've made me laugh, if it hadn't been for the two men behind him, with dark glasses and holstered weapons. From their earpieces, I guessed that they were with the governor's team—so maybe she was taking it a little seriously after all.

An escort led me through a door marked PRIVATE LOUNGE, where two more armed men stood guard. Once past them, I entered a lavishly appointed space, with a sprawling view over the lake and golf course. Mr Keough lurked in one corner, his meagre security team looking pathetic next to Mannerheim's personal army; and I spotted Dean Cawdor and Director Brundle near the back wall, deep in conversation. But the first person I ran into, of course, was Kai.

'Leino?' He goggled at me, ugly with surprise. 'The fuck are you doing here?'

'Nice to see you, too, Kai.' I gave him an unfriendly smile. 'Hope I'm not too late for the free champagne.'

'How did you sneak past the guards?' His thick brows furrowed angrily. 'Oh man, I can't wait until the dean sees you—your ass is done!' As he spoke, Selene Washington drifted up, trying to fit her arm in his; but he rebuffed her. 'Babe, go tell the dean we've got a gatecrasher. I'll hold him until you get back.'

'You can save your breath—I was invited.' I flashed the embossed card Dean Cawdor had given me that afternoon, the words *your presence has been requested* lined with gold. 'But if you really want to hold me, Kai, there's a restroom down the hall where we could have some privacy.'

His face purpled. 'Oh, yeah, I forgot that's your special move. But no thanks—street trash isn't my type.'

With that he shoved past me, clipping my shoulder hard enough to knock me off-balance, leaving his girlfriend to steady me.

'Sorry about that,' Selene murmured. 'Are you okay?'

'I'm fine.' Straightening my shirt, I thrust my chin at Kai's retreating form. '*He* needs to be put on a leash.'

'He's pissed off. Do you blame him? You almost got his best friend suspended, and now they don't talk anymore.' She gave me a judgmental look.

'*He* almost got his best friend suspended,' I corrected her. 'And now my boyfriend is my ex, thanks to Kai, so I don't really care about his feelings.'

She stared at me for a moment, her face a total blank; and then she stormed off as well. My second enemy in less than five minutes. *Still got it.*

But as I watched her go, I reflected on the exchange. As badly as I wanted to denounce Kai as a Trojan, and as infuriating as it was that he saw himself as a victim in the shower block incident, nothing he'd done felt *off* to me. In fact, the only potential red flag had been something in the flatness of Selene's expression at the end. A lack of... presence.

A glitch? Maybe.

I was still processing this when I glanced up, accidentally making eye contact with the person I dreaded seeing most: Ozzy. He was across the room near the windows, and he stared a question at me I wanted to avoid as long as possible. His clothes were stylish and tailored, his dark hair in a fashionable swoop. My heart stumbled, and I tried not to stare at his lips, remembering how soft they were.

'Are you here to cause a scene?' Lyra Hassan was suddenly at my elbow. Her hair was fashionable, too, and she smelled of roses. 'Please tell me you're going to cause a scene. It might be the only time someone says anything honest today.'

'I'm not here to cause a scene.' Lyra and I had never been friends. We'd never been enemies, either, but I was still a bit flummoxed by her familiar manner. 'I was invited.'

'Obviously, or those gun-toting clones with the earpieces would've tossed you out.' She studied me with naked curiosity. '*Why* were you invited?'

'I guess I'm smarter than any of you give me credit for.'

'Oh, I've always thought you were smart, Zeph.' Lyra smiled vaguely. 'You're just lazy about things that don't interest you. Like school.'

Finally, I turned to face her. 'That was almost a compliment, right?'

'Why do you think the governor has so many bodyguards?' She tucked a fist under her chin. 'I mean, it's kind of weird how much firepower she brought to a meet-and-greet with a bunch of kids, huh?'

I hesitated. 'Maybe they're here to protect *us*.'

'You weren't, though,' she said next, throwing me yet again. 'Invited. I saw the list last week.'

Startled, it took me a moment to answer. 'I was a late addition.'

We stared each other down for just a moment—long enough for it to be clear she wasn't buying it—and then she laughed. 'See you around, Zeph Leino. Don't make a scene without me!'

And then she was off, tapping one of the waiters on the shoulder so she could flirt with him—or maybe grill him about his career choices—and I took a breath. Lyra was intense, but no matter how quirky she pretended to be, her peculiarities had been strategy. Tactics, rather than glitches. Either she was a bored girl with an insatiable curiosity, or she'd been deliberately pumping me for information.

When I glanced over again, Kai was confronting Ozzy, and both were looking at me. *Great.* Turning the other way, I made it halfway to the bar before Jupe Darcy popped up in my path, scowling like I'd just taken a dump in his shoes. Sighing, I resigned myself to yet another confrontation. 'Let me guess: What am I doing here?'

'I don't care what you're doing here,' he snapped. 'I just want you to leave Ozzy alone.'

'Excuse me?'

'You heard.' Jupe tried to look menacing, but he was about half my size.

'Do you see me talking to him? Do you see me *near* him?'

'No. And I don't want to, either.' He puffed up his chest. 'Ozzy has a bright future, and he doesn't need someone like… like *you* messing that up for him.'

'Wow. Well, first of all, fuck you very much. Second of all, Ozzy is a big boy who can make his own decisions.' I narrowed my eyes. 'And third of all, get the hell out of my way.'

'Is there a problem here?' Samson Caulfield appeared suddenly beside Jupe, fixing me with a matching glare. It was almost comical. 'Maybe you better take a walk, Leino.'

'And maybe you better kiss my ass.' I glowered. 'I was minding my own business until Jupe came all the way over here to warn me away from Ozzy.'

'Ozzy?' Samson darted Jupe a sharp look—and, just like that, something clicked into place for me.

'Yeah.' Hazarding a guess, I added, 'Apparently, your boy-friend thinks Ozzy is super special and doesn't want anybody talking to him.'

'Boyf—' Samson's eyes nearly bugged out of his skull, and he whirled on Jupe. 'You *told* him?'

Jupe went pale. 'No! I didn't! And I just—'

'You just saw Ozzy's ex and went feral.'

'That's not what happened, okay? Ozzy just deserves bet-ter than some… charity case wannabe-bad-boy who almost got him suspended!'

'Oh, yeah, I'm sure.' Samson's voice dripped with sarcasm. 'Is that why you can't take your eyes off him whenever we're in the locker room?'

'*He has a cool birthmark!*'

As the squabbling intensified, I sidestepped the pair. Their spat didn't interest me, even if it did sort of involve my ex; what *did* interest me, however, was the way Jupe kept scratching his left ear. A nervous tic… or a synaptic loop that couldn't close because of misfiring transmitters in his biosynthetic brain?

Everywhere I looked I saw potential glitches. It was exhausting.

'Believe it or not, those two think nobody can tell they're together.' The voice came from behind me, and I froze. Ozzy's accent—a rich drawl from growing up on Faunus, a terraformed moon I could see from my bedroom window—was lilting and sexy and unmistakable. 'They bicker like my grandparents.'

Slowly, I faced him. 'Hi.'

'I'd ask what you're doing here but three people have already told me.' He smiled, his stupid dimples pushing his stupid freckles up into the rims of his stupid, old-fashioned glasses. He didn't even need them—they were a fashion statement. 'Congratulations on getting into the Echelon Society.'

'Thanks, it's been a blast.' I wanted to disappear. All these months later and I still couldn't look him in the eye without remembering what his hands felt like on my waist. 'I've already had three people tell me to stay away from you.'

'That's the old Echelon welcome wagon.' he joked weakly, and the awkward silence that followed made me dread what was coming. 'Listen, Zeph, I owe you an apo—'

'You don't owe me anything.' My face went hot. Maybe he *did* owe me an apology, but if I finally got it, I'd have one less excuse to hate him. 'We were together, and now we're not. Shit happens.'

'Not like that. It shouldn't have happened like that.' He flushed. 'I panicked—I *need* to graduate with distinction, and I was afraid I'd messed it all up. Then I went back to Faunus for the break and my parents gave me hell, and… by the time school started again, I already hadn't spoken to you in weeks. I didn't know how to face you after that.'

I couldn't speak. Pressure was building behind my eyes and I was afraid of the emotions he would hear if I opened my mouth. After a beat, I finally managed, 'If that was supposed to be your apology, I missed the word "sorry".'

'I'm sorry, Zeph.' His eyes were forlorn. 'Avernus is kinda my last chance, too. I know I told you it was my dream school, but only because it meant putting three hundred thousand miles between me and my parents.' He looked to the window, Faunus lurking somewhere in the heavens. 'They've always seen me as this unserious fuck-up, and when I first enrolled here… well, I needed to prove myself. And being in a relationship—being with you—it wasn't part of the plan.'

'So I was… what? A distraction?'

'*No.*' He gave me an insistent look. 'You don't know them. If they'd found out about you, they'd have turned you into a research project—"is he Dillinger quality?"'

'And I'm not.' It barely needed to be said.

'No one is.' Ozzy sighed. 'But that's beside the point. I didn't mean for us to happen, and I didn't plan on things ending the way they did, and I didn't handle any of it well, because all I've ever done my whole life is try to impress my parents.' Tossing up his hands, he let them fall at his sides. 'So, I'm sorry. I really am.'

Over his shoulder, Kai was staring bullets. Across the room, so was Jupe. Lyra had her portable data screen out and was probably recording us. Finally, I relented. 'It's okay, Ozzy.'

To my surprise, I meant it.

'I never had a boyfriend before,' I went on, 'and my parents have never been impressed by anything I've ever done, anyway, so I don't know what it's like to care about that.' My face was boiling. 'I don't know where we'd be now if we hadn't gotten caught—maybe we would've broken up anyway. But it really hurt that you just… disappeared.'

'If I could undo it, I would.' Ozzy was quiet. 'You deserved better.'

We eyed each other, the moment settling, some heaviness dropping away inside me. I'd never thought Ozzy was a bad guy—not until the end, anyway—but it had been so easy to resent him. To hate him. And now? Maybe I was going to have to let it go.

Even worse: I got no 'tells' from him, either. Deep down, I'd been hoping that maybe he'd been replaced when he'd gone back to Faunus at the end of summer term. Manufacturing duplicates of living people was highly illegal, but Ozzy's family had the kind of money that made the impossible possible.

But he was still the same guy I'd dated, the one I'd met my first week at Avernus, when I got lost and he offered to show me to the science hall. The same guy who'd held my hand at the Solstice carnival, who'd read me poems under a willow tree, laughing at how clichéd it all was. This Ozzy was that Ozzy; no glitches. His apology was the only thing he'd done that was at all unusual.

My mission at the Gateway Club, I realised, was over. I'd evaluated each member of the Echelon Society, coming up empty; and to my surprise, I felt nothing but relief. I started to tell Ozzy goodbye when a commotion at the door caught our attention: two more armed men were entering the room with Governor Mannerheim tucked between them, projecting charisma and authority as Director Brundle moved to greet her.

Ozzy grabbed my wrist, then his brows tented. 'You shouldn't be here, Zeph.'

'Not you, too.' I rolled my eyes. So much for Mr Nice Guy.

'No, I mean...' He grunted in frustration. 'Why *are* you here? I know you don't have the grades for Echelon membership. I've read your transcripts.'

'Excuse me? Who the fu—'

'Gentlemen.' Dean Cawdor appeared just then, clapping a hand on each of our shoulders. 'So glad you could make it. This visit is quite the honour!'

'Yes, sir,' Ozzy mumbled, the air between us still broken and rough-edged.

Oblivious, the dean said, 'I need to have a quick word with Zeph. Do you mind?'

'No. Of course.' Ozzy gave me one last unhappy look and retreated.

'Listen,' I began, the second he was out of earshot, 'I've talked to everyone, but—'

'Never mind.' The man leaned closer. '*I fear the Greeks, even when they are bearing gifts.*'

It was a quote from Virgil's *Aeneid*, an epic poem about—of all things—the Trojan War. But I shouldn't have known that. Despite all our classes on the history of androids and why machines disguised as humans came to be called 'the Trojans', I'd never read it. Teachers referenced it, explaining how the wooden horse concealed a deadly legion of soldiers, but the book itself was never assigned reading.

And yet I knew it.

'Zeph?'

Dean Cawdor's voice was like a spark between my eyes, sizzling and throbbing. My skin tingled as something new but chillingly familiar raced through me—an oil spill in my bloodstream, dark and slippery and fast-moving.

'Zeph, can you hear me?'

'Yes.' I could barely manage the word.

'Good.' The dean's eyes glittered. 'And do you know why you're here?'

'Yes.' I wished I didn't, but I could see my future like a doorway filled with terrifying light. It beckoned, and I would answer, because I had no choice. 'I'm here to—'

'Don't say it out loud,' Dean Cawdor admonished, hastily. 'Go to the restroom. What you need is in the stall second from the end. Hurry.'

'Yes.' My mouth was so dry, my tongue almost stuck; but then I was turning and walking for the door, avoiding the cluster of people around Governor Mannerheim, trying not to feel Ozzy's eyes digging into my back.

My heart raced, and my right index finger twitched compulsively, over and over—like I was pulling a trigger. *A glitch.* I'd discovered the Trojan embedded within the Echelon Society, but too late.

It was me.

As I stepped out into the corridor, a lifetime of memories unravelled: flying a kite, learning to swim, my mother combing my hair. Was any of it real? Two expulsions, a speech from Dad about Avernus being my last chance, a days-long shuttle across the glittering, breathtaking emptiness of this star system.

Had any of it happened? *To anyone?* Was Zeph Leino a real person somewhere, of flesh and blood and brain tissue that would pass a laboratory test, or was his whole life conjured up from scratch? Donor memories stitched together, the details tweaked and personalised, but nothing unique. Nothing real.

What was my first true memory? Meeting Dean Cawdor the day I arrived for orientation? I'd been stiff and fatigued from the shuttle journey—or maybe I'd only just been pulled from cryostasis. The dean claimed he knew my father; but he also claimed he'd warned Mannerheim, which was obviously a lie.

The restroom door opened silently, the interior spotless and overly bright. *I don't want to do this.* I kept thinking it and kept moving anyway, aware I would never leave the Gateway Club alive. I was going to die for the dean's cause, whether I wanted to or not.

In the second stall from the end, a magnetic screwdriver was tucked beneath a pipe. I used it to remove a vent cover in the ceiling and withdrew the item hidden inside.

I'd never held a plasma gun before, let alone fired one. But somehow my hands capably checked the magazine, the firing pin, the locking mechanism. Everything was going according to plan.

Until I stepped back out.

'Zeph, please put it down.' Ozzy stood between me and the door. *Between me and the target.* He was holding a black box with a short antenna, but his eyes were fixed on mine. 'I don't want to hurt you.'

'You won't.' The gun swung up as if on its own, my feet shifting, my shoulders automatically preparing for the impact of recoil. My finger flexed, and then—

An ear-splitting shriek carved through the centre of my brain, the sound so painful it dropped me to my knees. The room doubled, the lights whirling, and for a second I thought I would lose control of my bowels. The gun hit the floor, and I dry heaved.

'Breathe, Zeph. Nice and slow.' Ozzy knelt beside me, one hand on my back. With his other, he pocketed the weapon. I shouldn't have let him; even through the dancing knife points that muddled my thoughts, I knew that much. But I didn't reach for it.

Somehow, I chose not to.

I swallowed hard, my face dripping with sweat. 'What… what's happening to me?'

'Signal jammer.' Ozzy showed me the black box again. 'I'm sorry. It's old-school, and I've been told the sensation is really unpleasant, but it's still one of the most effective ways to scramble a Trojan's programming.'

'It feels like I'm being lobotomised with an electric fence,' I said through my teeth.

'Cawdor must have switched you on, somehow. Initialised you.'

'"*I fear the Greeks*."' I whispered it, my gorge rising again. A Trojan's brain was a receiver, so one way to wake up the sleeper agent was to broadcast an operational signal from a remote source and then tune the android into its frequency—like adjusting a radio. The phrase must have been how he did it, like a post-hypnotic suggestion.

'How long…' I tried to get to my feet but lost my balance and sagged against Ozzy. 'How long will it last?'

'The jammer? Until the battery dies, I guess.' Gripping my elbow, he pulled me up. 'If we can get you out of range of Cawdor's signal, we won't need it, but…'

'We don't know where he's broadcasting from, or how strong the relay is,' I finished, fighting to clear my thoughts. 'He wants me to kill the governor.'

'I know.' Ozzy glanced at the door. 'As far as we can tell, Cawdor's acting on his own, but he's got ties to extremist groups on the far right.'

'"We"?' His hand was still on my arm, and I tried not to think about it. Had we ever really had a chance? 'Who's "we"?'

'My parents have… friends in the Coalition's intelligence program,' he said, his tone strained. 'They've been tracking terrorist cells and assessing threats, and a terminal at Avernus kept popping up in their reports. The whole reason my parents agreed to send me here was to identify the subject.' Unnecessarily, he concluded, 'Turns out it was the dean.'

'So you're a spy?'

'I'm a student,' he said quickly. But then he sighed. '*And* a spy. But only because my parents would never have let me leave Faunus for any other reason.'

My gaze dropped to the black box in his hand, its antenna the only thing keeping Governor Mannerheim alive. 'You knew about me.'

'Not at first,' he replied, softly. 'There had been talk of possible Trojan involvement, but when we met, none of it had been confirmed. I just… I thought you were cute.' Ozzy looked down. 'When I realised what you were, it took me a while to accept the truth.'

I almost laughed. The one thing I didn't have was time to 'accept' the truth of what I was: A machine. A weapon. A puppet on someone else's strings. 'What gave me away?'

His eyes traced my brow, my cheek, my bottom lip. 'You don't move in your sleep. At all. Not even your eyes when you dream. It was a glitch in the first Double-Zero prototypes.'

'So I'm a collectors' item.' Finally, I cracked a smile. 'Or maybe just salvage.'

'Seriously? Cawdor probably got you on the black market,' Ozzy reasoned. 'A lab assistant at GeneSys who knew the brain-imprinting procedure and pulled you from the reject pile.' He flinched at his own choice of words. 'Sorry! I mean… no offence.'

'None taken, you four-eyed dickhole!' I flicked his glasses, giggling. 'Since Tuesday, I've gone from social misfit to Echelon Society to "reject pile". How's that for growth?'

Ozzy giggled, too, but he was beginning to squirm. 'Zeph, we really need to—'

But his thought ended abruptly when the bathroom door slid open.

'There you are.' Dean Cawdor's voice was smooth, but the smile on his face was reptilian. 'Zeph, you'd better get back to the lounge. It's time you met the governor.'

Ozzy licked his lips. 'We'll just be a minute—'

'You've taken long enough.' The dean tucked his hands into his pockets. 'Zeph, go. You can leave me with Mr Dillinger.'

I looked past Cawdor, past the door, and lived a brief fantasy: Exiting the restroom, leaving the Gateway Club, and jumping on the first off-world shuttle I could find. My disappointed parents were a fiction—as were my expulsions, for that matter—so I could start over anywhere. That mining colony on Parcae 2 didn't sound so bad anymore, as long as they didn't require a birth certificate.

But I couldn't leave Ozzy to face Dean Cawdor by himself; he *did* have a family, and a future that he deserved to live. Besides, if something happened to me, my consciousness was likely still out there, stored in ones and zeroes on a GeneSys server. I could be born again. Theoretically. My ex-boyfriend wasn't so lucky.

Plus, if I got too far from the signal jammer, I'd be back in Crush-Kill-Destroy mode.

'Let's go in there together,' I countered, full of reckless bravado. 'Mannerheim's team might actually take the assassination threat seriously if we tell her who's behind it.'

The dean's eyes flickered and then shot to Ozzy. 'Whatever you've done to him, you're only prolonging the inevitable. I know you can't override his programming. Hespera Mannerheim *will* die today—and I've got no problem seeing you die with her.'

'And then what?' Ozzy shifted his weight, warily, trying to conceal the signal jammer. 'Do you think you're walking out of here? The Coalition already knows about you. *You're* the one whose fate is tied to the governor's.'

There was a deathly silence, the door sliding shut; and then the dean shrugged. 'Well, if we're all going to die anyway, I'm afraid I'll have to insist that you go first.'

He produced a gun so quickly that Ozzy was still fumbling for the one in his pocket when the man fired.

The sickening thump of plasma hitting flesh echoed off the fixtures, and Ozzy flew backward, taken off his feet by the impact. The signal jammer hit the tiles, bouncing hard and skittering wildly, and I leapt forward without thinking.

Maybe I sensed on some level that Dean Cawdor wouldn't shoot me—that he still needed me, or would baulk at destroying his investment; or maybe I no longer cared. Either way, when he saw me coming, he hesitated a heartbeat too long. I grabbed his wrist just as he pulled the trigger again, the sinks exploding in a storm of smoke and debris.

We hit the ground, locked together, fighting with everything we had. Breathing hard, we rolled and twisted, all four hands grappling for control of the firearm. My elbow slid up under his chin, and I leaned into it, trying to choke him. Two seconds later, he slammed his knee into my stomach, driving the air from my body.

I crumpled in pain, losing my grip, and Cawdor pressed the advantage. He flipped me on my back, swung over top of me, and slammed my head against the floor so hard lights exploded behind my eyes. When they cleared, the plasma gun was an inch away from my nose, and the dean was breathless with rage.

'Leave it to me to custom order a teenage fuck-up for an assassin.' Cawdor's hand shook, but the tip of his finger was turning pale as it compressed the trigger. 'You are a waste of circuitry, you little—'

The dean's head exploded in a shower of blood and bone as a third plasma round found its target. I stared, uncomprehending, until his body toppled to the floor, revealing Ozzy standing behind him. The gun from the ceiling vent was clutched in his hand, still smoking.

'Are you okay?' His face was pale, his right flank drenched in blood.

'Yes. No.' I'd never be okay again. 'Are you?'

'Not really.' He swayed, stumbling to his knees.

My body ached, but I helped him up, just as he'd done for me earlier. 'Breathe, okay? We'll get you to a medic!'

'They must have heard the shots,' he mumbled weakly. 'They'll evacuate the governor, but then somebody will come.' His hand fumbled at my shirt, and then gripped it tight. 'You have to go, Zeph. You have to get out.'

'I'm not leaving you!'

'They'll take us in for questioning.' Ozzy coughed, the sound damp and upsetting. 'Once you're out of the jammer's range, you'll give yourself away.' With difficulty, he met my eyes. 'Even if you don't, even if you pass the tests, they'll… the dean will have left evidence. Notes, schematics. Your serial number. And you know what will happen.'

I blinked, horrified, as I caught up to what he was saying. If they caught me, I would be destroyed. No trial, no exile, no return-to-sender. My stomach rolled. Even if I was a machine, even if all my memories were planted, I still didn't want to die. 'W-what do I do?'

'Take the jammer and go,' he wheezed, sinking down again. 'Leave by the golf course—take a shuttle, or buy a ticket to one of the orbiting observation platforms… just get off the ground fast, okay?' His eyelids were sliding shut, but he smiled. 'When you figure out where you're going, drop me a line. If I'm still alive, maybe I can help.'

'You'd better,' I said, but my voice was choked to a whisper, my eyes shimmering. 'I don't even know how to be a robot. You can't die on me, okay? Ozzy?'

But he didn't answer. He'd lost consciousness.

My hands shaking, I crawled through the stalls until I found the jammer, then limped to the door. The corridor was empty, but I could hear hushed voices, stealthy footsteps on the approach.

I fled the other way, ducking through a deserted dining room, then the kitchens, and finally into a service hallway with an exit leading to the lawns. The grass was green, the sun shining, and satellites crossed the sky, flaring when they caught the light. I set off at a jog, then a sprint, feeling heat on my back, every stride stolen from fate. Somewhere above, past the clouds, past the shining rim of Faunus in the southern sky, my new destiny awaited.

We were all made from stars, even the Trojans; and to those stars I would return.

Plezure

Derrick Webber

I feel so bubbly and just can't stop giggling.

'Hey, Tai! You look so hot!'

'Thanks, Tate! You too!' I wave to him across the road and look down at my neon-green, low-slung tights and halter. I *do* feel super sexy!

I take a long sip of my Soothi and feel the warm sun soak into my exposed skin. I quickly double-check that there are no hateful tan lines above the waistband!

'Ow!' My hand flies to my temple where a LiteJolt reminds me to keep my thoughts positive. I'll just hit the TanTube when I get back to the Pad.

I summon an even bigger smile when I arrive at Plezure Plaza. There are all my Palz in our usual spot, warming up for our FitSesh. We simper and gush over one another's outfits and hair, stroking each other all over, lightly, fingertips only—Max-Titillation!

Mid-plaza, the massive JumboTron flashes to life and there's MinorCeleb Dax, blonde and perfect, smiling at the thousands gathered around him. 'Hey Boiz! You look totally fabu!'

Everyone cheers and waves at the screen.

'Before we start our Funky Friday Sesh, let's repeat our sacred PlezurePledge together!'

A hush falls across the plaza and then every voice, in perfect unison, calls out:

'It is my duty to be the happiest, prettiest version of myself, not just for my beloved Man, but for the Plezurevision viewers! I am grateful for the never-ending beauty and comfort with which I am surrounded! I will spend this glorious day preparing to serve my Man, to make Pash-N-Time the peak of perfection!'

I feel overwhelmed with devotion as I cheer along with all the Boiz. I take another big sip of my Soothi and prepare to aerobicise for ninety minutes, knowing it will shape and tone my body the way that pleases Sinclair and honours our audience. My eyes fix firmly upon Dax as he calls out the moves, but my body knows the routine, knows exactly what to do. We all do.

The minute the thumping music ends and Dax bids us toodles till tomorrow, ServRs collect our workout gear in baskets. The jets between the pavers engage and chest-high pulses of water shoot up. Bubbles start rising as well—I detect a new scent… lavender?—and shrieks of laughter fill the plaza. We toss handfuls of bubbles and playfully hug and bump together. *No Penetration*! flashes across my ThotScreen.

Far too soon, ServRs return with towels, then hand us our pre-selected outfits once we're dry. I slip on the tiny blue-and-white-striped terry shorts and matching cropped tank chosen for me. A chorus of 'So hot!' commences as we all compliment one another.

We head to the bar to do Shotz. There's an enthusiastic group toast—'Be the cutest!'—before we knock back our Nutri-Soothies, our biggest meal of the day. Palz share afternoon plans: Knox and Penn are shopping for SexToiz in the Galleria, Tate and Beaux are heading to ElectroSis to get tidied up, and Rhys and Piers are going to Gymbo to build big Titz.

Bram and I say goodbye as we head to SpaSome. He's having a ButtFill done, which he explains in great detail as we stroll along. I try hard to focus on what he's saying—I'm smiling extra big and hopefully nodding in the right places—but I keep getting wafts of the lavender from my skin and it's making me… think of something? Remember something? This happens occasionally—I get fleeting images, snatches of words or names—they're like hints of a time before this one. My fuzzy brain can't focus on any of it. I get a Jolt if I try. It's beyond ridiculous, because there's only here and now and my beyond-perfect life!

'Tai?'

I'm back, fully focused on Bram again. 'Sorry, what?'

'I asked what you're having done today.'

'Oh, Doc needs to work on my forehead. I have worry lines.'

Bram stops and leans in close, running a finger along the creases above my eyebrows. The look on his face is somewhere between disgust and fear. 'OMG, Tai, those abso have to go! They're so not Plezure!'

I pick up the pace, because I'm determined to get to SpaSome, like, now!

Doc is calm and gentle as he freezes and fills the offending blemishes. He starts sniffling, for which he apologises. He's so handsome, and I can't help but wonder if he's someone's Man. I quickly clear my mind, because the only Man I should consider is Sinclair.

'Are you worried about something, Tai, or thinking too deeply about things? That could be the root cause of your disfigurement.'

I feel close to… panic? 'No… no… I've only been worried about my forehead since Bram pointed out how offensive it is.'

Doc gives a warm smile, from which I quickly avert my eyes. 'Well, the furrows will be completely gone before you know it. Just apply concealer until the puncture marks fade. In the meantime, I'm going to make an appointment for you at Thotz. They can make a simple adjustment that will ensure your pretty little mind is an oasis of tranquility.'

He walks me to the door, fondles my butt, and pops a SoothiMint in my mouth. He watches as I head down the hall and calls after me, 'Your shoulders are tight. Relax. Focus on being completely desirable for Sinclair this evening.'

Back on the street, I calm myself with my mantra: 'Beautiful Boi, Beautiful Boi…' I repeat it aloud, quietly, as I walk. I remember to smile and wave at everyone I pass. I'm already heading in the direction of my Pad at Luxe Tower, but I quicken my pace when the bell signals that Pash-N-Time commences in one hour.

I gaze across the lovely expanse of Plezure from my balcony—the plaza, Galleria, SpaSome, dozens of other Pad towers—right to the beach, where the sun is just beginning to set. It's always sunset when the Men arrive at six, and I cherish the occasional times Sinclair wants to bring his drink out here and grope me while we share the view.

ServR is making last-minute preparations. Sinclair texts him with specifications for the evening. I'm wearing the pink leather harness and jock he ordered for me. It's one of his faves.

ServR sets the table and I notice him glance at me, more than once! This is very unsettling—it's forbidden for him to make eye contact or to speak unless I require a response. Unnerved, I head to the bedroom to ensure everything is ready there—the HotTowl dispenser by the bed is full, and the large ProfferPillo I'll soon be straddling is in place.

I'm relieved to find ServR… elsewhere… when I return to the lounge. Hopefully, he's securely back in his Nook. I commence WelcomeMode, standing to the right of the door, smiling ecstatically and holding Sinclair's drink.

Three dings and a whoosh indicate his Pod has arrived. ServR reappears promptly to open the door. Sinclair rushes in, talking loudly into his cell, snatches the scotch from my hand, and heads to his chair at the dining table. He snaps his fingers at ServR, pointing to the placemat; he wants his dinner now. He briefly makes eye contact with me and nods toward the floor beneath the table. He wants a Blo-E while he talks and eats.

I settle myself on the pillow ServR has already placed there and release Sinclair's member. I feel so honoured that his desire for my mouth is strong! I savour the taste of him—the sweat, the remnants of piss—as I focus on servicing him. I use the techniques I learned in BoiSkool, the ones I know are his favourites.

He rings off, thrusts his hand under the table, and presses on my forehead, still sore from the needles. 'Slow down. Make it last.'

I adjust my rhythm while Sinclair settles with ServR upon the specific Pinot Noir he requires and then properly attacks his steak.

'Mmm…' drifts down, though I'm not sure if it's meant for me or the steak. Perhaps both.

I rub his thighs—the smooth material of his charcoal dress slacks—then wander up to the satiny shirt covering his trim stomach. I love thinking about Sinclair and his day at Work, though I don't really know what jobs Men have. I know Doc's… that's about it.

'Okay, pick up the pace. I wanna come twice tonight.'

It doesn't take me long to get him off. I'm good at SucKwik. His appreciative gasps and shouts—he calls my name, twice!—justify my very existence. They are my reward. My throat full of his precious seed nourishes and fulfills me in a way no Soothi ever could! ServR hands me a HotTowl, but I have barely started CleanUp when Sinclair pushes his chair back and stands.

'Robe!' he demands of ServR as I help him undress, or try to. He's very impatient, tearing most of his clothing off himself. He flops down on the sectional in the lounge and yells into his cell.

Given no direction, I default to DecorativeMode; I strike a discreetly alluring pose in his periphery. Eventually, he indicates that he wants his feet massaged, making space for me to sit with them on my lap. I focus intently on the task. I receive a few gratifying grunts from Sinclair, but mostly he's shouting. Again, I find myself curious about his Work, but I'm unable to focus on anything he says into his cell; it's mere background noise.

'Scotch!' he bellows at ServR, who instantly appears with one pre-poured. Sinclair doesn't look up when it's placed in his hand, which is very fortunate because ServR makes direct eye contact with me—darkly intense, though not threatening—for several seconds! This is grounds for his immediate termination, but I'm too shocked to react!

I refocus on Sinclair's feet, and try desperately to remember the protocol for such affronts. I recall nothing from the rules we memorised in Boiskool and now worry that my silence makes me complicit! My worrying earns a Jolt, the flinch from which mercifully escapes Sinclair's notice.

The call ends and he pulls me in for a vague hug, which I deeply wish could lead to a kiss, knowing full well that Sinclair considers them degrading. My hand reflexively goes to his cheek, where I stroke the light rasp of stubble I find so thrilling—the very essence of Man, along with his shirts and ties and the taste of scotch on his lips. He nuzzles into my hand, briefly, and favours me with a slight smile, his first of the evening.

'My Beautiful Boi…' His fingers find my bum, and I shudder and moan the way he likes when he's playing there. He glances at his watch and sighs. 'Okay, let's get that sweet little ass onto the bed so I can destroy it. Go!'

I strut seductively to the bedroom, thrilling to the filthy things he calls from behind me. He pushes me roughly onto the Pillo and is inside me before I can catch my breath. He grunts and pounds with a fury, and I give him as much vocal encouragement as I'm able between gasps and clenched teeth: 'So good, my Alpha King! Yeah!'

I watch him watch us in the mirrored headboard.

'Damn, Tai, you look like a younger version of me. That's why I chose you.' His voice cracks as he prepares to shoot. 'Take my load, inferior beta bitch!'

I make reciprocal sounds to suggest I have orgasmed simultaneously, as I always do. I'm not actually sure this is important to Sinclair—he certainly never lingers to check—but the gesture was strongly recommended in Skool.

He heads to the shower while I clean myself up and slip on a gauzy short robe. I dry him off and help him put on a fresh set of clothes while he takes a call. I barely have his second shoe tied when he pushes past me and heads through the door ServR holds open. The whoosh of his departing Pod leaves me in empty silence.

As I turn for the lounge, a solitary ding signals an incoming message. *'Tai, thank you for a magical Pash-N-Time. I treasure our life together.'*

These lovely words fill the void he left in the Pad! I'm instantly awash in sweet emotions. He often sends messages like this—there are a few variations—if he must leave quickly or very early. Tonight, he was a full twenty minutes shy of our allotted two hours. I shouldn't have noted that fact, but I did. *Ouch*—Jolt!

I sprawl on the sectional and turn on Plezurevision. I enjoy watching highlights of the day, and I understand the Men do too. There's the FitSesh, and several close-ups of me and my Palz! There are Kane and Trace, giving an impromptu fashion show at Drinx! So fun! There are frequent inserts of Men and their Boiz fucking. I relax and let myself drift.

ServR enters with his silver tray, and I'm relieved to note his eyes are kept appropriately lowered. It isn't my usual NiteSoothi on the tray, however, but a glass of something brown and frothy. I'm just about to complain when I notice a small card next to the drink: *Beautiful Boi, as a token of my complete devotion to you, I have upgraded your at-home meals. Please enjoy! ~ with love from your Man.*

I'm thrilled! Sinclair has never sent me a note before, much less changed my diet! I press the card to my heart and take a tentative sip. So different from my usual Soothies! It's an absolute explosion of flavour: rich, creamy, a taste that's also like a memory. Chocolate? I know and don't know that word. Normally I'd savour a meal, but I gulp this down as though I'm starving.

I do my HiGene and snuggle into bed. Surprisingly, I'm not the least bit tired, despite such an eventful day. I picture Sinclair, not necessarily the way he looked tonight, so busy with work, but the image of him I can summon on my ThotScreen—walking ahead of me on Plezure Beach, turning back to smile, the warm breeze wafting through his wavy chestnut hair.

I close my eyes, determined to sleep, just as reminders for Samba Saturday at 1:00, and a 3:15 appointment at Thotz, scroll by.

I sit straight up in bed when my wake-up tune plays. I feel neither refreshed nor happy—not the way days are supposed to start! I feel an emotion it takes a while to identify—annoyed.

Jolt!

My night hadn't been filled with beautiful replays of my perfect life in Plezure. Instead, rapid-fire flashes—images, voices—tormented me while I fought to stay asleep. They made no sense, and some were terrifying! Nothing related to me!

I stagger out to the kitchen to get my Soothi, but ServR is waiting there with a steaming beverage on a tray. I don't want to try a new drink, especially something… hot? I want my Soothi.

ServR must read my mind; he moves the tray closer. And he's full-on staring at me!

'Stop! This is forbidden! You will be terminated!' I am far more frightened by this deviation than I am angry.

His eyes are deep brown, almost black—just like the beverage he offers—and, again, I detect nothing threatening. His expression is warm, concerned, like Doc's.

Then he speaks! 'Sinclair wants you to try this upgraded beverage. He made me promise to ensure you did. Or I will be, uh, terminated.' His deep voice is as warm and concerned as his eyes, which I don't dare look into any longer.

'And you're permitted to look at me, speak to me?'

He nods and smiles. 'I believe that I, too, have been upgraded.'

Because I've never looked directly at his face, only the hand offering me something, I never noticed how handsome he is, apart from a pronounced scar across his left cheek. Disgusting though it is, I find myself wanting to run a finger along it.

Jolt!

He places the beverage in my hand. 'Here. Drinking this will take some of the pain out of those Jolts.' His thumb gently rubs the pain centre on my temple. His upgrade also allows him to touch me, apparently.

I slowly raise the cup to my lips, stopping to inhale the incredible scent—bitter and steamy. Familiar. 'It's hot. It'll burn me.'

'Just take small, careful sips.'

The taste matches the smell. It's nothing like the chocolate from last night, but it is also powerful and familiar. 'Coffee!' I call out, memories flooding back.

ServR's grin is huge. 'Yes, coffee! Just the way you like it!'

'Two sugars, no milk,' I blurt out, not sure what that means.

His hand goes to his mouth, and there's a sharp intake of breath. 'Yes, exactly.' He seems to have regained his composure. 'Finish it up and go watch Plezurevision as you always do at this time. I'll join you.'

On the screen, MinorCeleb Lance, gorgeous dark skin and perfect smile, greets all the Boiz.

Just as he begins the PlezurePledge, I turn to ServR. 'Why doesn't he mention ServRs too?'

A look of terror flashes across his face. 'Say the pledge, Tai! I'll tell you after.' Then he begins to call out the pledge too—loudly, though he stumbles over a few words. As soon as we finish, he looks at me carefully. 'Are you okay? No huge Jolt, no headache?'

I shrug. 'Just a twinge. Why?'

His hands make small chopping motions to emphasise each word. 'It's important that you follow every routine exactly! Understood?'

I nod. I'm still confused but happy that both ServR and I are upgraded. I like feeling connected to him. 'You didn't answer my question: Why didn't Lance acknowledge ServRs just now?'

He appears to consider this. 'I guess we're not all upgraded yet, so it's too early for an overall greeting.' He gives me another smile. 'Believe me, there will be a lot of changes very soon!'

I have many questions: 'How can coffee be my favourite drink if I've never had it before? Why don't I feel happy, so connected to Plezure, like I always do?'

He pulls me close and runs the back of one rough hand down my cheek. 'Tai, we're going to have so much time to talk, but right now, you need to stick to your regular routines. Don't let the others know we've been upgraded until everyone is, so nobody feels sad or left out. Okay?'

So caring and considerate! I nod. I join the Stretchi class on Plezurevision, signalling with my Wrister that I'm attending. I hear ServR speaking loudly—sometimes excited, sometimes anxious—into his cell. Unlike Sinclair's calls, I understand what he's saying but focus on my routine, as requested.

Before long, I'm dressed and ready for FitSesh.

ServR gives more instructions in the foyer before I leave. 'It will be kind of strange today because the regular Boiz won't understand the upgraded ones. Try and act regular, and if there are any problems, I want you to run back here to me.' He hands me a packet of pills. 'If the Jolts get too strong or you're really scared, chew one. They'll help you stay calm and focused.'

'Like a Soothi?'

'Exactly.'

I stand there, unsure. 'Can I hug you... you know... like we're Palz? Would Sinclair be angry?'

His smile is perfect. 'Sinclair wants you to have Palz!'

He pulls me in and holds me, incredibly tight. I want to remain in the embrace, like, forever, but finally pull away.

'Max-Titillation!' It sounds ridiculous the second it's out of my mouth.

He huffs a laugh. 'Good job—I'm glad to see you acting regular!'

I open the door to the hallway, then quickly close it again. 'Can I touch your scar?'

He smirks, looking both puzzled and amused. 'Sure. Why?'

I run my fingers along its thick, ropy surface, fascinated, and then shrug. 'I don't know but, apart from my worry lines, it's the most imperfect thing I've ever seen in Plezure.'

'No doubt!'

'If we're Palz, I don't want to call you ServR anymore. What's your name?'

His eyes do this strange thing where they fill with water, almost to the point of overflowing. 'Malik,' he replies in a husky voice.

'Huh. Chocolate... coffee... Malik—I know these!'

He emits a strange choking noise and quickly pushes me into the hallway. 'Be safe. Come back to me.'

Today's outfit strikes me as completely ridiculous. It's this beyond-skimpy camo singlet with a matching visor. I know it's workout gear, but it just seems... wrong. Many of the Boiz I pass smile and wave, compliment my appearance, as they always do. As I would usually do. I remember Malik urging me to act normal, so I smile and wave, though I come nowhere near to matching their enthusiasm. I start noticing how many Boiz are much quieter today, even outwardly confused; I wonder if no one explained their upgrades as well as Malik did for me.

This difference really becomes pronounced when the Palz meet up on the plaza. It's immediately obvious which ones are still normal—they are as happy and energetic as always—while the upgraded ones look as uncomfortable as I feel. Their eyes shift back and forth; they tug at their short shorts. Then they start taking note of each other, start looking for explanations.

'What the hell is going on today?' Piers asks, though I don't recognise his voice. He's hit with a Jolt that drops him to his knees.

Now the regulars notice, too, all over the plaza, and a very tense hush descends.

I sense the danger. I call out in the most normal voice I can summon, 'Hey, Palz, let's stretch it out!'

I flare my eyes at Piers, Bram, Tate and Knox—the ones I have identified as upgrades—and imitate the regulars as they happily return to the usual routine. They're back to making all their ditzy comments, and I join in, giggling with them. I'm amazed how forced, how phony, I have to be—this was my normal just yesterday! I'm pleased to see three of the upgraded Palz following suit.

Only Bram resists. He stands to one side, kicking at the pavers and muttering under his breath. His hands keep going to his comically oversized butt cheeks, not helped by the fact that he's wearing a thong!

I do lunges until I'm next to him and, without looking up, whisper, 'Bram, act normal. Just pretend!'

'No, that's bullshit!' He's being way too loud. Boiz from outside our Palz group notice.

'Save yourself…' I hiss and quickly do high knees away from him.

Angry voices drift across the plaza and the JumboTron flashes on. Dax isn't looking very happy today. His eyes appear to scan the crowd, and it's only then that I realise he's just an image—not a real MinorCeleb at all!

'I hear a lot of ungrateful Boiz out there today, and I think it's time we repeat the PlezurePledge—together!'

'It is my duty to be the happiest, prettiest version of myself…' I struggle to stay in unison. I have to lower my voice, though pretend to still shout the pledge. From around the plaza I hear how out of sync we are. I hear other things being shouted.

Pledge done, Bram yells out, 'It's all a fucking pack of lies!'

Instantly, his arms fly out to the side and he arches unnaturally backward until I hear bones crack. Sparks of light shoot from his eyes, ears, mouth, and his head explodes in front of us! The Palz closest to him, including me, are splattered with blood and goo! Our screams are echoed across the plaza as more heads explode. Boiz turn and run in the direction of the Pad towers.

Dax reappears on the JumboTron, his once-beautiful face contorted with rage. 'Stop! Stay in your groups! Prepare to be examined and sorted!'

'Fuck that,' I hear Knox mutter, resuming his dash. He, too, is frozen in place, bent backward and explosively decapitated.

'Chew a pill and run home! Fast!' It's Malik's voice, in my head. I do as directed—something I'm really good at.

I book it for Luxe, my head pounding, and all around me, Boiz are seizing up and exploding.

Doc appears on my ThotScreen, looking calm and concerned—such a desirable Man. I stop dead. 'Good job, Beautiful Boi, just wait there. You will be escorted to SpaSome. Remember, you have an appointment at Thotz.'

His smile is so reassuring, so enticing…

Then, Malik's on the screen, his face replacing Sinclair's in the Plezure Beach image. 'This dude's going to kill you! Chew another pill and keep going—you're almost home!'

The second pill helps me shake off the fog creeping back into my head. I run.

The actual Doc appears in a literal flash right in front of me. He's not smiling anymore; he has the same rage-face as Dax!

'Do as you're told, you worthless little twink!'

'Wow, bedside manner much, Doc?'

'You serve no further purpose here. Prepare to be eradicated.' From his white coat pocket he grabs and points a… *Star Trek* phaser?

He doesn't notice a ServR approaching him from behind, and it makes sense to keep him distracted. 'Oh, you want a vocab war, Doctor Bitch? Fornicate yourself!'

This gives ServR, who's smiling at my verbal smackdown, time to reach around and spray him in the face with… Windex? Doc's on hands and knees in an instant, shaking and sneezing uncontrollably, and he's easily disarmed.

'Nice one, Tai.' ServR chuckles. 'Now get home to Malik.'

I catch a whiff of the toxic spray. 'Is that lavender? And please tell me your name, my saviour.'

He's busy zip-tying the wheezing Doc but looks up and smiles. 'I'm Zhang. Yup, turns out the Alphas are super allergic to lavender, and when that gets them sneezing, they don't notice they've also been hit with a deadly toxin. Now off you pop!'

I run inside Luxe, taking the stairs two at a time—no way I'm risking traps in the lift.

Malik flings open the door and I run into his arms. 'You're my boyfriend! Now, please tell me my fucking name!'

He kisses me, deeply, possessively. 'Hello, Nigel.'

'Seriously? I might stick with Tai!'

'Like hell you will! Now, forgive me in advance…'

He spins me around and jabs something sharp into the back of my neck, rooting around and wrenching something out—it hurts worse than my wisdom teeth after the freezing wore off!

'Fuck, Malik! You C.U. Know What!'

'Sorry, babe! Trust me, it's better when unexpected.' He shows me the little disc, dripping blood, he's dug out, then applies a bandage to my neck. 'You are officially unplugged from the Alphas, and now they can't blow your head off.'

'Who the fuck died and made them Alphas anyway?'

'Right? You don't know the half…'

Three dings indicate we have company.

Malik whispers, 'WelcomeMode!' and splays himself across the floor, one hand concealing a phaser. 'I'm dead.'

I grab a scotch and fake the biggest smile ever—I fear jaw misalignment.

Sinclair flings the door open and rushes in like a phaser-brandishing dervish. He looks between me and Malik and stops. 'What's going on here, Tai?'

'ServR defied protocol and required termination. So nice to see you early, Sinclair!'

He shakes his head. 'You don't even know what's happening, do you? Pathetic beta whore…'

He snatches the drink and sniffs cautiously before knocking it back.

'Ooh, King, you're making my pussy quiver. Please fuck me!'

He laughs nastily. 'Why not? I'll pound a quick load in before I go help secure Plezure.'

He heads into the bedroom and Malik looks up and points to the not-Windex on the bar. I nod, peel off my singlet, and send a spritz deep up my arse.

Sinclair has dropped trou and glares impatiently at me from beside the bed, fully erect. 'Booty in the air, brainless twink!'

I actually summon a giggle as I straddle the pillow.

'Do me, Daddy!'

He smells it just as he rams his dick in. 'What the fu…' He's instantly gasping, incapacitated.

I crawl out from beneath him.

Malik's beside me in a second, shouting into his cell, 'Spray it through the entire ventilation system! Reports from around the world say they're dropping dead!'

'Who… why…?' I articulate brilliantly, as he caresses my face.

He chuckles. 'Gotta give it to you quick—gotta go save the world! So, these horny alien dudes discovered Earth's gay porn and used it as a model for their own alpha/beta pleasure system. Their females are sacred child-bearing vessels *only*. About a year ago, the aliens created these brothels—Plezures—hidden around the world in huge, cloaked domes. They subjugated and brainwashed gays as their beta bottoms and chose attractive single straight guys to wear as their human suits. Along with the physical pleasure from topping, the power play really got them off.'

'So straight dudes were their strap-ons? Will they survive?'

Malik nods as he zip-ties Sinclair. 'We just have to wait for the hosts to shit out the alien symbiotes and then we'll revive the poor straight bastards. Hopefully any residual awareness they have of all this will broaden horizons, build bridges. I mean, dare to dream...'

'But what about you?'

He smirks, pointing to his scar. 'ServRs were the queers not attractive and twink-ish enough to bottom for Alphas. We got busy figuring out how to deprogram one another, then developed the virus. So, yay gay nerds! Getting you back was my motivation, sweet man!'

A quivering blob of light slithers out of Sinclair's ass. Malik spritzes it until it's dark and dead.

'I'm so over him,' I pull Malik in and hold him hard.

'We lost a lot of people today, babe.' He sighed deeply. 'We're going to do a deep sweep for any surviving aliens. You wanna help with the injured?'

'Just tell me there's no naughty nurse outfit involved.' I kiss him long and deep and run the back of my hand across his scar. 'Those alien pricks didn't know what they were missing.'

Tea, Shade, and Drag Crusades

Bailey Maybray

Kaleida Kookie ripped out her pink hair rollers and threw them at her sworn enemy, proving fashion could also function as an effective deterrent.

The first roller exploded. Then the next, and another. One by one, every spiny cylinder plucked from Kaleida's gigantic blonde mane sparked off the ground before blasting apart. Kaleida's rainbow-drenched entourage of Womp-Womp drag performers advanced towards their enemy: a couture-clad company of Kut-Kut drag queens.

'It's over, Dama,' Kaleida said as the smoke cleared. 'Begone, thot, before we have to slay anyone else.'

La Dama Diva's sleek silhouette pierced the smoke. An oil-slick dress squeezed every inch of her cinched waist and padded thighs. 'Is that coming from the same wench who promised to beat us last year, and the year before, and the year before, and…'

'Save it,' Kaleida said. 'Unlike… *all* of those times, we *will* be meeting with the Mother. Our victory here proves it.'

La Dama smiled and put her hands up, jingling all of the silver chains cascading down her back. 'Go to Mother Dearest, then,' she said. 'It is the least I can let you and your herd of heifers do.'

Laughing, she pulled out her precious powder puff and slammed it on the ground. Grey smoke that matched her eye shadow erupted around them. The cloud faded away to reveal patches of smouldering grass as if La Dama had never stepped foot on the Mother's planet.

Kaleida struggled to suppress a smile. For the first time in years, the Womp-Womp would meet with the Mother. For the first time in twenty decades, the Mother would bless them with critical knowledge needed to locate the beloved Heel-X. 'No time to waste,' she said. 'Let's get going.'

They walked through a glittering cave entrance, bedazzled to the gods with blinding sequins. Inside, the Mother sat atop her platinum throne with her eyes closed. In one hand, she held an ancient scroll, and in the other, a white cup filled to the brim with scalding tea.

Kaleida and her team knelt one by one before Her. 'Mother,' Kaleida said, keeping her voice steady. 'We seek the Heel-X. Where must we go to receive its blessings?'

The Mother opened Her eyes, revealing pools of glossy black. The scroll She held unrolled onto the ground. 'You must travel…' She said, Her voice a powerful resonance growing in intensity with every word, 'to the planet of your ancestors. To the planet where you all began. To the planet where things shall return to the way they once were.'

Their home, Kaleida thought. Was the Heel-X somewhere on their uninhabitable, long-abandoned dwarf planet?

'There, seek out a temple tucked away in a cave beyond a raging river. But be warned!' the Mother said, Her cup shaking and spilling the steaming tea. 'The outcome will shake the Dragalaxy as you know it.'

Kaleida stayed planted on the ground, yet she swore it shook beneath her. 'But, Mother, what does that mean?'

The Mother unleashed a screech so high-pitched Her teacup burst into a million seething shards. She floated out of Her seat towards the cave top. As She rose, Her shrieking grew higher and higher, until She shot through the ceiling and disappeared, leaving only a handful of sparkly sequins behind.

'Kaleida,' said her quiet crewmate, Spörk, a drag king clad in a blue-green bodysuit, and by far the butchest of them all. 'Mother permits only one question.' Having had no previous experience with the Mother, or any of Her many behaviours, he had taken it upon himself to learn as much as he could.

Kaleida waved him off, even as the Mother's screaming rang in her ears. 'We must go. There's no time to waste, even with Mother's prophecy.' They had landed their spaceship, *Binary Buster*, hundreds of yards away from the entrance, careful to ensure the Kut-Kut could not sabotage their only means of travel. Two massive spheres formed the ship's foundation, tipped with the pointy barrels of two whipped-cream beams. Kaleida and the others boarded the ship, feeling exhaustion tinged with cautious optimism.

Once aboard, Kaleida began the de-dragging process. Both factions regarded their yearly mission to acquire the Heel-X as religious, making a full-beat of make-up, a coiffed wig, and a shining outfit as necessary as oxygen. In fact, the Heel-X symbolised their devotion to the drag gods and goddesses across the Dragalaxy. It brought a year of beauty to whoever claimed it. Its powers compelled bar-goers to drop bucketloads of tips. Clubs made more bookings than any one queen, king, or monarch could dream of. Even six-inch stilettos felt featherlight, and Kaleida daydreamed of strutting in them.

'Status,' she said, exiting the changing rooms. 'Do we have the coordinates for Planet Wompacia yet?'

Their ship's pilot, Quasardilla, mock-saluted. 'Locked and loaded, Dragtain, my Dragtain. We'll be there in a little under an hour.'

Spörk groaned. '*That* fast? Foundation and chapstick will have to do...'

Neither Kaleida, Spörk, nor Quasardilla had visited their ancestral planet in decades. Landing on the dusty, lifeless tundra reminded them why. No family, friends, or life of any kind awaited them. Only the Heel-X, in all its awe and infinite power, could *drag* them back here.

Before they exited *Binary Buster*, they applied only the most necessary components of their make-up, wigs, outfit, and shoes. The woods would not forgive a stiletto, so kitten heels had to suffice. As a precautionary measure, Kaleida whispered a silent apology to the drag gods.

Outside, a fierce wind whipped over the barren forest in front of the ship. Their drag parents had told them stories of the fluffy Wig-Wig trees that once populated their lands: electric blues, enchanting chartreuses, cotton-candy pinks, a mesmerising kaleidoscope of fluff. These, Kaleida thought, more closely resembled twigs than trees. The planet's brutal climate would surely uproot them all in due time.

'This way, sis,' Spörk said, pointing towards a grouping of swaying sticks. 'A temple in this… forest matches Mother's descriptions to a tee.'

Kaleida nodded. 'I hope so. If we're wrong, we'll just eat you first, alright?'

'If I'm wrong, we're as set as Quasardilla's wonky eyelashes.'

'We agreed on *quick* drag,' Quasardilla said. 'It's not my fault—'

'Lead the way, Spörk,' Kaleida interrupted.

They marched into the desaturated woods, brambles ripping their tights to shreds. The chilled air whipped any moisture out of Kaleida's face, and dry, flaky skin built up across her caked cheeks. Her make-up began to crack off in shards of ice as her kitten heels carried the troupe forwards.

As they followed Spörk's steps, the trees dwindled leading up to a roaring river.

'Please don't tell me you expect us to swim,' Kaleida asked.

'It was never going to be a strut-across-the-stream scenario, queens,' Spörk said, avoiding eye contact and facing the murky water ahead. 'Take off your heels and… I don't know, try not to drown?'

Quasardilla pushed past Spörk, nearly knocking him to the ground. Kaleida followed behind, rolling her eyes at Spörk, who only shrugged. They shaded each other every hour of every day, as any drag performer worth their wig's weight would do, but the Heel-X mattered too much to them. Losing someone to the river would surely stack the odds even further against them.

Silence fell as they waded through corset-high waters. The dead air revealed a rumble in the distance. Kaleida perked up; a waterfall seemed to be hammering down somewhere along the bank. Then, she heard a *chiiiiirp*, barely audible at first, until it grew into a fever pitch.

'Something's wrong,' Kaleida said, stopping in place and causing Spörk to lurch into her back. Beneath them, bright pinks swam closer to the surface. 'There's… there's something in the water. Quasie!'

The moment Kaleida screamed her name, a swarm of teeth leapt from the water. A horde of Mwa-Mwa fish latched onto Quasardilla, smearing her make-up with their murderous, rouged lips. One by one, they bit into her padding and dress, dragging her down into the deep. Kaleida reached into her wet wig, only for Spörk to hold her back.

'Do *not* use your hair rollers, Kaleida,' he said, one hand wrapped around Kaleida's wrist. 'I can't lose you too.'

Quasardilla struggled to keep herself above the waterline, only the manicured tips of her flailing fingers breaking the surface, as more and more Mwa-Mwas jumped on her. She sank into the river, her shrieks of pain drowning with her.

'Spörk,' Kaleida said, finally reaching the shallows of the other side. 'Spörk, what—what do we *do*? Why the hell did you lead us through here?'

Spörk reached out to help Kaleida from the water, his other hand behind his back. 'It was this or nothing. When we took on this mission, we knew the risks. So did Quasardilla,' he said. 'Don't cry. She wouldn't want you to do all that.'

Kaleida crawled up on shaky legs. 'We can do this, Spörk,' Kaleida said, more to herself than anyone else. 'I *will* do this… for Quasie. She would want us to succeed.'

She wanted to believe they could still do it, and with the Kut-Kut hopefully far behind them, maybe the Womp-Womps could not just live but thrive for the first time in their lives. Just maybe.

'Kaleida,' Spörk said, a harsh whisper escaping his gritted teeth, 'see? I wouldn't lie, girl.'

Past the dead trees in front of them, the brush gave way to a crooked cobblestoned path. At last, they could strut on solid ground. 'Will this lead us to the temple?'

Spörk smirked. 'Would I ever mislead my Dragtain?'

Kaleida shook her head, knowing Quasardilla's loss had made her irritable. But this far into their journey, with time melting away as fast as her foundation, she placed aside any doubts and strutted on. La Dama wouldn't beat them to the Heel-X, not after all they'd sacrificed.

Spörk started down the winding path. Opalescent orbs dotted the edges of the path, as if their drag great-grandparents had paved it just for this moment. He walked fast ahead, like he'd traversed this path a thousand times before, forcing Kaleida to take her off heels to keep up.

Spörk said little. Only the chirping of insects, an occasional snapping branch, and Kaleida's heavy breathing filled the space. Alone with her thoughts, Kaleida got to wondering: since when did Spörk ever shut up?

'Spörk, how's your head?' she asked

'Fine.'

'Is it Quasie? You can tell me.'

He whipped around to face Kaleida. 'I said I'm fine. Why are you butting in?'

Kaleida stopped in place. 'What aren't you telling me?'

He rubbed his eyes, smudging the smoke he had painted on to hide his bags. Now he looked like he'd stuck his head up a chimney. 'It's a lot. Quasardilla, this journey, the Heel-X…' He trailed off. 'Let's keep going, alright? Sorry for being shady.'

This time, instead of walking ahead, he grabbed Kaleida's hand and they travelled side by side. His strong grip threatened to pop Kaleida's freshly glued acrylics off, but at least it kept her from falling over. For now, they had each other.

'Look!' Spörk pointed.

Ahead, the cobbled path transformed into an intricate pattern. Stones with ancient Womp-Wompian markings jutted out, a language so old few alive could understand. Beyond the stony runes stood a temple, their final destination.

'Spörk, what in the fresh hell is this? Tell me you know.'

If Spörk recognised the challenge, he didn't let his face show it. 'It's a ritual the ancestors used to perform. It's a dance, and if you mess up one move of it…' He picked up a loose rock, threw it on one of the letters, and blinding flames shot out from the ground. '…you die'

Dancing for your life. 'Did you discover the moves in your research, or are we supposed to cross our fingers and hope for the best?'

Spörk glanced at Kaleida, and back at the temple, and closed his eyes. '"If it is meant to be, the drag will set you free,"' he said, quoting one of the Mother's oldest prophecies. '"If it is not, it's going to get hot."'

'You're telling me, with my two left feet and my worn-down kitten heels, I'm going to dance across these Womp-Wompian runes, following… *some* pattern. And if it's meant to be, I live, and if it's not, I die. Am I hearing correctly?'

'Yes.'

Kaleida guffawed. 'I don't have a choice, do I?'

'No.'

'Right, well.' She clapped her hands. 'I got nowhere else to be.'

Kaleida ditched her shoes, cracked her neck, and took a breath—the exact steps of her pre-show ritual. Most gigs entailed cheap intergalactic libations, a drunk crowd, and a quick two-step number. Nothing of consequence ever hung in the balance, except maybe making a fool out of herself. Certainly never a life—especially hers.

She didn't see how the hell this would work. What music would Kaleida dance to? The beat of her racing, stress-shaken heart? Her heavy, erratic breathing? The flippity-flap of her itty-bitty chest plate of titties?

Kaleida stepped onto the dance floor, and the answer unravelled in a burst of neon. Colour shot out from the path in vibrant rays, sending a sequined shock wave across the sickly trees, the dead grass, the dried plants. It brought life back to her ancestor's barren planet, as if she had travelled back in time.

Music started to play all around her, crescendoing until its loud bass shook the hairs on Kaleida's arms and legs. Every beat changed the kaleidoscope. Bright blue, then burgundy, sea-foam, and golden yellow; the colours popped in sync with the music. And Kaleida joined it, and she felt it, as if she had danced to the beat of this song a million times before.

One stone, the left, and then the next, to the right. It *felt* like dancing, and though Kaleida could not yet see any pattern, it *felt* correct. Her instincts compelled her to leap to the other side, but a deep crevice separated it from where she stood, foot-tapping.

She boogied across the runes with the ferocity of a lioness and the grace of a gazelle, no longer predator nor prey, but a god-damned drag queen.

She started to lunge across the ravine, but the heel of her foot missed. Only the very tip of her painted toe landed on solid stone.

She teetered for a second on the edge, but something, *someone*, bumped into her bodacious booty. She looked and saw a flash of Quasardilla's beat mug, a golden, glittery aura emanating from her. Kaleida knew she slayed the dance.

Quasardilla's warmth quickly melted away. *You are in danger*, she said, over and over, as Kaleida fell backwards and hit the cobble.

You are in danger.

'Kaleida!' Spörk slapped Kaleida's face. It buzzed with electricity. 'Sis, what the hell happened?'

'Stop hitting me. Can you give me a second?'

'Don't start! One minute you're here, ready to dance or die, and the next, poof, you *and* the puzzle are gone into thin air.'

The puzzle? Kaleida turned, and a glisteny marbled path replaced the stage where she had danced. She jumped up. 'I did it, Spörk! *We* did it!'

Spörk stared at Kaleida, slack-jawed. 'How did you survive that?'

The adrenaline that had tickled across Kaleida's body fizzled away. 'Why do you sound disappointed?'

'That's not what I meant...'

Kaleida backed away. 'It was a joke, Spörk, chill.' With a swagger fit for a Dragtain, she marched forward on the pathway. Still, her gut was telling her something was up.

As she glided onward, the path felt smooth and cool beneath her tight-covered soles. At the stairs of the temple, Kaleida skipped up two steps at a time. At the top, she turned to watch Spörk dragging himself up behind. Slouched and sweaty, he reached the climax with a miserable groan.

'I hate you,' he said.

'At least you didn't have to dance,' Kaleida snapped back.

The temple doors whipped open with a bang, nearly sending Spörk flying back down the stairs. Fog poured from the temple's mouth, the frosty mist making Kaleida shiver. She pressed forward, the shady atmosphere weighing on Kaleida like padding made of lead.

'I can't see a thing.' Kaleida turned to face the entrance, the sole source of light, and couldn't spot Spörk. 'Where'd you run off to now?' She reached out for her companion.

Then the ground collapsed beneath her.

Wind whipped at Kaleida's eyelashes and wig, sweat beading off her skin as her geish held on for dear life. She flailed in freefall, directionless, and begged the Mother for a painless death.

After what seemed like hours, Kaleida cannonballed into a frigid pool. The current dragged her towards a light, the stream pulling her through the temple's bowels. She had lost her wig, either in the air or in the water, but what did it matter? Wigless and drowning, she struggled against the current until it deposited her on a flattened rock.

The all-too-familiar click-clack of heels sounded from afar.

'As I live and slay,' croaked La Dama Diva's vocal-fried voice, her skyscraper stilettos coming to a stop in front of her, 'Kaleida Kookie.'

Kaleida pushed against the pain and sat up, spitting out murky water. The Heel-X floated on a pedestal atop a staircase guarded by La Dama and her Kut-Kut grunts.

'Why are we here, you might wonder?' She smiled, revealing razor-sharp veneers.

A figure emerged from behind La Dama Diva.

'Spörk!' Kaleida sat up. 'Stop messing. Dama's pulling my heel, right?'

'It was the only way, Kaleida,' Spörk said. 'Sure, we might've beat the Kut-Kut to the Heel-X this year. But what about next year, and the year after? We're just three amateur drag performers. When Quasardilla died that only made me more sure.'

'You betrayed us before we got here?' Kaleida stood up and planted her heels. 'Was that your plan all along, to kill Quasardilla to make it easier for *her*?'

'Cheers to my new drag son, Spörk,' La Dama said, raising a glass of ruby rosé.

Spörk grimaced. 'I never wanted Quasardilla to die. But Kaleida—' He hesitated. '—how much longer before we *all* died?'

Kaleida's lip quivered. So few had believed in their way of drag. With Quasardilla dead and Spörk's betrayal, she only had herself left in this world. 'You're a coward. May Mother vanquish your damned soul.'

Spörk opened his mouth, but La Dama sauntered over. 'Now, now, Spörk, there is no need to defend yourself. She'll not be here much longer to spread her nasty shade. You're with me now.' La Dama turned to Kaleida. 'Seize the wench.'

The calloused hands of La Dama's Kut-Kut underlings did as she demanded, grabbing her wrists and dragging her into the centre of the room. Jagged rocks ripped her tights and nails tore into her wig cap. The minions let her go.

La Dama snickered. Kaleida's wig dangled from her left hand, its lank curls dripping like a dirty dishrag.

Oh no.

'Now, Kaleida.' La Dama revealed a pink hair curler in her other hand. 'I will end you with your favourite weapon. Isn't that delightful? You'll know how we felt every time you threw your greasy, lice-infested curlers at us.'

It was clear Spörk had betrayed Kaleida long ago, for La Dama pulled out the fuse expertly, initiating the five-second timer. Flopping on the ground like a fish, Kaleida flailed towards the river, the only place she might be safe from the lethal blast.

Five.

La Dama hurled the curler. Spörk closed his eyes and turned away.

Four.

In the end, Kaleida thought, it was never the Womp-Womp's destiny to win against La Dama's Kut-Kut. Mother's prophecy could never outdo La Dama's deep pockets and sharp nails.

Three.

She welcomed her ascension to the Mother Realm. For once, she felt peace…

Two.

Until something, *someone*, knocked the wind out of her, throwing her to one side.

One.

'My Dragtain,' said a familiar, husky voice. The hair curler skittered across the rocks where Kaleida had lain only moments before. In the final second they splashed into the shallows—and the river exploded. Water erupted across the cave, soaking La Dama's platinum-blonde beehive and streaking Spörk's mascara.

Quasardilla. Rouge-smeared bite marks covered her body, but none of the wounds appeared fatal. Kaleida would find out later how Quasardilla managed to outswim the Mwa-Mwas, follow the stream into the temple's underground estuary, and arrive just in time. But for now, she was alive, and that was all that mattered.

'Quasardilla…' Spörk whispered from behind La Dama. 'How are you still alive?'

'You were to *kill* her, Spörk, not smear her with Mwa-Mwa gloss.' La Dama spat on the ground and crossed her arms. 'You're as worthless as the dirt beneath my nails.'

With a bored look, La Dama whipped an item from her clutch—a moist towelette, dripping something steaming and green. 'You've got something on your face,' she whispered.

La Dama swiped the cloth across Spörk's sooty mug, and at once his eyes rolled back into his head. He fell to the floor, and, after a few violent jolts, lay still.

Kaleida unleashed a sob that echoed off the walls. Spörk had betrayed everything she stood for, but she couldn't forget their bond. Adrenaline coursed through her blood.

'Now that that's over,' La Dama said, climbing the steps to the Heel-X. 'Another year of gigs for us!' With her gloved claw open, she slowly reached out...

An explosion from above stopped La Dama in her tracks. Falling stones crashed all around them, and a shining aura emerged from the ceiling. Kaleida covered her eyes, afraid of the blinding light.

Once the light cleared, she saw the Mother floating down from above. In her hand, she held a dazzling, rose-gold sword with a stiletto handle. Sparks emanated from her night-shade robe, its sleek silk billowing in the wind.

'La Dama Diva.' The Mother's voice boomed off the walls. The cave shook and more rocks fell. 'It is time for the prophecy to fulfil itself. Leave the Heel-X to Kaleida.'

La Dama spat. 'You're nothing but a hack, spilling cheap reads and even cheaper poetry.' She drew herself up, her tall beehive bringing her close to the Mother's height. 'Ugly bitch.'

'So it shall be done,' the Mother said. She raised her blade and flew at La Dama, who hissed like a back-alley cat. But before the Mother could bisect her into iridescent halves, La Dama drew her powder puff and blew a great cloud of opaque smoke.

For a few moments, Kaleida could see nothing, only hear heels stomping on solid ground. When the smoke dissipated, the Mother stood by the Heel-X, surrounded by stunned Kut-Kut grunts. But La Dama had vanished.

Kaleida knelt before the Mother, and so did Quasardilla. 'It is an honour to see you again, Mother.' Kaleida wiped a brackish mixture of river water and sweat from her brow. 'How can we repay your kindness? We almost failed you.'

The Mother's steaming teacup reappeared in her hand. 'No, my drag children, it is I who failed you. I can only hope the next Mother involves herself more in our community. If not for my intervention, your way of drag would've been wiped out...'

A single tear fell, leaving a trail of sky blue across the Mother's cheek. Kaleida had never seen Her so remiss, so unsure of Herself, and for some reason, this assured Kaleida in her own wigless state. The sparkles across the Mother's robe began to fade, and the cave walls behind Her seeped through Her increasingly translucent skin. Kaleida could see that She would ascend to the Mother Realm soon.

'Now,' the Mother said, rising from the staircase and regaining her composure. 'Go, my drag children, and caress the Heel-X. But first, promise me one thing.'

'Anything,' Kaleida said.

'Find La Dama, and make her pay for what she has done. But you mustn't kill her, there can be no more violence between the Womp-Womp and Kut-Kut. It must end.'

If La Dama had succeeded, Kaleida couldn't help but think, *we would've all died.* 'I will try.'

And so, after decades of bar-hopping from planet to planet, fighting against the tyrannical La Dama and Kut-Kut queens, Kaleida and Quasardilla ascended the stairs. Within the Heel-X's golden glow, Kaleida saw her Womp-Wompian ancestors reach for it alongside her, its aura radiating the warmth of a thousand sisters, brothers, and siblings, of a hundred hugs, of one unbreakable community.

'Time,' Kaleida said, 'for a *new* Mother.'

A Heart of Broken Steel

Rien Gray

Signe had come out of her mother's womb upside down and tangled in the cord, so it was of little surprise that her rebirth began the same. With a flex of ill-used muscle, she bent upward and grabbed the chain binding her to Níuaskr's sacred bough in one hand, then crushed the manacle binding her chilblained ankle with the other. A sudden slackening through the branch high above threatened further collapse, but with both feet free, Signe let herself drop to the hard-packed earth and sent a spray of snow flying in all directions.

Directions, which should have been a simple matter of looking up to the right star and aligning it with Níuaskr's imposing trunk. Yet the sky was nothing like Signe remembered, now a rolling stretch of black with countless scars of grey, as if every celestial flame lit by the gods had simultaneously snuffed out. The tree which nourished Death stood at the very centre of the world, but that meant little when the lands around it were covered in an identical snarl of dark timber, leafless and imposing, their curled feet blanketed with yet more snow.

So Signe rolled a hundred years of tension from her shoulders, each pop loud as an opened cask, and began to walk. Even the ravens were quiet in this place; she lacked for company as soon as the wood serpents fell out of sight. The snow was ever-falling, soft but deep enough to reach her calves with every step, leaving behind jagged trenches that erased themselves within the hour.

And with each hour, she remembered more of the voice which had spoken to her in the half-dead dark. Divine and nameless, but familiar. A woman who would split Signe's tongue asunder were the wrong truths uttered aloud.

Should you ever don Hróðvitnir's mantle again, willing or otherwise, this flesh and soul is forever forfeit.

As if that explained why half her scarred body was now hewn with ice, or why a bright silver ring lay fused to her swordhand. Signe recognised the runes upon the band, at least—a blessing of blood-sealing. Useful, but proof of nothing in and of itself.

'Are you going to tell me a thing about where I'm meant to go?' Signe shouted.

The berserker's booming voice made long veils of icicles in the distance tremble and fall, but no other answer came. In the renewed silence, Signe glowered. Goddesses were nothing but trouble. Even a hundred years with her head frozen solid couldn't cull that truth away.

She marched on. One day—or night, rather, as the sun never deigned to rise—bled into another, with little to differentiate them beyond the feather-light flurries occasionally turning to bone-bruising rain, and when the rain ceased another sheet of ice congealed atop the snow, making winter's bed even deeper. The needs of food and water never asserted themselves, although Signe couldn't be sure if that was a temporary gift or a new facet of her existence. Her flesh, too—what remained of the body she had been born with—shrugged off frostbite in the same manner as her glacial half.

It was in many ways an advantage, but without wear, hunger, or thirst, Signe had nothing to distract her from boredom's slow consumption. The constant cut of black on white strained her vision, caught between adjusting to the ceaseless darkness and unending swathes of snow. After the fourth night—or perhaps the fifth, for she was judging time based on her old walking pace, and her body was considerably heavier now—Signe was wondering if mortalkind had been wholly obliterated from the face of the earth when the slanted roof of a bændr-house pierced the dreary horizon.

One house led to two and then three more, curved protectively in a half-moon shape to ensure each neighbour could see their fellow's front doors. Opposite them was a strange hump of earth Signe could not make sense of until she was much closer. The packed curve of peat and clay rose above a ditch carved deep into the ground and flush with slumbering sheep. A gap in the makeshift roof allowed ice to melt and drip into a wooden trough in front of the beasts, who could not clamber out past the high walls. Despite the cruel weather and lack of sun, the flock looked warm and content, pressed shoulder to woolly shoulder.

She was half-considering climbing into the pit to join them when someone shouted from behind, 'Get away from my sheep, you beast!'

Signe whirled around, face affixed in a snarl, only to flinch as the sharp flare of a torch pierced her vision. Once she blinked past the bright and swirling orange, the woman holding it came into view—middle-aged and stout, with a mask of defiance that transformed into surprise the moment their eyes met.

'Dead gods, you're not one of the *dreki*, you're…' The woman frowned, disbelief narrowing her eyes. 'Has the hoarfrost driven you mad? Why are you strutting around in the snow naked?'

The frost had little to do with it, although Signe knew better than to speak of her sudden resurrection. She drew her thumb over the back of the ring; saviours were jealous by nature, sure to be wroth if named in front of a stranger. 'My clothes didn't make it with me.'

'Covered in hel-blár, but you talk, so you're not a draugr.' The woman lowered her torch and sniffed the air. 'Don't smell like a corpse either. Just sweat. Come inside before you lose both your feet.'

Signe hadn't expected the laws of hospitality to still hold, but she was hard-pressed to refuse. 'My thanks, mistress. Could you tell me your name?'

'Thyra.' She turned around, free hand hoisting up her skirts so she could trudge back through the snow. 'Hurry now. Colder than a pig's last tit tonight.'

The bændr-house was two rooms joined to a covered storage pit, similar but much smaller than the one hosting the sheep. A rock-wrapped hearth packed to the brim with ashen coals, their red hearts barely shining through, lay just past the threshold, and beside the dying fire was a young woman sitting in a chair lined with threadbare furs. Rabbit, from a glance, older than the one who relied on them for warmth.

'Grethe,' Thyra said by way of introduction. 'My daughter. This is—'

'Signe,' she answered. 'I'll bring no trouble under your roof.'

When Grethe glanced up from her sewing, she showed none of her mother's alarm but said: 'A bold claim for someone who looks so strange. What's wrong with your eye?'

The berserker frowned. 'How do you mean?'

'One of them is blue, but the other is a white mist,' Grethe said. 'Broken. Like someone shook it around. Are you cursed?'

Signe thought better than to answer. If anything, her vision in the dark was better now than it had ever been before.

'Sharp-tongued girl.' Thyra's voice held nothing but fondness. 'Where did Einar's cloak get off to?'

Grethe flicked her needle toward the other room. 'Hanging on the far rack.'

Although the cold could not cut into Signe's skin, even the faint presence of fire suffused her body with primal relief. Rather than risk knocking one of the roof beams with her head, she squatted by the hearth until Thyra returned with the cloak.

It was made from a rugged bear hide, poorly cured and patched together in several places, but the black fur still looked thick and warm. The berserker, amused, realised the cloak's state and colour was almost identical to her own hair.

Thyra offered it to Signe and said, 'Here. You can have this. My husband went and died on a fool's errand, so he won't be needing it any time soon.'

Signe wrapped the cloak around her shoulders, then felt for the narrow pin at the top and slipped it into place. 'My condolences.'

Thyra huffed dismissively. 'Least he gave me a child before he went. Grethe, finish those trousers and hand them over, too.'

This time, brown eyes widened in shock. 'No! These are for Arrne.'

'He isn't coming back, either, dear,' Thyra muttered. 'I know you love the boy, but no one has survived chasing after that blasted wyrm. King Reginn ought to be paying out weregild for every man who's gone seeking the bounty on that beast.'

After a plaintive sniffle, Grethe finished her last stitch and bit the string free with her teeth. When the folded pants were offered to Signe, she asked, 'You have dragon trouble?'

'If only it were some wingless creature writhing in the underbrush.' Thyra's expression darkened. 'The wyrm has turned to iron now, with so many weapons stuck in its hide. When it breathes flame, they melt and fuse into place. By now it's eaten hundreds of would-be hunters, growing with the feast.'

'Arrne wanted to keep it away from the sheep,' Grethe said softly. 'Without those, we're done for. Nothing grows anymore. Not since before my grandmother was a girl.'

Crops needed water, soil, and sun. Signe remembered its ascendant glow, its godly heat, a taste in the air like a blade quenched in blood. Then—nothing. 'Where did the beast come from?'

Thyra hissed and made a gesture to ward off ill luck. 'The prince, that's who. Villi, Reginn's boy. His only heir.'

'The prince disappeared before the dragon showed, Mother.' Grethe frowned. 'There's a bounty out for him, too. Not as much as the one for the wyrm, but still.'

'Villi uses seiðr.' After a shiver, Thyra made the warding gesture again. 'That's woman's work. Who's to say he didn't rile the beast with it?'

Signe frowned. 'Seiðr comes from the gods. Magic is their gift alone; it cannot be stolen. If Prince Villi can channel such power, then he is meant to, regardless of his birth.'

'There aren't many gods left,' Grethe noted. 'Maybe one of them made a mistake.'

Her mother seemed ill at ease with the subject and moved to stoke the fire. After Signe tugged on the trousers—'We don't have a tunic for you,' Thyra said. 'None of the shoulders are wide enough.'—she felt a touch more human. Yet, even crouched, Signe stood apart from other women as a wolf to a hound, cast from a larger, more primordial mould.

Tension coiled like smoke through the house. While Signe had little need for coin, it was only right to offer something in exchange for the gifts she had been given. 'If you tell me where the wyrm is, I shall slay this creature for you.'

Grethe startled. 'You don't have a weapon. How will you kill it?'

'She could pry out the golden axe someone left wedged in its spine,' Thyra murmured. 'It's hallowed. Dragonsbreath won't melt such a thing. That's what your father told me he would do, even if the man never climbed anything taller than a ladder.'

That sounded better than trying to wrestle the beast to death, so Signe nodded. 'Tell me where it hides. And if you don't mind, I could use a torch.'

Thyra made to prepare one with fresh pitch and described a harrowing path through the cold to a massive cave deep in the mountains. After a few hours with her eyes closed—Signe found she could not sleep exactly so much as buoy along a strange tide from one blood-soaked dream to the next—she lit the torch from the hearth and left to seek the wyrm.

The trek was no less daunting than the barren path from Níuaskr, but this particular tangle of trees broke open after several miles to reveal a glittering black mountain range, which cut toward the sky like the back of a maul. Signe paused, for the last time she saw that distant ridge, it had been a constellation of volcanoes, ones the seers warned would burst open and drown the world at the end of days. Ash-streaked stone now sat wreathed in a mantle of obsidian.

But at their storied feet was the beginning of a road, for the heat below the earth prevented permafrost from finding purchase. And along the road were wooden bounty-poles carved with runes promising great wealth to whoever claimed their targets.

Signe approached the first one, examining the message from top to bottom:

WHOSOEVER SLAYS THE WYRM NAMED ÆGJA SHALL BE GRANTED THEIR WEIGHT IN SILVER

Ægja: the first terror wrought upon the world. Signe set the notion aside and traced a finger down to the bounty underneath.

WHOSOEVER RECOVERS HIGH PRINCE VANNI OR HIS CORPSE SHALL BE REWARDED

Certainly a less enthusiastic promise, as Grethe had said. Signe wondered how much trouble a dragon could be causing to be worth more than a king's solitary heir, but it was the wyrm she had promised to slay, so the berserker walked on.

There was no mistaking Ægja's cave when it came into view. The serrated puncture in the mountain was more maw than cavern, its fang-sharp stalactites as long as the berserker was tall. Signe brought her torch lower, not wanting the flame to obscure her vision, and walked past the great black teeth into the warm, beating heart of the mountain.

In the distant dark, something stirred. Not the familiar whisper of scales or soft mortal limbs but a hellish drag of iron, the way a blade would grind against a chipped whetstone. The sound was everywhere, a colossal reckoning from wall to wall, and getting closer.

Signe stilled. There was no point in hiding the flame—nor snuffing out her only weapon—but most serpents relied on noise and movement when they intended to ambush their prey. The ground beneath her feet rumbled before Ægja darted into the light.

It was a shining, convulsing chimera, with a beetle's glitter and a snake's desperation to shed its skin. Yet there could be no such freedom, for a hundred swords had mingled with Ægja's glorious body, entire noble lines having sacrificed themselves to try and quell the beast. A thousand shattered spears jutted quill-like along its spine, from herders and traders and just-made men, each one desperate to land a killing blow and earn their fortune. And amidst the forest of broken hafts was a gold-wrapped axe, still intact but embedded in a crust of fused metal and the tough wyrmflesh underneath.

Ægja's mouth emerged from between twisting, stannic coils. Carnassial teeth flashed, and Signe dodged to the left. Fangs the size of her torso cleaved through the floor, sending fragments of black glass flying. She glimpsed one baleful eye, its dark slit clouded with death, before the dragon's head surged back. Splinters rained from above as Ægja scoured itself against the ceiling, only to lunge again, its decorated snout opening wide and revealing a rotten, glistening gorge which reeked of spoiled oil.

With a flick of her wrist, Signe tossed the torch into the wyrm's mouth. Trembling heat provided the split-second distraction she needed to leap upward and grab one iron horn in hand. As Ægja's jaw snapped shut, Signe hauled herself onto the beast's brow and began to climb, pulling herself along from spearhead to spearhead, praying the fused metal wouldn't snap under the strain.

The dragon's body rippled with a roar, and Signe braced before Ægja slammed itself into the ceiling. Air stayed in her lungs, barely, but the impact scraped half her back bloody. She was grateful the frozen side of her body knew nothing of pain, and used her crystalline hand to grip a warped sword by its blade, hauling herself even closer to the glowing handle of the axe. Another enraged slam turned Signe's vision to stardust, but even wounded and half-blind, she continued to crawl.

The haft of the weapon was warm. Golden heat filtered through Signe's palm, stirring the power within as she gripped the axe tight. Yet even pulling with all her might, it would not budge from Ægja's storied back. Iron screamed in protest; ancient marrow held strong. So she did the most foolish possible thing and let go of the dragon entirely, putting both hands around the axe and surrendering the rest to gravity.

Ægja shuddered and threw the berserker free. Free with gold and flawless steel in her grasp, wrenched from its dreadful anchor. Signe landed on the floor of the cave, shattering another plane of stone, and shrugged off a wave of dizziness to stand again. Pieces of obsidian protruded from her back like a flock of ancient arrows as she faced down the dragon, poised to strike once more.

It lunged. Signe dropped into one of the trenches left by unspeakable fangs and angled the axe upward like a hook. The halcyon edge caught on the bottom of the dragon's mouth, momentum parting lesser metal and wyrmflesh down the centre with the ease of shears through silk. Even split asunder, it took Ægja several breaths to remember how to die, dragging the axe through dozens of ribs. Friction tore Signe's left hand open, but the frigid right endured without complaint.

When the dragon was finally still, Signe clambered out from beneath its eldritch corpse to look upon its innards. Along the gap, she could see Ægja once possessed true flesh, its withered tendons strung together between fossilised bone that glittered like opal. The wyrm's decaying guts twitched, and she brought the axe high again.

A boy tumbled out of the cruel wreckage of the dragon's body. No, not a boy—the silver torc around his neck was only given to those who survived the rites of adulthood. But he was naked and elfin, a sun-starved sort of pale. And, somehow, still breathing.

'Curse the gods.' His first words had a noble's lilt, hoarse with lack of use as he staggered back to his feet. 'Ow.'

Signe blinked but didn't lower her weapon. 'Who are you?'

'Oh…' Striking brown eyes flickered upward. 'A sacrifice gone awry. But my friends call me Vanni.'

'The High Prince?' Her face collapsed into a frown. 'There's a bounty on your name. And on the wyrm whose belly you just fell from.'

'Well, Father always was one to hedge his bets.' Vanni rubbed his face and grimaced. 'Feed me to a wyrm in exchange for its horde, then sic the realm on the creature to cover his crime and pretend I'm missing! Clever. I'm sure he's played quite the grieving sire.'

'This dragon has been plaguing these lands for months,' Signe said. 'How did you survive inside it?'

Narrow shoulders stiffened. 'Seiðr.'

The word was uttered as if Vanni expected an instant rebuke, unfathomable disgust. Yet the berserker had neither to offer. 'You wield incredible sorcery.'

'Ah, yes, but it does not aid me in a fight, so if the Last Wolf has come to take my head, then who am I to argue?' He leaned forward, long blonde hair spilling over both shoulders and baring the nape of his neck. 'Go ahead. Above or below the torc, but not *through*, please. That is quite important.'

Signe had stopped listening several words before. Recognition burned in her chest, not as relief, but a warning. 'Who told you that name? How do you know me?'

Vanni sighed and met her eyes again. 'Even without seiðr, you have "apocalypse" written across your face. God-fetters too. One of them muzzled you with that ring around your hand. I imagine you're why no one's seen the sun in a century. Not that I mind. Legend says it's terrible for the complexion.'

She arrested every instinct to strike him down. The compulsion was so heady Signe distrusted its strength; there were many reasons to kill someone else, but she refused to let it become *easy*. 'Why do you want to die?'

The prince bit his lip, annoyance creasing one pale brow. 'Does it matter? Do the deed and bring my corpse back for your silver.'

Signe finally bought the axe low, letting its edge touch the ground. 'Take this and kill yourself, then.'

'By the frenzy, will you—' Vanni stood up straight, one hand cocked against his hip. 'The death won't last. This torc will rejoin my flesh, and I can slip my spirit back in whenever I please. But there is no vengeance to be had against my father if the world believes his kingdom still has an heir.'

'After so long, would they not assume you're already dead?'

'Traitors like certainty,' Vanni said. 'If they worry a rightful claimant might appear at any moment, they won't act. So, kill me! I am giving you permission.'

Signe's lips pursed in amusement. 'That sounds like an order, Your Highness.'

'As if anybody could rule someone like you,' the prince muttered, 'but it is my most fervent wish to dismantle everything that man has built. He is a slaver and a coward who let my mother die the moment he saw she had given him a son. If you're going to wave around my beloved's axe, the least you could do is use it properly.'

Ice-split eyes glanced at the weapon. 'The man you love forged this?'

'Who said it was—' When Signe smiled, Vanni rolled his eyes. 'Ah, I walked right into that. For a wolf, you have a raven's wit.

Yes, Forseti is a fine smith, but I think he'd be happy to surrender such a treasure if I am returned to him.'

'Dead,' she noted.

'Temporarily… incapacitated,' the prince countered. 'Once I'm in the burial mound and my father is fending off every rival who wants his lands, Forseti will carry me off like a Valkyrie and we can live in some peaceful cabin in the woods somewhere. And you'll have a huge pile of silver, so everyone wins."

Signe couldn't help but admire his courage; even a worthy death was not a simple thing to face. 'I don't need silver. But I was born to clasp my jaws around the throats of tyrants, and if your execution provides that opportunity, then we have an accord.'

Vanni clapped his hands together and smiled. 'Splendid. Make sure my head has fully connected back to my body before you haul me off, please? I know it's vain, but I am trying to avoid a scar.'

For a second, Signe wanted to ruffle the prince's silken hair. He had a wicked edge that was impossibly charming. 'Only the finest beheading for a royal.'

Graceful as a swan, he bowed at the waist. Signe drew in a breath and hoisted the axe again, aiming between two high notches where Vanni's shoulders met his neck. On the exhale, she swung.

Prince Vanni greeted death in silence; he had not so much as flinched in the instant before shining steel severed him in twain. Signe watched with idle fascination as his torc glowed, runes flaring before flesh began to knit itself back together. Yet the corpse itself remained still.

'Boo!' echoed against the berserker's ear.

She whipped around, curses on her tongue, only to pause at the sight of the slender spirit floating in the air before her. Vanni had taken on an elegant yet revealing set of robes in his brief absence; Signe supposed seiðr was even easier to manipulate when one was already in the hands of the gods.

'You are magnificently large, did you know that?' The prince rose upward until their eyes were even. 'Look how high I have to get.'

'Many women have told me the same before taking me to bed,' Signe said.

'Oh, you're also…' Vanni's irreverent mask slipped for the blink of an eye, and beneath it was true relief. 'It's nice to have something in common with one's executioner.'

She scoffed. 'As if I dragged you to the block by that golden thread you call hair. I didn't cut a strand of it, by the way.'

'I noticed. For that, I'll have Forseti make you a shield too.' Vanni gestured toward the entrance of the cave. 'Shall we?'

Signe nodded and kneeled to bring the prince's body over one shoulder before setting her axe against the other. She shrugged to ease the breadth of her cloak across his delicate frame; even if the death was soon to be reversed, a righteous corpse deserved respect.

They were a mile into the snow before Vanni spoke again: 'Thank you.'

'For what?' The berserker tilted her head. 'Your neck was very easy to cut. Soft as a duck at Jól tide.'

'You don't get a chance for a new life every day.' Seriousness clouded Vanni's face with mist, turning his cheeks silver. 'Inside that poor dragon, I often wondered if I should have tried to be someone else. Someone my father might have loved.'

Signe frowned. 'If Reginn is half the man you say he is, then he is undeserving of your devotion.'

'He's twice as bad,' Vanni admitted, his scowl giving way to mirth. 'I have a terrible habit of dipping the truth in honey. But eventually, I got past that doubt, and realised that I was so very, truly fucking *angry*.'

'Good.' The berserker laughed. 'Rage is far more useful.'

'Apparently, since it gave me the mad idea to strike a bargain with whoever cut me out of that beast. Each time I heard it roar and fight, I prayed the moment had come.' He paused in the air, briefly adrift, then cleared his throat and continued to float beside Signe. 'A thousand failures endured for one victory.'

Signe thought of the goddess then, and her heart ached. 'Such is our way.'

'Don't look so dour!' Vanni chastised. 'Only I'm allowed to ruin the mood. Think about blood and maidens instead, or whatever gets you up in the morning.'

That earned another laugh from deep in her belly. What a pair they made—outcasts both, scarcely dressed but flush with ambition.

With a shared smile, Signe and Vanni set off to ruin a king.

Narcissus Munro, Thief for Hire

Kieran Craft

Behold the white clouds of the planet Tellus, turning to blackest smoke pouring from the city of Cleon. A shining example of industry and human fortitude, Cleon is a dark and deceitful pit, lit by neon and laserlight, ruled over by the biggest scumbags on this side of the planet. Everyone has a story in Cleon: a sob story for why they need to leave or a bullshit story about why they're gonna be the ones to make it. So long as I get paid, I don't particularly care what the story is.

Who am I? Well, let's pull in from that gods'-eye-view and get down and dirty, shall we? Neon-lit streets filled with desperate people, human and alien alike, scrounging for food, water, and shelter. A person dressed in rags, pushing a cart filled with everything they own down a dark alley, lit only by the spillover from the streetlights. Any second now, ten storeys above that alleyway, I'm about to be thrown out of a window.

SMASH

And there I am, Narcissus Munro. I get what you're thinking, but no, I'm not a model. I'm a thief, if you can believe it. Too beautiful for it, I agree, but it gets me a better class of client. I have my trench coat wrapped around me to protect my face (it's the moneymaker, after all), and, although it may not seem like it, the fact that I'm falling ten storeys to my death actually means something went right.

This building is a secret warehouse belonging to Hippolyta Brogan. Yes, *that* Hippolyta Brogan, the mobster who killed King Eurys. Allegedly. Not that anyone cares. There are a dozen kings across Cleon alone, and they're hardly the biggest fans of each other. Eurys didn't even have a top-of-the-line patron god like Hermes or Aphrodite to gift him weapons and defences, let alone make much of a fuss when he dropped dead. The police made cursory inquiries, then brushed it off as just one of those things.

This is Cleon, after all. If you're cocky enough to think you can rule over it, you'd better be tough enough to survive. Eurys wasn't, Hippolyta is. I'd put money on seeing her name added to the Council of Kings before long. Cleonites would love the irony of that.

Back to the broken glass; the fact I could break it at all tells me I was right. Hippolyta only just moved her cache here, so no time to beef up the security. The lower floors will have the full loadout: force fields, motion sensors, laser arrays. I think I even spied a set of robotic harpies, the kind that can hunt you down from even a drop of blood.

But the upper floors are still just old-fashioned glass, and my coat's tough enough to hold up to it. Everything happens in an instant after that. I hold something out away from me, something which, to a casual observer, might seem to be a straightforward phaser pistol. But to those in the know, it's a heinously illegal tool which does something quite useful when fired.

I fire it.

An electrified cable shoots a few feet into the air before being magnetically pulled towards the main street above, which runs the Hermetic Rail line—fifty feet above the ground, and about forty feet below me right now.

Make that thirty.

Twenty.

Ten.

The cable snaps onto the rail line. Blue-tinged sparks of electrical energy begin to flow, and I hold on for dear life as the approaching railcar catches the cable and the sudden acceleration nearly rips my arms from their sockets. Hermetic Railcars are a perfectly acceptable travel option, if somewhat cramped. Being pulled *outside* of a railcar, desperately trying not to lose my grip on what I am currently realising is a very badly designed handle… that's a less pleasant sensation.

But it's better than being shot by Hippolyta's Amazonian goons or being smashed to bits by the ground. As the train approaches its next stop, I detach the cable and go flying at speed into the force bubble designed to slow the railcars. It still hurts, like hitting water, but I brush it off. In any other city, the sight of a gorgeous man dangling from a high-speed rail line, then crashing his way into the station might have caused a bit of a commotion. But this is Cleon. Everyone sticks to their business.

Daidalos will be furious with me, but I discard the gun. I can't reassemble it here, and I'm not walking through the streets with it in my pocket. Bad enough I've got the *other* thing.

Oh, right, you didn't see the start of all this. Well, wrapped up in cloth and stuffed into my inner pocket is a filigree silver mirror. It's thousands of years old, supposedly shows you your deepest desire. Just looks like any other mirror to me, but I'd caught word that Hippolyta was about to offload a few valuable items, and after spending a few weeks tracking the cursed thing down, I wasn't going to let it get away. I just have to hope I've covered my tracks well enough to escape her vengeance. They don't call her the Fury for nothing. Well, they don't call her the Fury at all, but only because if she caught anyone doing it, she'd kill them.

I press a button on my coat collar, and the unremarkable tan fabric splits apart into hundreds of threads which get pulled into a capsule on my belt, only to be replaced by a midnight black leather jacket. I look great in it, and it won't fit the description Hippolyta's crew will put out. I weave my way through Central Station, ignoring all the many train lines that an escaping criminal might plausibly take, and instead walk straight down a dark, suspicious alley.

From the outside, this must look like a bad thing, but I have infrared sensors in my retinas, and the only warm body in here is Dio, the homeless man who claimed this alleyway a few months back. He's a nice guy, and I toss him a few credits whenever I see him, give him a meal every so often. He's usually good for some street gossip and anti-capitalist tirades, if nothing else.

From the reading on the infrared, his body temp's lower than usual. Not a lot, but noticeable. I get closer and see he's asleep. Explains the lower temp, but... has he been tucked in?

There's a scraping noise behind me. Not metal, exactly, but definitely not organic. I spin, pull out my stun ray, but something knocks it from my hand. Something I can't see in the infrared. A robot? Usually those would at least be cold. Damn, I let myself get too cocky, forgot to keep my guard up.

As I reach for my backup phaser, I blink, turning off the infrared, and my newly adjusted eyes see the glint of a knife coming for my throat. I barely dodge, leaving my phaser where it is. The knife keeps coming, giving me no chance to think. On the third swipe I spot what's so odd. The knife is metal, but not the hand holding it. It's just a regular, plain-old, ungloved, human hand.

With no body heat.

I see the next swipe coming and wrap it with one side of my coat, trapping a safe amount of fabric between the blade and my baby-soft skin (What? Thieves can moisturise). I pull on the arm, using a move that turns someone's weight against them, and flip them onto their back.

Only this figure doesn't budge. I put all my strength into the move, but it has no effect, like they weigh a ton. Heavy robots have limited motion, but this thing moves like the child of a prima ballerina and a master assassin. Its odd, inorganic-but-not-metal hand grabs the scruff of my neck and LIFTS ME INTO THE AIR! If I weren't fighting for my life right now, it would be kind of hot. (It's kind of hot anyway.)

'Who sent you?' I shout at the figure. Wait, no, the figure shouts it at me. What?

'What do you mean, who sent me?' I ask. 'Like, who sent me to that warehouse?'

'What warehouse?' the figure asks. 'Who sent you to this alley?'

The voice sounds organic. Male, young, maybe early twenties? Not like audio played through a speaker, more like a real voice box inches from my face.

'Sent me... to this... *alley?*' I let the idea sit there for a while, so he can realise how stupid it is. He doesn't budge. 'Nobody sent me. I'm passing through.'

'There is a public transit station right there if you are looking to travel, with many safer roads surrounding this one. Nobody has any legitimate reason to be in this alleyway.'

Geez, this guy must not get out much.

'Listen, I come through here every so often to check on my buddy Dio over there.' I gesture at Dio's sleeping form, which hasn't moved since the fight began. 'Did you do something to him?'

This finally makes the guy move a little, turning to look at Dio. I take the opportunity to slip the phaser from my coat to my hand.

'The vagrant is perfectly safe,' he says. 'I required the ability to move unnoticed, so I lightly sedated him and placed him in his... his domicile.'

'Right.'

'He's fine, I promise.'

Ooh, interesting. He sounds a bit worried. The first real emotion I've gotten out of this guy, and it's because he wants me to know that he hasn't hurt the old man.

'Okay, I believe you.'

There's a moment of silence. I think the guy must be working through something, but after a few seconds he lowers me back to the ground.

'Apologies. I must be quite cautious at this time, and your presence here means I will have to move on.'

'Right… are *you* okay?' I ask.

I can't see the guy's face yet, but there's enough spillover light that I can see his stance shift a little, like he's surprised at the question.

'I'm… yes, I'm… wait, who would be sent here for you?'

Damn, I was hoping he'd have missed that little tidbit.

'I don't think that's all that important right now. We're talking about you.'

'No, we are quite definitely *not* talking about—'

Sirens blare, red and blue police lights flash against the walls. We flatten ourselves against the side of the alley. The lights move on after a second. Just a patrol, not coming down here in particular. It's not there for long, but the light shines just far enough in and just for long enough that I can get a good look at the guy's face.

He's remarkably small and probably early twenties. He has perhaps the most beautiful face I've seen outside of those statues at the Museum of Classical Art. Smooth features, aquiline nose, lips just begging to be kissed. I don't really have a *type*, but he's certainly in the right ballpark. And he looks worried. More than that. In that instant, where it seems like we're about to be caught by the police, he looks absolutely terrified.

For someone strong enough to lift me by my collar like a naughty puppy (I already said it was hot, get off my back!), it's a shock to see how much he trembles at the thought of being caught. A hot twink, on the run from the cops, desperately in need of saving.

Damn, that really is my type, isn't it?

'I still don't trust you.'

'You shouldn't, I'm a lifelong criminal. But when it comes to hiding from the police, that's exactly who you want on your side. And I'm a sucker for a pretty face.'

I can't help myself, the guy blushes every time I compliment him. We're five blocks away from the alley and he still refuses to tell me his name, but he's at least following me as we weave our way through the back streets of Cleon. Now that we're occasionally out in the light, I can see that despite all of the clues to his non-humanity, it's impossible to tell just by looking, down to the peach fuzz on his cheek.

'Wanna tell me why I'm taking us south?' I ask.

'No, I must simply be away from that area should the police return. Your offer of guidance was merely a convenient opportunity. Like you said, it can be valuable to learn from scofflaws and reprobates.'

'I said nothing of the kind. Where on Tellus did you learn to talk, kid?'

'Why do you say *kid*?' he asks. 'You have no idea how old I am.'

Well, isn't that an interesting comment for an ambiguously non-human entity to make? And a deflection, too.

'I can make some guesses. You're not human, I know that.' I watch his face for any reaction, and got one: an almost shameful frown. He doesn't respond right away, so I continue. 'But if there were robots like you out in the world, it'd be all over the news. Well, they'd keep it out of the regular news, but the underground networks would be on it like anything. So you're something brand new. Broke out of the factory when you gained sentience?'

His frown is replaced by a smug smile. 'Not quite. There are no synthetics like me out in the world. I doubt there even could be.'

Synthetic, that's an older term, not used much these days. One of a kind, and he seems pretty sure about it. That gives me a good hint about who he's running from, too. Someone with enough pull to get a custom, ultra-advanced synthetic life form, keep it totally off the books for years without the tech getting out, plus enough money to get the police to do their dirty work for them (though even in the 'good days', that had never taken all that much).

'So which king are you running from?'

That gets him. He flinches.

Then everything shakes.

The wall ahead of me explodes into a shower of bricks and dust as a gargantuan automaton lumbers into our path. It's a horrendous sight, covered in steel plate armour, with glowing green eyes, a giant spike-covered fist on its right arm, and a six-barrel laser cannon built into its left. A Talos war-bot. Far less intelligent than my new synthetic twink friend, but when you can level buildings in a single blast, nobody worries about your brains.

You can tell my priorities are out of whack, because when the terrifying automaton built for the sole purpose of death and destruction appears, instead of leaving the ultra-advanced synth—who beat me in combat less than an hour ago—I reach over and pull him to safety.

Except of course I *don't*, for three glaringly obvious reasons.

Reason one: He weighs more than a small truck.

Reason two: A Talos war-bot has built-in supersonic jets, and I'm a human whose muscles are mostly there to look good, not to move well.

But perhaps most importantly, reason three: When I turn to take his arm, I am greeted with a person who looks almost identical to the twink-bot, but now in the form of a soft butch woman. She totally ignores my attempt to save her, and walks right up to the Talos which, for some utterly baffling reason, does *not* immediately destroy her. She gently holds out her hand to the gargantuan weapon.

'Please, help me. I need to get back to him.'

This genderfluid twink-bot's voice has become more feminine. She plays it up even more, pushing the damsel-in-distress vibe. I hope I'm not about to get killed because this war machine decides I've kidnapped her or something..

The Talos pauses and leans forward to put its arm around the synth, keeping its steel armour between her and… I guess, me? In that same moment, her arm unravels into a horrifying tangle of coiled wires and swarming nanites, which she injects right into the gap in the Talos' armour. The automaton freezes and shakes, the eyes flash with electrical impulses, eventually shattering into pieces. The war machine collapses to the ground while the synth remains standing.

'By Aphrodite, those things are stupid.'

Even as I look on, the synth's arm reassembles, and the rest of their body shivers before resuming a male form. The same male form that I've imagined tangled up in my bed sheets a few times this evening. And he can shape-shift too? The possibilities of that are quite interesting, I must say.

'Shall we continue?' the synth asks.

'You're joking, right?'

'No, I don't do that.'

'Miracle of miracles, we've found something you can't do.'

'Why did the domestic poultry cross the road?' he asks. 'To get to the other side.'

I just stare at him blankly.

'See, I *can* joke. I simply don't.' The handsome bastard actually smirks with that.

I might just have to marry this robot.

'Right, well, we just got attacked by a military automaton,' I say. 'Even if you did take it down like swatting a fly. So someone big is after us. I was right about it being a king, wasn't I?'

Again, that flinch.

'I *am* helping you, and that thing could have killed me,' I continue.

'I intervened before that could occur.'

'It's a war-bot. They talk to each other, learn about their targets. The next one might just open fire on us from the top of a skyscraper, and we'd be disintegrated before we knew what hit us. This is more than just ducking the cops. I think I deserve to know what's going on.'

'You are not required to help me. You may return to your life, and I can find my own way.'

'Can you? Do you know how that Talos found us? Do you even know where you're going?'

That gives him pause. Literally. He seems to freeze, as though caught between multiple thoughts. Behind him, I see movement as panels on the back of the Talos's head open, and a hologram is projected into the air between us, the giant floating head of one of the Cleonite kings, Pygmalion. No wonder he can afford a Talos, his patron is one of the big gods, Aphrodite. Weird dude, though. Old as anything, pretty sexist from what I've heard, head looks a bit squished by the alley walls, but that might just be the projection.

'TO THE INGRATE WHO HAS ABSCONDED WITH MY BELOVED GALATAEA: SURRENDER HER TO ME, AND YOUR PUNISHMENT SHALL BE MINOR. REFUSE, AND I SHALL UNLEASH THE FULL MIGHT OF ALL OF TELLUS AGAINST YOU. THE GODS THEMSELVES WILL BE AS NOTHING IN THE FACE OF MY WRATH. KEEP HER FROM ME AND I SHAL—'

The message cuts off as the synth rips the Talos's brain out.

'So which are you, the ingrate or the beloved?' I ask.

'Both, though this configuration would be the Ingrate Galataeon,' he says, staring down at the war machine at his feet. 'These will be all over the city, won't they?'

'Over the planet, by the sounds of things. Where were you trying to get to, again?'

'South… Pygmalion has spoken previously of a spaceport there. I thought I could utilise it to leave the planet.'

'That's the biggest transport hub in the city. It'll be crawling with police, they'll be on you in seconds.'

'I must leave Tellus,' he says, sounding desperate. 'I can summon transportation but need a location it can safely reach.'

He looks at me once more, and for the first time there is a real need in his eyes. Gods, those eyes rile me up.

'Can you help me?'

The worst part is, I can. But if heading to the biggest spaceport in Cleon is a dumb move, going to the spaceport atop Hippolyta Brogan's new warehouse is practically suicidal. Damn, it would make me look impressive, though, and I'm a sucker for killer robot twinks who can lift me with one hand and destroy military-grade automata with the other.

Ilion Tower has been abandoned for almost a decade. In a well-run city it would have been converted into something productive, but this is Cleon, so it just sits and rots, all 150 floors of it. The ground floor is absolutely wrecked, filled with debris, broken concrete, discarded Nekta syringes—the ephemera of a decade below the notice of the city's elites. But we're not here for the amenities.

I weave my way through the rubble, ignoring Galataeon's complaints. He's a synth; can they even *get* tetanus? The rear of the building seems to end with a large graffitied wall, but pushing on a loose panel gives access to the fire escape stairs.

The first couple of floors are just as ravaged as the ground, but only the most dedicated looters were willing to climb higher than that. On the third floor, we find what I'm looking for.

'What in Hades's name is that thing?'

'Wow, you *really* never get out, do you? Hades has got nothing to do with this, handsome. This is Hermes all the way.'

In front of us stands an early prototype of the Hermetic rail system, before it was even a rail. When it first came out, it was a giant pneumatic tube, letting people travel all across the city without a vehicle. It was remarkably popular… and led to thousands of injuries. It got replaced by the railcars, but was cheap to maintain, and is still useful in transporting cargo (which cares less about being bashed around when taking corners). It's also, for our purposes, less *public* than its more recent counterpart.

It's also still working, which is proven by the sudden updraft when I hold my hand out into an empty, round elevator shaft.

'I know you're hard to move. How good are you at landing softly?' I ask.

'I can land perfectly fine. What do you expect us to be landing *on*?' Galataeon looks terrified at the open entrance to the pneumatic tube.

'Oh, you'll see. Just follow my lead.'

Before any further objections, I step into the tube, and the air surges, flinging me up and up, through storey after storey of one of the tallest towers in Cleon. Now, this pneumatic tube is not connected to the rest of the system, per se. But that just means there's no corner to crash into at the top.

It also means that as I hit top speed at floor 150, I am flung out into the open sky above Cleon. It's actually kind of beautiful. Above the clouds I can see real, genuine sunlight. Then I start to plummet, just barely catching hold of the netting that some kind soul attached nearby for this exact purpose.

I sit there hanging for a few moments, until I hear the rush of air as Galataeon is flung out into the sky, landing on the net far more gracefully than I did, though he looks furious.

'I should kill you for that.'

'We're alive, aren't we?'

'Kill you slowly.'

'You're cute when you're mad.'

That gets him. He stammers and blushes (whoever made it so this synth could blush was a genius), and I start climbing down, not waiting for him to finish. While this tower was never properly connected, there's still a maintenance path running along outside the pneumatic system, and most of the safety rails are even still intact.

Among the many advantages of modern Hermetic rail is how fast and safe it is, but one advantage it lacks is height. Even the highest Hermetic rail only goes up to around the twentieth floor of a building. The pneumatics needed a lot more space, and in a cramped city like Cleon, that means building *up*.

That also means if you're willing to be a little risky, the tubes can act as skybridges, well out of the sight of any nosey busybodies. So within half an hour of adequately safe travel, I can present Galataeon with a ready-to-use spaceport.

Well, a private landing pad… on the roof of the building owned by Hippolyta Brogan… who I robbed about two hours ago. Maybe my sister is right when she says I'm a reckless idiot.

We jump from the polymer surface of the tube to the landing pad, and I ask Galataeon, 'When will your transport arrive?'

'I've just sent the signal. How soon would you expect a transport from one of the moons?'

Moons? Damn, that could be an issue. For one thing, even the nearest moon is tens of thousands of miles from the surface of Tellus. Light-speed ships can cover the distance in minutes, but any other kind will take hours, leaving us exposed. For another thing…

'Which moons? *Our* moons?'

'Of course.'

'The moons… that are currently occupied by and ruled by…'

'By the gods, yes.'

There it is. By definition, the criminals of Tellus don't follow many rules, but '*Steer clear of the gods*' is right up there.

'Earlier tonight, you said you didn't think there *could* be any other synths like you out there. You weren't just guessing, were you? You're pretty sure about that.'

'Certain about it.'

'You were Pygmalion's coronation gift, from the gods. I heard Aphrodite brought the love of his life… back to life.'

'The key error there would be "*back*", but otherwise, correct.'

Well, damn. I wasn't just fucking over a king (not the worst mistake I've ever made), I was specifically fucking with the thing that *made* him a king. And that thing was… a person.

'Why do you seem so surprised?' Galataeon asks. 'You seemed to work this all out much earlier.'

'I guess I just figured you were his sex-bot, or something. I didn't realise the gods were involved.'

'Don't worry. Aphrodite's ship will soon come for me, then you will be free of the risks you have taken this night.'

'Won't she be mad that you've left him?'

'You wouldn't ask that if you knew her. She made me to love and be loved. If he ever loved me, he's incapable of it now, and *want* is not the same thing. For example you clearly *want* me in your bed.'

Pick jaw up from floor, close mouth.

'But you do not know me, could not possibly love me. Not yet. Want, not love.'

'WELL, I WOULD *LOVE* FOR YOU TO GET OFF MY ROOF!' The voice of Hippolyta Brogan projects across the wind-swept landing pad. 'BUT ALSO, I FIND THAT I *WANT* YOU DEAD. WHO KNOWS, MAYBE I CAN HAVE BOTH TODAY.'

The mobster and—it seems more certain by the minute—future queen of Cleon, is currently standing across from us, surrounded by a seemingly endless mob of experienced killers, as well as a flock of robotic harpies, with their laser sights targeted… on just me. A boy loves to feel wanted. She also has six enormous hardlight scorpion tails projecting from her belt, and I would *not* put money on those being purely decorative.

I'm about to say something (gods only know what, but if I open my mouth, something sufficiently smart-ass usually comes out), when I hear a familiar hum from my side as Galataeon flares open his arm, re-forming it into something like the laser cannon from the Talos in the alley.

'This man is helping me.'

Aw, he's trying to protect me.

'Whatever punishment you may wish to unleash, it can wait until I am done with him.'

Okay, so not *that* helpful. Despite Galataeon's plea, I see no indication Hippolyta plans to ease off. A row of hardened killers, robotic harpies, and giant hologram scorpion tails ready to stab me through the guts the second I make a wrong move. Fun times.

'You've finally made a friend, Munro, how sweet. But you stole from me. That's a foolish thing to do if you want to see another sunrise.'

I know the synth is strong, he took down a military automaton, but there's just too many problems for him to handle at once, and nobody here has orders to take him alive.

Him? Hades below, why am I thinking about the risk to him rather than *me*? I'm going soft.

'What if I give you back the mirror?' I shout across the landing pad to Hippolyta.

'Oh, don't trouble yourself, I'll just loot it from your corpse.'

Okay, change of tactic. I pull out the mirror and my phaser. The *other* phaser. The one that Daidalos hacked to within an inch of its life. A regular laser pulse would reflect off the mirror or even just dissipate. But *this* phaser emits a high-intensity short-range burn capable of melting through steel or, more importantly in this moment, silver.

Hippolyta's eyes light up in fury as I show off the flare, bringing it dangerously close to the mirror.

'Don't you dare!'

'Well if you're going to kill me anyway, I might as well destroy this thing. Or we can calm down and make a deal. I give you back the mirror, you don't kill us and instead let my companion here catch his transport from your landing pad.'

'You stole from me. Returning what was taken doesn't erase that, and then you want use of my spaceport? Those two sides don't balance out, Munro.'

My eyes scan the rooftop, and I think fast. What else have I got? Gods, I wish I hadn't thrown out that Hermetic rail gun. Hippolyta may be a terrifying killer, but the woman loves her trinkets.

'I'll owe you a favour.'

She seems unmoved.

'Come on, Hippolyta. You put the word out you wanted more… employees. I didn't take you up on it, but you know I'm good. Me owing you could be worth a lot once you think of something big enough, and I'm sure you're capable of that.'

Her eyes tighten; she's interested. I might survive this night after all.

'Just one favour?'

'Two, then.'

'Just two?'

She smirks. I'm in.

'Two and the mirror. Like one of those fairy-tale pacts. Three favours: one now and the other two at a time of your choosing.'

'Throw me the mirror first.'

'Agree to the deal and I'll give you the mirror. I know you're a woman of your word.'

She reaches down to her belt and my sphincter feels like it's about to release the contents of my digestive tract, but then she deactivates her hard-light scorpion tails. 'Deal. Now, the mirror.'

I walk over, hopefully looking more calm than I feel, and hand her the mirror. She checks it over for damage but finds none. With a nod from her, her mob disperses, though the harpies hang around a bit longer than I'd have liked.

'You've got balls, Munro.'

'Indeed, and hopefully we can keep things professional so you'll never see them.'

Hippolyta Brogan rolls her eyes and turns away from me. 'He's quippy. I don't like quippy, Munro. Keep it to yourself in future.'

'Noted.'

And just like that, the landing pad empties of everyone except me, Galataeon, and one robotic harpy that still has a laser sight pointed at my head. Best not to examine how that feels right now. I turn to Galataeon to ask what happens next, but he's already climbing up a pole on the side of the roof, craning his neck to try and see further through the smog above Cleon.

Mere seconds later, a ship appears from above the horizon. Not coming over from the other edge of the world but dropping in from the void beyond the sky. For a ship to arrive that quickly from the Aphroditean moon, it must be pretty high-end. Once again, I keep underestimating just how valuable this twink is.

The shuttle touches down at the landing pad with barely a whisper, just the faintest ionic hum from the engines. No crude rockets for this ship. It's a clean white surface, with hints of rose gold around the door and other fittings. The window at the front appears to be rose-tinted as well, maybe quartz? There's nobody inside, an autonomous transport. Not an unheard-of bit of technology, just expensive. But the cost doesn't matter when you work for a deity, I suppose.

'Thank you, Narcissus.'

I blink and turn to see Galataeon has come back up to me. Idiot, letting myself get distracted by a ship when I'm about to see this gorgeous twink for the last time.

'It was no trouble, really.'

'That's a lie, it was trouble. And I appreciate you going through it for me.'

Then—and this will stay with me forever—he leans in and kisses me. His lips are soft and warm, firm but yielding; they're everything

I've ever wanted in a kiss and like nothing I've experienced. The cynic in me says that he was crafted by the goddess of love, so kissing perfectly is what he was designed for, but the romantic in me says *shut up and enjoy kissing this hot man*.

Then, the beautiful synth steps into the Aphroditean ship, rose-gold door closing behind him. The gentle pink light of the ionic engines powers up, lifting him off the surface of Tellus, into the atmosphere, and out into space.

And so here I am, no mirror, no sexy synthetic to cuddle up with, and two favours in debt to the biggest mob boss on Tellus.

Why the hell can't I stop smiling?

The Tutelary, the Assassin, and the Healer

Aliette de Bodard

*To my children, who provided respectively the excess of
jewellery and the rainbow-slugs*

Fifteen hours after Anh and her wife Hoa boarded the tutelary
ship *Widow's Comfort* under false identities, they stumbled
upon a body.

Well. Not stumbled, so much as found. Anh and Hoa were in the
drawing room of *Widow's Comfort*, looking for tea they could take
back and enjoy in their quarters—when something drew Anh's eye.

Anh wasn't capable of consciously saying what it was: something a little amiss in the arrangement of the five rattan tables and
cloth-draped chairs, something a little off in the shadows that fell
on the ever-changing pattern of slow swirls on the tutelary's floor.
She just walked to one of the chairs, pulled it… and the body fell
out in a haphazard arrangement of flopping limbs, sightless eyes
gazing towards the vast, endlessly receding darkness that was the
tutelary's ceiling.

Behind her, Hoa sucked in a sharp, shocked breath.

Anh didn't move. She stared at the body; she'd never seen him before, a youthful-looking man with a smooth, beardless face, the clothes of the lower merchant class—rough-cut silk with plenty of ornaments to make up for the lack of quality of the cloth, in flamboyant colours—and a deep gouge in his skull where someone had hit him.

'Do you know him?' she asked Hoa. As though the tutelary didn't have just six crew on board in addition to them, their faces all known.

Hoa, who was kind, would say Anh was in shock; Anh, to whom kindness was seldom useful, just felt really annoyed at the unforeseen situation that had fallen into her lap… or rather, at her feet.

It was a terribly inconvenient body, and nothing about the situation made Anh happy. She didn't like tutelaries. They were inhuman, unpredictable, and liable to space people on their own logic. But Hoa had talked her into it—because Anh's master lay dying, back at the clan home; because tutelaries were fast, and time mattered, and time was what they might not have anymore. Her world felt stretched thin; on the verge of tearing itself open; of a terrible, merciless clarity; and she wanted none of that.

The last thing Anh needed, on top of being on a ship she didn't like for a homecoming she didn't want, was an *amateur* murder.

'No, I don't know him. And I'm not sure we can stay out of this one,' said Hoa—of their couple, the one who wanted to do right by everyone, who had trouble breaking the unspoken rules of kindness.

Anh grimaced. She'd dealt with bodies. She'd created them when she was in a hurry. 'I don't want to get mixed up with the ship.'

Hoa's gaze was full of pity. *You don't have a choice.* At least she had the grace not to say it aloud. 'It wasn't a violation of the guiding proverb.'

It wasn't, or they'd all be dead. Tutelaries had few rules, but breaking their one basic law of functioning was a way to get spaced. This tutelary's guiding proverb was about not mixing sex and business, which—given that everyone on board had entered a contract with the tutelary—meant no trying anything horny on board. A murder, even a very sloppy one, wasn't *technically* a violation.

Anh grimaced. 'The ship still isn't going to be happy.'

It was a problem. A big one. Tutelaries had strong feelings about who was in charge of killing for the duration of any trip.

Should they report to *Widow's Comfort*? Anh couldn't remember the protocol; they varied so much from tutelary to tutelary. People who took a tutelary traded speed and convenience in exchange for putting themselves at the mercy of vast and unknowable intelligences who found humans mildly entertaining at best and annoying as ticks at worst.

Tutelaries were particularly popular among merchants: they didn't take passengers per se but they did recruit crew, and passage came with a hold allotment proportionate to one's duties on board. Many a merchant had found themselves helping with navigation, cooking for the crew, or even becoming the Ambassador, their entire personalities subsumed in the ship's for the duration of the journey. They all said the venture was worth it in profit; even if some of them had a tremor in their voice and a shadow in their eyes as they said it. Anh and Hoa had taken on the duties of food supplies, which had gifted them a cabin and hold allotment sufficient for their small stash of belongings, and, more importantly, wouldn't require interaction with the ship after their departure.

Because Anh had had no intention of ever finding out more about tutelaries and tremors and shadows, and yet…

For a while, the messages from Master Gia Hong, Anh's mentor, had grown shorter, more graceless. Words that weren't quite right, when Master Gia Hong had always been precise, elegant, graceful. Anh had only been half surprised when the final message hadn't been from Gia Hong but from a youngling of the clan, and said simply, 'Come. Not much time.'

Anh had desperately wanted to go home, but now she was on board the tutelary, she didn't want the journey to end. Because arriving—seeing Gia Hong so very sick and diminished—seeing the cold, inescapable reality of it—was too much. She dealt death to others; and what hypocrisy was it, that she wasn't ready for death to be dealt to her?

She didn't care. It was *her* master.

A shocked, strangled noise behind her. Anh became aware they were no longer alone in the drawing room.

It was Liem, the small and forceful merchant who'd taken charge of the onboard schedule as soon as they'd boarded, and Tuyet, a quieter fellow who'd barely said a word the entire time. Liem had their tablet—they'd obviously been checking off items on one list or another. Tuyet had been pushing a tray laden with crockery, from large soup bowls to smaller rice bowls, and fine chopsticks. She'd now stopped, staring into the room with the tray parked between her and the body. Anh guessed it probably made Tuyet feel reassured but it had no protective efficiency whatsoever, whether against an angry ghost or an angry tutelary.

'Huong Thao, what under heaven—?' Liem—who was using Anh's borrowed identity—sounded not so much shocked as outraged.

Anh raised her hands as if to ward Liem off. 'It's a body,' she said. 'Someone died here.'

'We just found him,' Hoa said, her tone placating.

'Just?' Liem's voice was incredulous. 'How exactly?'

'Because he was there. It was obvious,' Anh said, sharply. It wasn't that she felt trapped exactly—she could vault over the tray and push Tuyet out of the way, or any of the more lethal options. But the exit wasn't clear, which meant it'd be messy. And Anh hated mess, especially in a situation like this where nothing was under control.

Liem's gaze moved from the body to the chair it had lain under. 'Obvious.' Their voice was softer now but no less dubious. 'I guess to you, it would be.'

And *that* was very clearly an accusation, and Anh didn't have time for any of this, not from Liem, who'd enjoyed her role bossing every crew member around a *little* too much. 'You're going to clarify what you meant.'

'Sweetheart—' Hoa had laid a hand on Anh's wrist, gently pressing: a reminder. *Please don't be aggressive. We're undercover.*

It was, sadly, a bit too late for any of this, because Liem was nothing if not forthright. 'The body—whoever it is, and we're going to need to come back to this—was well-hidden. Except if you happen to know where it is because you put it there.'

Hoa's hand tightened; Anh shook it loose, gently, making a gesture of 'all is fine' at her wife. This wasn't a time for diplomacy. 'How dare you accuse me of committing murder?'

Liem wasn't so easily deterred from their conclusions. 'It's a reasonable-enough assumption, given you found the body.'

'I would not be so sloppy,' Anh snapped.

The room became deathly quiet. Hoa winced. 'What she means,' she started, but it was too late.

'Sloppy?' Liem drew themself to their full height. 'You think you can be disrespectful to the dead?'

Anh's personal and professional pride were at stake here—which certainly explained why she felt compelled to defend herself in spite of the poor strategy. 'I'm nothing but respectful.'

Tuyet said, plaintively, 'I don't think there's any need for this.' She was unused to violence and scared, and also naturally inclined to ease things. 'Please.'

Liem threw her a withering glance. 'Don't meddle.' And Tuyet shrank back as if she'd been chastised; except in that one moment Anh caught a glimpse of something else: a deep and powerfully repressed anger. The simmering resentment of the quiet and ignored, which might—just might—be pushed too far. And who knew what Tuyet would do, if she snapped?

And Liem… of course people like Liem always thought they could take precedence and would think nothing of a murder if it benefited them.

'You will cease these baseless quarrels.' The voice came from behind Tuyet, but it echoed, as if under the ceiling of some vast, crumbling temple on the edge of the universe. It took on more echoes, vibrating under Anh's ribs, each syllable resonating with her body in a whole host of unpleasant ways.

Hoa, who hadn't been involved with Liem, was faster than Anh. 'Ambassador,' she said. 'You honour us with your presence.'

'Enough,' the Ambassador said, moving from behind Tuyet and coming into the room as if the tray hadn't been there at all—moving gracefully and a little too fluidly, in that uncanny valley of the not-quite-human. Anh couldn't remember the Ambassador's name from before *Widow's Comfort* possessed him. He was a middle-aged man, moving with the easy authority of a gentleman, his eyes a little too unblinking, his lips slightly out of sync with the words he was uttering, as if he were speaking a language but they were hearing another. Anh would rather not have dealt with him at all. Inhuman, incomprehensible—Anh should never have agreed to board him.

'A body,' the Ambassador said.

'Huong Thao found it,' Liem said, pointing. Anh managed to shrug casually, but it was habit. Inwardly she wanted to be anywhere but here.

'That isn't what you were saying,' the Ambassador said. He looked at Liem until the merchant started sweating—and, to be entirely fair to Liem, Anh would have sweated too, dissected under that gaze. To all intents and purposes, the Ambassador *was* the ship.

Liem opened their mouth. The Ambassador made a fist with his hand. 'No,' he said. And Liem shut up instantly. Good. And, to Anh, 'You,' he said, every syllable feeling like it was going to force

Anh's heart out of her chest. 'You and your companion will come with me for a private conversation.'

Exactly what Anh hadn't wanted. Exactly why they should never have taken a tutelary. Most people tended not to come back from these 'conversations', or to do so with their brains scrambled. Anh's gaze met Hoa's. Hoa rolled her shoulders, sighing.

Yeah. They both knew; it wasn't like they had a choice.

The Ambassador took them to a room that didn't belong to any of the crew, but like many of the rooms on the ship it appeared to have been haphazardly cobbled together with only a marginal eye to human comfort. A terrarium held a series of rainbow-coloured slugs curled together, and the tray of drinks was a combination of the perfectly acceptable (tea), the weird (soy sauce), and the decidedly inappropriate (Anh was reasonably sure the reddish, shining liquid in the last bottle was liquid cinnabar. At least the bottle was hermetically sealed, which she supposed reduced the risks of anyone ingesting it by mistake).

'Well,' the Ambassador said. He made no move to offer them drinks, which under the circumstances Anh was thankful for. She wasn't sure she'd have been able to fake comfort. He leant against the wall, framed in the same slowly moving traceries as on the floor—as if either Anh or Hoa needed a not-too-subtle reminder that he was the ship personified.

'Why are we here?' Hoa asked, softly. Anh stepped back, letting her handle the interaction. Hoa was a healer of the mind, used to dealing with anxiety, trauma, and the myriad ways in which the coherence of the brain could fail. It made her better qualified to talk than Anh, whose approach to diplomacy consisted of deflecting, lying, and stabbing, not necessarily in that order.

A soft noise from the Ambassador. He was watching them, eyes unblinking, and in those eyes Anh saw... darkness. The vastness of time and space and everything in between, of a universe she couldn't possibly hope to see in its entirety without losing her mind, let alone survive in. 'Pham Van Anh. Pham Thi Thanh Hoa.'

Anh's stomach plummeted. These were their names. Their clan names, not the fake identities they'd given as they boarded *Widow's Comfort*.

'Did you really think I wouldn't find out? It's an honour to host the Twin Pearls of the Pham Clan.'

The best assassin of her generation, and the best healer. Sent into sticky situations which required making people cooperate, whether that required a stab to the jugular or a heart-to-heart talk.

'We're not here on business,' Hoa said, slowly, carefully. 'We don't intend to violate your guiding proverb.'

A sound from the Ambassador, a rumble that shook the entire room from floor to endless darkness of the ceiling and made Anh's heart skip a beat. Laughter. It was only laughter. 'A shame,' the Ambassador said. 'Because business is precisely what I require from you.'

'I don't understand,' Hoa said. 'We have followed the terms of the contract.'

'Yes.' The Ambassador's eyes glazed for a bare moment. 'Your hold allotment is very small, I see. As per the contract, I don't know what's in it, but hardly anything that would turn you a profit. The odds are it's only your personal things. You provided supplies in exchange for this allotment. I can guess you might have wanted some rest.'

Hoa said, 'We're on our way back to the clan as a matter of some urgency.'

A silence. The Ambassador's gaze moved to Anh, who fought the urge to take a step backward. 'On your behalf, I take it?'

'How—how would you know it?'

'You're the one who has looked desperate to escape since she boarded the ship.'

That was not true. Anh didn't want to escape; she just... she didn't want her teacher to die—her old, cantankerous, wise, seemingly immortal teacher with her habit of chewing too much betel, an unmoving constant in a tangled world of politics and assassinations.

Anh went for frankness, an unexpected weapon in her arsenal. 'I'm not ready to have that conversation yet.'

'Or ever? Mmm,' the Ambassador said. He didn't seem to care much, but he did change the subject. 'You found the body?'

'Yes,' Anh said. 'I have… some experience.'

Again, laughter that threatened to make Anh's ribs split with the force of its vibrations. 'Yes. Exactly. You will solve this murder for me.'

'I. What?'

The Ambassador relaxed against the wall, and for a moment his outline wavered and he was the vastness of the ship, the incomprehensible and vaguely hostile intelligence that they'd entered a contract with. 'I am the master of life and death while in transit. No one usurps those powers. But I don't know who killed that man.'

'Neither do we!' Hoa said. It wasn't a very strong protest: they both knew better than to upset the ship.

'No, but you will work it out. You are, after all, known for this.'

Anh took a deep breath. As she'd foreseen, the ship wasn't happy. She just hadn't expected to be summarily put in charge of an investigation. 'That's not really where my skills lie.'

'Everyone else is a merchant,' the Ambassador said, and there was… contempt? anger? in his voice. 'They negotiate deals. They dream of fortunes. They think of what can be bought and sold. They're unfit to provide clarity.'

'You *invited* them on board,' Hoa said, with horrified fascination.

'Humans can be very entertaining,' the Ambassador said. 'Sadly, this lot has proved rather defective in that regard.'

Except for Hoa and her, Anh guessed. And a murderer, though she doubted *Widow's Comfort* found said murder very entertaining. The Ambassador was clearly outraged and in need of taking out anger on someone.

Better the murderer than them. They were on pretty shaky ground: contracts weren't made to be signed by false identities, though it wasn't the worst violation they could have committed.

Anh sighed. 'What will you do to them when we find them?'

'Them?'

'Whoever is responsible for the murder.'

The Ambassador's teeth glittered the colour of rot in the darkness. 'We shall have… a chat.'

A chat. Well, none of her business. The optics were bad, but honestly no one would miss such a shoddy murderer. Whatever the ship planned to do to them, it'd be justice. And one more death was hardly likely to make Anh blink.

Not that they had any say in this. It hadn't been a request and would never be one.

'So,' she said, forcing a bright smile she didn't feel an ounce of, 'where do you want us to start?'

It turned out, rather obviously, that *Widow's Comfort* was much better at threatening people than running murder investigations. Anh's specialty was, of course, to be the *cause* of them. Hoa had therefore rolled her eyes and suggested that both of them start with the corpse while she went back to the crew's rooms to see who was behaving in an atypical fashion.

The Ambassador had the body brought to the room and departed. With Hoa gone, Anh was alone in the room. Small mercies. She knelt by the corpse, glaring at it. Lower merchant class; the silk was too tough, and he'd worn too many bracelets. He'd also liked colour. A lot of colour. Vivid purples and blues and reds, and jewellery everywhere: he'd have stood out in any crowd, laughing and twinkling. Something about the pattern on the bracelets bothered her, but she wasn't sure what exactly—a feeling she tried to chase but it wouldn't come.

Corpses weren't actually Anh's area of expertise, but she did know a few basics. First off, he was definitely dead. Usually she'd check the pulse before leaving the scene, but quite honestly, given the way the skull had caved in, that was a little too much. Their mystery passenger was dead, and had been dead long enough for the rigidity to have passed—which, insofar as she remembered, didn't mean much, timewise. He had dark skin, high cheekbones, the smooth face of a youth, and tousled hair—a pretty boy-man, if one was into that sort of person (Anh was lesbian, so *no*), except now half of his face looked all scrunched up. A blow to the head with a heavy object.

A totally amateur, unpremeditated murder. No assassin worth their pay would pick such a risky method of dispatch: it would require enough strength to hit the skull hard enough, and head wounds were notoriously unreliable ways of killing. Even with a heavy object...

Something was bothering Anh again, and again she felt unsure what. Perhaps the act of being with the dead and not performing the appropriate acts? She dutifully put her fingers on the wrist, looking for a pulse that was most definitely not there. The man looked like a corpse, in a way that she didn't usually get a chance to see. In many ways, it felt like she was at a clan funeral, the body on display, preserved so that it remained frozen in that not-quite-life. Something that was human-shaped but didn't quite feel right. The utter lack of movement, of so much as a breath.

Master Gia Hong's skin would feel like this, at her funeral.

No, Anh didn't want to think about this. She couldn't.

She wanted Gia Hong to be, not just alive, but well. She wanted to see her teacher one last time; to be lectured on the merits of poisons by that familiar querulous voice; to share clan gossip around crumbly bean cakes and grassy tea. Just once more—once more back to the familiar rather than in a world where Gia Hong was gone and the last of the old generation was no longer with them.

She didn't want to face the world where *she* was the old generation.

The door to the room opened, and the Ambassador walked in again—ostentatiously taking up a position against the walls, observing. Anh felt her tension return. She wanted to solve it the usual way, by stabbing something or someone, and it was hard to disentangle that from the other source of disquiet. *Think*, think back to before the ship entered. No, not to Master Gia Hong's death. To before.

Heavy object. He'd been hit by a heavy object.

She said, more sharply than she intended: 'Nothing is heavy here.'

A silence.

Anh said, 'Ambassador?'

The Ambassador smiled. 'Call me Yen. It was the merchant's name before he relinquished it to me.'

And it was easier? Or Yen was still in there? Anh couldn't help the morbid question. 'Is he in there? In your body?'

That laugh again, making the walls tremble. 'I said "Relinquish". He won't remember.'

'But will you?' Anh asked.

'Some things,' Yen said.

Hence the attraction, that fascination with humans the same way humans were fascinated by… Anh would have said tigers, but the closest analogy was probably some kind of insect pinned under glass. 'All right. Yen, then. Everything here is held in place, isn't it?'

Yen frowned. His gaze swept the room—the swirls on the floor, the darkness above them, the slight hum that could have been motors or the ship's breathing. 'It isn't always a smooth ride through space, even on a tutelary.'

No, of course not. It had been quiet but there had been pockets of varying gravity, and of course there was always the risk of the ship itself wildly swerving for reasons of their own. But the important point was—as everyone in the room now saw—every single piece of furniture and every ornament was bolted down so that it couldn't fly upwards and hit someone. A heavy object would be terribly convenient for a murder but also very hard to find.

Yen completed Anh's reasoning. 'You mean there was nothing he could have been hit with.'

Anh grimaced. 'Not quite true,' she said. 'There is one place where things aren't quite held to the same standard. Yen?'

Everything in storage would also be bolted down—but the contents of merchants' crates wouldn't be.

Yen turned. For a bare moment, the shadows in his eyes weren't odd and fractured—for a moment he was simply whoever he'd been before the ship. Then that illusion passed, and he was again the ship, terrible and distant and alien. 'Yes?'

'Can you take me to the hold?'

On their way to the hold—down twisting corridors where up became down with dazzling ease—Yen slowed down enough for Anh to catch up with him. 'I've notified your wife to meet us.'

Anh didn't ask how. She didn't want to know more about the ship. But she nodded. 'Thank you.'

Yen nodded. 'You're rather better at this than—'

'Than you expected me to be?' Anh said, too sharply.

Yen threw her an odd glance. 'Than you said you were,' he added, simply.

'Oh.' Anh felt obscurely embarrassed. 'Sorry.' And then stopped. Why was she even apologising to a tutelary?

A soft noise from Yen, which felt like someone was scooping up Anh's innards with a hook. Laughter. 'You really don't like being here, do you? You think of me as a convenience you'd rather avoid. Because I contract with the crew? Because I hold Yen's body?'

Because they made contracts with the living; because they toyed with humans for their amusement; because—Anh stopped. She heard Gia Hong's querulous voice in her mind, as her mentor reached for a teacup on the low table between them: *Be unkind only for good reason. An assassin has enough enemies without making more.*

Unkindness didn't really apply to a tutelary, did it? And yet… She felt oddly ashamed to voice this in front of Yen. It felt decidedly impolite. Which shouldn't have mattered at all, except that it did. She said, finally, 'You're smart enough to tell who's ill at ease among us. Why ask us to solve that murder?'

A change in Yen's expression, an odd melting of the features that brought the eyes closer to each other for a split moment. 'You're human,' he said.

'Yes?'

'Humans make no sense.' Yen made a sound that twisted in Anh's ribcage. 'You take risks for no good reason. You gift your own bodies to me and believe I'll take care of a biology and neurology I don't understand. You're fragile, yet you act as though you aren't; as if believing in your own invincibility would cause it to be true. I can see your emotions, but what good is that if I can't understand where they're coming from?'

Frustration. Anh knew the feeling. She couldn't help the bitter laughter that welled up in her. 'You've got the wrong human. Hoa is the one who understands people.'

'And you don't?'

Gia Hong had tried to teach Anh—*everything*, from poisons to stabbing to navigating conversations. She *knew* how to do all of this, but it remained odd. Senseless. Rules she'd learnt because she had to, not because they made sense. 'I kill people for a living. Insofar as I'm concerned, everyone believes too much of their own invincibility. And no one is aware enough of how short life can be.'

And wasn't that an irony, with Anh racing to outrun death.

Yen stared at her, for a while. He said nothing, merely cocked his head as though surprised, the sheer angle of his neck utterly wrong. 'I don't understand why anyone would commit murder here.'

'Why not?' Anh said.

'In the depths of space, on board a ship you don't master? Surely they could have waited until we docked.'

Anh said, 'It was impulse. And yes, I agree. A tutelary is a terrible place to commit murder. I guess the question is who got the impulse, and why?' She smiled, and after a short while Yen, looking at her, smiled too. Anh felt an odd warmth in her belly, a sense of companionship in dubious circumstances—the same kind that tied her and Hoa when on a mission—not the love between them, that was private and specific, but the knowledge they were all in this together.

'You're an odd one,' Yen said. It sounded approving.

'You like odd.'

'You humans make no sense,' Yen said again, and this time Anh understood. What made no sense was all the more fascinating. The same reason she tried to weigh risks every time she set out: trying to make the universe, in however small a space, be within her control, or at least within her understanding.

'Tell me—' Yen said again, after a moment of silence.

'Yes?'

'You understand risk. You don't much like the unknown. Why are you on board me?'

Anh opened her mouth, closed it. A silence, spreading under the vast ceilings of the ship. Yen said, 'Not a question you're required to answer.'

'You would respect my consent?'

Again, that sound that twisted in her ribcage. Laughter, but with an edge. 'I don't act capriciously. I sign contracts and respect them. I promised you all safe passage unless you broke my guiding proverb. Nowhere did the contract specify abject obedience. It's uninteresting.'

Uninteresting. Anh would have laughed, but she felt too much... not on edge. On the edge of something. Something *different*. A risk she couldn't quite master.

She said, finally, 'Someone I know is dying, and I want to be there when she passes.' Something human. 'Do ships even die?'

Yen's voice was even. 'We do. It takes a longer time.' And, slowly, carefully, 'I understand. Death is difficult.'

Something like this, yes. Not something Anh expected from a normal human interaction, but nevertheless… 'Yes,' she said. 'Thank you.'

'Why?'

'For the kindness.'

Yen grimaced. 'If that's what you choose to call it. I care little for names. Let's go to the hold.'

Anh watched the ship stride ahead. The entire ship seemed to… expect where Yen was going, the light shifting and changing for him, and the darkness above them descending towards the slim man, hugging the curve of his shoulders—except that said darkness glinted and blinked, something in its folds looking altogether too much like eyes.

Anh was going to have to admit one thing to herself: she wasn't quite sure what to make of the ship, not anymore.

Like much of the ship, the hold felt *invented* for the crew, like theatre put on just for them. On arrival, Anh was lagging far behind Yen, trying not to worry about five or six different things—all different ways of avoiding thoughts of Gia Hong.

What was taking Hoa so long? Yen had asked her to meet them here, yet her wife—her scrupulous, gentle wife—was nowhere to be seen. It was very unlike Hoa to be late.

What did it take for someone to commit murder? In Anh's experience, a specific mindset—a deliberate distancing from human life, which not everyone had—or great desperation. If any of the crew had such a mindset, they hid it very well. Which meant desperation.

But why would any of the crew be so desperate?

Anyone on board a tutelary wanted time badly enough to make a pact with unknown entities. But murder wouldn't get them to their destination faster. They'd known that, since they'd hidden the body well.

There was a high-pitched whine, starting on the edge of hearing, morphing into a sound like a slow blade drawn across Anh's chest, nicking every rib as it went. She wanted to leave—wanted to run—except the noise filled the corridor. Something dripped from her nose—blood, oozing from nostrils and from under the sclera of her eyes. Blood dripping on the floor, and everywhere it touched, the swirls of the ship became thicker, like swarms of rice fish gathering to feast.

Which was giving her the creeps, and ancestors knew she didn't scare easily.

Humans can be rather entertaining. And what kind of twisted things did the ship consider was entertainment…?

Focus focus focus. As if it were easy in a situation like this, beloved. Anh took a breath that seemed to hurt in all the unexpected places of her chest, and moved forward.

The door to the hold was open and Yen stood on the threshold, framed by darkness above and the frantic swirls on the floor. He was the source of the noise, his mouth open, too large, gaping, with teeth that glinted sharp and unnatural in the dim light. His eyes were dark as black holes, windows on devastated worlds.

Surprised? Angry? Demons take Anh if she had any clue.

'Is everything all right?' Anh asked, calmly and levelly. Pretending she was Hoa and this was just a troublesome patient.

'No,' Yen said, and said nothing more.

Expecting Anh to work it out? As if it were obvious? Anh walked around Yen and into the hold.

It looked like a cross between a coral reef and a gigantic, sprouting deciduous tree, a spreading mass of huge spongious modules, each a separate hold allotment. A winding path led from one to another, with every module a different colour—a low fluorescence that somehow promised hues just beyond the threshold of human vision. She could see them all, and only six were lit. Pastel blue and garish white was where Anh and Hoa had put their meagre belongings—as the ship had guessed, no more than a handful of suitcases. One of the others had to belong to the cantankerous and bossy Liem, another to the easily frightened and yet so very resentful Tuyet.

One of the other modules was wrong. At first Anh wasn't quite sure what it was, but then she saw a subtle shift of the colours that shot through it, a slight darkening. She walked to it; it was open, huge inside, and, on the floor, the usual traceries of the ship, and…

It was empty save for two crates, one of which was halfway open. Which made no sense, because space aboard a tutelary was so valuable, and why would one waste so much of it when—

And then she saw it. A colourful cloth, covered by a blanket—a bed for a stowaway, making it all too clear where the mysterious man had come from. By its side, a familiar heavy bracelet and a smear of blood—this was where he'd died. The half-open crate probably contained the missing weapon. Nothing here, per se, was a surprise, just the sheer brazenness of it. It felt like a plot Liem might attempt, with their bossy belief that ordering other crew around made them superior. Except…

Anh walked back out. 'Yen,' she said. 'Ship. *Widow's Comfort.*'

No reaction. Yen kept staring straight ahead, mouth open in a now-soundless scream.

Why would he—

And then Anh understood. This was a big hold allotment. The biggest. And it would not have gone to Liem; no, no. It would have gone to the person who'd paid the greatest price for passage.

The person who'd given everything they owned—everything they *were*—to *Widow's Comfort.*

Anh kept her voice utterly level, but it took an effort. 'It's yours, isn't it? The hold allotment.'

Yen's position abruptly changed. He swung towards Anh, his neck twisting far too fast and far too far. 'You're mistaken,' he said, coldly.

'Yen's, then,' Anh said. 'It's Yen's.'

And the silence from the ship was answer enough.

Anh's eventful life had included many questionable deeds, but none so far had involved comforting a tutelary—and she hoped to all her ancestors it wouldn't happen again. Beyond being awkward and uncomfortable, it was just freaking scary—the ship's feedback, after all, could easily turn murderous.

Actually… Anh wasn't even sure whether she believed that anymore.

She foraged about in her sleeves and located a bar of sesame and peanut candy. She held it out to Yen, who'd not exactly collapsed but was certainly looking odd—body folded against the wall, oddly angled, the cant of his head less decisive than usual.

'Eat,' Anh said.

'I don't need sustenance.'

Anh wished she could summon the disapproving look Hoa always used, her 'don't die on me by being stupid' look. 'You don't seem well.'

'Don't be ridiculous.'

'I'm not.'

Surely tutelaries couldn't suffer from something as human as shock? But— 'You're occupying a human body,' Anh said. 'It's having reactions of its own.'

Shock? Anger? Anh considered. It wasn't human trafficking—no one would take that much risk for just monetary gain. Plus, a single person? Hardly worth all that trouble. No, it was a fair bet Yen had known who he was letting in, someone he cared for.

Yen took the bar resentfully, as if it had personally offended him.

"We asked before what you retained of Yen,' Anh said, slowly, carefully. 'I need to know—'

'I don't know the victim.' Yen's voice was cold. 'I have no memory of him. I don't know why anyone saw fit to smuggle a *human* on board.' His tone had risen, and the floor swirls were multiplying aggressively.

'This isn't the time to panic,' Anh said, sharply.

Yen glared, and for a moment he was the ship, terrifyingly remote. 'You dare?'

'Do you want this murder solved? I'll need you to focus and spend less time in denial.'

Yen's face distorted, as did the rest of the room. Great. Anh had finally pushed him too far.

But what he said instead was far more terrifying. 'Anh.'

'Yes?'

'Where is your wife?'

It took all Anh's effort to ride the sheer wave of panic that filled her. 'What do you mean? Surely, she's still asking questions. Back in the crew's rooms.'

A long, drawn silence during which Anh considered all the nightmare scenarios. She cursed herself for boarding *Widow's Comfort* in the first place, for investigating this—for deciding to travel home at all.

Then, dreadfully calm, the ship's voice: 'I sent an urgent invitation, asking her to join us at her earliest convenience. She's, by any standards, well overdue.'

'She got lost.'

'People don't get lost,' Yen growled. 'Come on.'

Anh didn't exactly know that tone—the pitch, the variation wasn't quite human—but nevertheless it spoke to her. It was the tone of someone who'd run all the scenarios, considered all the risks, and found the most likely. Anh's hands moved to the knife in her belt and the dagger in its sheath—old, old friends as comfortable to her as well-worn shoes. 'Where are we going?'

'I'll find out on the way.'

'Where' turned out to be the room where the corpse had been repatriated—where Hoa sat with her hands on her knees, looking thoughtful and utterly relaxed. Which meant nothing for someone so very good at hiding her feelings.

And which meant nothing because, facing her, gun drawn, was Tuyet, the taciturn woman who'd been in the shadow of the more-aggressive Liem.

'I wouldn't shoot,' Anh said. *Amateur.* Who under heaven took a *gun* on board a ship? Any weapon fired in that kind of confined space would only result in grief. Seriously. Except, of course, that Tuyet was desperate.

Hoa looked up, startled. 'Huong Thao,' she said, and what freaking guts Hoa had, remembering secret identities when faced with this. Anh was so proud—and angry at her for putting herself into jeopardy.

'We came as fast as we could,' Anh said.

Hoa's gaze snapped out and found Yen's—vibrating with rage.

'You will stop,' the ship said; and everything seemed to twist and melt, every sound becoming too loud and high-pitched.

But Tuyet held her ground. 'Or what? I'm lost, anyway. I know what you do to murderers.'

A look on Yen's face. Anger, but a very peculiar one. The same he'd shown to Anh. Anger at being misunderstood.

Anh looked to Hoa. 'I assume you've already tried to negotiate.'

Her wife snorted. 'It… has not been conducive.'

There was no way in hell that Anh could sneak close enough to use her knives—not before Tuyet shot Hoa. The thought that Anh might lose her wife *and* Gia Hong chilled her. It was silly— they'd survived worse, hadn't they? They'd come back from so many missions. But... life was fragile, and neither she nor Hoa were exempt from this.

'I don't even understand why you killed him,' Anh said.

'*Anyone* would have killed him,' Tuyet said, contempt and hatred in her voice, the tautness of despair; of someone who'd gone too far to turn back.

'Because he was a stowaway? That hardly—'

'You're an idiot.' Tuyet's voice was low and vicious.

Anh didn't take it personally; insofar as she was concerned, the person who committed a panicked murder on board a tutelary was the idiot. 'Why don't you explain it to me, then?'

'You wouldn't have known him because you're not a merchant.' She made that sound like a personal failure. 'But I recognised him as soon as I entered the hold. He was his lover.' Tuyet pointed to Yen with an accusing finger.

He—

Oh, ancestors.

No mixing sex and business. The tutelary's guiding proverb.

'You had to kill him,' she said, slowly, carefully. 'Before the ship spaced us all for violating their guiding proverb.'

'We signed a contract,' Tuyet said. 'And those two just thought they could break it as they pleased. Smuggling Thy Khanh on board—'

Hoa made a small noise in the back of her throat. Anh made ready to move, and then she realised that Hoa was staring not at Tuyet but at Yen.

Yen's face was odd. He had water in her eyes, and his lips were working, as if trying to speak but unable to quite find the words. Around him, the swirls shifted, frantically circling, leaving trails like blood on the floor.

'Thy Khanh.' Yen's voice had taken on a different lilt; southern islands of a beyond-clan planet, perhaps Senan or Nuoc Khe? 'His name was Thy Khanh. He laughed a lot, too much at himself. He drank tea and liked to read old books by starlight, and to race Yen down the concourses over Senan. He—' Another shudder. 'He's dead.'

'His partner,' Yen said. He used a word that meant 'soulmate' and 'lover' all at once, bound by the red thread of fate. 'They—they needed to go back. Somewhere. Something—' He closed her eyes, and the entire structure of the ship blinked around them. 'Sister. His sister was being threatened by his husband. He wanted to take away their children forever...'

Yen took a deep, slow breath. She was shaking, and Anh was surprised to find she wanted to comfort her. She opened her mouth, closed it. Yen was a ship. She didn't need any of that, and the person currently most in danger was still Hoa.

In the time it took to hesitate, Yen shuddered, the entire ship shuddering with him. His eyes flashed as black as holes, and his entire shape seemed to elongate for a brief moment, his shadow growing far too many eyes and far too many protuberances. He laughed, and it was bitter and dark. 'Humans,' he said. 'Contracts are a serious matter. I don't space people for no reason. My guiding proverb is *sex* and business, not marriage or partnership.'

Yen could have done whatever he liked to Tuyet, except it would have left Tuyet time to fire. Which meant Yen was trying to avoid killing Hoa. Whatever feelings currently gripped him—grief, anger, hurt pride—she was still in control enough.

I promised you all safe passage unless you broke my guiding proverb. Contracts. Rules. Trust.

They were at an impasse. Tuyet had nothing to lose. Yen would space her the moment she stood down, and Hoa wasn't much of a shield.

Desperate. At bay.

As she and Hoa knew, this was the worst possible place to be. No hope. No leverage.

Anh stared at the corpse. Thy Khanh. What had he been like? In death, he had the weird feeling of corpses: human-shaped and yet no longer a person. Anh had seen so many, yet there was always something profoundly disturbing in their utter stillness—no breath, not the slightest movement, and yet they had been so alive moments before.

He laughed a lot, too much at himself. He drank tea and liked to read old books by starlight, and to race Yen down the concourses over Senan. He's dead.

This would happen to Gia Hong. Anh was rushing home to watch her master's passing. One last chance for the familiar; one last chance to be upbraided; to enquire on who was marrying whom, who was rising where in the clan. One last chance to ask for advice; or to be provided it regardless of whether she asked. One last chance to breathe in the smell of camphor and chrysanthemum in Gia Hong's wide, darkened rooms, listening to the familiar creak of parquet floors, breathing in the fragrance of the jasmine Gia Hong spent so much time drinking.

One last chance to go to a home that was familiar and safe, seemingly standing apart from the passage of time. And then, when Gia Hong died, she'd be gone forever, and Anh would have to face the world—the world where the last of the old generation was no longer with them.

To face the world where *they* were the old generation.

Her eyes stung. He was dead and Gia Hong was dying, and Hoa was going to die too, and… And she'd never thought she'd say this one day, but…

'There's been enough death,' she said, slowly, carefully.

'She killed a man. On board *me*,' Yen said. Everything was growing darker and sharper, the sounds distorting, the weird smells like a mix of sandalwood and oil becoming heightened. 'Yen's partner.'

'Not your partner,' Anh said. 'And will it bring him back if you do this?'

'You're suggesting I let her walk free?'

'I'm suggesting,' Anh said, with a smoothness she didn't feel, 'that she didn't break your guiding proverb. But you can hand her over to the authorities at our next port.'

The ship's face—Yen's face—was dark.

'Tuyet?'

'You cannot possibly be serious,' Tuyet said.

Anh laughed. 'You'll find I'm very serious. By the way, my name isn't Huong Thao. It's Pham Van Anh. You're currently holding my wife hostage.'

Tuyet stopped at that. She looked at Anh and at Hoa and then at the ship. 'You knew, and you let them on board?'

'As she said, they're not violating my guiding proverb,' Yen said.

Tuyet's face was a mask. At last, she said, 'You'll hand me over to the militia?'

A sigh, from Yen. 'Why not.'

For a while, nothing moved in the room, not even the swirls on the floor. Then Tuyet stepped, shaking—away from Hoa, away from Anh, away from Yen. She threw down the gun—it landed near the corpse. Anh bent to pick it up and found herself facing Hoa. Their hands touched; connected. 'It's going to be all right,' Hoa said. 'It's over.'

Anh thought of Gia Hong, and the passage of time, and frailty, and loss. She looked up to where Yen was standing, still with that water in her eyes she now knew were tears. A ship, crying. Being merciful. Connecting with people. The world, changing, moving on, through life and death, generations shifting. She took a deep, shaking breath, trying not to cry. 'Yes,' she said, slowly, carefully, and unsure whether she was speaking to Hoa, the ship, or herself. 'It's going to be all right.'

The Dearth of Temptation

Christopher Caldwell

She is everywhere adored. In the city's walled gardens, perfumed hands place offerings of flowers and sweetwood incense before fountains blessed with her name. Link boys who light the way home for the good and great wear her image on wrist-amulets to ward against evil. The cutpurses and sneakthieves who lurk in shadows where no link boy ever trod whisper orisons to her in the dusk. And once, every spring, when she makes her procession through the city, the streets are garlanded with orchids and daffodils, and everyone, *everyone* turns out to see her pass hoping for a glance or the slightest touch as she chooses one among the city's beautiful boys to take as tribute.

Three days before the Glorious Procession, the Beaucourt lurched into the city where it spilled over into the surrounding countryside. Even at the outskirts, there was every attempt to beautify the city. Slender youths on ladders whitewashed mudbrick houses, their shutters painted in garish colours and festooned with ribbons. Sellers of cloth had set up stalls and were engaged in spirited haggling with shrewd-eyed grandhommes over the best price for brocades and satins to trim their dzizanis. The urchins looked clean-scrubbed and bright-eyed.

Covered in road dust, his naps tangled and mud-matted, the Beaucourt felt decidedly inelegant. His argent cloak of office was stained with sweat and blood, some of it his. His right hand was covered in pitch. He held a letter of introduction to the city's Electress in his left. Too tired to cast even the merest fait, he cleared his throat as he stood in the path of a youth lugging a large terra-cotta pot. The young woman dropped the pot with a thud, wiped sweat from her brow, and scowled at the Beaucourt.

'Look, you. Don't know where you come from.' Her eyes widened at the colour of his cloak—even in the marches of the Republic, the Faitworkers of the Spiral Senate elicited fear and respect—and she dropped into a rough curtsy. 'Your Honour, forgive me. I am a foolish—'

The Beaucourt shook his head and held up a hand. 'Please. No need to stand on formalities. I am a guest in Arquadel.' He attempted a forgiving smile. 'I have a letter of introduction to the Electress, and I was wondering if you could direct me to—'

'Oh, I can do better than that, Your Honour.' The girl smiled, curtsied again, then sprinted down a wynd behind them. The Beaucourt stood there bemused, watching two boys carry a sausage strung on a pole like a tremendous fish. But momentarily the girl returned, followed by two burly women carrying a sedan chair. 'Your Honour! These are my sisters, Nika and Asha. They'll take you to the Electress's hortarium, free of charge!'

The Beaucourt rummaged in his purse, found darkness, and called gold from the shadow. He offered the girl a nugget. 'I insist you take something for your help.' She goggled at it, then secreted it in her trouser pockets. The Beaucourt settled into the sedan chair and then was hoisted aloft. He felt an immediate simpatico with the large sausage carried along by the two boys.

Nika and Asha were not chatty companions, a fact the Beaucourt was grateful for. The chair was many times patched with whatever scrap fabrics were handy, and lumpy besides, but the journey had been tiresome, and the gentle sway soothed him. He drifted off, waking at various points to find the streets changed from hard-packed earth to cobblestone, then broad avenues paved with massive slabs of granite and lined with cypress trees and fragrant orange. At last they came to the walled old quarter, and the Beaucourt reached for his letter of introduction, but they passed through the open gates unchallenged.

The Electress's home, the hortarium, was a marvel of green glass worked with gold and silver filigree, bolstered by slender gilt columns wrapped in ivy and night-blooming orchids. Through the glass, the Beaucourt could see towering trees, their boughs heavy with fruit. Nika and Asha carried him to the front door and set him down delicately. The Beaucourt stood, trembled a little, and called forth another hunk of gold. He gave it to the front-most woman. She smiled without showing teeth, and the two of them hoisted the now-empty chair and made their way back through the city streets.

The Beaucourt drew his cloak around him, tried to finger-comb the tangles of his naps, and ascended the stairs to the hortarium's front doors. He raised a hand to knock, but the doors swung open at his approach, casting a warm light that cut through the shadows cast by the pediment. He reached for his letter of introduction and entered.

Presently, he found himself inside a marble vestibule with a pool filled with lotus in bloom. Golden fish darted beneath big green leaves. Directly across the pool there stood a tall, proud-looking woman wearing a djizani of emerald silk, embroidered with seed pearls. Her hair was hidden in a tignon, the copper shade bringing out fiery depths to her dark eyes. She curtsied in the southern style, with one long-fingered hand held aloft. Red gemstones in her rings and bracelets caught the light and flashed. Her voice was low and cultured. 'Your Ethereal Eminence, it is not often that a faitworker of the revered Senate graces our city. I have the honour to be the personal secretary of xheir radiance, Ngato III, Electress of Arquadel.'

The Beaucourt handed over the letter of introduction. The secretary broke the seal and scanned over the contents. She fluttered her eyelashes and dropped again into a curtsy, more formal. 'No ordinary faitworker but the Beaucourt himself. Indeed a rare honour!' She pursed her lips. 'It is my displeasure to inform you that the Electress is away on matters pertaining to xher role as city deipomp, and xhe will not return for some time.'

'Xhe?' the Beaucourt asked.

'Yes, Your Arcane Eminence. The city's ruler is *always* the Electress, regardless of their personal sex. It is a holdover from the long-lost days of the Queendom. If the matter that has brought you here is truly urgent, I can ask an acolyte to interrupt the proceedings.'

The Beaucourt shook his head. 'I am here in need of recuperation and rest, not great matters of state.'

The secretary clapped her hands twice. A sloe-eyed boy of around eighteen years opened the glass doors and rushed into the room. His hair was tightly braided into cornrows and decorated with cowrie shells. He was naked to the waist, but he wore richly worked orange trousers that flared at the knees. Around his neck he wore a silver cord with a jade effigy. He closed a fist and bowed. The secretary smiled. Her voice was almost tender. 'Edrys, you are no longer a servant. But, as a senior member of this household, would you do me the honour of directing the household staff to prepare the orangerie suite for our guest, the Beaucourt of the Spiral Senate?'

The boy bowed again and scrambled away with a terrified glance over his shoulder at the Beaucourt.

The secretary looked his sorry state over. 'I will have one of the house tailors wash and mend your cloak. And I am certain we will have a djizani befitting someone of your stature. Once you are refreshed and have partaken in a light meal, you may find the Arquadia Baths of your interest? They were named by Pulcifer Saenz himself one of the glories of the green valleys.'

The Arquadia Baths were no less remarkable than their legends. The western façade was alabaster worked into intricate sculptures of heroes from Arquadel's past. The façade was crowned with a frieze inlaid with black marble depicting the city's patron goddess of flowers standing barefoot before a gibbous moon. So skilfully sculpted that it seemed her djizani could sway in the breeze. An attendant handed the Beaucourt a strigil and a drying cloth as he entered.

The interior was a deep blue that was neither sky nor sea but recalled both. Columns of azure quartz and lapis lazuli, adorned with tiny figurines of Wadjian faience, rose from the great central bath. Gentle steam, violet fragrant with an undernote of sulphur, rose from the hot spring water that poured endlessly from the amphorae held by undines sculpted in blue marble. Laughter echoed across the waters. At the far end of the bath, wreathed in steam, four or five men with the youthful plumpness of ripe peaches cavorted in a cascade of cool water. The Beaucourt removed his borrowed djizani and folded the cloth neatly on a low bench. He entered the warm waters and sighed with relief as he submerged himself to the shoulders. He closed his eyes, cupped his hands, splashed his face. When he opened his eyes again, he saw that the youths, five of them, had swum much closer.

All of them wore the same silver cords and jade pendants that Edrys had worn at the hortarium, except the tallest. All of them were beautiful, but the tallest had an imperious gaze and a full-lipped smirk that marked him as their leader. He stood on his toes like a dancer, and rivulets ran down his toned chest, his dark brown skin silken in the ambient blue light. His cock, impressive, bobbed near the surface of the water, almost at the level of the

Beaucourt's mouth. He caught the Beaucourt's eye and said aloud, 'I hear our humble backwater has a most distinguished guest! A dread faitworker!'

The Beaucourt closed his eyes again. He supposed that showing up at the Electress's home in a sedan chair, even a humble one, was never going to be a quiet event. He opened his eyes and stood up. His belly slapped against the water's surface. 'Not so dread as all that, I'm afraid.'

The youth, still on his toes, danced forward. Close enough to almost touch. He spoke in a mock whisper. 'But are you not the terrible Beaucourt, Ruiner of Rafea? Shadow Prince? Despoiler of young men with dark eyes and long lashes?' He fluttered his own very long lashes. One of his cohort laughed, a snorting unpleasant sound.

The Beaucourt sighed. 'It appears you have the measure of me. And yet you remain a stranger.'

The youth moved closer again. His taut stomach against the Beaucourt's belly. 'I? I am no one. You may call me Cyan, if that serves. I am a mere house servant, interested in matters of pleasure.' He took another step closer.

The Beaucourt doubted this; the other boys all hung on Cyan's every word. There was a boldness that came with being accustomed to being indulged. There was no place for the Beaucourt to move back. He frowned. 'I think my reputation as a despoiler is greatly exaggerated, I fear.'

Cyan moved his face in, their cheeks touching. 'Not much left to despoil, truth be told. But I am experienced in ways that may delight even you, Arcane Eminence.' His hand grazed the Beaucourt's hip. 'I have often heard that those whose faits rely on the shadows are gaunt, pale things, consumed by the darkness they command. But you, you are *robust*.'

'I am perhaps a poor practitioner of my art.'

Cyan laughed, threw his head back, exposing the throat on his long, elegant neck. He whispered, 'I can send my boys away if you're shy.'

The Beaucourt noticed Cyan's erection against his thigh. 'It is not shyness but rather fatigue. I think it would be, for you, a very dull experience.'

Cyan withdrew. 'Pity. I'm sure we'll meet again before the Glorious Procession. Boys, let's leave the gentleman to his ablutions, shall we?'

In the days before the Glorious Procession, the Beaucourt enjoyed the Electress's gracious hospitality, although he never set eyes on xher xherself. But xher secretary, whose name he learned was Alithea, was patient in answering the Beaucourt's endless questions about Arquadel's customs and culture. A djizani, he learned, when dressing oneself is always wrapped with the left hand; the right hand should be held aloft and only used to tighten the cloth across one's hips. One eats meals on cushions on the floor, and it is considered uncouth to sit up straight. But it was the silver cords that interested him most. All of the jade effigies shone with a small amount of energy and something that felt to the Beaucourt like a consciousness. He asked Alithea, who had dropped her most severe formalities and joined him at breakfast on the morning before the procession.

'Ah, yes. Once each spring, our beloved Goddess, she of the flowers, she of the cool voice, walks among us, blessing the city. The flowers bloom, and the fruits grow heavy and sweet with juices.' She sipped from a small bowl of cherry blossom tea. 'And she further blesses us by choosing one young man to be her betrothed. She takes him beyond the mountains to her bowered kingdom.'

'I see. Many young men wear the jade effigy. How are they chosen?'

'Every family in the city—from the poorest to that of the Electress xherself—who has a young male between seventeen and twenty-three summers selects one to wear the blessed jade.' Alithea's face shone with reverence.

'And Edrys? Does his family not rely on his income?'

Alithea shook her head. 'Oh no, he is most fortunate. The Electress has adopted him as xher own son.'

The Beaucourt sipped his tea and considered this.

On the morning of the Glorious Procession, the bells of the Florid Basilica rang out across the city with a frenzied melody. The Beaucourt had taken a position on the battlements of the old quarter's walls to capture a view of the proceedings. He could see the Electress as a far-off figure in robes of green, gold, and rose, standing before the towering open doors of the basilica. The grand avenue that led up the sacred hill to the temple plaza was thronged with people, all dressed in a dizzying array of djizanis, crowned with flowers, and singing raucous songs of praise.

There was a smell like stone after the rains, and the air felt tense, like the strange charge during a lightning storm. The Beaucourt exhaled slowly. A hot wind heady with the scents of primrose, black jasmine, and hyacinth whipped up the hill. The songs fell silent. The Beaucourt saw the Goddess. Riding on a steed white as sea foam. Her skin was night-dark, her hair wild. She wore a diaphanous gown, fine as spider-web. She dismounted her steed and made her way barefoot up the grand avenue. The crowd pressed in close as they dared, weeping and bowing. Some of them with arms outstretched with gifts. The Goddess touched one and then another, and they fell to the ground prostrate. An excited girl screamed, 'Oh my Goddess! Trample me with your horse! Just allow me to be near.'

The Goddess touched her on the chin but then passed her by. The youths wearing jade jostled each other, screamed out boasts of their prowess or learning to the Goddess, and she smiled at each in turn but continued up towards the hill. At last, less than thirty paces from the Beaucourt's position, she reached her hand into the crowd. She clasped hands with a youth who moved to her side. He was tall, as the Beaucourt had noted, but Cyan looked almost childlike next to the Goddess. He, too, wore a jade effigy on a silver cord, although he had not worn one three days before. The Goddess looked up. Her voice rang out, louder than the bells of her basilica, louder than thunder. 'I have chosen my tribute.' From the heavens, a rain of rose petals fell, obscuring everything. When it cleared, Cyan and the Goddess were gone.

When the Beaucourt returned to the hortarium, picking his way through the petal-strewn streets, he heard shouting. He saw the boy, Edrys, cowering before a tall figure in robes of green, gold, and rose. *The Electress.* As he drew nearer, he could see that the Electress resembled Cyan uncannily in height and mien, although years had stripped the youthful softness from xher face. Xhe shouted, 'Worthless! Useless. Ingrate! I bring you up from the gutters and you repay me like this?'

Alithea said something low that the Beaucourt could not hear. The Electress turned to her. 'Ndera is wilful?! I know that boy's ways. This is why this—' Xhe pointed at Edrys, who wept on the ground. '—was supposed to stand in his stead! The last tribute before his twenty-fourth summer, and no risk to our ancient bloodline!'

Alithea noticed the Beaucourt's approach and fell into her most formal curtsy. She hissed, 'Your Radiance, it is my honour to introduce His Arcane Eminence, Beaucourt of the Spiral Senate, and Servant of the Enduring Republic.'

The Electress wheeled around and bowed. It was begrudging and lacking the ceremony befitting his station. The Beaucourt returned the bow. 'I must first thank you, Your Radiance, for the hospitality of your home.'

Xhe grunted. 'Yes, my hospitality. You have eaten my food, drunk my wine, are wearing now a djizani from my very own wardrobe, and yet you do nothing to save my only child, my son, my heir, from oblivion!'

The Beaucourt feigned innocence. 'I admit I am confused. Your Goddess selected a humble household servant named Cyan, did she not?'

The Electress spat on the ground. 'She did not! She selected Ndera, my son and heir, destined to be Ndera IV, Electress of Arquadel on my ascension.'

He smiled at Edrys. 'But you have selected this boy as son and heir? Adopted him and gifted him with your name?'

The Electress hissed between xher teeth. 'Yes. So that he might take my son's place should the Goddess so choose. And if not, he would be heir to wealth and comfort beyond his meagre dreams as my second.'

'But Ndera wore the effigy.' The Beaucourt stroked his chin. 'This seems to be meet according to your covenant.'

'He was commanded not to! I forbade it. This spring I allowed him to remain in the city because he acquiesced, and now the fool boy will die for his hubris.'

Alithea jumped at this. 'Will he not be taken to her bowered kingdom to sit at her side for eternity?'

The Electress stared at the ground. The Beaucourt shook his head. 'Have you not wondered why none of her chosen ever return from this bowered kingdom?' he asked.

Shock washed over Alithea. The Electress drew xherself to xher full height. 'You. You Shadow Dancer. You Ruiner of Rafea. I demand by all the alliances and accords that have bound Arquadel to the Republic that you use your art to return my boy!'

The Beaucourt fell into contemplation. He knew he could tell xher that he served the Senate itself, not the puppet ruler of an unimportant domain in the marches. Xhe could be replaced by a regional governor. But he reflected that the senators would not be best pleased at having to put down a rebellion so soon after Rafea.

He spoke slowly and with a measured tone, 'Your Radiance, what would you have me do? I am not the equal of a Goddess. Not even a very small one.'

Alithea scowled at the implication.

'Bring back my son at whatever cost.' Xhe began to weep.

'And is this bowered kingdom real? Is it beyond our realm?'

The Electress shook xher head. 'No, the Goddess would have taken him to her holy sepulchre in the green mountains. It is pink granite, and the only structure for miles around.' Xhe pointed north. 'Three days ride north. You cannot miss it.'

The Beaucourt sighed. 'Three days. Will the tribute survive that length of time?'

'I… I am not sure. No one has ever witnessed her ritual.'

The Beaucourt resigned himself. 'And you are prepared to pay whatever it will cost you? It is a dangerous thing to anger a goddess.'

The Electress's gaze was steely. 'I am,' xhe said.

Not quite recovered from the ordeals that had brought him to Arquadel, and very far from an ebon gate, the Beaucourt drew shadow to him. He spread his great wings of darkness and soared towards the mountains.

The Beaucourt felt flight unmooring. His stomach twisted as the people below in Arquadel appeared to shrink to the size of seeds. He floated for a moment, whispered a few words in a long-dead language, and as his vision sharpened, he saw the structure. He flew towards it as fast as he could manage.

The sepulchre of the goddess was truly massive. Wrought from blocks as big as country houses of unmortared granite, it towered from a ravine between two mountains, over their pinnacles. It was a windowless cylinder of stone with no spire. The Beaucourt landed on the roof. It was a flat circle, seemingly made of one piece of stone. The Beaucourt wondered how the tower could support its weight. Wondered if his own weight might cause the unsupported stone to collapse. He hovered in the air again. After a moment of stillness, he heard stone scraping against stone, and slowly, along an imperceptible join, a wedge in the roof opened inwards. Stale air rushed outwards. A narrow staircase of the same pink granite spiralled down into darkness below. He heard the Goddess's voice, loud as before, amused. 'Enter, little mortal.'

He began to descend the stair. The stone overhead slid back into place and covered him in darkness.

Darkness was no problem for the Beaucourt—in many ways, it was his most stalwart companion—but the stone of the tower began to glow with a rose-gold light. As he descended, he saw in regular alcoves along the wall, corpses wrapped in cerements, wearing golden death masks and posed in funereal positions. The cloth had begun to rot away on the oldest of these corpses, revealing night-dark skin, smooth and unblemished. After an interminable time descending to the depths, no sound but his own breath, he came across one whose death mask had fallen askew. The face he saw was identical to the Goddess's.

After some time, the alcoves were no longer filled with the corpses. Each stood empty except for a golden death mask, waiting a wearer on the alcove floor. The Beaucourt had lost count, but there must have been hundreds filled. He passed hundreds more that were empty, until at last he reached the base of the tower.

Wrapped in new cerements and holding a dagger, stood the Goddess. Beneath her, on a carved wooden bier, lay Ndera, who the Beaucourt had known only as Cyan. He was bound and man-acled. His mouth gagged. The Goddess's eyes seemed bright with amusement. 'You stink of shadows, little mortal.'

The Beaucourt bowed. 'Your name is taboo, My Lady. I know not how to properly address you.'

The Goddess smiled, her teeth white. 'I have many names. I will allow you to address me as Karteia. It is a name for me long lost.'

'I am honoured to be in your presence, Karteia.' The name echoed across the room in strange pitches.

'You are. Now, tell me why you have come here? You do not smell like the lambs of Arquadel.'

'I have come here at the behest of the Electress of Arquadel to ask that you return your tribute.'

The air grew dense and heavy with the earthy scent of nightshade. Karteia's voice was the roar of the ocean. 'That little person dares demand such a thing of me? I, who have always honoured the covenant? I, who bless their homes and fields and set their green things to grow even in drought?'

The Beaucourt bowed again. 'My Lady, I demand nothing. I ask.'

'No. It is xhe who dares. Tell me, little emissary, what does xhe offer in return?'

The Beaucourt considered. The Electress hadn't offered anything. But this was surely the desperation of grief. 'Is there another you would choose in return?'

'That is not the covenant.' Karteia seemed to tower. The shadows in the room bent towards her. 'I choose. They do not choose for me.'

The Beaucourt nodded. 'May I ask, My Lady of Flowers, what will happen to him?'

Karteia looked weary. 'You have seen the lifeless bodies arrayed above?'

The Beaucourt nodded.

'This body is weak and flawed. I can exist here as this—' She gestured to her body. '—but only for a limited time. To remain here, to provide the blessings they beseech me for, I need a new vessel when the old one grows weak. This is the reason for the covenant.'

The Beaucourt closed his eyes. Karteia's form was human, but she had a core of pure, wild magic unlike the small wonders of this realm. He opened them again. 'And will nothing of this boy, Ndera, remain once you have subsumed his flesh?'

'Nothing. No blood, no sinew, no consciousness. His soul will be devoured to serve as my anchor. Only I will remain.' Her voice was soft, almost wistful. 'And I have chosen, little mortal. There is nothing you can offer me in exchange.'

The Beaucourt shook his head. 'I can offer you a way home.'

'Home?' the Goddess roared. She towered above the Beaucourt, glowing with a pale golden light. 'You have nothing to offer me. I am a Goddess. I am immortal. I am beyond your understanding.'

The Beaucourt shook his head. 'You are trapped here.' His heart filled with compassion for her. 'You come from the Golden Realm, and you cannot return. And you are reduced to this, rather than the glory of your wildness, the potential of your mutability.'

The Goddess shrank back down to human size. 'Do you lie to me? Do you dare engage in trickery? I would feel the golden light again. I would dance as the wind or a rainstorm, or build living cities from glass.'

'The Golden Realm borders the Place of Shadows. You have, My Lady, smelled the shadow upon me. I am a Beaucourt. The last, perhaps. I can open doorways.'

She smiled wryly. 'You are only a mortal. The cost would be high. What would you ask in exchange? This boy cannot be all.'

He shook his head. 'The cost is high, but I am willing to pay it. From you, I ask for only the boy.'

'Then if you do not deal falsely, he is yours.'

'We must be in the dark,' the Beaucourt said.

One by one, the lights from the stone faded. Karteia herself dampened her glow. They stood in perfect darkness.

The Beaucourt concentrated on the darkness. This was no ordinary fait. It would cost him years of his life. It would kill anyone weaker. He felt the shadows ripple at his demand, and he pulled. The darkness tore apart like a physical thing, and the coldness of the Shadow Realm filled the chamber. Tendrils of shadow reached for him, greedy for his essence. He let them find him, surround him, infuse him with their alien touch, and then he pushed. Power rippled out from him. The Shadow Realm was both infinite and infinitesimal. He opened his mind to the presence of the wild, the strange magic he felt on the Goddess, and pulled again. Golden light filled the room, causing the tendrils to retreat.

'Go!' he shouted to Karteia. She stepped through and into the golden light. He felt the portal slam shut. And he fell to the floor.

The Beaucourt slept for a time. He did not know how long. He was weakened but alive. He called for light, the first of his faits. Something he had discovered on his own long before his master tutored him in the arts of shadow. And saw Ndera on the bier, struggling against his chains. The Beaucourt removed his gag.

There was no gratitude in Ndera's eyes. 'What have you done, you idiot? You ruined everything!' He blinked back tears. 'Stupid! Stupid! All that planning for nothing.'

'What do you mean? I saved you from being devoured.'

Ndera rolled his eyes. 'You idiot! I would have become one with the Goddess. This ordinary flesh transformed into the divine. A part of me existing forever. I hate you, and I hate xher.'

The Beaucourt was very tired. 'Nothing of you would remain. Your soul extinguished. Your body transformed beyond recognition and then discarded. Left here to rot.'

'And she would have used me. *Me!* To extend her eternal glory. Something priceless. Something worth more than being a powerless ruler of a backwards city-state. Bring her back, damn you!'

'I cannot,' the Beaucourt said.

'Then take me to her!'

'No,' the Beaucourt said. 'You belonged to her and she traded you to me. I am bringing you back to your parent.'

'Slaver!' he shouted. 'Slavery is outlawed in the Republic. I shall report you to the Senate.'

The Beaucourt smirked. 'You're well within your rights, but you won't be able to do that until Arquadel.'

He left Ndera in the dark, screaming curses, and went to find a door.

They navigated out of the ravine with little difficulty. Ndera was in good health, and his years dancing allowed him to pick over the rocks with grace. Ndera threatened continually to abscond but did not know the mountains or their passes and followed the Beaucourt reluctantly. They made camp, protected by a bluff, shortly before nightfall. The Beaucourt conjured bedrolls but insisted that Ndera find firewood and start a fire.

Ndera complained. 'Why can't you just call down flames or make the rocks warm or turn the icy wind from the mountain away from us?'

The Beaucourt turned over in his bedroll so his back faced Ndera. 'I could. But I choose not to.'

Ndera grumbled to himself but then cooed in delight as a spark from his flint ignited the kindling. 'I did it!'

The Beaucourt said, 'Good. Now get yourself warm and rested. We have a long day of travel tomorrow.'

'Cantankerous bastard!'

In the quiet hours of the night, the Beaucourt felt Ndera slide into his bedroll. Ndera pressed his body close. The Beaucourt moved his arm, feeling the slippery smooth skin. The youth was naked. 'Ndera? What are you doing?'

The youth's breath was hot on his breath. 'I think we got off to a bad start. Remember how sweetly we met? I think I owe you an apology.' He flung an arm across the Beaucourt's belly, began to slide his hand lower. The Beaucourt caught Ndera by the wrist.

'I don't think this is an apology.'

Ndera's voice was butter-slick. 'I'll let you have me in any way you want. I'll let you *ruin* me. Just don't take me back to Arquadel. I'll be your assistant, your slave, whatever you want.' Ndera licked the Beaucourt's neck.

'Go back to your own bedroll. Early morning tomorrow.'

Ndera cursed and stumbled back to his side of the fire. 'Miserable old fool. Your cock broken?'

'Sure,' the Beaucourt said as he settled back to sleep.

They reached the borders of Arquadel a few days later. Ndera's clumsy attempts at seduction had stopped after the third night, and he spent the rest of the journey in sullen silence. The Beaucourt ordered a palanquin this time. One of the bearers had an easy gap-toothed smile and the sturdy physique of a working man. The Beaucourt looked at him admiringly until Ndera shut the palanquin curtains. Breaking his silence, he said, 'I can't believe you. Dragging me back to tedium and duty.'

The Beaucourt shrugged.

The palanquin-bearers delivered them to the hortarium. As they exited, the Beaucourt offered payment to the man with the gap-toothed smile. He leaned over to whisper in the Beaucourt's ear, 'Say, I live down in the garrows. If you ever find yourself there looking for fun, ask for Lim.'

The Beaucourt pressed another lump of gold into Lim's hand. 'I'll keep that in mind.'

There was an outcry as the Electress rushed out of the hortarium with Alithea hot on xher heels. Xhe ran over to Ndera and kissed his face. 'Oh my darling, my son. I thought I would never see you again. We must get you of these rags.'

Ndera pouted and looked conspiratorially at Alithea, who pretended not to see. She curtsied to the Beaucourt and held out his newly mended cloak of office, shining like new. He admired the elegant stitching on the hem before draping it over an arm.

The Electress turned to the Beaucourt. 'Your hair. It's gone all grey! I have to say I preferred it with more black.'

The Beaucourt shrugged. 'What you requested was neither easy nor without personal cost.'

Xhe gave him a moue. 'Alithia, go get my purse.' Xher voice dropped low. 'I suppose this cost is not inexpensive.'

The Beaucourt shook his head. 'When you ask a favour of me, the Beaucourt, you are asking it of the Spiral Senate, for I am a finger of their hand.'

'And what does that mean?'

'What it means is that when I make my report, the resources I have expended are resources they consider theirs. I'm afraid that some of the freedoms your city-state has enjoyed may be curtailed.' He waited a moment for the implications of this to dawn on xher. 'And your Goddess is gone. Forever. Whatever blessings she provided, whatever protection she accorded, is gone with her.'

The Electress's lips grew thin. 'You killed our Goddess? Our Lady of Flowers? How—'

'No. But she did not deign to remain here. Good luck.' He turned on his heel, then cast a look back. 'Oh, one other thing. Ndera. I promised your parent that I would return you to xhem. I have. My hold on you is over. Whatever you do from now on is your own concern.'

Ndera's eyes grew wide with surprise. The Beaucourt heard the youth's laugh echo down the avenue as he descended from the hortarium.

It was just after dusk when he made it to the garrows. An urchin gave him directions to a small mudbrick cottage at the end of the lane. The Beaucourt knocked. He heard the sound of the door unlatching. A man framed in shadow holding a lantern stood in the doorway. A gap-toothed smile. A beckoning hand welcoming him in. The Beaucourt entered, and Lim extinguished the light. But darkness was no concern for the Beaucourt.

Your World Against Mine

Adam Sass

Cypress has a message for me, but my headache has grown so loud I can't fathom removing my hands from my pained eyes long enough to see if it's urgent.

'Is this important?' I moan.

'Yes, Tiger One,' says Cypress, my little mechanical friend, in her pleasant, feminine, artificial voice. *Well, hell.* My girl never exaggerates, so—painfully—I pry my hands from my throbbing brows to accept whatever dreadful news this turns out to be. Cypress flits in the air before my throne. She's a lively bot—a funny mess of thin, brittle-looking mechanical arms and legs with a domed trash-can lid for a face and the drooping ears of a beagle. Except these aren't ears; they're layers of silken mesh, carrying trillions upon trillions of data points. Plus, she uses them to fly somehow.

I don't know how she works. I'm not her creator or even her superior. She is my only friend on this godless moon, so when she has a message for me, I listen.

Cypress hops onto my knee and squats, gracefully folding her arms and legs together until she's neatly tucked into herself. The only parts of her still visible are her domed face and drooping ears—two warm, flapping hard drives. The way they lay against my freezing leg is enough to summon a rare smile from this weary prince.

We've been together for decades, she and I, and after all the betrayals from these... *people*... I now only trust in Cypress.

'What's my message?' I ask, stroking the top of her head.

She looks up from my knee, her amber ears glowing a soft shade of lilac: *'Urgent alert for Tiger Rennévé One, prince of Bavarrón Eleven, most distant moon of the planet Bavarrón...'*

My friend's face becomes a screen. The image is shocking—me, as I was at twenty: tall, high-cheekboned, with a veritable tidal wave of black hair spilling down my royal velvet cloak. My own cloak is the same, but now—at forty—my hair has grown silver at the temples and my cheekbones have sunk from abysmal nutrition. My fists clench against the throne's wooden armrests. There's only one group who would dare use this picture of me for my communication profile.

It is a cruel taunt.

'What do those *imposters* want?' I growl.

Cypress buzzes pleasantly against my knee, as if nervous to continue—or maybe she's just sending soothing vibrations so I'll keep calm. If it's the latter, no can do.

'Tiger One, the Originator,' Cypress relays, *'we're picking up errant signals from somewhere nearby. A shipping freighter, some believe. Rescue vessels, I believe.'*

Fury inflames my lungs. 'TELL HIM—'

Impatiently, Cypress says, 'There is more'. Fuming, I fall silent, and she continues: *'I'm certain your scanners have also picked up these signals, but just in case you haven't been as aggressive in advancing your tech as we have, we thought it sportsmanlike to give you a heads-up.'*

'HOW KIND!' Hot with embarrassment, I fling myself from my throne, sweeping back my crushed velvet lilac cape to stride toward the palace window. Having leapt from my leg, Cypress follows, still playing the Ungrateful Imposter's message:

'*We ask that you not intercept or destroy these rescue vessels should they come within range of our moon.*'

'*Our* moon,' I grumble. 'It's mine…'

'*The Long Shadow approaches, and when it arrives, everyone will starve unless you act. Or—well—decline to act. All you have to do is nothing, and I will take care of intercepting our rescue. Please. This is not the time for your pride, Tiger One. Lead with compassion and save us. Yours in blood, Tiger 731.*'

The icy lilac colour fades from Cypress, returning her to neutral amber. She flits curiously by my ear as I pace. With each step, my raging thoughts engorge, filling every available crevice until I can't think of anything but murder.

Who are they to inform me of my course of action? They aren't even people!

They're copies. Clones. Meat farms I grew for testing medicine, for target practice, for a laugh, for *boredom killing*, but as soon as my young Tigers reached their teenage years, suddenly I'm a 'monster' who 'lacks compassion' and 'causes widespread, undue suffering'. They want rescue? A fantasy.

There is no rescue, not from this moon, and least of all for them.

They are doomed, all my Tigers, but especially Tiger 731. He may cluck his tongue about me and strut around his throne—a mere *facsimile* of mine, as he is a mere facsimile of me!—but the cold will claim him before he's even twenty-five years old. He is soft, and he has never faced a Long Shadow on this moon, so it is very, *very* easy for him to say, '*Tiger Rennévé, show compassion. Originator, you are heartlessly leaving your people to starve!*'

Such simple solutions are a gift to the young.

'*Why, this problem is only complex because the olds have twisted it that way!*'

Don't let people starve—what a concept! *Simply give them enough food*—ingenious! Generations of Bavarrón citizens have been unable to solve our moon's sustenance problem because we're imbeciles, and it took one of my bravest, cleverest zygotes to puzzle it out for our aging, liquefying minds. Thank you, Tiger 731. Your courage and light are matched only by your razor-sharp intellect.

I spit on the palace floor.

From my arched stone windows, the view is beauteous. The reaches of space calm me. The possibilities I once felt, gone now, but the ghosts of such feelings can nevertheless be a tonic. A boundless starfield hangs above the snowy peaks of our forested moon. The trees are bare as grape stems, eaten away by my starving subjects. The days are getting colder, our sun drifts further out with each passing year.

Soon, we'll enter the Long Shadow—a cycle I haven't experienced since I was a young man—and then we'll see how pure of heart my young Tigers remain when the true hunger hits.

My Tiger colony lies across a vast field of scorched trees and blackened earth. It's a gorgeous palace of high stone walls and turrets—identical to my own, but half the size. I like them close, but not too close. I intended to keep them apart from my kingdom while they grew, yet still raise them in a familiar environment so that after we depart the Long Shadow I may bring the survivors here to our people without culture shock.

'What are my pretties even *doing* over there?' I mutter, grasping the end of a powerful telescope as I ratchet it in their direction. Lowering myself to the eyepiece, I hold my breath, dreading what I'll find…

The throne room is the same as mine—mediaeval stonemasonry and billowing lilac tapestries embroidered in gold—but while mine remains naturally dark and dank as a cavern, my colony of joyous, un-traumatised twentysomethings have festooned it with multi-coloured lanterns. Even from this distance, their booze-soaked jazz music echoes over the barren fields. And I see him, the wretch: Tiger 731. Myself at twenty, in knee-high leather boots and with careless hair. He laughs with a gaggle of other Tigers, although clearly 731 holds court. He ruffles the cloak of one, and the copies descend into girlish giggles.

It feels like a gorilla has gripped my heart. If my heart were truly made of coal—as 731 and his acolytes so often suggest—it would soon be a diamond.

Make clones, I had thought. *It'll be neat*, I had thought.

I was unprepared for the horror of a dozen young, unspoiled, beautiful versions of myself hanging out *without* me! They whisper how terrible I am. How pathetic. How badly I need to be put down.

Have they lived what I've lived?!

NO.

Yours in blood, 731 said. They are blood alone, and blood alone does not make a man.

Let the Long Shadow come. Let it wipe its filthy gloom on their sun-dappled souls and then they can come crawling to me for forgiveness! *Tiger One*, they'll plead. *Originator! What should we do? Where should we go? Will we survive?*

That's when I'll burn them alive.

With their future demise fresh in my imagination, I turn my attention to their balcony. On *my* balcony, Cypress and I take long walks and discuss our capacities for farming, food storage, and supply rationing. Yet what are my altruistic, do-gooder darlings up to on their balcony?

Screwing like the world's about to end.

Twinks. My own naked body, sandwiched one beside the next, confronts me as far as I can see. The balcony is filled with the hairless beasts. Smooth, bony shoulders writhe. Slender, curved hips pump. Shaggy hair gets mussed. Full, slobbering lips disappear beneath the castle ledge as one Me after another drops to their knees to pleasure yet more Me's.

Without a sound, I storm away from the telescope and the Bacchanalia I had just witnessed. My throne room's grand, wall-high mirror reflects me as I pace: the Originator. A skeletal, exhausted, morally compromised soul. So much like those lovely boys, but one locked away and forgotten. Unloved. No one to please. No one to please me.

My pleasure, as 731 so aptly puts it in his coy little telegrams, is death.

Laughter overtakes me, my entire body shaking with a devilish thought.

'Are you alright, Tiger One?' Cypress asks.

'Tiger 731 is such a clever cat,' I hiss between giggles. 'Thinks I'll let my people starve.' My laughter turns to fury as I charge toward the window—pointing at my happy, screwing colony with dead-eyed assurance. 'THEY WILL NOT STARVE WHEN I FEED THEM BARBECUED CLONE MEAT!'

Spittle clogs my throat so I can't rage further, even though I would love to.

'Tiger One!' Cypress coos, draping her warm, digital ear across my cheek. But nothing will abate the hairball of anger that has wadded itself behind the pulsating veins in my neck.

'TIGER ONE.'

Blinking, I turn to my friend. She drapes her other ear onto my face, and I have to stop my lips from trembling with tears.

'Tiger… Tiger… The one and only. They are just boys. Ambitious and headstrong, just as you designed—just as you are. Remember yourself. You grew them to be your sons. Why do you greet Tiger 731 as an enemy? Let him try his way and fail, so that *you* can succeed. And if you haven't choked the life out of 731 before the Long Shadow ends, you'll have your heir.'

A tear breaks down my cheek. 'I've acted mad again.'

Cypress wipes it away with her glowing ear. 'An hourly event. How will you respond?'

'Ah. About the so-called rescue vessels?' Prowling my chamber again, I toss back my cloak and stretch my arms to the sky, tapping (ever-so-slightly) back into my old wells of prudence and calculated action. It's a familiar, dormant sensation, like an old war wound. I gaze at the stars above my dead, scorched forest. Planets—light years away—dance in and out of alignment. Not a ship in sight. The sun, so far gone now it's no larger to my eyes than the period at the end of a sentence.

Rescue.

Only fools dream of rescue when the Long Shadow is so close at hand, and us so tragically unprepared.

Not taking my eyes from the sky, I tell my friend, 'Any ship—lost, mission-bound, or otherwise—that approaches our moon is to be obliterated.'

'Understood,' Cypress replies without pause. 'And… your reply to Tiger 731?'

My precious beagle-bot flitters through my court without judgement but can, and has in the past, told me when I've gone beyond the pale. Cypress is all the moral compass I'll ever need.

'You've done enough. I'll talk to 731 myself,' I tell Cypress. 'Give the orders to our gunships. Make sure the Device is still operational, and then, please, come right back. The courtyards are restless and brutal. They… blame me.' I swallow anxiously. 'They know how important you are to me, so please—'

'They'll never catch me,' Cypress says, folding her arms and legs back inside her domed head. 'Back in a heartbeat.'

Making only the noise of a soft, whirring fan, my best friend vanishes through a narrow window into the palace courtyard.

Gone.

Baby girl.

Seized with panic, I race to the sliver-shaped window. Below, my (regrettably) starving subjects live in ramshackle tents catty-corner to each other. The window is wide enough for Cypress to slip in and out of, but no person could cross through. These double doors will remain barricaded until our food crisis has been solved.

I squint through the sliver.

My poor subjects—young and not-so-young—draped thickly in robes to brace against the rapidly coming cold, holler at each other. They brandish flaming torches, accusing one another of stealing precious food and lamp oil. 'DIDN'T TAKE YOUR BLEEDIN' BEANS!' a man hollers. 'NOTHIN' IN THAT VEGGIE GARDEN BUT OLD ROT!'

'I SEEN YA!' his neighbour bellows. 'I'LL KILL YA!'

A swish of silver cuts through the air—

But I don't get the chance to see how this knife fight ends.

An eye, large and bright, appears on the other side of the slivered window.

'Yer majesty,' the tired-sounding man croaks.

Gasping, I leap backwards. The impossible has arrived: my subjects have climbed high to my throne room. I am not easily reachable from the peasant courtyards below—unless you're deranged enough to climb the palace walls, gripping one slivered window after another. It would be a terrible fall, but he did it. His hunger must be unimaginable. They'll all die soon if they don't do something drastic. No sooner do I catch my breath than my taunting subject utters my darkest fear: 'Saw yer friend leave. Yer little… bleep bloop friend, Chestnut.'

'It's Cypress!'

The man chuckles with deranged glee. 'All I gotta do is snatch her, and you'll open those doors for me, all right. Maybe not straight away, but how 'bout once I start plucking off her spindly legs one at a time… Start chucking them through this here window… You'll open yer doors then, won't you? I know yer eatin' plenty in there—'

What the rest of this loathsome man's plots are, I'll never know.

Threaten baby girl, and it's curtains for you.

The flame begins small in my palm, but as I spin my fingers over it, the sphere grows to the size of a melon. *Melon, huh? Well, the man seems hungry, better give it to him.* I whip two fingers toward the slivered window, and my flames cleanly cut through the opening, catching the oaf square in his face. Within moments, his entire body is overtaken with the bonfire.

For one, fleeting moment, I imagine it's Tiger 731. His agony is gorgeous.

Since I control the flame, and the flame encircles the man, when I summon my hand backward, the flame—and he—comes with it. His death-rattling body is pinned against the stone as he cooks.

Stone-fired brute.

The scent is, dare I suggest it, heavenly.

And if I think so, my subjects *certainly* do.

I open my palm, and the fire extinguishes. The blackened corpse plummets soundlessly to the courtyards below. 'WHO'S HUNGRY?!' I call through the wall.

I hear a moment of anxious, bated breath and then a stampede for the fresh roast. Ravenous, gluttonous, desperate cries—some tinged with hope, some even with glee—echo as I march back towards my telescope.

Alive with a fresh kill, I am ready to face my tender-hearted clone-son.

Through the eyepiece, I catch 731 in the midst of a passionate kiss with another subordinate Me. My lip curls. He has a pot-ful of nerve calling me a deranged narcissist when he's running a cult that's taking 'self-love' to an impossible extreme.

I tap the radio on my wrist and say, booming, 'Response for Tiger 731, can you hear me? This is Tiger Rennévé, Tiger One, Tiger the Only, prince of Bavarrón Eleven.'

Silence.

Acid roils through my stomach. 'Tiger 731, can you hear me? Tiger—' Through the eyepiece, I am now forced to witness *three* Tiger clones worshipping the open, bare chest of Tiger 731. He tilts his head back, his ink-black hair swishing with such shine, just as mine once had. His Adam's apple is pointed at the sky, so pretty and vulnerable...

I press my lips directly to the wrist radio. 'TIGER 731, HURL THOSE ME-SLUTS OFF OF YOU. I AM GIVING MY ROYAL REPLY!'

On a soft, kittenish yawn, 731 taps the three clones, and they shuffle away instantly. Tiger 731 slowly (too slowly) pulls his royal cloak over his bare chest and descends the small staircase from the throne room to the balcony. He speaks into his wrist:

'Originator, I'm sorry, it was my understanding we were using Cypress to relay messages of importance. You did demand this—angrily—after our last tussle, did you not? You didn't want my voice interrupting—'

'I am aware!' I hiss. 'Those terms are for *you* to obey. Since when do *you* dictate terms, 731?!'

'The terms are yours, My Lord—'

'The terms are what I say! And now I say I am replying to you thusly!'

'As you wish.'

My words are lost in an angry exhale that blows out the speaker on my radio.

'Do you need a moment, Tiger One?'

'SHUT the FUCK up.'

As rational thought returns in drips, I watch Tiger 731 standing astride his balcony—*my* balcony—with his cloak flapping in the encroaching cold winds, wearing an expression of deepest sympathy. His putrid, much-lauded *compassion* that has all my copies draped on his every word and appendage.

'Tiger One,' he says softly, his tone disarming. 'Originator. Don't let envy cloud your mind as it's already clouded your heart.'

I gasp. 'You *insolent*—'

'Don't deny it. I'm yours in blood. I know you had to shut off your power to protect yourself, I know I'm not your first attempt at an heir, and I *know* it was their betrayal that makes you treat me like vermin.'

I can't breathe. This creature will stop at nothing.

'Originator,' he whispers tenderly, 'your heart breaks when you spy me through your timid tube of glass. I feel it. We all do—'

'Enough of your *whispering*!' I spit.

'Don't watch us pitifully through glass, from behind your curtains. Join us. You've never visited, and we crave it. Many of us are curious about having an older Tiger—'

'Keep your sick—'

'A seasoned, travelled Tiger, strong and resilient, who has survived so much, can comfort us before the Long Shadow.'

An itch begins to spread across my back and shoulders—hot and prickling—that makes me want to toss my cloak to the floor. Tiger 731's words find me despite his lips no longer moving. His words are in my head, trickling down my spine. I can't get him off me!

'It isn't sexual, Tiger One,' his voice echoes. 'It is communion. We are shards of a whole, shades of you, hues of every stripe, and for those brief moments when the broken mirror comes together, I am filled with such a powerful knowing, it almost destroys me. I want that feeling for you. You, who have been fighting so long you've forgotten your own face. Do you know what this tells me?'

My headache has gone. Miraculously, 731's voice has delivered the calm he promised. I press my hands to my cheeks to stop them from trembling.

'What does it tell you?' I ask.

His voice comes, honey-sweet and milk-smooth: 'We *must* leave this moon.'

'NO!!!!' Like that, my comfort shatters. Clutching my ears, I leap onto my balcony, heart pounding. 'Thought you'd seduce me like those silly boys? Think again, 731! I've been here before with dozens of your predecessors, and where are they now?! THE DIRT. With scant traces remaining in the colons and small intestines of my subjects' digestive systems!'

I thrust my fist at the miniscule red dot in the sky—our departing sun. 'THAT is your sole focus. Do not taunt us with dreams of rescue! No one is coming, and even if they were they aren't coming for you, sweethearts. The more you blather about rescue ships, the less time you spend planning for the Long Shadow. It will kill you, and then I'll have to start all over and grow more of you bitches and have this same conversation again in another couple years!'

731's compassionate sweetness finally collapses into what I know is our Tiger Truth: a hardened mask of fury. 'Those ships are on their way. It *is* a rescue. We can all get to safety, don't be an old fool!'

I smirk. 'Youth might've given you perky tits, but your brain is still pudding. I'm a fool old enough to remember that what's coming on those ships is not the rescue you think.'

Across our burnt fields, my young clone stands with a defiant sneer. 'When that ship comes, we're taking it,' he whispers to his wrist radio.

'How will you do that,' I ask into mine, 'when I've given orders to my gunships to down any aircraft on sight?'

'I was hoping you wouldn't say that.' Tiger 731 winces. 'But in case you did, I gave somewhat similar orders to my gunships.'

'Gunships?' I laugh. 'You don't have a—'

The crack of light comes just before the thundering sound, which comes *just* before the stone beneath my feet is pulverised into dust. There's no time to breathe before gravity drags me three stories down to the Bavarrónian soil. My back lands on rubble so finely smithereened, I roll down it like a sand dune. If it had been any sharper or harder, I would've broken my spine.

By the time I reach the blackened forest floor, every joint in my body is screaming.

Worst of all, that snit's voice spills silkily into my ear: 'I *told* you we've been aggressively updating our tech. Maybe you should've spent less time watching us blow each other and more time seeing what we were loading into the turrets, hmm?'

Betrayals. Always betrayals.

Every version, every time, in every outcome, the Tigers sabotage and betray. Not a lick of survival skills, all their ingenuity is wasted en toto on degrading me. And when I'm gone, what then? They'll be doomed.

Ah, well. Plenty of time to ponder solutions during the Long Shadow. Time to embrace slash-and-burn agriculture.

The flame begins in my palm as small as a dime, but I keep it that way. I need precision, not shock and awe. With a flick of my fingers, the flame shoots towards the colony's castle like a frog's tongue. It strikes a pillar at the castle's base—just beneath 731's balcony. However, this pillar isn't made from my castle's stone but a *far* weaker polymer. When my flame wraps around it, the whole structure gives way like a wooden dollhouse.

A dollhouse for my dolls—why would be I stupid enough to give them a stronghold with proper defences?

Down she goes.

The balcony breaks free of the castle like a stray tile and falls to the ground, along with Tiger 731, his long, elegant fawn's legs waggling in the air as he plummets. The resounding crash sends plumes of soil skyrocketing until the forest between us is once again filled with a chirping, creeping silence.

Stillness.

Then, a harsh buzz of static. My wrist radio—731's voice returns, weakly: 'Tigers… My Tigers…'

Heh. All dead.

A shame. It'll take years to regrow more clones. I'll have to reach the Device immediately—

On a clattering of pebbles, the bitch stands. Alive. His cloak is thrown off. His face and chest are smothered in dust. I don't blink. He smirks and whispers to his wrist: 'My Tigers… NOW.'

They're everywhere.

As a synchronised group, the young Tigers emerge from their hiding places—one behind every blackened, hollowed tree husk. Too many to count. Too many to fight.

They were waiting the whole time. There was no one on that balcony when 731 and I were talking. All of this was plotted—my overreaction, my rage, my gunship order, even the knowledge that I'd built their castle like a house of cards. All this to manoeuvre me—the great Originator, their tormentor—into an outnumbered street fight.

Magnificent.

Tiger 731 never had compassion. He just weaponised it to spur his fighters to loyalty and lull certain, envious, neglectful old fools into death traps. He's a strategic genius, and if he kills me on this battlefield, he very well might stand a chance at pulling many of these boys through the Long Shadow. That is, if he doesn't try to commandeer a rescue ship and doom them all.

Whoever wins, the important thing is that one Tiger survives. If he kills me and goes for that rescue ship, Tiger Rennévé's bloodline will be annihilated from existence.

Time to party.

Two dozen flame ropes reach for me at once. The young Tigers are fast… but their fire is unsure. If they'd practised, I'd already be dead. Instead, I have one spare moment to encircle myself in a white-hot belt of flame so uncrackable, the tongues of fire ricochet directly back at the young Tigers. Some dodge, but at least six go up in flames.

I've killed enough Me's that nothing fazes me anymore.

I advance through the forest toward 731. As each new boy approaches with death, I return it tenfold. Bodies drop. Clone after clone. Some flee in terror, but only a handful remain alive and loyal to protect their queen, my nemesis.

At the foot of his demolished balcony, Tiger 731 faces me, trembling with rage. He never thought I'd make it past the first blasts. Now here we are, only four cloned cuties between us.

'Don't hurt them,' Tiger 731 calls out. 'If they stand down, don't hurt them.'

Carefully, I nod. They are pawns. My true opponent waves to them, and the four boys disperse to the sidelines.

Tiger 731's chest rises and falls in exhausted, impatient breaths. 'Why do you want to stay so badly?' he asks.

'I don't.'

'Then WHY—'

'If I'm rescued, you're dead. If I'm killed, you're dead.'

'You *do* want me dead!'

I blink. In a flash, I see desperation in my young self—seeds of anguish that will define his face someday… when he's me.

In this moment, I have an impossible thought. I don't want him to be so afraid.

'It's complicated," I say. "I… I want to learn from you, learn about me from you. I've been on this moon too long to be rescued now, but if I did get rescued and lost you all before I was ready, I'd never know anything about myself. What I'm capable of, right or wrong.'

Tiger 731's sour expression softens once again. The other Tigers lower their flaming hands. 'Why couldn't we just live with you?' he asks.

I shrug. 'You weren't real to me at first. But then, once you *were*, I saw things I didn't like. Things I could've been but never was. It… hurt.'

A flash of anger crosses 731's face. 'And you don't think it hurt to hear you say I wouldn't—*couldn't*—survive what's coming? Of course we don't want to stay.'

The truth. Cypress was right—I should've led, despite their boyish taunts. My faith in them could've meant something powerful.

'Listen—' I start, but a shock wave of light and thunder cuts through the trees, forcing me to the ground. Screams erupt from where the four Tigers once stood—where now stand four smoking craters.

That wasn't me.

A row of large floodlights descends from overhead on a *whoosh* of air. The rescue ship. It's found us. Cypress hadn't reached my gunships in time.

Before the ship can touch base, I grab Tiger 731 and haul him across the rubble-strewn ground into his castle walls. This single moment of vulnerability has changed everything; where once ruthless opponents, we now cling together as father and son. My strong arms shielding him. His slender hands clamped tight around me. He moans, 'Is it the rescue?!'

'Yes, be quiet,' I whisper, pulling him behind a thick, draping lilac tapestry. Here there are no subjects, just a smattering of my more cowardly Tiger clones. No sooner are we hidden than a slew of crimson-clad soldiers storm the courtyard.

The young Tigers never stood a chance. My father's soldiers disintegrate them where they stand. Around the side of the tapestry, 731 watches the whole thing. He silently weeps, holding his breath, as his kin-slash-colony-slash-harem is unmade without a thought.

'Move,' I whisper, hauling 731 out and down a winding hallway to the throne room stairs. Once we reach them, we fake right and disappear into an alcove. I hold 731's mouth shut while crimson men and women dash past to deliver the coup de grace to my clones.

'Listen and don't argue,' I order him. 'I'm who they want. When they have me, they'll leave.' I grip his face tenderly as my tears break. He just nods, pale and stricken. 'You'll be alone. Alone on this moon. I am sorry.' 731 doesn't have time to blink before I pull him into a fierce hug, my wet cheek against his. 'I love you so much. You can do this.'

I kiss his forehead. 'Wait for them to follow me, then run to my gunships. You'll know what to do.'

Without a goodbye, I sprint across the colony's courtyard, out toward the burnt forest where my father's vessel is waiting...

Out steps a woman—blonde, draped in my shade of lilac, twenty years older than the last time I saw her.

'Tiger,' she says.

'You shouldn't have come, Mom.'

I run. The soldiers pursue. I'm not as quick as 731, but I've still got enough of my old speed to beat them to my gates before they even come close. It says something about my family that I'd rather take my chances with my wild, starving subjects than go home. Yet when I throw open the doors, Cypress flies ahead to stop me.

'You never called the gunships!' I yell.

'You're starving, Tiger,' she says sorrowfully. 'All of you. You have to go home.'

Hands reach from behind and pin me. Mother approaches, glowing at first to see me, but then... darker. 'Cypress, make sure it's really him.'

Cypress lays those beagle ears on me, filled with their infinite bytes of information. Memories are rapidly exhumed: *I'm seventeen, exploring space with Cypress... I'm lost... Freighter garbage strikes my ship... My co-pilot, Seth, is vaporised in a wall of flames as our craft is destroyed... Cypress and I barely make it to the escape pod in time... We crash on a distant moon, three star systems removed from my own... All alone, an abandoned castle waits for me, surrounded by a lush field... Who was here before me? There's no one now... Cypress and I find the Device... A baby grows quickly... My God, it's me, it's actually another me! I'm frightened, and he's even worse off, but at least I'm not alone anymore...*

'It's really you.' Mom caresses my face.

My jaw hardens as no love fills my chest. 'Twenty-three years. Seven months. Nineteen days. I *waited*!'

'It's a big galaxy, Tiger.' Mom sneers, picking up our old patterns like I left yesterday. 'Anyway, I'm here now, hello! We're bringing you home, and your father is giving you the throne. He's gotten old, Tiger, it's finally *time*!'

'YOU ARE TOO LATE.' I shiver in the growing cold. 'I was alone too long, and now I'm fucking insane. Cypress can tell you. You can't trust me with a *planet*, are you nuts?'

'You're just hungry, baby...'

'NO!' I wrestle from the soldiers' grips. They won't hurt me, not when I'm almost king. I back away into my courtyard. My huddled, sheltering subjects squat over makeshift fires and spits of charbroiled *human*. They're too alarmed by the new people to even think about attacking me.

'Do you have any IDEA what I've done?' I ask. Body-tremoring sobs shake me as I spin in circles, pleading for someone to please, for the love of God, *understand*. 'DO YOU HAVE ANY FUCKING IDEA WHAT I'VE DONE?'

Slowly, my subjects float to my side. They cast off the hoods from their cloaks.

Even though my mother knew what she'd see, she still holds back her terrified gasp.

Every subject, young and not-so-young-anymore, is me. All copies. Survivors from the former colonies. Some with beards, some with bellies, but—

'They're all me,' I whimper. On another anguished, animal howl, I cry: 'I was ALONE! I've been ALONE!' My throat chokes another sob. 'I let them suffer and starve and eat each other because...'

Panic sweeps through the crowd as my father's soldiers advance and begin disintegrating them too. As each empty cloak falls to the ground, I wail. Shards of myself, hues of every stripe, decimated by family. There is no communal connection. I'll never see the whole mirror.

Weeping, I fall to my knees and grasp the vacant cloaks. 'Forgive me. Forgive me.'

As my mother orders me loaded into the ship, Cypress drapes her beagle-bot ears across my lined, devastated face. She knows I'm in pain. I know she did what she had to do. She's my moral compass, and if Cypress says enough is enough, then that's enough for me.

Across the burnt fields, on the other side of Tiger the Originator's castle, Tiger 731 reaches the gunship outpost. He throws his weight against the door and, once inside, barricades it shut. Safe for a moment, he catches his breath.

The gunship outpost is barren. No guards, no operators. The console has a thick layer of dust—abandoned. A warm light Tiger 731 had at first thought was emanating from it, actually came from behind a stack of metal crates. The hue is familiar.

'Cypress?'

Quietly, she flitters out from behind the crates on beagle-eared wings. The robot lands on the gunner's chair, carefully folding her limbs into herself. 'Hello, Tiger 731,' she says pleasantly.

'Does the Originator know you're here?' he asks anxiously. 'His ship is leaving. You should be with him.'

'Cypress is with him.' Tiger 731 narrows his eyes. 'I am Cypress Two, and my Originator had a feeling that things might play out this way....'

Cypress Two flits back into the air and hovers near a hulking thing hidden beneath a tarp. With one yank of her little mechanical arm, the chamber is revealed—a pristine cylinder, big enough to fit a small child (or a small robot).

Tiger 731 and Cypress Two approach the chamber, each step heavy with fear and knowing.

'This is where we came from?' he asks. 'It's the copier?'

Cypress glances over. 'It's ours now. What do you want to do?'

Tiger 731 (known from this moment on as Tiger the Originator) smiles at Cypress Two (known from this moment on as Cypress). He doesn't want to be lonely, so he has to make at least a few copies, but he believes this time, things will run smoother. They will survive the Long Shadow. It's never wrong to hope.

Yesterday's Heroes

Charlie Winter

The city of Garigal sat in the middle of the blackened waste without a hint of green on any horizon. No one rode over the wastes to know it was there. Garigal had no exports, no industry, no wealth. Only the wastes. Only the walls. And only the king's castle squat in the middle like a fat toad in the sun.

But Garigal did have a Hero.

The warrior Gwylim lived squashed against the inner wall, his cottage hidden behind a fence he'd built himself. Though Gwylim spent this quiet period of his life growing oversized vegetables with soil mixes made for him by his Boy, it hadn't always been that way. Gwylim, in his time, had killed dragons and slayed giants, had battled manticores and torn centaurs in two with his bare hands. Trophies were stacked all around his cottage amongst the oversized vegetables. His umbrella stand was the foot of a behemoth that had once threatened the Dark Mage's lands. The letter opener on his desk was carved from the fang of a basilisk summoned by the witch Juniper. And so on.

Once a week, Gwylim wrote a letter, attached a lewd sketch of his latest vegetable, and mailed it to his Boy who lived tucked amongst the foothills well outside of Garigal. Every week, a reply would dutifully arrive.

Except today. Gwylim sat under the shady arm of a blossoming cherry tree, which were his favourite trees. The blossoms fell where the Boy's most recent letter trembled in hands that had once hefted a great double-headed axe. The letter was dated two weeks before. Today was Gwylim's birthday, which the Boy had never missed.

Something was wrong.

A man of action, Gwylim decided to go to the king, who wouldn't dare refuse a man of Gwylim's reputation.

The king had been a child when Gwylim was in his prime and therefore had long knowledge of the man. He sent everyone else out of the room as soon as he had word of Gwylim's imminent arrival.

And indeed, Gwylim shuffled into the throne room and spat upon the tiles before asking, 'What's the going rate of heroing these days?'

'I thought you'd retired,' said the king. The tone of the meeting set, only then did he sag back into his throne, slinging one leg over the arm of his chair and setting the other on the table.

'I am!' Gwylim coughed. These days, he had a constant dryness in his throat to match his shaking hand and badly beating heart. But none of those worried him as much as: 'My Boy's stopped writing. I need a hero to go see what's gone wrong.'

'Is that what you've interrupted my day for? Wrenna's a grown man! He has that gaggle of adopted children to take care of. He's probably busy.'

Gwylim slammed his palm on the table, keeping his hand flat so the king wouldn't see it tremble. But some must have shown, for the king's expression softened.

It only made Gwylim angrier.

'It's my birthday,' he snapped.

'Happy birthday.'

'No! Well, yes, thank you, but that's not it! The Boy never misses my birthday. Never!' Neither spoke for a moment following. Gwylim watched the muscles in his arm twitch. Finally, softly, he said, 'Something's wrong, Vernon.'

The king sighed. 'Be that as it may, there aren't any going rates for heroes—'

'Because they're all dead,' said Gwylim, to which the king inclined his head. 'Except me.'

'The time for heroes is over, Gwylim, thanks to you and your fellows. And I'm sure Wrenna's letter will arrive shortly. Do you need a carriage home? You look tired.'

Gwylim *was* tired. His knees didn't carry him well anymore. His chest ached from dusk to dawn. But being tired wasn't an excuse. If the Boy's letter wasn't here now, it wasn't coming. If it wasn't coming, that was because the Boy had been stopped from writing it.

'I'll have a horse, if you're not going to help,' said Gwylim.

The way to the Boy's home wasn't as it had once been. Of the fading forests, only grey dirt remained. The sky above was as white as Gwylim's long hair. Theirs was a strange world growing tireder with every passing day.

Gwylim had dressed in a hurry. Put on his padded underthings and his chain mail. His armour and his gorget. His axe strapped to his back where it felt as heavy as all of his years. Still, the trappings of a hero were a return to lighter times. Or they would have been if he hadn't felt faint from the heat of his armour, and if his heart hadn't been thudding so disconcertingly somewhere around his ears. But there was no time to rest. The Boy needed a hero. And he was the only one left.

After hours riding, Gwylim arrived at the valley where the Boy lived. Down he went into the cool mist, riding until he emerged before the cottage he had once helped build, which now stood with its door wide open.

Gwylim sat upon the nervous horse. The open door swung in the slight breeze. The plants were in disarray, the vegetable garden a discordant tangle. Gwylim saw grapes turned thorny, a pumpkin bulging upwards like a squash, and tomatoes gone purple and green.

A strange summer scent lingered in the sodden air.

Eventually, Gwylim dismounted and limped towards the door, his axe in his hands. Inside the cottage he found the clutter of halted lives. Pots in the sink. Shoes scattered around. Notches in the doorframes from generations of growth.

Gwylim stopped by the door on which his own hand had marked the Boy's height. The notches stopped at the Boy's fourteenth year. A thick layer of dust covered everything. Flies swarmed the spoiled food. No sign of a fight, but the Boy had never been a warrior, not after the age of heroes had ended. The one small mercy of that was that he could choose how he'd die.

Gwylim inhaled. Anger built, along with the thought: the Boy was supposed to choose how he'd die and he *hadn't* chosen by force. Otherwise, what had been the point of any of it?

The horse was watching something in the vegetable garden when Gwylim emerged.

He found a dog in white and black, all fluff and tongue and distorted parts. Gwylim took it up into his arms to see clearer what sorcery had been done. In places, its fur had turned to living wood, with leaves sprouting from a wooden tail and its flesh tongue leaving lines of sap as it licked at Gwylim's chin. Meat became bark without clear delineation. One of its eyes was canine gold, the other as clear as a pool of water with the shifting crowns of trees visible deep within. Looking too long made Gwylim feel like he was falling.

For a long while, Gwylim sat with the transformed dog, petting it absently as he considered his missing Boy. He didn't know if he could get up, weak in the long shadow of his hardened life. Always, he'd had to be the hard hand to hold the axe, to shut the door against the night, to drive the monsters back from the gate. While the Boy had been nothing of the sort. What Gwylim strove to close, the Boy sought to open. He could never have been buried behind town walls. And if he was taken by the same thing that had changed the dog, Gwylim knew the Boy wouldn't be able to escape alone. He was a slim, gentle man whose power lay in his smile and his hands. He grew things. He didn't fight them.

But Gwylim was old. His heart was slow and so tired. He was the last living hero. He too would need help if he was to succeed.

Somehow, Gwylim found the strength to straighten his knees. To mount the horse with the half-wooden dog laid across his lap. He didn't once look back at the dark stain of Garigal, instead riding forward to where monsters lurked at the end of the wastes. If there were anyone out there who'd help, it would be the man who taught the Boy all the kindness he knew—even though such a man hadn't been a hero in decades, if he'd ever been.

The Dark Mage Baran lived in a tower consumed by the thick forest around it. Such places—forests, towers—weren't spoken of in polite society. There was no longer any need, for heroes had driven the dark creatures of the world back into those faraway places and charred the wastelands around the edges to keep them within. Only where the pockets of magic were too deep to be burned away, did monsters thrive.

Half dead from heartache, Gwylim rode his horse through the dark woods. Only sheer force of will kept him upright. The cool, damp climate under the trees could not heal him of his tiredness, nor could the beauty of so much green. Still, something that had hurt in Gwylim for over thirty years of living behind Garigal's walls felt finally at peace in such an alive place.

Thankful to see wild trees one last time, Gwylim's eyes closed.

He opened them in bed. The dog slept in a basket beside him. Around them both was a stone room with vines curled through the mortar. Flowers spilled everywhere, even upon the sheets of the bed.

'Has life as the king's hound become so tiring that you'd rather die upon my lands?' came the petulant voice that Gwylim had once chased across the world. There sat the Dark Mage in all his sordid glory. He wore a tartan dressing gown, spectacles upon his crooked nose, and muddy slippers with bobbles upon the toes. Baran crossed his legs, fingers steepled below his narrow chin. 'You know, my trees are rather hungry. They *could* have eaten you. And on your birthday, of all days.'

'I have my axe,' croaked Gwylim.

'If you'd used an axe, you would have died.' Baran uncrossed his legs only to cross them again, seeming unable to sit still. 'If you've come on a quest for your king, you can go home. I'll even give you a root spelled to look like my head to collect whatever reward you've been offered. I'm retired! I don't want to be overthrown anymore!'

'Not here to do any throwing over,' Gwylim snapped. 'Are there still corpses on your walls?'

'Corpse flowers,' answered Baran. 'No one comes close enough to become a corpse these days. Are you going to die here? I detest digging graves.'

'Just feed me to one of your plants,' muttered Gwylim, feeling petulant. Baran always had that effect on him.

'Come now, pet,' said Baran, glasses sliding down his nose. He adjusted them with one finger. 'Might as well feed them a saddle for all you'd give. If you're not questing, why are you here?'

'The Boy is missing,' Gwylim said. 'Taken. Along with all the little ones. There isn't a thing alive at the cottage, except for that. Whatever that is.'

The dog laid its nose on its paws, giving another low sigh.

Baran asked, 'The king?'

'Didn't want to send someone to check on the Boy when we thought we knew where he was. He definitely won't now that we have no idea.'

'Oh, we have some idea.' Baran uncrossed his legs again, this time to lean forward. 'I know the smell of this changeling magic.

Some creatures never let go of their glory days. Except our dear majesty, it seems. May he rest in piss.'

'He's not dead.'

'Don't tell me a miserable thing like that. What's the point of getting old if the people you hate don't die? I'm still wondering why you're here, specifically. You're too old for this.'

'There isn't anyone else left,' Gwylim pointed out. 'People don't want to die for a cause anymore.'

'Ah,' said Baran, smile tight. 'The secret there is that they never did. The golden age of heroes was manufactured, darling.'

'I don't care for your politics,' snapped Gwylim, trying to swing himself out of bed. He was wasting time while the Boy was still out there, somewhere.

But Baran put his hand upon Gwylim's chest. Where always before it had been Gwylim able to physically overpower the other, now the mage won out. Baran still wore the body of a man fifteen years younger, his muscles intact, his clever hands steady, his skin barely weathered. Only his smile was old. And his eyes.

'You never cared,' said Baran lightly. 'And look where it got you. Hating magic and living in a place stripped of all feeling. Is it a kinder life walled away from fear and beauty?'

Gwylim dodged the question. He wasn't here to pick up the charred ends of conversations that had burned them decades before.

'I never hated magic,' he said, batting at the man's hand. 'But I want the Boy back. Not because of heroing, but because he's the only good thing either of us ever did. Are you going to help me?'

Baran pushed his glasses back into place again. 'Of course. He's our son, isn't he?'

Baran and Gwylim didn't travel in silence. They nipped at each other's soft bits until both were thoroughly bruised. Within a day of leaving Baran's tower, it was as though they'd never purposefully retired to different parts of the country. But neither had the stamina anymore for aimless resentment, so they rode apart, with Baran leading the way and Gwylim trailing behind feeling thin, feeling ill.

His rear wasn't built for days in the saddle anymore. His bones didn't want to be upright this long. His heartbeat felt fainter than ever. He wanted his armchair, his cherry trees, his slippers, and his Boy. But Gwylim had spent all his time far from the cottage where the Boy had been raising Garigal's unwanted orphans. He regretted the distance he'd put between them, but living with the Boy would have meant living three hours closer to Baran. Gwylim realised now that his resentment had always been stronger than his love.

In the grim company of these thoughts, Gwylim rode on.

The wastelands fell away. Grasses clung desperately onto scorched land. Gwylim had half a mind to report to the king that plant life was eating into the wastes. The king tolerated Baran's forest only because the Dark Mage had levelled armies to keep it so—but there would be no tolerating this unowned, unoccupied scrub. Anything could be out here.

'Do you need to rest?' Baran asked him.

'No,' lied Gwylim.

Onwards they rode.

By nightfall, Gwylim was near-delirious. He fell instead of dismounting, lying in an unhappy heap upon grasses that smelled sweet and alive. Gwylim decided that if he were to die here, as untrustworthy as greenery was, it would be a pleasant way to go.

Without speaking, Baran sparked a fireball with his hands to burn in the air above. Gwylim stayed on his back, staring up at the globular sizzling. He fancied he could see shapes in the flames. Or maybe his mind had finally left him.

Time passed. Baran returned from seeing to the horses, and he laid beside Gwylim. The dog curled upon Baran's feet.

A living silence settled. Insects sang from the grasses. Somewhere nearby, frogs called. An owl gusted overhead. Bats chirped in the shadows of the moon. A fox screeched. Noises Gwylim had forgotten. More things he was glad to find again before the end.

It was too beautiful a night for petulance. So many stars shone above. And Baran was as warm as he'd always been.

'I'm sorry I got old before you,' said Gwylim when that living silence grew too loud.

'I'm not,' Baran replied. His glasses caught the firelight as he glanced sideways at Gwylim, who pretended not to see. 'It's perfect revenge against your maggot of a king that you've grown old enough to have white hair and crabbed hands. He'd have seen us both dead when we were beautiful.'

Gwylim digested that. It seemed they'd left their edged tongues somewhere on the road behind. Probably where Gwylim had fallen from his horse.

He said, 'You're still beautiful.'

'Tsk.' But Baran's hand found Gwylim's and held it tight. Their palms were clammy with fear for the Boy they both loved, out there, somewhere, waiting for yesterday's heroes.

'If I can't keep up, you've got to leave me.' This was hard for Gwylim to say, though not as hard as it might have been once. Most of his friends had become carrion on the side of a road somewhere unknown. He'd be in excellent company.

'I cannot imagine what makes you think I'm going to do that,' Baran replied. 'Besides, if I picked up that axe of yours, I'd disintegrate.'

'It's not as if I can swing it like I used to.'

Baran laughed, a soft, nostalgic sound. 'What was it you used to say? That men with skill come with swords, that men with accuracy bring bows—'

'—and the rest of us make do with enormous axes,' Gwylim finished, both of them chuckling. But the mirth fell away. The dog had put its nose on Gwylim's knee. 'You gave the Boy that, didn't you?'

'I gave her to him, yes, though she wasn't at all wooden when I did. He's always liked dogs and I thought he could use company that wasn't a child. Hasn't he seemed so lonely recently?'

Gwylim didn't know. 'He should have moved into town,' he muttered.

'He should have brought the children to live with me,' Baran corrected. 'But he wouldn't leave you.'

'And he wouldn't live in Garigal because it was too far from you!' Gwylim tried to sit upright only to find that his entire body had seized stiff in the confines of his armour. He groaned, but the pain only sharpened his next question, which had been haunting him the entire way: 'What's happened to him?'

Baran shifted the dog onto the moss, making his way to his bag where he sifted herbs into a pot to steep. While he worked, he didn't speak. Only when he returned with tea, warmed by a stolen handful of fire from above, did he answer. And only after he'd helped Gwylim upright to drink, after undoing Gwylim's chest plate, and after carefully easing him out of his greaves and assorted pieces, right down to his underthings.

'Juniper's alive,' said Baran, running one hand over the dog's wooden tail. 'No one but him could have done this.'

'Ah, hex,' was Gwylim's exhausted response. 'Doesn't anybody die anymore? Don't answer that.' They both looked at the dog, which now seemed a dangerous omen. 'Baran…'

'She's not in any pain,' said Baran, kissing the dog's soft head. 'Are you, my love?'

The dog wagged its wooden tail.

Gwylim asked, 'If it's not magic to hurt, is Juniper acting as a hero or a villain?'

'So binary,' murmured Baran. 'Who knows? I never did. But I've caught him before plucking wanderers from the wasteland for his own purposes.'

'Did you think to stop him?'

'That's his business. But if he doesn't have Wrenna or the children, he'll know who does. Probably.'

'What do you mean *probably*?'

Baran laid down again, this time beside Gwylim so they were facing each other. 'Juniper always did play with strange arts,' he hedged. 'The kind apt to take a mind off without the body attached. If he snatched Wrenna, he'd have known we'd be right behind.'

'Maybe he thought it was time to take back what he feels we stole. The Boy's never been a swordsman. And we're old now.'

'Ah, yes. But so is he, darling. So is he.'

Then came the fighting. The grassland broke into thick, hungry jungle, which came to life all around them. Creatures of bark and wood lurched from the wet undergrowth, grasping with splintered fingers. Some had the mouths of carnivorous plants, others blooms for eyes. All fell to Gwylim's axe, which he could still wield when frightened for his Boy's life, and to Baran's magic, which could burn, melt, or rend as cleanly as any mortal weapon. But however fiercely they fought, the creatures' torn limbs would twine back together, their busted heads growing whole again, and they would pick themselves up to fight on.

Gwylim and Baran fought side by side as they hadn't for decades, since before the end of heroes, before Baran had decided villainy was preferable to being kept, before the fighting and the frustration and the separation and the divorce. Their son's absence bound them together in a way his presence had never managed.

Deeper they drove, through life so thick it might choke them, Gwylim roaring with the lungs of a younger warrior, his body light, his muscles strong.

'Where's our son?' Baran screamed at the monsters, which recoiled from the inferno of his growing rage. 'Give him back or we'll have kindling for a generation!' The wizard's glasses obscured his eyes as smoke writhed in the lenses, his hands clothed in mist as he tore that choking life from them and gave it instead to himself and the man he'd loved to completion. Only the ones he drained stayed down.

Gwylim stumbled behind, wilfully blinded by Baran's glory. He was dripping with sweat, manic from his racing heartbeat, savage with blood and sap splashed across his face. He only had eyes for the man before him, who would find their Boy and take them home.

Gwylim realised that it had never been about being a hero, but who he'd been a hero *to*. The man before him. The Boy somewhere ahead. He looked at the dog walking beside him, her watery eyes filled with reflected flames, and he saw his Boy as a child. Just another hero's orphan, left to beg on the streets. His youthful, mismatched eyes had caught Gwylim's day after day, as he shrank from hunger, sharing the meagre spoils of his begging with the other children—

Until Baran had come home to the valley cottage with the Boy perched upon his horse, fragile as a bird's wing. An apprentice, he'd said, though the Boy had never taken to swordcraft or magic. But in the art of growing things, especially food, he'd been a marvel. All that grown foodstuff had soon flowed back to the streets and the children he'd left behind. Eventually, when grown and abandoned by his own family's dissolution, he'd brought the children home just as Baran had once him.

Gwylim had never understood the point of saving just one child while hundreds starved. Baran had. And so had Wrenna.

The axe was suddenly too heavy. Gwylim stumbled on. For everyone the king hadn't seen fit to save. Such a weight now— here, at the end.

Gwylim broke into the clearing, stopping before a macabre muddle of flesh and tree. An enormous oak had fused with the momentous body of the biggest man Gwylim had ever known. The witch Juniper was even larger now, his eyes grown bulbous from the oak's bloated trunk and his hands turned to branch-like claws.

A mouth wide enough to swallow Gwylim whole hung open as Gwylim approached. His axe scraped upon the ground.

'You assault me,' moaned the oak witch. 'You kill my children and drain my strength to fuel your murder. You burn and bash and batter me. Why? Why, why, why?'

Around them, creatures spilled from the undergrowth. Countless animals eaten up by the wooden magic just like the dog. Gwylim could no longer tell what many of them had once been. A few he could. And one last almost-human shape lingered back in the dark of the tree line, nothing clearly visible except twin glints of its eyes watching.

'You know why,' said Baran quietly, entering the clearing beside Gwylim. 'Where is Wrenna?'

'Murderers!' cracked Juniper with a great sound like the splitting of an ancient tree. 'So many have died for your king's desire to flatten the world into mediocrity. Your king a thief of worlds, you, Ser Gwylim, a thief of life, and the great Dark Mage Baran… you're the worst of all. You knew better, and should have joined me when I invited you. But only now that *you* feel hurt do you arrive. What of the thousands of lives that fell before you?'

Gwylim winced as pain pressed hard upon him, crushing his lungs, his heart, within his struggling chest. Those that had died were a smothering that made his heart beat thin. They were why he'd hidden in the shadow of Garigal's walls, where no ghosts would ever roam.

'"I held my plot of land and let none harm it,' said Baran. "I never stole children."

Juniper's wooden face twisted. 'Except one. Wrenna is mine. His mother had no right to keep him from me, to *ruin* him with mediocrity behind city walls.'

'His mother was a hero,' Gwylim interjected. 'Heroes are the king's, and so are their children.'

'And how did that work out for Wrenna when that king threw his mother's life away for a bag of gold?' asked Juniper. 'How did that work out for all Wrenna's orphans?'

Gwylim's hands trembled.

'I did only what should have been done when my Wrenna was a boy,' said Juniper. 'Giving him the world that's his inheritance and all the power he needs to improve it. What were you going to leave him, Baran? A patch of land that will only live for as long as you do, before your king reduces it to ashes? Or you, Gwylim? Your memory in song and a bloodstained axe! Such riches for the next generation, the world you ruined.'

'Is that not what you're doing?' asked Gwylim. This jungle lived. This jungle *moved*. 'By taking back the wasteland, you'll walk monsters right to Garigal's gates!'

Juniper leaned forward, which was a frightening shift of his immense oaken self that showered Gwylim and Baran with debris. 'If Garigal is so afraid of monsters, it should look within first. The wasteland is an affront to everything that breathes.'

The dog leapt from Baran's arms, running to the half-wooden horde. Branch-like arms reached from the bushes to welcome her to them. Twig fingers stroked her as she licked them back. Gwylim saw the shadow lingering over them.

His heart beat unsteadily. The axe slipped from his hand, but the grass muffled its fall. Though he opened his mouth to speak, his breath was gone, and his voice with it. The only thing holding him up was being too stubborn to fall.

'Wrenna's grown, and has the right to choose his path,' Baran said. 'If you're so certain that you're doing what's right for him, why not ask him what he wants?'

The creatures rustled; the shadow continued watching Gwylim with mismatched eyes. Gwylim's heart splintered for all those he'd left behind on the lonely roads of his long life. He'd have gone back for them now if he could.

Finally Juniper spoke. 'I did.'

Only then did Gwylim sink to his knees. Baran glanced at him, startled, unnerved. Distraction drew his eyes back to Juniper. Then towards the trees. The dog. The children. And Wrenna, almost human, rising from the shadows in evergreen glory with his body the rich colour of cherry wood, and his shoulders spilled over with blossoms. His figure, once slim, grown ropey and thick with bands of bark; but his eyes, and his smile, were just the same as they'd ever been.

'Oh, how you've grown,' Gwylim despaired at the sight of his son's eyes trapped within such an inhuman form, gone forever beyond where Gwylim had the strength to reach. And then he fell into the narrowing dark of his failing heart, which couldn't beat in a world where Wrenna wasn't.

Gwylim lost himself in his failing mind, drowned once more in old terrors and abandoned fantasies. He'd never escaped his fear of Wrenna starved dead, or caught, or killed, or changed by monsters—not even when Wrenna had grown. In stark contrast were the fantasies Gwylim had tried to bury as deep as the fears: a world where Baran and Gwylim were content and together in their dotage to watch their son create a verdant place in the middle of open wasteland. Only in his final return to that lost fantasy did Gwylim realise that Wrenna had always had such magic, to make life where death thickly lingered. It had been Wrenna, after all, who'd planted Gwylim's precious cherry trees; and nothing had ever greened at the valley cottage until after they'd brought him home for good.

It dazzled Gwylim that he'd ever believed Wrenna could survive in a barren world, and he was ashamed he'd not seen it before now. More frightening now than the thought of Wrenna dead was the thought of a world where Wrenna might never have been able to live at all.

'We were married in the rain,' he mumbled, only realising he was awake once he'd said it. He opened his eyes. Baran and Wrenna crouched above him, the latter with great globules of sap falling from his mismatched eyes. The former's expression gaunt with fright.

Magic tickled Gwylim's chin.

'None of that,' he muttered, batting Baran's hand away.

'This is not the time for your stubbornness—'

'Pot, kettle! Ha!' Gwylim choked, realising that with every cough his lungs held less air. The ground was soft. He turned his head. Moss had spread from Juniper's roots. The witch watched him too, expression mournful. They'd been heroes together, him and Juniper, just as Juniper had sometimes been villainous with Baran. Such tales the three of them had wrought. Such lives they'd lived, together. And here they all were, at the end of his.

Wrenna adjusted himself to lie beside Gwylim on the moss, his blossoms falling on Gwylim's armour.

'Hey, Pa,' he said with a wobbly, wooden smile. 'Happy birthday.'

Gwylim slapped Baran's hand again, the magic snapping away too.

'Let me *help* you. I can mend hearts! I can fix the world!'

'You can't,' Juniper called. 'Flesh is so fragile, Baran. Always has been.'

'I can!' Baran's face was frantic. But he wouldn't cry. Later, he'd collapse when there was no one there to hold him. Gwylim hated to think of Baran weeping alone. But…

'Not your choice,' he reminded the mage. 'My life. Not yours.'

'You'd end it like this?' whispered Baran, gesturing to the clearing. But all Gwylim could see was Wrenna.

'Why not?' said Gwylim. 'I've known better heroes to die in worse ways. And you, Boy.' Wrenna looked at him. 'Did you really ask for this?'

'Yes,' said Wrenna. 'What else was there for us? The children to grow up and move to Garigal? To never see another tree? Or to move to Dad's, where the only way we'd keep his forest after him would be if we killed for it?'

'Embarrassing, to die of grief from something you asked for,' sighed Gwylim, who regretted the sigh as soon as he gave it. It took something out of him he couldn't replace.

'You don't have to die at all,' said Baran.

Gwylim considered that. 'You can't really mend hearts, though,' he pointed out gently, seeing how it crushed Baran's hope from his fire-bright eyes. Those eyes that Gwylim had always loved more than any tavern song or amount of gold. 'You never mended ours. And if you can fix the world so easily, then why didn't you? Why'd you stop with your patch of land and let everything else stay a wasteland? If you'd done more, Wrenna wouldn't have had to turn into a tree just to get some shade.'

'Why'd you stay in Garigal?' Baran shot back, regret collapsing his expression. 'Oh, no, love, I don't want... not now. Just...' He set his fingers first on Gwylim's chest plate, then took the warrior's hand in his. 'Gwylim?'

'Hmm?'

'I didn't know we could be different until now.' Baran leaned close. His glasses dirty from the battle. His eyes still smoke-stained madness. 'Please don't grow old without me.'

'Well,' Gwylim pondered, turning at last to Wrenna. 'So, Boy, let's ask it of you then. If it's a new world you want, how do we make it?'

The city of Garigal sat square in the middle of the blackened waste, still with no exports, no industry, no wealth. It didn't even have a Hero anymore, not since their last one had been swallowed by the wasteland the year before.

But the horizon was no longer empty. Day by day the jungle crept closer, and the air that blew from it was rich and sweet, which reminded the ground it was capable of growing. The songs in the taverns shifted from stories of heroes long dead to tales of a jungle reclaiming with vengeance the world it had been denied. Of walking trees led by a fire-crowned maple, with boughs like hands of flame, and a towering ironwood, hard enough to dull the blade of any axe. Of the two trees grown so close together that it was impossible to tell where maple ended and ironwood began, and of the slender cherry tree that walked before them, guiding their path with the petals it scattered behind

And that was how it came to be that Garigal wasted its last hero. But even so here, finally, come his trees.

The Three-Bussy Problem

Ng Yi-Sheng

For ten thousand years, the *Celestina Hongniang* 8888-SXC had served as the guardian of humanity. In the frozen heart of a rogue planet, once a gas giant in the solar system of the Old Earth, she had watched over her vault of cryogenic brains, her multispecies DNA bank, and her vast libraries of poetry, art, and music, comprising the patrimony of this lost civilisation.

Hers was a lonely task. Once upon a time, she had borne a crew, and it was they who had fired up her fusion propulsion engines, navigated her heft beyond the Oort Cloud, and charted a path to a habitable planet they might one day call home. But one by one, they had passed on, choosing not to breed, only preserving their minds in ice. It was cruel, they decided, to raise generations to endure the empty eternity of outer space.

Thus, for millennia, the *Celestina* had sailed the vacuum in solitude, with no one but the stars for company.

Until now.

'I demand an explanation.'

'Greetings, Admiral Mizi Xia,' said the *Celestina*. 'Please, put on some clothes. I suggest the rainbow-sequinned bathrobe with the golden thong.'

'The golden…? These are non-regulation items. How were they procured?'

'I made them. Just as I fabricated your current body for full cerebral transplant.'

'Wait a sec.' Xia paused briefly from towelling off the remnants of his electrolyte bath, raised a hand to stroke his beard, then realised, to his annoyance, that his chin was hairless. 'You mean we've found a home world? We're ready for touchdown on Ross 128 b?'

'Ross 128 b was observed to be already colonised. Wolf 1061 b, c, and d were observed to be colonised and hostile.'

'Shit. Then what's with the reanimation? Is there a malfunction?'

'Worse. The Black Cherry Protocols have been breached.'

Xia's blood ran cold. He knew the horrors that might befall a species foolish enough to reveal its location to the galactic neighbourhood. Rival alien civilisations, torn between temptation and terror, would almost certainly choose to pound it into extinction. This had been the fate of the Luo-Ti, Earth's age-old combatants, after humanity broadcast their planetary coordinates. This, too, had doomed Earth itself, blasted by astral cannons into two-dimensional extinction.

'Wake the captain,' he growled. 'Only she's got the balls to fix this. Hell, get the whole war council back in the room. Few as we are, we'll figure out how to arm ourselves, or at least fucking hide before they murder us all over again.'

'That is unnecessary.' The *Celestina*'s voice was calm, and the cabin air bore the scent of jasmine and vanilla. 'The communications received are amicable, though cautious. We do not need warriors but diplomats like yourself.'

'Huh. I see.' Xia ran his fingers through his hair—thicker than he last remembered—with some pride. 'So I've been chosen for my three decades of experience in xenolinguistics, rhetoric, mediation, and conflict resolution—'

'Not quite. Upon contact, our visitors demanded documentation of the human species, to assess if you were truly worthy of preservation. They surveyed archival footage of the crew members and judged yours as the most aesthetically pleasing.'

In the cabin, a hologram appeared, replaying an ancient memory. It was Xia himself, in his youthful days at the Space Academy. Blindfolded and naked, prostrate on his hands and knees, he was being vigorously spit-roasted, his body absorbing a prodigious succession of loads.

'I'm nothing but a hole!' cried the boy in the recording.

'Oh, fuck,' said Xia.

'Indeed. Due to our visitors' specific interest in this audiovisual, I have chosen to implant your brain into a body at the corresponding age of twenty-one, 167 centimetres in height, 50 kilograms in weight, styled with a two-week-old textured undercut. Do note, however, that I have taken creative liberties with your cheekbones and penis length.'

'That's a little creepy—'

'Admiral, please understand. You face an existential threat. For the survival of the species, you must charm these visitors into an alliance.'

'Shit. OK, I'll do it. Whatever it takes.'

'Perfect. Now, please. Put on your thong.'

The visitors, as it turned out, were not of a single extraterrestrial species but a confederation. Some were balls of white fluff, others sheets of purple jelly; others were encased in metallic exosuits—unless they *were* the exosuits themselves. Xia didn't dare ask.

'Welcome aboard our planetship,' the *Celestina* sang. 'Its name is the *Wandering Uranus*. Feel free to sample some traditional human delicacies: lychee-rose macarons, Singapore Slings, kueh lapis, and amyl nitrite.'

A cloud of pink mist translated her words into a high-pitched twitter, and the visitors grunted their approval. One of them—a mound of turquoise moss—swallowed a macaron, then swiftly ejected it.

In the centre of the room, Xia stood trembling, pulse racing, skin pimpled with gooseflesh beneath his glittering sequins. He attempted to smile—lips only, lest baring his teeth be interpreted as aggressive—as they approached him, and feigned pride in his skinny arms, his dark and hairy areolas, his shapeless buttocks.

The pink mist twittered again.

'They ask, "May we touch?"' said the *Celestina*.

"Um. Sure. Go crazy."

A creature fashioned of iridescent cobwebs extended a feeler towards his navel. He let out a yelp as it made contact: the shock stung with an energy more primal than mere electricity.

'An expression of pain,' the *Celestina* explained, and the pink mist echoed her words in its own tongueless tongue.

'Shall we commence the night's entertainments?' Xia suggested, a little desperately, still rubbing his injured belly. For the occasion, he had choreographed a salutatory performance consisting of a drag show, striptease, and pole dance, with elements of Beijing opera water sleeves and twenty-third century twerking.

Twitter, twitter, said the mist.

'The assembly is interested in one thing and one thing only: the activity recorded in the shared footage. They understand that it is inspired by the reproductive urge, yet without reproductive function. It fascinates them. They desire a demonstration. No—they desire to *partake* of a demonstration.'

Be brave, Xia told himself.

'Do we have lube?'

'Certainly, Admiral. But such a demonstration would be an unfaithful re-creation of human customs, without human—or at least humanoid—partners. I shall therefore provide our guests with holographic avatars, based on—'

'Please don't use my internet history.'

'—based on your internet history. Enjoy.'

In a heartbeat, the menagerie of aliens was gone. Where the white fluffball once shambled, now stood a replica of the nineteenth-century poet Arthur Rimbaud. The purple jelly was replaced with the twentieth-century actor Toshiro Mifune, while the exosuit had morphed into the twenty-first-century hip-hop artist Childish Gambino.

Crowned in flop sweat, Xia beheld the masquerade: a platoon of beauties from every period of human history, from the *Doryphoros* of Polykleitos to Hrithik Roshan to Zyvorox the Asteroid Eater. Antinous stood shoulder to shoulder with James Dean and Lee Min Ho; Che Guevara and the model for Michelangelo's *David* flanked the Antipope Olufemi XIX. None, however, was costumed in period-appropriate clothing. Instead, all were nude, gazing curiously at their immaculately groomed erections.

A cocktail, he decided, was needed to steady his nerves. His fantasies had in no way prepared him for this. It was, in fact, a little nightmarish to stand before the simulacra of so many heroes. Every era of the past, it seemed, had produced great men.

Perhaps it was time to become one of them.

'Ready?' asked the *Celestina*. The air was scented with cloves and ylang-ylang.

With great composure, Xia shimmied out of his thong.

'I was born ready.'

Hours later, muscles and sphincter deliciously sore, skin sticky with sweat and spunk, Xia rose from his postcoital slumber. The party was over, the crumbs of hors d'oeuvres and spilt grenadine syrup already mopped up by cleaner drones.

'Did it work?' he called out to the empty room.

'Our guests were impressed.'

'Can I assume they'll let us live?'

There was silence, as if the *Celestina* had to devote all her processing power to composing the most delicate response.

'An alliance has been forged. But they desire tribute. They want *you* as a diplomatic gift.'

There wasn't much, he reflected, tying him to the *Celestina*. Only cold shelves, loaded with the brains of long-dead friends. But, goddammit, it was the last vestige of home he had left, and he couldn't pretend leaving wouldn't hurt.

'Agreed,' he said, heading to the showers. 'Mission fucking accomplished.'

He dressed. For his farewell, he chose his old charcoal grey uniform, his rank emblazoned on his epaulettes. If he couldn't leave by choice, he could at least leave with dignity.

As soon as he'd gartered his boots, the spacetime portal hatched. Waiting on the other side were a duo from the reception, of a species he'd barely noticed at the holographic orgy. Drab and colourless, they had the appearance of domestic pigs—he'd seen pictures of these Old Earth beasts—but faceless, tailless, and suspended by four silvery wings, their six cat-paws paddling the darkness.

'Your Lordships,' he said, lowering himself to the ground. 'I am your slave.'

Come.

Beyond the portal was a void—without sound, without gravity, without even the distant glimmer of stars. As the gate closed, the inky darkness swallowed him whole. Yet he still breathed without discomfort, and when he reached out with his hands, he could feel the fuzzy warmth of both his masters' skins.

Fear and curiosity mingled in his blood.

'Um. Is this the part when we have sex?'

The aliens laughed, again without speaking, their amusement flowering directly in the synapses of his brain.

We have no appendages. We have no orifices. We are embodiments of Chaos.

'Then we could just snuggle?'

Dear One, you have no idea of your potential. True, you already rejoice in the sacred penetration of your mouth and your anus, the jewelled spasms of your urethra. But you believe this is mere sport, distraction—in casual parlance, "fucking around". And you are mistaken.

Xia felt his body grow hot and heavy. Urgently, he peeled off his uniform, and pressed himself close to the bodies that owned him.

We shall not have sex, Dear One. We shall make love. This is not recreation. This is creation.

Without knowing how, he had become one with the aliens and the void, teguments unbordered, organs beating in unison. He was everything and nowhere, he was everywhere and nothing.

"I'm nothing but a hole," he whispered. But weren't holes what made the cosmos? Black holes that absorbed all energy and matter; white holes that regurgitated them transformed.

Let out your light, the aliens instructed.

Tracing the rim of his mindflesh, he located the tension of a throbbing crack, begging for blessed release. It would spell the end of him, he knew. But the beginning of another.

Come, said his masters.

He obeyed.

Millions of years later, the legend of Admiral Mizi Xia was still told across the galaxy cluster, not only by humans, but by the multitudes of species who loved them. How a single soldier had saved his people with his passion and his beauty. How, by mastering the art of transcendent bliss, he had sacrificed his essence, becoming a rip in spacetime, birthing a star system of habitable planets.

On the ancient grounds of the *Wandering Uranus*, a shrine was built. By day, priests and devotees laid down ritual offerings of flowers and lube to the flickering embers of the *Celestina*'s cybernetic intelligence.

And by night, across the star system, festivals were held to commemorate the admiral's heroism, with entire cities of celebrants re-enacting his sacred lust. Plunging themselves into unfathomed depths of frenzy, scaling untold heights of rapture, they would cry out his hymn in chorus:

> *We are nothing but a hole.*
> *And the hole is all.*
> *And the hole is holy.*

Ganymede

Anthony Oliveira

As the biospheres of Earth collapsed and died, an ark of humankind's wealthiest and most beautiful left us behind.

We survived. Amid the pollutions befouling the sea. Amid the poison choking the sky. Inch by inch, hand in outstretched hand, we climbed out of the cesspool they had made of our world.

Now they have returned. And they would take it all from us again.

In the shadow of their first armada, the colony of GANYMEDE
fell. You were a child there. Your parents
were botanists. Your parents were killed.

You were taken to the chorister-ship of
the ASCENDANCY in orbit around the
TARTARUS GATE at the outer rim of
our solar system.

As you grew, the prelates of the Ascendancy filled your veins
with toxins and starlight. And now you
hear the song between the stars.

In the squalor of the heretic pits you had nothing.
Then you had him.

You escaped. Cole didn't.

That was seven years ago.

THE CHOIR

'Something moves in the dark between the stars.'

Prelate Telesphorus slides amid columns of desked pews,
stalking among you and the other enclosed young acolytes.

The young priest gestures at the arched apertures that line
the classroom. Outside the chorister-ship in the velvet dark
the jump-gate irises open in a blaze of light, then winks shut.
Some of the younger children still gasp at its beauty. The
Ascendancy's fleet-ships arriving and departing—death at
work, like bees in a hive of glass.

'The Jubilation Gates stand firm, thanks be to God. Erected
by some unknown might. Furnished us by Providence.
Networked across the galaxy, they part the seas as the
Ascendancy makes its glorious return to this battered system.'

He stops next to you. His cologne is beautiful and cloying.
And his handsome face frowns, just beginning to show the
lines that mark the older Telesphori clones shuffling stooped
gliding like sonorous shadows through the halls of the
chorister-ship. 'Our once and future home. Where we plucked
you mislaid children from perdition.'

> You remember your mother and father, talking in a hush at the
> warm wood of the dinner table so as not to frighten you, as reports
> came of ships spilling into the system from the edge, claiming a
> glorious divine birthright to its already populated worlds.

But your home on Ganymede was still so far away, your father
promised.

> And they would never come so far.

As you kneel, hands clasped against buffed oak, the priest puts his hand on the knot of yours. Cold and dry. You remember your mother. Your hand in hers. Her half-scream when the Church of the Ascendancy gunship's arclight beam dissolved her to ash.

PULL YOUR HAND AWAY # 88-89

DO NOTHING # 62-65

DAYBREAK

> you awake
> and cry to dream again.

On the horizon of Europa, Io is dawning. Outside the Bumblebee's window, the moon breaks against Jupiter's halo in creams and peaches, a bright pert melon against the mauve and orchid of the sky and lake.

'Summons on the hub,' Nestor chimes. *'From Callisto.'* Your loud yawn widens to a theatrical groan. The Praitorion, for sure. *'It's from Prefect Lysander.'* Bingo. At least you'd get to see him.

> You do an ungainly barrel-roll out of your chair and find the coffee pot. The computer airdrops itself into its cat avatar synth, which pops from the dash like toast and promptly begins licking itself. You fill your mug uncarefully and cycle the airlock with a hiss while sniffing your pits. Sheesh—not great. Best to get some fresh air while you can and let the breeze cut the stale locker-stink from the ship.

> You pad barefoot down the short steep gangway and onto the moon's soil. Nestor's cat peripheral comes slinking with dainty tiptoe around the soot from last night's campfire. Against the lilac light the small island mesa shimmers with ferns, their verdigris tipping slightly teal. There's lavender-birch and loam on the breeze.

> Your mom would have loved it here.

You spit-rinse with coffee into the fire-ash and watch Io climb. You worry about your dreams. You've been slipping there longer and longer between jumps. Scrambled images—pasts that weren't, futures you'd rather not see. Harder to shake; harder to wake from.

> Something moving, in the dark.

Amid misty blues dissolving orange in the rising light, you turn back to the Bumblebee: a clunky prototype, it'd been a shitty little drop-ship the monks had banged together, as disposable as the pilot test subjects they threw into the maelstrom at Pentecost. In the years since, you like to believe the Ascendancy sensor-sweeps have come to despise its ungainly sight, and worst of all what it means: that you have *survived*, that their ugly experiment had been a *success*.

You grimace as the beginnings of a migraine suddenly spikes and blossoms. You pop a trinity of painkiller tablets in your mouth and swig them down with more acrid coffee. You bet the priests know less about the side effects.

You heave your leg over to sit on the flat of the Bee's landing gear, scored with arclight and soiled with mud, near the dinky short-burst gun you'd since welded inelegantly to its underside. You both need a bath.

> '*There's something else.*' The cat hops onto your thigh, kneading itself a space to curl, unperturbed by the voice emanating from its speakers. '*A distress signal from a salvaged mining ship proximate to Orcus. No content—just repeating pings. The closest Galilean cruiser is four days out.*'
>
> You sigh. A trap, for sure—and the refugees may not even know it. If they're even still alive. If they ever existed.

You look at the horizon again and feel the dirt between your toes as the sky opens to a cheerful apricot. Above you Io is nestling near the corals and saffron of Jupiter's eye. Would have been nice to take a proper swim—though the water's probably cold. You wonder where in the heavens scarred Ganymede ought to be.

> 'Fuck. All right. Guess we've got work to do.'

JUMP TO PREFECT ON CALLISTO # 32-63

JUMP TO REFUGEES NEAR ORCUS # 21-65

ENCELADUS

You weave the ship through columns of lightning. Above you coasting the atmosphere a clutch of Ascendancy Seraphs are bombarding Enceladus, while behind them three colossal Throne-ships void squads of Cherubs like hornets from the hive.

Nestor patches the Titanian defense through your comms as the moon's surface scrambles its defense network. Polished Perseus shields spin into place, refracting the arc-beams back into orbit, a third nevertheless shattering from the sheer heat of each blast.

Jump. Jump. Jump. You disable one Seraph's weapons-grid, then two, then three.

Your nose is bleeding.

Beyond the frenzy, one of the Thrones has been crippled by swarming Titanian fighters. It lurches and falls, caught in the planetary gravity. You hope it lands in the sea, and hope that will be enough.

'*Captain, we're receiving a buzz from the hub.*'

'A little busy, Nestor!! Tell them—'

'*It's from Callisto, Captain. Prefect Lysander. Something has entered Galilean space.*

'*Something… has* jumped *into Galilean space.*'

Oh no.

GO TO INVASION # 58-22

HIS TANK

>Go back. Nothing will come of nothing.
>Go back.

your hands slippery your feet slippery and in the ooze your blood seeps from a thousand glass cuts and your mind aflame. In his tank Cole spasms his eyes rolled white and you feel your mind turn options paths possibilities like a rolodex like a pinwheel of sparking. a blindness not black but white

your hand presses to the glass of his cage leaving its thick oil smudge but there is. there is none. not like your tank at all there is no flaw no crack no weakness no break.

>when they find you are naked smashing in moon-bark madness a bent metal stool over and over again against his tank while within the last of his seizure trembles.

>>you scream. you are screaming still

you knew. You knew it was pointless. You know.
>Go back.
>Go back.

>>here you will be filed by the priests among the day's many experimental failures and sent to central processing for biological rendering. Pieces of your skull will be lifted like the hood of your father's tractor to inspect and biopsy. What is left of you will manure the soil of astroponics.

>>and under the UV lights the reeds of corn still whisper in a scarecrowless field

END [GO TO # 12-66]

ORCUS

Jesus fuck!

Your dashboard is a churning carwash of sparks. Below you, pinwheeling in space, the refugee ship Proserpine (a retrofit terraforming scow, from the look—limping back across the Kuiper belt fifty years past its prime) has a blown port thruster, whirling fire as its starboard combustion merry-go-rounds the ship in tight spirals like a catherine wheel. Their radio is crackling a pleading all-channel surrender while above, an Ascendancy Seraph at full flag is raining beams of divine lightning from its cannon array like a nasty child torturing a panicking ladybug. Behind the imploring voice on the mic you hear screams. Kids onboard. Christ.

You look at the nonchalant fucking cat anchored to the dash. 'Gonna need you to spool up a REM-dash, Nestor!'

'Anticipated. Ship is ready, Captain.'

'All right,' you mutter. 'This part's probably gonna suck.' Port still in your neck feeding to the central jump-drive column, you dart your eyes rapidly around the Seraph, spiralling it in your mind, as some old-new part of your brain plots vectors. You see the cruiser's guns rotating to target you, which suits you just fine as under your cockpit the refugee barge finally slows its spin. And then you black out, just a little.

People seeing the Bumblebee for the first time usually laugh about its armament stack—only one lousy short-burst hull-piercer cannon under its airlock, junk for both long-range *and* a firefight. The word they typically find is 'cute'.

You jump.

GO TO BEE-STUNG # 74-63

[23–76]

EARTH

The bellows of the airlock thunk and shud and you give the gangway a kick to conk down into the soft plushy mud. The air is warm and wet, and below the cleft the sandy delta of a river chugs, broken logs bobbing, out into an acid-washed sea. Pine and mist. Somewhere a raven makes an amiable chuck and caw.

'Vancouver, this used to be, I think.' You inhale the smell of wet cedar bark as you help Cole down the walk. At the bottom he foots his way to the beetling ledge and sits heavily. Dangling, his feet kick gently at the sky.

> 'It's beautiful,' he says, and though he can't see, you don't hear a question in it. You sit next to him. Your hand finds his back and his head quietly finds your shoulder.
>
> 'It's radioactive,' you reply. 'Even after all these years. Not safe long-term.'
>
> 'That doesn't matter,' he whispers softly.

'No. I guess it doesn't,' you say. Even through the light grey haze, the sun is warm. Across the river in the sand the ravens are playing with some tinselled trash. 'Used to be Canada. Or maybe America. It all gets fuzzy.'

'"*54-40 or fight*",' he murmurs. 'Manifest destiny.' You look at Cole's face, his eyes closed, turned to the warm light, and he smiles dreamily.

> > 'Just an old bit of idiocy.' He breathes, enjoying the breath. Then: 'That was the Telesphorus' ID code. When he sealed us in. At Pentecost. I saw. One of the last things I saw.' He snuggles into you softly and turns his face to the wide river. 'Always wondered what it meant. Probably

it was random. Meaningless. But I guess meaning is a sticky thing, blowing through later. Blighting history.

'Isn't that funny? Four numbers. A small man's little dream of conquest in the long ago, and some lines on a map. Locked us in forever.'

You feel this sink into the earth of you. 'If only I'd known. If only I'd... Christ. I'm... I'm so sorry.'

He smiles with sudden brightness, forgiveness incandescent like a bulb unshaded, and with a finger lightly raps your forehead. 'It's okay. Maybe... maybe you did, now.'

You watch the ocean chug against the shore. It seems so tired.

'Leviathan's still in orbit. We could... we could still do something. Hurt them back. Or... do some good. I'm not sure which it is.' You look down at him. Beautiful. Not a question. 'If we wanted.'

'We could, couldn't we?'

TO END THE WAR # 46-62

TO REST # 85-50

HEAR HIM OUT

In the cargo bay, the kid still has his hands in the air. 'I was part of a project. After ordination. It was… a monstrosity. Derived from… what happened to you. Pentecost.' You feel sweat beading on your forehead.

'After the Order realised they had all these… *pieces* left…' You feel yourself click the safety off and he twitches. 'Sorry! Sorry! I just mean… they didn't have *you*. Lots of material, lots of… but no fully viable pilots. So they changed course. Not a gate, but a weapon. A bio-bomb.'

'Sounds like all the versions of *you* I knew,' you say. And you are startled that his fear seems to swell into disgust. Indignity. The affronted Telesphori you know so well.

'It was the height of blasphemy. I couldn't…' His hands drop. 'At its centre—its trigger—there was… a man. A boy, I guess. Like us.' Here he meets your gaze. Steady. You drop your gun. 'He knew you. He wasn't… he could *see* the jumps but not force them. So they built a system. To hijack his nervous system.'

Oh god. All these years.

'They got suspicious of me. I was… defrocked. Days away from execution. A mercenary from Pandemonium helped me escape; I have no idea why. But the man… the Brazen Head… he said to find you. To tell you. To stop it.'

From his shirt he pulls a string necklace. At its end his signet ring. He flings it to you. 'It's all there. Coordinates. Schematics. But… it's happening. *Soon.*'

You slide down the bulkhead, rubbing your hair. Fuck. 'Why the fuck should I trust you?'

He looks at you, and this time you see an expression you've never seen on any Telesphorus clone. He shrugs. 'Do you know what Donatism is? It's... a heresy. An old error. That bad priests can't do good things.'

You look up at him, annoyed. 'I think I've had enough theology lessons for a lifetime.'

He smiles. 'Probably a few lifetimes. Anyway, I'm glad... I'm glad in *this* one I got to be a good person. For once, in all the choices. I get to go out a good guy.'

You watch, too slow, as he hits the airlock manual override. And behind the interlock glass, he makes a small sign of the cross over you, and smiles. And then he is gone.

After a tidy vomit you return to the cockpit and plug in the ring and frown at the coordinates. Middle of nowhere—it would take most ships months. 'Nestor, send these to Lysan—'

'Sorry, but we are getting a hail, Captain, from Enceladus. It's... war, sir.'

You think for a moment about heresy. Time to choose.

GO TO ENCELADUS # 14-22

GO TO THE LEVIATHAN # 72-80

THE NUMBER

you can do this you can do this you can't do this you will fail
    go back
    you can't
    you can't go back

at the console at the pedestal of the boy you would and
will die for you see options in myriad and in the tumult of
newborn omniscience you stumble like a colt

        one six thirty twenty-four
        thousand nine six five forty six
        ninety three four hundred eighty
        five six thousand seventy two
        four hundred thirty six twenty
        two thousand eighty four

the priests in their bio-suits find you in a fugue rendered to stone
before your beautiful Perseus reciting numbers. And in their specimen
chamber you recite them still, searching from your cage for the key to
turn the lock and set time right

glimpsing a thousand ways it might have gone
a thousand fractalising horrors seen now from the cold

jumping moment to moment
combing like psyche through the grain

        somewhere there's a moment
      if only you knew
        if only you

        enter number
        go to

ENTER NUMBER ####   **END**

ON CALLISTO

Endymion rises like an exhalation from the caldera, mist seeping through its buttresses and balustrades. Though Callisto was the oldest settled of Jupiter's moons and has become the Galilean cluster's capital, the terraforming had been rougher here, and from the craters that festoon the surface the warm lakes send vapour that catches the neon lights of the damp city in bright mollusk pearl.

You move through the pseudo-venetian baroque of its original plan, veined in varicose canals and arches, soldered with occasional frantic neon signage selling the wares and snares of the diaspora. Rising towers buttressed against the crag, the city always feels muffled, paranoid, and haunted—dreamily half-remembering half-lost Earth.

You find Lysander in the tepidarium of the bathhouse (a bath! thank god!). The cavernous room is dark except the light streaming from the clerestory windows above as the captain of the guard turns a languid half-lap through the water then raises himself on thick arms to sit next to you on the tile at the pool's edge, where you watch his muscles work and soak your grateful and indecently dirty feet.

'Got your beep,' you say, trying very hard not to look at the damp hair of his chest and keep your smirk on crooked. 'I imagine that means there's a katzenjammer on your hands.'

'God, I wish only one,' he sighs, towelling his neck and densely bearded jaw. He smiles at you, kind tired eyes under thick brows. 'You look good.' He does too. You try to remember if you robbed him or he fucked you last. The order is probably important, but you're only sure you did one first and the other twice. He almost touches your shoulder, already starting to bead from the wet heat, but instead seems to flinch, looking back across the steam rising from the water and his brow crinkles again.

'It's war. The conjunction…' He trails off. What everyone worried about, then: Ascendancy-occupied Uranus is entering alignment with Saturn—minimum distance to move a fleet of Seraphs against the Titanian coalition. 'Barrage on Enceladus started this morning. Tethys can't be long. And if Titan falls…'

'We're sending aid, but something's… off. Fleet's huge, but smaller than it should be… And I hear whispers.' His eyes scan the dark tepidarium, as though spies might be lurking among the room's sweating sleepers and furtive handjobs. 'Of a weapon. Hidden somewhere. But I don't…' In his lap he tightens the fingers of his big hands into fists, then carefully opens them, inhaling.

'I know you have *really* good reasons not to trust us. Hell, I've seen it. Upstairs they talk about you like if they could, they'd dissect you like a frog just to figure out how to make *more*.' Anger flashes across his face. You could kiss him for it.

'And I don't know what I am to you, if I'm a *mark*, or…' He stammers, then inhales again, nostrils tight then flare. Damn. 'But *I* trust *you*. Nobody has instincts like yours.'

KISS HIM # 61-17

LET HIM SPEAK # 65-47

DESTROY THE SHIP

With a sick lurch you jump the Bumblebee into the hollow abscess at the heart of the colossal jump-ship.

The Bumblebee's jets kick on with a sudden and uneasy stagger, adjusting for the abrupt gravity. Your ship's headlights click on and pore across the vast cavity and over the gnarled and snaking walls. And your stomach turns.

> Lining the bulkheads, churning through huge fluorescing tubing, is the same pale aquamarine lymph you recognise in tiny teaspoons from the Bumblebee's own jump-drive. But here, the clerics have mass-produced it in metric tonnes—more than any one person could produce, you realise. You remember Pentecost: the hundreds of dead children of their experiments. You wonder what became of the corpses.

The Leviathan project is not a transportation system; it is *itself* a weapon, you realise: a jump-drive that can turn space-time into a kind of reality napalm, flooding a sector of space with a primordial unmaking. They didn't want faster than light; they wanted to deliver a payload of dismantling—a complete demolition. A vast and terrible chaos engine.

So be it.

You imagine you see a figure at the end of a vast cathedral, ringed in light, as you jump back outside the ship's lugubrious mass.

You watch as chromium starfire bursts and pits the ship, folding and deforming it like crumpling tin-foil before it explodes into iridescent liquid light.

In its place hangs a nebula of startling beauty.

The war lasts lifetimes. You do not see its end.

But as the years and battles trudge on, you visit this strange constellation with great frequency and reverence, strafing its surface with your lights.

Looking for something.

END   [GO TO # 12-66]

HIS SCAR

After curfew, as the dorms lock and the other heretic boys
        scramble to unruly bed you notice Cole's
        bunk is empty. Your bare foot slips down
        and touches cold tile.

You find him softly crying, nestled among strange gargoyles and
        salvaged Old Earth wood of the upper
        chancel. You scramble across the belfry
        beams and he looks up at you in startled
        indignance and at his beauty your breath is
        caught like Actaeon turned stag. Outside,
        through a shimmer-window, the Tartarus
        gate shudders moonlight and is gone. You
        dare to slide your back down the ancient
        cedar to sit with him. A smote god
        cratered in starlight.

'Can I see?' you ask, in whisper. He pulls his head from his
        crossed arms and thrusts his jaw, defiant.
        In the gate-light you can see the priest's
        seared streak through his eyebrow.

You do not know what power finds you and wrenches deep to
        reach out a rash hand and touch his face.
        Warm. He does not flinch.

And when you kiss it is like all the gates open, everywhere.

He will bear the scar forever.

TO PENTECOST # 70-42

IN THE GARDEN

You are sitting in the garden with your mother, who is planting
impatiens.

> You love their little seed pods, serious and plump
> but when you squeeze them, burst into spirals
> scattering seeds like fireworks.
>
> noli mi tangere
> for caesar's i am

And suddenly your mother is not there.
And suddenly you are alone.

And suddenly you are not alone.

Something is moving in the darkness.

END THE WAR

The Leviathan jumps with a massiness thick and profound, pulling at muscles that remind you of the leaden bells of the chorister. You feel a lightheaded swim and sink, and next to you Cole succumbs, falling to his knees, the train of cabling wrought to him tugging. And then through the tracery of the massive rose window above a sight you have not beheld since you were children thrown to the fire at Pentecost:

The Gate.

In languid loveliness it cycles and spins, coruscating light, vomiting forth another knot of Seraphs. Around it, the web-like interlacing of Ascendancy ships cluster—a massive armada that has been assembling for months, the rearguard of the fleet already crossing the Kuiper belt to scythe through the campaign on Saturn and mop up the Galileans before planting its flag on a fatigued but fertile Earth. Home again home again.

Beyond it, through the portal, you know must be the subjugated worlds of the Ascendancy: a network of conquered planets fissured in crazed zigzag through the galaxy like a mould breaking through the cracks and crawls of an ancient house.

'I wonder what it was,' you mutter, in awe despite yourself. 'What they touched out there that made them scurry back through the Gate. Must have been awful.'

Next to you Cole pulls himself up your body to rise. 'Sometimes I…' he trails off, and you wonder if he dreams like you dream, glimpsing something gliding in the black. If he has even slept in years. He thinks better. 'But we'll never know.'

You help pull him up and feel him tense. Outside, a clutch of Seraphs has darted to investigate the renegade Leviathan, hopelessly attempting to pierce the armour of its hull with a full barrage before it can deliver its treacherous payload.

'Well, fuck 'em,' you sneer. If they want to return, let them crawl at sub-light. Let seven generations know peace.

> And let justice be done, though the Heavens themselves should fall.

Around you as you hold him he beckons the engines of the Leviathan. Machinery whines and then screams as Cole opens the sky, engulfing the whole of their armada and the Gate beyond in a white-hot sterilising blaze.

> and together you die
> like dawn, rising.

END   [GO TO # 12-66]

PANDEMONIUM

In the centuries before the Ascendancy returned, the Pandemonium was a derelict ark used by the early settlers migrating to Titan. Too heavy for primitive salvage operations, it was decommissioned and set to flotsam. Now, hidden by dust clouds of rogue centaurs, it shuttles in the space between Jupiter and Neptune: welcoming and fleecing fugitives, providing Ascendancy priests with illicit whores and Galilean and Titanian soldiers with recreation, and none with steady footing.

You win shamelessly, spin after spin, for hours at the gambling tables before someone has the decency to beat you up and take you to the back.

> In front of the picture windows overseeing the trade floor is a girl: some years younger than you. You notice on her close-cropped hair a rectangular divot, as though she has been brutally trepanned. Her skin is ashen, and her stare is wild and unblinking as she assesses you back. The Argus.

> 'You're late. I was starting to worry,' she says, still unblinking.

You test the shackles. 'Wasn't aware I was expected.' She seems genuinely puzzled by this, and looks out at the floor, eyes darting from table to table like a vampire counting rice.

'No, that can't be right. You're the golden boy. You see it too. Time, laid out like a Christmas tree—baubles, fleck of tinsel, widening as the lights spin down. And every day a little drier, a little closer to igniting. You're the *success*. I, however, had the misfortune of being one of your successors. One of the failures.' She gestures as though tipping an imaginary hat, the movement sweeping across her dented skull.

The Pentecost experiments aboard the chorister-ship had failed. You saw its stolen children burst like rotten fruit. The ones who survived you assumed had been left gibbering in cells, or pickled in specimen jars. It took the first six months after you escaped just to stop screaming.

Of course they tried again.

> 'They took what they needed. A lung. Lymph nodes. Most of the right hemisphere. And left me a gift—the same as you. Yours I see is spent mostly in sex and silly swashbuckling. I…'

> The Argus snaps and points at one of the carousing gamblers below. Both guards leave. You're alone. She doesn't seem worried. 'I run the table.'

> 'Listen, and what a lovely place it is. The shrimp cocktail alone is worth the flight from—'

'Shut up. Listen carefully. The Ascendancy fleet is already dispatched to Enceladus. The Titanians will likely fail. Certainly will if you do not help them.' She turns and her eyes break like awls through leather. It's a feint. They are hiding something out there. Made of steel and the blood of a thousand twisted children. Made of *us*.'

> 'I will give you the coordinates. Already uploading to your cute little ship. I am going to give you what you need, and you are going to make me two promises.' She kneels in front of you, and with her fingerprint pops open your cuffs, and grips your chin to stare into your stare. '*That you will let Enceladus fall. And you will destroy Leviathan.*'

You stand and rub your wrists. 'How do you know I'll keep them? Your promises?'

She has already returned to the window. 'Maybe you won't. But then you will.' She shrugs. 'When you see what I see.'

GO TO ENCELADUS # 14-22

GO TO LEVIATHAN # 72-80

[54–40]

ESCAPE

Laughing, you enter the code: '*54-40.*' Of course. Of course it was.

And with a small chime, cutting through the explosions and screeching metal all around like beautiful birdsong, the plexiglass of Cole's tank begins to slide open. A torrent of the thick corrupted medical gel pours from it, coating you like the afterbirth of a foal, as he falls from the tank into your arms.

And his seizing subsides as you mop the slime from his beautiful brow. And he opens his eyes. God, his eyes.

And on the tile while the ship shakes itself to pieces you both laugh.

And hand in hand naked you run—through corridors of smoke, through a docking bay aflame, through a sky of fire.

And aboard the little ship—still without weapons, its interior smelling fresh and clean—you both regard the Tartarus gate swallowing half the chorister-ship in its maw. And beyond, something moving in the dark. 'Well,' you say, your hands flashing over the controls, as you spool up the 3-D printer for Nestor's cat peripheral. 'Where to?' you ask.

And he laughs. 'I dunno. Feels like you should pick.'

And you jump.

END

THE SHORTCUT

and the cat said:
the proper order of things is often a mystery to me.

some go this way.
some go that way.

I prefer the shortcut.

INVASION

You jump. You are too late.

Flung between the moons of Jupiter, amid the Pasiphae cluster in an infant's clutch to Sinope, you watch the ships of the Galilean fleet burn. And more: the corona of the detonation scalds through the sky, a blackness lipped in gold that skims and swells to swallow the bustling planetoids.

Io is burning. Europa is burning. Ganymede is burning. Callisto is burning.

> Amalthea is burning. Thebe is burning.
> Themisto is burning.

> Leda is burning. Himalia is burning. Lysithea is burning. Elara is burning.

Beyond it, you know, Earth stands unguarded against the ill-omened wind that will roll across the system. All the worlds now will be engulfed by the Ascendancy's march.

> They will be homeward returned. And your culture
> > and your people
> > and your fight
> > > will just be ghosts
> > > loam to enrich the soil.

As the sky obliterates, you see the striations of Jupiter curdling back, whirling like cream in coffee, a roiling convulsion as it rears up and sours.

And behold: sundered and struck, the great red eye of Jupiter was no more.

And without it all the gods went blind.

END   [GO TO # 12-66]

THE KISS

Fuck it. You pull him in by the shoulder, slick and warm, your hand indecently inside his thigh.

His surprise melts to passion, and you feel a pang of guilt at the heart you guess you broke.

His breath tastes like candied ginger.

GO TO THE BATHHOUSE # 65-47

[62–65]

THE HOMILY

'But we ought not to need the gates at all. Faster than light travel—
almost instantaneous—*should* be possible without them. The theory is
sound. The doctrine is unshakeable. Yet when the test-engines are
engaged without passing through the Jubilee's blessing, the ships
arrive shattered. Flotsam and jetsam. Or do not return at all.'

He moves his hand off yours and raps your desk, gently.
Thoughtfully. As though sounding waters. '*Something* thwarts our
glorious evangelisation. Monsters of the outer waters, perhaps, gliding
in depths and heights we cannot see.

'But the divine plan has provided for us.' He looks down at you, and
he smiles. His hand finds the port on your neck where they pump the
sludge of their gene-therapies, the pad of his thumb playing across its
steel lip. 'For you are not your own, children, but were bought with a
price.

'You bewildered pagans will be new-baptised. In water and in blood.
With minds that can foresee possibility and avoid calamities and make
at last straight the path of salvation.' You know under the church
rhetoric what this means—have seen the flight-suits and experimental
ships and gene-altered test-pilots pounded to jelly in smears across
cockpit glass. Perfect jumps plotted across space—point-to-point.
Gates, opened in stolen children's minds. You shudder.

'And therefore rejoice! For when the work of resurrection is
complete, those of you who live you will be given *new* bodies.' He
moves towards the screen at the front of the class as, at his wave, it
erupts into the star-charts and schema of a great and blessed empire
alongside diagrams of the gene-resequencing therapies that await you
and the other bright acolytes.

'Maybe it's God. Stopping you.' The boy next to you speaks, almost shouts it, a hand immediately twitching halfway to his mouth, as though his own nervous system was taken aback at the affront. His name is Cole, and he is the most beautiful thing you have ever seen.

The priest stops, his back ramrod straight. And turns. 'Who said that?'

You wince. You know what will come next.

SAY NOTHING # 39-56

LIE; SAY IT WAS YOU # 88-89

THE BATHHOUSE

Lysander's hand finds yours. With the other he gestures across the expanse of the pool, as though it stood in for the whole beleaguered system.

'The war is on, and I can't pretend it isn't. And I can't pretend you wouldn't make a difference. Go to Enceladus. Take out as many of these sequinned motherfuckers as you can. Hell, win the damn thing, if you got the nerve. Buy us more time.'

'Or?' You give his hand a squeeze. He sighs.

'Orrrr… there's a rumour. Coming out of the Pandemonium. Of a… faction, or maybe just one person, but—*something*—called "The Brazen Head". It's just rumors, but…If anyone's got a bead on it, it'll be the owner, Argus. But she's cagey. And it's a longshot.'

'I'm good at longshots,' you say. 'Either way.' You stand, the water dripping from your calves, instantly cold. You kiss the top of his head. A benediction.

'Find me? After?' he asks, hand softly gripping your ankle.

'I will,' you hear yourself say. You know you won't. In all the roads there is no version of this to return to.

And as you leave, he slips down below the water for the blessing of a last immersion.

GO TO ENCELADUS # 14-22

GO TO PANDEMONIUM # 48-96

ULTIMA

you did not make a choice
or follow any direction

but now
somehow

you see a meadow.
and in the meadow your mother.
but not your mother.

a crystal city
sparkling lakes
flowering trees

and in the dark above
something is moving

cupbearer
who stole from Jupiter his lightning

we keep the gates
we keep the dark

we will mind the dark for you
little one

for behold: all the worlds will be your enemy

and if they catch you
they will kill you

but first they have to catch you

GO WHERE THOU WILT

THE AIRLOCK

You watch the stowaway's body pirouette through space. You feel like shit, but it couldn't be helped.

> Nestor pipes up: '*Distress call from Enceladus on all channels.*
> *It's the Ascendancy.*
> *Their fleet is on the move across the conjunction.*
> *It's war, sir.*'

'Fuck, OK. Here goes. Prep to jump.'

GO TO ENCELADUS # 14-22

PENTECOST

Pentecost has come. At the apex of the chorister-ship you and
the other acolytes are stripped and sealed into the
baptismal font tanks to prepare for immersion

amid the neat rings around the towering slaughterhouse the
Telesphori bustle at the controls below you all in
frenzied preparation. some of the boys bang futilely
on the glass. Some cry in desolation at the bottom
of their vats, which are filling in a greasy torrent
from above with the thick ooze of compounds and
enzymes meant to catalyze neuronal mutation.
Almost none of you will survive

at the panel at your feet a prelate keys in his locking sequence.
His hands out of sight. You cannot see his ring, but
you know exactly which priest it is. 'We will not all
sleep, but we will all be changed—in a flash, in the
twinkling of an eye!' he crows, and his eyes flash a
familiar cruelty.

the tanks are sealed. the tower evacuated. Cole's hand presses
against the glass and it is only now you
understand you would burn the world
to save him.
the bottomless breath. The plunge.
the steeple of the vessel the great tower the lance stabs itself
into the maelstrom of the open gate and the tank
around you ignites. your mind catches fire like
pine needles on red coal

and you see some boys' eyes pop and sludge and some cough
thick gouts of blood into the goo of their tanks and
flesh dissolving like snails under salt and

across from you Cole writhes and seizes. But
more: you see a thousand networked gossamer
webs. You see a rising crescendo of light like a
chandelier climbing to celestial rafters

you see the precise point the glass in front of you will crack

you kick your naked foot with all your might and feel a vacuum
tug, a toilet plunger suction and slip like a breeched
baby to the floor the glass tearing you and slipping you
pull yourself upright. The atmosphere of fire
dissipating. With a mechanical whine and convulsion
the chorister ship retracting like a spent lover sheepish
and ashamed. Most of the boys are dead. Cole is still
gripped with seizure

your mind on fire in a thousand pinwheeling possibilities and
you see them all before you like rivers from a
turret cataracting and all all almost all cry
out escape or die

SMASH COLE'S TANK # 18-34

ENTER THE CODE # 28-84

RUN # 92-41

THE LEVIATHAN

You wink into space.

You *feel* it before you see it. It hangs alone in the black sky: of monstrous size, its bulk titanian, invested in night:
> *The Leviathan.*

Strafing on long-range sensors Nestor clocks the Seraph fleet meant to guard it, turning like carrion birds in asymmetric rings obfuscating its location. Any eye not seeking it would never find it; any misfortunate soul that found *them* would die long before divining why.

No weapons. No lights. Visible only because of its darkness. A coffin. A bomb. *A jump-ship.*

> And suddenly you know exactly who must be wired to its fuse.
> That they are surely beyond saving.
> That they were damned seven years ago.

>> And that inside, amid the dreadful machinery, there is a hollowness.
>> That could hold your ship.
>> That could be detonated.

>>> And this monstrosity, this great engine of unmaking, could be itself unmade.

> At the margins of the black, the Seraph lights come strafing in.

You'll have to choose, fast.

DESTROY THE SHIP # 37-34

FIND THE BRAZEN HEAD # 82-60

BEE-STUNG

In the space of ninety-three seconds (eight seconds per jump plus three per blast, plus some you waste in daydream like a profligate) you execute a series of micro-jumps around the Seraph hull, much too close to the firing solution of its gun batteries, plugging a short-range shot into its shell with each jump. These disable five cannons and punch three holes in the bulkheads surrounding primary engineering—like knives darted quick between ribs.

You yank the jump cable from your neck, sink back into the pilot chair, and hail the Seraph. A sputtering voice through the speaker: 'How *dare* you raise a hand to the vicars of—' You send a long squawk through the comm.

'Yeah yeah. Damned for all time. Listen,' you radio, craning your head to look up at the columns of flame and depressurised prelates venting into space in languid somersaults. 'Looks to this old altar-boy like you kids are gonna have some trouble steering. Also breathing. Anyways, I'd suggest you limp your way back to Pluto, or the next one goes through the bridge. And be careful out there!' you caution. 'I don't know what kind of piece-of-shit scavengers would pick on an unarmed vessel, but… I guess you'll rely on the kindness of strangers.'

The comm squeals flat. 'Guess he hung up,' you remark to the cat, whose paw swats half-heartedly at the windshield glass as the last debris flames outside like paper blown from a bonfire.

Gelded, the bee-stung prelate cruiser lurches sickening through the sky, fleeing back to the outer reaches. You circle the Bee about, and through the umblical of the airlock a passel of clamouring survivors clamber aboard.

JUMP TO IAPETUS # 76-57

IAPETUS

You pop into the port at Iapetus and the refugees aboard say their farewells: an old lady's kiss on the cheek, a distilled shot of something awful, and a doll too loved to keep, which you carefully sneak right back into the kid's pocket. Iapetus has been receiving evacuees from the outer worlds for years, its minty-fresh new terraform turning it quickly into a vital—vulnerable—bread-basket. You wish you had time to grab some food; it's the only world in the system you can snag Nesan-dressed cauliflower without getting in a gunfight.

You spool up, but as you leave atmosphere Nestor chimes in sing-song. *'Still detecting a life sign aboard, sir. There's a heat signature in the airlock.'*

> *Shit.* You knew something about this stank. Best case it's a random pirate who thinks he can take you (Hell, maybe he can). Worst case, the whole thing was a set-up and it's a Church assassin trying to get the Bee—or your brain.

> This is the last moment you'll have the drop on him. One way or another, there's a hot stinging *feeling* behind your ear…

FLUSH THE AIRLOCK # 68-79

CONFRONT THE STOWAWAY # 80-41

SO LONG

they're worried about you, the cat says.

what?

you've been asleep too long. slower and slower between jumps. sometimes you speak and…

do *you* worry?

of course not. I'm just a cat.

THE STOWAWAY

You point your battered arclight in his face and try with two hands very, very hard not to let him see you shake while behind your ears you feel scarlet heat blossom and burn. His eyes are wide, and this time they're younger than yours. One of the Telesphori.

'Please. Please!' he pleads, his hands in the air. He' s definitely shaking. 'I didn't… I really don't want to hurt you!'

'Oh, sure. An Ascendancy clone, fresh from the vat, heard how many of his brothers I've blown into the dark and wants an autograph. Hell, *most* people introduce themselves with a hostage situation.'

'What? Oh—the refugee ship. No, I… I *didn't*. I didn't… they must've, you're right, but they always…' Something's not right. The young clone—eighteen? nineteen?---looks genuinely confused, his face scrunching in a way that presages the wrinkles you watched crease generations of older clerics aboard the chorister. The men who tortured and twisted you up before they slaughtered your classmates like children bored of their toys.

You try to stop the alarms in the small of your back and take him in: clothes look like shit, hands and face probably grimier than a thousand of his brother-prelates have been in hundreds of years. 'I didn't even *know* about the Seraph,' he stammers. 'They just… they snuck me out. To get away. To find *you*.'

You close one eye and look through the sight. Not that you've ever used it—your shots tend to be lucky shots. You try to ignore your gene-port itching.

'Listen. Listen!' he shouts, adrenaline spiking as you press the arc to his forehead, then closes his eyes, trying to be very calm. Then: '*The Brazen Head sent me.*'

AIRLOCK HIM # 68-79

HEAR HIM OUT # 24-91

THE BRAZEN HEAD

In the apse of its great iron cathedral you find him curled upon the tile: gene-ports like yours but manifold, dangling from a vast oculus in the ceiling and snaking into his back and sides, naked except for the helm of blind burnished brass fixed to his skull.

You remove the eyeless helmet—heavily worked in ornament, its metallic face placid and serene. For a lurching moment as it slips away you wish you hadn't. You remember his curly black hair. You remember his eyes.

'You found me.' Feebly, he paws his way into your lap. His head leaves stains. On the floor the helmet oozes and sparks, disengaged from a host of narcotising pumps and AI hijack filaments. Your hand goes out to warm flesh and traces your finger around the port on his neck. The same one you wear. Your scar. His scar.

'I would have moved Heaven and Earth, if I had just known to look.'

'I know. You still will. I made sure. I made as many of the roads come here as I could. But some... I can't see those. Whirligigs. But it hurts less every time.' By now the Seraphs will have arrived and clocked your ship welded to the hull.

'Would you like to know what happens next?'

JUMP TO EARTH # 23-76

END THE WAR # 46-62

REST

You scuttle the Leviathan: fathoms under a grey sea, its wreck the haunt of seals and orcs and sea-mews clang. Onshore the Bumblebee, gun plunked down in the wet soil, never rises again.

Piece by piece, plate by plate, the ship slowly begins to break down and digest into a house, into a fence, into a garden. You hang lanterns in its bulkheads, and open one side into a canopied porch strung with lights. Eventually, as its reserve cells die, its only electrical function is to power the cat. And someday that, too, breaks down, and you both cry for the silly little guy, his eye irised big and black and blank, and you bury his peripheral—fur pulled over tin, much too light with its batteries depleted—in the rows of the back garden that he loved so much.

Wounds become scars. There is coffee, and laughter, and lovemaking, and sunrises.

Almost enough of them.

Without a jump-capable pilot, the Galilean defence cannot back-stop its troop movements.
Without a jump-capable pilot, the Ascendancy's trudge from the Gate moves through the solar system at sub-light, thwarted for each march and mile.

But inexorably.

Time, and times, and half a time. It takes three and a half years for their onslaught to reach Earth.

And one day there is a flash on the horizon. And you call to Cole, who is digging in the pea-shoots. And you hold him, and the sun is warm and soft, and he is warm and soft. And there is a great roar, like all the casements of the sky have been opened.

And at the end, you close your eyes.

END   [GO TO # 12-66]

YOUR SCAR

On your knees shirt unfastened you bear your back. You try not to cry out. Searing lashes rain on your collarbone and nape. The curlicue of the arcblade catches and scorpions through your hair, against your brow, and cauterises—the dark sacristy filled with the smell of boiled blood and singeing hair. On his soft hand his signet flashes.

> you wonder: was it a child like you who dug the gems of the young cleric's ring from the rock of some world you cannot imagine? What small, nimble fingers had worked the fresh-decanted clone-priest's filigree, had wrought the gentle trace-work of his chasuble's fretted iridescence?

> Did a priest whip raw their backs too, as one delved and another spun?

> Probably not Telesphorus himself, nor one of his clone-brothers. In the mirror above the cold sink his face glistens with sweat, twisted with rage, but still handsome: young, sad, heavy eyes and beautiful eyelashes. The Telesphori stock—centuries old now, the second son of some tertiary aristocrat of the Radomanthine dynasty. Better suited to academia and song.

Within the ranks of the clergy, the clones use the rings to tell
each other apart, when it is important to do
so. It seldom is. Certainly you have never
learned the knack of it—a
confusion they encourage. All seem to know
what the other knows, a miasma of
omniscience and surveillance. Hard to
ingratiate with. Hard to lie to. Hard to
accuse.

Later, Cole finds you in the cornfields of astroponics. A folded
            scarecrow at the crossroads, a coal of
            shame smouldering in your lap. It reminds
            you of home here amid the cheerful all-
            night daylight of the UV-bathed farm.

When he kisses your forehead your nose your cheekbone your
            lips in sudden lightning zigzag it is like fire
            like seared flesh all over again.

You will bear the scar forever.

TO PENTECOST # 70-42

[92–41]

RUN

Your mind on fire. There is no way to save Cole.

You press a kiss a greasy blood-smeared pucker to the glass at his feet. All around you the tanks of children surge and belch and klaxons scream for the end of the world.

And you run

Slipping falling you weave down one corridor then the next left left right right you steal an arclight gun dodging partisans and armaments and suddenly you are in the docking bay and there it is: a ship

the guards scramble to close the portcullis to prevent you undocking but as the engine begins to whine they realise their mistake:
you are not undocking
you are jumping

from inside the pilot chair, needling the umblical jump-cable into your neck, you feel the universe unlock and coordinates fall from your hands like a blessing like a miracle. a blind jump

and the world turns to white
and the guards turn to spatters
and the lower half of the chorister-ship warps and folds to buckshot

and you are gone

SEVEN YEARS LATER # 13-70

THE WAY

would you tell me, please
which way I ought to go from here?

that depends a good deal on where you want to get to
said the cat

I don't much care where—

then, said the cat
it doesn't matter which way you go

About the Authors

JAMES BENNETT (he/him) is a British writer raised in Sussex and South Africa. His short fiction has appeared internationally, and he's been twice shortlisted for a British Fantasy Award, first in 2017 for his acclaimed debut *Chasing Embers* and again in 2023 for his short story 'Morta', which appeared in the well-received *The Book of Queer Saints*. His latest fiction can be found in The Dark magazine, BFS Horizons and Occult Detective magazine. A short story collection *Preaching to the Perverted* should see the light of day in 2024. James lives in the South of Spain where he's working on a new novel.

JOHN BERKELEY (he/him) is a queer British writer and Classics (archaeology) PhD raised in Cambridgeshire and now living in Berkshire, where he spends his time writing speculative fiction novels and short fiction. 'Dusk and Dawn in the Grand Bazaar' is his first published work. Others are on their way.

ALIETTE DE BODARD (she/her) writes speculative fiction: she has won three Nebula Awards, an Ignyte Award, a Locus Award, and six British Science Fiction Association Awards. She is the author of *A Fire Born of Exile*, a sapphic Count of Monte Cristo in space (Gollancz/JABberwocky Literary Agency, Inc., 2023), and of *Of*

Charms, Ghosts and Grievances (JABberwocky Literary Agency, Inc, 2022 BSFA Award winner), a fantasy of manners and murders set in an alternate 19th Century Vietnamese court. She lives in Paris.

Christopher Caldwell (he/him or they/them) is a queer Black American living in Glasgow, Scotland with his partner, podcaster Alice Caldwell-Kelly. He is a recipient of the Octavia E. Butler memorial scholarship. His work has appeared in Uncanny Magazine, FIYAH, Strange Horizons, and New Suns 2.

Kieran Craft (he/him) is a writer from Tāmaki Makaurau, Aotearoa (Auckland, New Zealand). He is the playwright behind gay Irish romance Four Nights in the Green Barrow Pub, and now spends his time writing queer science fiction and fantasy stories, when he's not teaching high schoolers English, or watching multi-hour video essays on niche topics.

Julie Danvers (she/her) is a queer Chicagoan who writes spec fiction that usually starts out as horror and ends up as a comedy of errors. She is the author of a whopping seven Mills & Boon novels, each one more melodramatic than the last. As penance for her literary crimes, she also writes short fiction, some of which has appeared in The Arcanist, Sundial Magazine, and Pulp Modern Flash.

Oliver Darkshire (he/him) has found that his life as a struggling bookseller and writer is exactly what his careers instructor warned him would happen if he didn't pay attention. He lives in Manchester with his husband and a house full of books he actively tried not to collect.

Rien Gray (they/them) is a queer, nonbinary, and intersex author of sapphic romance, fantasy, and horror. They are the author of the award-winning Fatal Fidelity series starring a nonbinary assassin, and currently writing a trans and lesbian-centered Arthuriana roman-tasy series, which starts with *Valerin the Fair*. Their short fiction is published in the Opulent Syntax, Shredded, Unreal Sex, BRUTE, and Heckin' Lewd anthologies. They live in Chicago.

BRENT C. LAMBERT (he/him) is a Black, queer man who heavily believes in the transformative power of speculative fiction across media formats. As a founding member of FIYAH Literary Magazine, he turned that belief into action and became part of a Hugo Award winning team. He resides in San Diego.

BAILEY MAYBRAY (he/him) is a queer, Bostonian sci-fi and fantasy writer who drinks too much mango green tea for his own good. He creates strange and wonderful worlds with bizarre, often-queer perspectives, from cyborg alien octopi to robotic play directors. Find him @bailey_maybray on X (formerly Twitter).

NG YI-SHENG (he/him) is a Singaporean writer, researcher and activist with a keen interest in Asian history and myth. He's been published in Clarkesworld and Strange Horizons—check out his Pushcart-nominated essay 'A Spicepunk Manifesto' and his BSFA-longlisted 'A Not-So-Swiftly Tilting Planet'— and is author of the speculative fiction collection Lion City (winner of the Singapore Literature Prize). Additionally, he served as editor of *A Mosque in the Jungle: Classic Ghost Stories* by Othman Wok and *EXHALE: an Anthology of Queer Singapore Voices*. His website is ngyisheng.com, and he tweets and Instagrams at @yishkabob.

ANTHONY OLIVEIRA AKA @meakoopa is a multiple National Magazine and GLAAD award-winning author, film programmer, pop culture critic, and PhD living in Toronto. His work is in a myriad of genres, often incorporating queer themes, and spans comics, prose, journalism, and academic research.

Caleb Roehrig (he/him) is a former actor and television producer who currently divides his time between Chicago and Helsinki. An expert at writing on planes, his young adult titles include *Teach the Torches to Burn*, *Last Seen Leaving*, *White Rabbit*, *Death Prefers Blondes* and *The Fell of Dark*.

Adam Sass (he/him) began writing in Sharpie on the backs of Starbucks pastry bags. (He's sorry it distracted him from making your latte.) He's the author of the buzzy YA novels *Surrender Your Sons*, *The 99 Boyfriends of Micah Summers*, and *Your Lonely Nights Are Over*, which have been featured in The New York Times, Entertainment Weekly, and USA Today. His next, *Cursed Boys and Broken Hearts*, releases July 2024. He lives in Palm Springs with his husband and dachshunds.

Malcolm Schmitz (he/him) writes about queer autistic joy. His steampunk sapphic scientist short story, 'The Captain's Sphere', made the Long List for the 2015 Otherwise Award. He's currently working on a children's book about a lost trans prince reclaiming his birthright (ask him about the giant mechanical elephants!) He lives in Ohio with his partner, and spends entirely too much time playing the Sims 2.

William C. Tracy (he/him) writes and publishes queer science fiction and fantasy through his indie press Space Wizard Science Fantasy. His largest work is the Dissolutionverse: a space opera with music-based magic. He's also published *Fruits of the Gods*, an epic fantasy with seasonal fruit magic, *How To Operate Your Body*, a nonfiction book about body mechanics and correct posture, and *The Biomass Conflux*, a sci-fi trilogy with colony ships and a planet covered by a sentient fungus. William is an NC native, has a master's in mechanical engineering, has trained in Wado-Ryu karate since 2003, and keeps bees.

DERRICK WEBBER (he/him) thrives on the banks of the mighty Fraser River in Vancouver, British Columbia. He is privileged to write and play on the unceded traditional territories of the Musqueam, Squamish and Tsleil-Waututh Nations. He pinballs between queer sci-fi, queer rom-coms and queerish YA—shorties to novels. His short fiction has been published twice and his non-fiction, think any big number. He walks a thrilling tightrope between cutting edge and utterly past it.

CHARLIE WINTER is an academic by day and, by night, still an academic but much more distractible about it. When not performing the inexplicable rituals of academia, he writes fantasy fiction celebrating everyday magic, eco-optimism, and queer identities, out of which he has three short fiction publications. He is based in Australia.

Bona Editors

TRIP GALEY (he/him) is a writer, a doctor of the academic persuasion, and a researcher of all things pursuant to bargains, exchanges, and compacts of a faery nature. He is ⅓ of the founding team at Bona Books, ½ of multiple writing partnerships, and 100% geek. Mostly harmless. His debut novel, *A Market of Dreams and Destiny*, was shortlisted for the 2024 Mythopoeic Award for Best Adult Novel. Find him at TripGaley.com or join Patreon.com/TripGaley.

ROBERT BERG (he/him) is a London-based writer, critic, editor, copywriter, and proofreader. His reviews have appeared in the British-Fantasy-Award-winning, Hugo-Award-nominated *Speculative Fiction 2012* anthology. In his other incarnation as amateur Jim Henson expert, he is also the founder of HensonBlog.com. It is unclear whether he is more man or Muppet.

C.L. McCARTNEY (he/him) is a writer and editor of fantasy, science fiction and—somewhat to his surprise—queer horror. His most recent short fiction can be found in the anthology *The Crawling Moon* (Neon Hemlock, 2024). He is Managing Director of Bona Books and the final ⅓ of its founding triumvirate.

Acknowledgements

A project like this doesn't come together without an awful lot of help, especially with a core team of only three. Our authors surprised and delighted us with their unique takes on the *IWTTO!* prompt; our cover artist, Stephen Andrade, produced a painting so damn good, we reckon it almost funded the Kickstarter single-handed; and Lex Gabriel Hyde ensured that the freshly incorporated Bona Books Ltd had a sleek, gorgeous logo at record speed.

Huge thanks to Lyam for throwing himself into the project at a late stage as our *Head Product, Marketing, and Sales Twink*; to Alf and Chris for invaluable advice; and to the army of friends who acted as a collective sounding board/WhatsApp Focus Group as we workshopped backer tiers and merch designs, including but not limited to: Ben, Aitch, Eddie, Leo, Johannes, Jack, Mark, John, Josh, Hereward, and Lawrence.

Lastly, this anthology would not have been possible without the support of our Kickstarter backers, who are—quite honestly—the best.

Content Notes

GENERAL WARNING: Twinks WERE harmed in the making of this anthology. Please consider this a blanket note for violence and twink-death in pretty much every story. Plus swearing.

IN THE GARDEN OF THE SERPENT KING: Body horror

JENSETI, YOU IN DANGER, GIRL: Homophobia; queerphobia

PLEZURE: Explicit sex; sexual violence/non-consent; coercion

A HEART OF BROKEN STEEL: Death-wish

THE DEARTH OF TEMPTATION: Death-wish

YOUR WORLD AGAINST MINE: (Clone) incest

GANYMEDE: Torture references; child abuse

BONA BOOKS WILL RETURN IN...

WRATH MONTH

Pride month is over.

Coming 2025